LIAR LIAR

HOUSE ON FIRE

Sara,
Thank you for shopping
small & supporting small
authors with big dreams!

[signature]

Liar Liar
House on Fire

Liz Gordon

Malisa

I've never met someone with more fire than you

ONE

MIRANDA

I STOP LESS than five paces from the fire and release the breath caught in my throat. It billows upward in a cloud, folding into the puffs of smoke as they dissipate and blend in with the night.

Flames skip outward from the carnage and inch closer as they lick at my damp cheeks. The beams of wood that once made the home solid and formidable crack and fall, showing just how fragile the structure was all along.

I slowly close my eyes, and my bottom lip quivers. A feeling of warmth creeps over me as I remember the weight of a wool shawl being draped over my shoulders.

"Montana winters are tough, baby. But you're tougher," the echo of dad's voice reminds me.

My lips curve into a smile just as the tiny hairs on the back of my neck spike. The piercing sound of a small child's wailing echoes in the distance. I open my eyes and turn toward the noise.

My daughter's different sounds have become engrained in my memory, down to the octave. It's inevitable when you become a parent. If I'm doing laundry or making dinner, the pitch of her cry dictates my response. Do I have to drop everything and rush to hold her, or if she can soothe herself?

In an instant, my mom brain decodes the noise overpowering the pops and sizzles of the hungry fire. *That's a come and hold me cry. She'll be fine.*

Piper's whining inside the running car tears my gaze from the fire. The home is gone, and the battered water hose coiled in the front flower bed won't be enough to bring it back. Nor would I really want it to.

The heat radiating behind me dissipates as I step toward the sedan and prepare myself to seal the chapter of my life that I spent over a decade building. *Life will never be the same again.*

Reality sinks farther in. I'm the one reliable thing my daughter has left in the world. Everything is up to me. My shoulders raise as my lungs fill with the smoky night air.

"Piper needs you. It's time to move on," I whisper with a melodramatic exhale.

The crying escalates as I draw closer to the car. A throbbing pang thumps beneath my breastbone, and each shuddering breath leaves me on the brink of tears. I push forward and shove my emotions away, burying them deep. *Now isn't the time to break down.*

My car's headlights are still beaming into the thicket of trees where I'd left it. I grab the door handle and rest my other palm on the snow-dusted roof. *Clink.* My wedding ring hits the metal and catches my attention. I slide the gold band off my finger and set it in my palm.

Not once had I ever complained that the pawnshop ring had something engraved on the inside from its previous owner. I thought the inscription gave it character. I tremble slightly, bring the band to eye level, and watch the fire burn through its center.

"Forever and ever, huh?" I mutter with a breathy chuckle as I read the phrase.

My chest grows tight. The house is quickly crumbling, but all I see is Jake, and all I hear is the painful words he muttered only a few hours earlier.

JAKE SAT ON the hearth and rubbed the tip of his thumb along the edge of the brick corner, his foot tapping incessantly. I sat on the couch as directed, facing him and waiting for him to spit out what was on his mind.

"What, Jake?" I asked, irritated that he wanted to have a conversation before I'd had my coffee.

"I met someone," he said as a hint of regret hung in the air.

I stared across the room blankly as I tried to comprehend his words. *Good God, he's serious.*

"What's her name?" I asked, praying it wasn't someone I knew.

"Don't worry about it. You don't know her," he returned.

"What is her name?" I repeated, my voice raised.

"Allie."

A chill ran through me as the name rolled off his tongue. *Allie.* I nodded to acknowledge that I heard him.

"She sounds lovely," I finally returned with a smile. A sarcastic scoff slipped from my lips.

The once charming and charismatic man that delivered self-written vows before God and a county judge had finally reached his breaking point in our marriage. Three simple words and our relationship was over.

"Miranda?" he pushed, trying to evoke a reaction.

3

I ignored him and gazed off into space with my jaw clenched. I tried to block out his voice as I sunk into the couch's worn-out cushions and imagined Jake's mistress.

My picture-perfect replacement stood tall with long model legs that looked even more incredible in heels. Her smooth, unblemished skin showed no signs of aging and was pulled tight over blush dusted cheekbones. The mystery woman had a full head of long hair that hung in loose curls and boasted a natural shade of auburn with sun-derived highlights.

She's not real. I shook off the moment.

I looked back at Jake. My cheating husband stood before me and rambled. His mouth was moving, but to me, every word was muffled as if my head was sunk below water. Repeated apologies slipped from his lips for close to an hour as he kept saying the same thing differently. His entire dialog went in one ear and out the other.

"I'm really, really sorry. I didn't mean for this to happen," Jake said repeatedly. "Miranda, please say something."

I sat in front of him as the tears I was trying to fight finally fell from my eyes. His infidelity was the final straw for us. For years, our marriage had been a roller coaster of ups and downs, screaming along a broken track while we both anticipated its inevitable crash.

I wasn't too daft to acknowledge that I was no longer the youthful woman I was when Jake and I had met. My once brown hair now had scattered greys that I had stopped coloring, and my eyebrows no longer got professionally shaped every month. The size four pants I refused to part with had gone baggy and left me with the "no-ass-at-all" disease my mama always joked she'd passed on. Raised veins have begun to poke out all over my thighs, and I often wore pants to cover them.

"Sorry? That's all you have to say?" I responded, my tears ceasing almost instantly as I became more enraged.

"Mere," he said coolly as he laid a hand on my wrist.

"No, don't you Mere me."

I brushed his hand off my arm, my anger forcing him away, and accidentally hit the items on the end table next to the couch. A thrifted lamp, a family photo of us three, and a small clock passed down to Jake fell to the floor.

"Seriously, Miranda?" he said as she gathered the fallen objects and placed them back on the table. "You and I both know this isn't working out, and it hasn't been for a while."

I stood quickly and tucked my bottom lip between my teeth, trying to silence the whir of anger brewing in my mind. I wanted to scream, collapse, the idea of hitting him even crossed my mind as I ran through a gambit of emotions. But Piper was nearby, so I chose to maintain my composure.

With my arms crossed, I turned around and took a deep breath. *We're not great, but it works. I thought it worked.*

"Miranda?" he pushed.

Jake stepped forward and reached toward me. I could feel his hand approaching my shoulder.

"Just don't," I replied as I shrugged away from his inbound touch.

"Whatever. Of course, we can't talk about this. We can't talk about anything anymore."

Talking about something would require you to actually speak to me occasionally.

"No, no. I just can't do this with you right now. I can't, okay. Piper has an appointment, and I have some errands to run. I'll be back to get some stuff tonight, and we'll go stay with my mom for a week or so," I explained. "I'd prefer it if you're not here when we get back."

"But, what about Piper?" he asked. We both looked to the back of the living room at our two-and-a-half-year-old little girl asleep in her play yard.

"We'll be back for the Wagner wedding. It's only a week from now. We can talk after that," I replied. "I just need some space. Can you just please give me that?"

Jake muttered something indiscernible under his breath.

"What was that?" I asked.

"Nothing, fine. We'll talk then."

"No, what did you say?"

"Nothing okay. If you're gonna go, just go. I guess I'll see you then."

"You guess?"

"Yeah, I'll see you there."

I stared at Jake for a moment. His eyes were sullen, and his expression looked scattered. Our many years together had helped me learn how to read his facial cues, but the empty profile he wore was foreign. His overall presentation and tone felt incomplete like I was missing something. But I didn't have the time or determination to wrangle it out of him.

"Whatever," I scoffed.

Jake leaned down and kissed Piper atop her head and offered a rehearsed apology again. With a slam of our bedroom door, he left the room and the conversation.

I grabbed up sleeping Piper, marched down the house's front steps, and tucked her into the car. Through the rearview mirror, I caught sight of Jake in the window, watching us disappear down the long drive.

When I figured he'd vacated the house, I made the trek home just after the sun had found its way behind the snowy mountain peaks. *Just grab a few things, and we'll go see mama.*

Gravel cracked and shifted beneath my tires as I traversed the quarter-mile driveway and neared our quaint farmhouse tucked away in a thicket of woods. After the last turn in the windy path, I saw an unusual light bouncing off the rocks and filtering through the trees. An unmistakable smell worked its way through the car's vents.

The bend straightened out and formed a circular parking area, and our home finally came into sight through the dusty windshield. *What?* I blinked twice to reassure myself that the image playing before me was real.

The two-story wooden structure with its idyllic front porch and American flag in the yard sat at the back end of the circular drive. But, instead of being strung with icicle Christmas lights and a wreath adorning every window, it stood tall and engulfed in violent flames that danced high above its peaks.

"No, no. What the hell, Jake?" I asked in a panicked tone. I wrapped my fingers tighter around the wheel.

"But seriously, babe. Just think about how much it's worth," Jake's voice resounded in my mind. "Think of what we could do with it all."

"Jake, come on. That's not even funny."

"Well, it's a little funny... and it's true," he responded.

As I stared at the smoldering wood, a scoff escaped my lips when I thought about the many times Jake had cracked dark jokes about what a fire would mean to the old farmhouse. The house wasn't exactly "up to code." The septic would have to be dug up and replaced, and the asbestos shingles needed to be taken off before it was ready to put on the market, all repairs Jake didn't want to front the cost to make.

Multiple times he had laughed about increasing the payout amount and even once visited the insurance agent to pick her brain. Still, I never took his subtle actions and jokes as something he was seriously considering until I pulled up to the blaze before me. I knew the fire wasn't accidental.

"No, no. I'm not getting wrapped up in this," I mumbled as I climbed out of the car and ran my fingers through my hair. "This is your mess."

Jake's job as a deputy at the local sheriff's department gave him the knowledge of the ins and outs of a crime scene. *He would know how to make this look like an accident.*

His relationship with the obnoxious and overweight fire marshal always struck me as odd but suddenly seemed to make perfect sense.

"You're going to slip him some of the payout, aren't you?" I mumbled. "Let me guess, faulty wiring?"

For close to ten years, we'd shared the three-bed, two-bath home far outside the city limits that was willed to Jake after his father passed. We'd held each other close and danced to old country hits in the kitchen, chuckled as we watched Piper throw spaghetti on the kitchen walls, and ignored each other as our marriage slowly grew cold. The mortgage had been paid in full long before I met him, and it was no secret the vast property was worth a small fortune.

"You bastard," I scoffed.

A LOUD POP sounds, and a chunk of charred wood shoots from the house. The smoldering piece lands near my foot and snaps me back to the present.

I slowly unclench my fist and release my wedding ring. A soft jingle rings out as the jewelry hits the driveway and becomes one with the damaged property. As I move toward the car, I step on the band and dig it farther into the earth.

I sigh, wipe my damp cheeks, and yank the door open, allowing Piper's crying at total volume to waft out. I bend over and weave my cold fingers through her short tuft of hair and see tears rolling down her cheeks.

"Shhh, shhh," I whisper.

I sing a slow church hymnal from my youth as I slide a purple knit cap over Piper's head and ears. The light from the fire outside casts its illumination on her round face and the tears falling from her eyes slowly decrease while they begin welling up in mine. Piper flinches as I press my cold lips onto her cheek.

Thank God she doesn't know what you did.

"I love you, baby. Mama loves you," I whisper as her screaming finally mellows.

Staring up at me, Piper's bottom lip quivers, and she reaches forward as far as her five-point harness will allow. She latches onto her milk cup with shaking hands and lowers it into her mouth.

The car finally slips into silence now that Piper is settled. An exaggerated breath escapes my mouth as I sink into my well-loved sedan's driver's seat. The tiny hairs from my side bangs tickle my cheeks as the breeze coming through the vents blows past me. The heat sends the smoke smell embedded in my hair flowing throughout the car while I sit with my hands on the wheel.

"We can do this."

I glance at the fire in my side mirror one last time and read, "OBJECTS IN MIRROR MAY BE SMALLER THAN THEY APPEAR."

Just hours earlier, the house had felt large and indestructible, a fortress that would withstand the tests of time and the elements. But in its reflection, it looks insignificant as it crumbles to pieces.

A solitary tear slides down my face and is quickly wiped away with a sleeve. I wrap my fingers around the steering wheel and slowly press the pedal, my attention fixated on the darkness ahead.

"It's gonna be okay. Everything will be okay," I repeatedly mutter, unsure of who the hell I'm talking to.

Piper sits quietly in the back, strapped tightly in her seat. The suspension shakes and squeaks as we traverse the bumpy path toward the main road.

Less than a minute after joining the unlit highway, two blaring fire trucks pass as they speed toward the burning house. Their lights bounce off the trees and briefly blind me as I try to focus on the road's edge lines.

"He's gone," I mumble in a singsong voice to myself as the speeding emergency vehicles' lights fade in the side mirror. I continue heading north, pretending the screaming trucks and subsequent ambulance mean nothing to me.

The newly resurfaced road feels longer than ever as I head farther from town and deeper into the darkness. Streetlights disappear, and the four-lane highway turns into a two-lane. The gentle flurry of falling snow slowly becomes heavier in the beams of my headlights until I'm forced to flip on the wipers. Piper remains motionless in the back after being swiftly rocked to sleep by the car's gentle vibrations soon after we left the driveway.

I push northbound, pull my elbows close, and rest my chest on the wheel. The reflective lines have fused themselves into a never-ending stripe, and my eyes see them running without end in my peripherals. The haze of the road and the mesmerizing glow of the paint leave me feeling like someone forced their way into my head and is controlling my every move.

An hour from our home's crumbling ruins, a slight pull to the right stops my car in a gravel cut out in front of a dark open field. The headlights dim, and I rest my forehead against the steering wheel as I take a moment to regroup. *Just relax.* Tiny rustling sounds come from the back seat as the vehicle's motion pauses. I cringe, thinking Piper will wake from the stillness, but two minutes of silence is only broken by the hum of her soft snore resuming.

I slowly rotate my hand and manually roll down the window to ensure the door won't lock behind me. A sharp breeze blows across my forehead as it comes through the minute crack. I twist the heat knob to full blast to compensate for the chilly draft before stepping into the cold night air.

The door shut louder than I expected.

"Shit," I whisper through clenched teeth. I peek in and see Piper sleeping soundly, unaffected by the sound.

I step away from the car and pull a crocheted cap down over my ears. I close my jacket but still feel the breeze fighting its way between the zipper's teeth. The snug fleece-lined pockets welcome my hands as I relax and let my head fall backward.

The Montana sky, unobstructed by light pollution, is enough to make you feel both overwhelmed and completely alone. It's a vast blackness that feels infinite. Flurrying snow dusts a thin layer on my face as I stare at the stars and feel like the earth is pulling me toward its core.

11

A couple of chuckles break from my mouth as I amble into the middle of the country road. I place one foot on either side of the subdued yellow lines and reach out perpendicular to my body.

"You're losin' it, girl," I say with another snicker as I twirl around.

In the thirteen years since graduating high school, I've worked odd jobs around town but never found a concrete career that fit. I worked as a maid at a small bed and breakfast for a while, then tried being a nanny to two small boys who ended up having a handsy father. Finally, I landed a job working as a secretary at a local elementary school but was laid off due to budget cuts. Unfortunately, I had never been particularly successful at any of the positions I held and couldn't find my calling when it came to employment.

When the pregnancy test unexpectedly showed two pink lines, I abandoned any idea of educating myself in the same manner my mother had and her mother before her. Instead, I set my sights on being a stay-at-home mom, a job that proved to be more work than any office I had tried. Over time, Piper and I established a routine that worked for both of us, and I learned to savor being able to watch her growing up without missing a minute.

But now, here I am in the middle of nowhere wearing a thin jacket, the night cold and gusty. There's no house to go back to, no job to tie me to the area, and very little money to my name. I feel alone and misplaced in the world. The barren highway feels more welcoming than the house I abandoned.

"Mama's all I have," I mutter. I look upward and see only the burning stars glaring back at me.

"I hate you," I belt out on repeat upward into the quiet night sky three times, wishing the darkness would answer me back.

"Say something!" I scream into the air as I feel my throat go dry. I wait in silence for a voice to call back to me, knowing good and well none will come. The only semblance of a sound that returns my yelling is the sharp whistling noise of the wind whipping over the car and the low hum of the engine I'm praying won't give out.

I step off the highway and walk back to my car. The muscles in my legs involuntarily go weak and force me to my knees near the trunk. As the rocks dig through my jeans, all my emotions release in unison and flood in like the first amplified note of an orchestra. I feel pathetic and alone. Tears stream down my face and sting my cheeks as the freezing night wind rolls over my face. *Everything is changed.*

After throwing myself a suitable pity party, I return to my feet and wipe away my tears. I glance at Piper through the fog-filled window and see my toddler still sleeping quietly, her thumb wedged in between her lips. The car's warmth welcomes me back as I climb into the driver's seat of the '89 Accord with rosy chilled cheeks.

"On the road again," I sing quietly as my tires spin against the snow-dusted rocks.

My northbound drive continues, and the road remains mostly vacant. A glance at the wobbly gas gauge shows it bouncing up and down at just below half a tank as if it's teasing me. "You're gonna make it... Just kidding," it keeps repeating.

"Please get us somewhere," I say to the instrument as I survey the lonely highway with no infrastructure in sight. *We'll stop for the night at the next town we hit.*

There, I plan for us to stay in a motel overnight, call and tell mama we're coming, and try to get ahold of Jake and ask him what the hell he was thinking. *Guess it'll do for now.*

The white noise of the FM radio's static that the middle of nowhere provides fills the car. The depressing melodies of eighties country songs are typically my music of choice, but the scan button fails to catch a signal. The feedback I do snag drowns out the sound of my tires rolling along the pavement.

The sharp winds repeatedly catch my car's side panels and push me back and forth between the lines like a pinball while I allow the gale to play with the vehicle. The swaying is helping me stay awake.

Vivid caution lights for a railroad crossing appear suddenly off in the distance of the Montana countryside and pique my intrigue. I rub my eyes and widen my stare as I snap out of a daze.

The crossing's arms light up and lower themselves to signal the arrival of an inbound train just as my car arrives at the painted halt bar. I stop at the appropriate place and watch the lights flash back and forth in a harmony that's just slightly out of sync.

In the distance, I hear the train's rising whistle rolling over the landscape as it draws nearer. I close my eyes and lean back into the headrest as I hum along, trying to match the horn's octave.

My car slightly shakes as the train speeds past, and I hear Piper mutter, "mama." I keep my eyes closed and enjoy a short daydream that Piper and I are riding the Amtrack toward a new life.

We're gonna be okay. I know we will. We don't need him.

TWO

MIRANDA

THE HIGHWAY'S BLACKTOP rolls on continuously. The repeated landscape and lack of turns leave me feeling like the road will never end. If I just keep chugging along, I might eventually circle the earth and end up right back where I started. *he last place I want to be right now.*

I'm exhausted, both physically and emotionally. Jake leaving me for someone else had often crossed my mind, but now that I'm alone and reflecting on the day's events, I'm shocked at how much his infidelity surprised me.

The sound of my tires pushing ten over the limit is repetitious. Occasionally a tiny rock causes a pop and changes the tempo, but besides that, the rolling rubber plays a gentle hum that's trying to lull me to sleep. I fight to stay aware.

I'd once played the big bad wolf in an elementary school play and briefly dreamed of being on a Hollywood screen. As I grew up, I admitted California wasn't an attainable goal, but I still joined the drama club and performed in front of larger crowds.

The stage lights were always my favorite. I could never see the people sitting in front of me, and all I could do was imagine the faces the audience was making over my missed notes and skipped lines. The glow was blinding but gave me the confidence to perform.

The open road in front of me now reminds me of the stage illuminated by the harsh lighting of my car's headlights. I can say or think whatever I want, and I won't see how anyone reacts. I can break down or shine.

We pass by a cattle farm, and the reminiscent scent causes my mind to wander.

I CAME INTO the world in the same small county hospital where both of my parents had been born. They brought me home in the dead of winter and raised me in the sleepy town of Butte, Montana, on old, handed-down farmland that sat well outside the city limits.

Although my mom kept a scrapbook filled with magazine cutouts of landscapes from around the world, we only left the state once for a two-day family vacation to see the Wyoming side of Yellowstone National Park. Yellowstone had it all: geysers, buffalo, big horned sheep, waterfalls. It was the most beautiful place I'd ever seen. I begged to go back; we just never had the money.

My parents grew vegetables in a field that stretched out for nearly a mile against a mountainous backdrop. My summer days were spent outside finding flowers to press between pages of a notebook, and when winter snuck up, I stayed inside and stoked the coal stove and dreamed of spring.

The peaks surrounding our land were doused in countless shades that faded into one and gave the ranges a watercolor appearance every season. The acreage just past the family garden was level and surrounded by a wooden fence my father constantly repaired by hand. Cows were always grazing in the green pastures, ready to be butchered when the freezer's bottom began to show.

A shanty chicken coop sat near the barn and always looked to be on its last leg from being battered by the rough springtime winds. Yet, no matter the season, I was expected to wake up before the sun, gather the loose eggs, and eat a freshly made breakfast before catching the bus that took me to the school close to town.

For as long as I could remember, we had been grouped in with those labeled as the poor people in town, even though mama always said we were *rich with love*. While the other girls in my grade had nice new clothes to start a new school year, most of the apparel shoved into my falling apart wardrobe was purchased from the thrift store's clearance rack or donated by women at the church.

I had always been slightly ashamed of being the kid wearing Goodwill clothes and eating peanut butter sandwiches surrounded by the popular girls who had it all. I walked the halls with my head hung low and avoided their affluent herds whenever possible. Although I hated to admit it, I envied their first-hand purses and makeup they didn't appreciate.

Life took a bright turn when I moved into town and got a job working as a hostess at a chain restaurant right after high school. Mama and dad did the best they could, but I was ready to figure out what I wanted to do with my life (and it wasn't farming).

Want ads in the paper hooked me up with two single female roommates that felt like my first real friends. They told me about college, the classes, boys, and parties. They made it sound so fun and alluring and I thought maybe one day I'd go. We also cooked dinners together and talked about our futures almost weekly. They were saving up to leave town after graduation. I was just getting by and waiting to see where my life was headed.

After working for a few months, I finally had the money to spend on the niceties my life had lacked since birth. With my earnings, I was able to get a haircut from someone who wasn't family, dine out at restaurants more than once a quarter, and eventually purchase a gently used car.

Then there was Jake.

He came in and swept me off my feet before I could begin to comprehend what was happening. I had always envisioned a guy like him wanting the superficial girls from school I had envied, but he genuinely appreciated me for my plain Jane wardrobe and introverted personality.

Jake constantly complimented me on how beautiful he thought I was, but something inside never allowed me to accept his accolades. My insecurities refused to let me believe the girl in the mirror was good enough. Even when I purposely dressed up and felt somewhat attractive, I continuously perceived Jake as the better-looking one.

When we went out to dinner or just walked around town, I saw the attention he got from other women but tried not to let it bother me.

Jake was a handsome guy with a face that I always said would look magnificent starring in a soap opera. Tall, dark, handsome, he checked all the boxes.

He stood at just over six-foot tall and methodically purchased clothes that hugged his figure in all the right places. He kept his dark brown hair neatly buzzed into a high fade that was long enough on top for him to run his fingers through its ends. Every morning, his face was clean-shaven like clockwork, but a smoky five o'clock shadow was poking through by mid-afternoon. He topped his looks off with a sharp jawline and long natural eyelashes that flipped above his blue eyes.

After work, he spent an hour or two at the gym maintaining a commendable physique. The outline of his chest showed through his shirts, especially the fitted white ones, and hints of the muscles just above his knees could be seen poking through his work pants when he walked. His fit figure and striking eyes lured me in from the beginning.

We met at a bar when I was in my early twenties. I was out with some friends for a booze-filled bachelorette party, and Jake and his coworkers had walked into the same dive bar for some drinks after a full day's work.

My eyes met Jake's from across the room, which was cloaked in a thin haze from the people smoking inside. He flashed me a toothy smile that caused a kaleidoscope of butterflies to take flight behind my ribcage. I shot a muted smirk back.

Before I realized it, the man across the bar was behind me.

"Hey," Jake yelled in my ear, trying to talk over the bar's booming music.

"Hey yourself," I replied, pulling my lips off my cocktail straw.

"Are you here with friends?" he asked as he waved to the girls who were drunkenly dancing beside me.

"Huh?" I responded.

"Do you want to go outside?" he replied, getting closer. Jake nudged his head toward the door.

"Oh, yeah. Um, okay, sure."

He grabbed me gently by the elbow, and I felt a warmth rush up my arm. He pulled me toward the door. I followed the stranger's lead willingly and only stumbled once in my unfamiliar heels and intoxicated state.

"Okay, now this is better," Jake stated when we made it outside.

"Wow, yeah, it is," I yelled, still trying to overcompensate for the bar's volume.

Jake chuckled at my raised voice and gently shook his head. I quickly shivered as the summer wind rolled over my exposed shoulders.

"Here," Jake said, offering me his windbreaker.

"Thanks," I replied with a broad smile and stared into his cerulean eyes.

"I'm Jake."

"Nice to meet you, Jake. I'm Miranda."

We found a wooden bench near the bar's entrance and sat outside and chatted. Jake placed one ankle on his opposite knee and gently rested his arm on the seat's back. He looked comfortable.

We talked and talked some more, and I leaned into his rib cage a few times when he made me laugh. Jake let me lead the conversation and didn't contribute much. Instead, he sat next to me, wearing a faint smile, and seemed to be enjoying my drunken rambling.

When one A.M. came around, the heavy bass from inside the bar finally stopped thumping. Someone switched the glowing sign to CLOSED. The manager held the door open as the bachelorette entourage stumbled out of the building in a drunken pack with the guys that Jake had shown up with.

Jake scribbled his phone number on a business card and passed it to me. I fumbled around with the sides of his jacket until I finally came across a pocket and tucked it away.

His smooth lips gently met my cheek as he grabbed my elbow and helped me fall into one of the girl's cars. It was either his kiss or the half-gallon of tequila sloshing around inside of me that made my stomach do a cartwheel.

"Can I see you again?" he asked hopefully.

"What about right now?" I replied with a sloppy wink.

"I don't think now is the best time." He was even cuter when he laughed.

"You're probably right. Then some other time, uh, yes."

Jake quietly smiled and shut the car door. He began walking back toward the closed bar when I yelled at him from a rolled-down window.

"Hey, you. You forgot your jacket."

"Just keep it. Give it back to me next time," he yelled back, bringing a smile to my drunk face.

I woke up the next day with pulsing temples when the sun beamed through the curtains. I choked down the urge to vomit before collapsing back onto the mattress. With my head buried inside my pillow, I closed my eyes and tried to remember the night's events that led to the miserable hangover. Vague memories popped into my head as scattered images played inside my closed eyelids: *pregaming, dinner, some more shots, the guy at the bar. Oh my God, that guy at the bar.*

"Ow," I groaned as I climbed out of bed.

I fished his number from the borrowed jacket I had dropped with my pants. "Deputy Jake Thacker."

The card's reverse side had a seven-digit number scribbled on it. I pinned it to the corkboard beside the phone. Seeing the name Jake, my memory was instantly triggered, and I remembered the handsome man I spent the night talking to outside the bar.

After waiting two days, I finally called the number on the card. I pushed my hand against my pants to silence its shake as I heard the line ringing. *What if he doesn't remember me? No, he will. He has to. Right?*

Sure enough, Jake did remember. He even sounded excited by my call and quickly asked me out to dinner.

Our first date went great. Jake loved that I ordered a beer and cheeseburger with all the toppings instead of a salad and vodka tonic. He laughed as I made a mess of myself with my dinner and even offered his napkin when mine ended up ketchup soaked.

The whole night, we bantered back and forth as the conversation rolled on organically. Jake talked, I talked, and we found many things we had in common.

"Don't even think about it," he said when I tried to grab the check.

Our smiles met across the table, and I felt my stomach turn inside out.

Jake walked me up to my apartment's front steps as the evening ended. He leaned forward and brought his hand to my cheek before gently bringing his lips to mine. Upon contact, I felt every synapse in my body fire in rapid succession as I kissed him back.

"Goodnight," Jake said as he pulled his face back. The rough brush of his stubble grazed my chin.

"Goodnight," I replied with a smile, my eyes readjusting to the light.

We continued dating and tried to see each other every day of the week. I quickly fell in love and found any reason to be around him. He was gentle-natured, soft-spoken, and the first boyfriend I had ever felt was worth my time.

As time went on, I often slept at his house in the woods more than I stayed at my own. Jake would pull my naked body in close under the comforter when the slightest draft worked its way into the bedroom and run his fingers from my shoulder to my waist and back, sending a natural chill down my spine. In the morning, he always had a fresh cup of black coffee with a splash of cream chilled to room temperature waiting on the counter when I finally moseyed into the kitchen.

After a year of dating, we combined households, and I made the cross-town move into Jake's parents' old house. It wasn't long before we realized the headache of learning what sharing a home meant and tried to perfect the art of compromising. Our relationship had its natural ups and downs, but we often found ways to have fun together. When the winter weather kept us inside, I shared my deep love of classic board games, and Jake taught me how to play PlayStation.

Jake finally got down on one knee at the peak of a mountain at our favorite ski resort. I didn't even take a breath before tears rolled down my frozen cheeks, and I accepted his proposal.

The next day, we ran off to the courthouse and signed the papers as fast as possible to begin our life together. As the newly minted Thacker family, we hosted an intimate party with close friends to celebrate our engagement and hurried marriage before going home and rolling around in our queen size bed.

The first year was blissful, and the honeymoon phase felt like it would never end. Jake was consistently romantic and attentive, and I reciprocated that love daily. Flowers, date nights, romantic wine by the fire, we did it all. From an outside perspective, it looked like we had all the answers for love wrapped up in a tiny package.

Our lives became increasingly busier when Jake was promoted to sergeant. Multiple overtime hours were quickly tacked onto his already busy workload, and the job seemed to wear on him. I tried to find something to occupy my time, which led to my bouncing from workplace to workplace, trying to figure out my ideal career.

We came into financial struggles that strained our marriage when we had to take out a personal loan to replace the roof after a nearby tree took out a chunk of it. We bickered for a week about selling the place. I was consistently irritated that Jake refused to sell and move just because the house had belonged to his parents. They were gone, and it was time to move on with *our* lives.

Even though it was dated, the entire estate was worth a small fortune. We could easily take that money and buy a house closer to town and have my mom move in so she wouldn't be living on her own three hours away.

Jake's parents' house worked well when we started out, but it was time for something new. I dreamed of us living in a more modern home in the city that didn't have unending leaks and drafts and didn't have the apparent influence of his mother's decorative style lingering in every room.

"We'll sell when the time is right, Miranda," I constantly heard him say.

"Sure," I always responded, knowing the time would never be right.

As our troubles and fights grew, our distance slowly increased. The life we had vowed to share was split in two. As much as we tried, Jake never returned my attempts to get back to how it was during the happy years of our marriage. We went through the socially proper motions of everyday life, but the fire of love that once burned passionately in our hearts had died.

We played the happily married couple game for years when we found ourselves out in the public eye. I would attend his work functions and weave my arm in his while I laughed at his jokes and forcefully played the doting wife role. On the surface, I was content, but deep down, I just wanted to go home, slip back into my pajamas, and watch the newest episode of Friends.

With our convincing fake smiles and tender kisses on the cheek, no one would have been able to know that behind closed doors, our relationship was cold and empty. We had become professionals at putting on the rehearsed show, and no one caught wind of the farce.

At one point, I contemplated asking for a divorce but never got around to talking to a lawyer. I was unhappy but comfortable with my world and didn't want to deal with a massive change. I still loved Jake, but I no longer felt a longing to be with him. We went out for dinner now and then, made small talk, and occasionally had sex just to curb one another's desires, but there was very little love that wafted between us.

When the little plastic stick surprisingly showed two pink lines, I begged Jake to stay with tear-filled eyes. He seemed to hesitate at first, like he wanted out, but he finally agreed and promised to make our relationship more of a priority. Being a good dad was important to him, and he planned to be there for his child, even if that meant he had to remain in a stagnant relationship.

His efforts to return to the happy couple we had once been were visible. He paid more attention to me and found little acts that he could do to help out while I was pregnant and uncomfortable. Our sex life improved from the special occasion only event that it had become, and our home's evident happiness was palpable for the first time in years.

But, it wasn't long before we fell back into the same jaded lifestyle we had become accustomed to before Piper's birth.

Our life became one of ignorance, and we often went about our days without saying a word to one another. When we did talk, it wasn't harsh but friendly, as if we had become roommates. Jake helped with Piper, and it was obvious he loved his daughter, but the romantic relationship between him and I grew further apart with every passing day.

Even though things were rough, I had never expected him to drift so far that he would leave me. I was callous enough to believe we could just move through the motions of being a family forever. I was okay with that, and I thought he was too.

But, his affair was our end. *I met someone* was my breaking point.

"We're leaving," I whispered to Piper as I grabbed her from the play yard.

As soon as my foot breached the house's threshold, the chilled air that blew across the porch felt fresher than it ever had before. The stress and anxiety about our relationship seemed to blow away with the cold Montana gust that sent a shiver down my arms. A half-smile formed on my face as I stepped down the stairs and secured Piper in the back of the car.

We spent the afternoon pretending like everything was right in the world. Piper had a dermatologist appointment, we ran some errands, grabbed some snacks, and went to a playground in the heart of town.

Piper's youthful happiness as she played in the midday sun was delightful. I watched her smile and heard her candid laugh as she flew high in the child swing. I blinked multiple times as if I were trying to record the images in my head like a film, desperate to remember the moment. I wanted nothing more than to shield Piper from the emotional heartache I was dealing with internally. *She deserves better.*

As the sun began to set and the early winter night rolled down off the mountains, I met a friend for an early dinner. I desperately needed a welcoming ear to vent and hoped Kirstyn could offer solid advice.

"Hold on. He did what?" Kirstyn asked with wide eyes.

Kirstyn set her fork down and rested her chin on her fist as her eyebrows inched in toward one another. I rattled off some obscure details of my relationship that I had never shared. A knot the size of a golf ball formed in the back of my throat as I spoke. I took purposeful breaks in my speech and talked slowly while keeping my emotions bottled up. Crying in public felt weak like he had won. I tried to fight off the tears attempting to pool in my eyes.

"I'm so sorry," Kirstyn replied as she gently placed her hand on my arm.

"Thanks, but really, it'll be okay, we'll be okay," I said as I looked at Piper, making a mess in her plate of spaghetti.

"So, what are you going to do?" Kirstyn asked.

"I'm gonna go stay with my mom for a while, figure things out. I just don't want to be at home anymore," I answered.

"So don't go back there, now or ever."

"I need to grab some stuff. I just need some time to cool off before we start talking specifics."

"Yeah, if he hasn't ridden off into the sunset with that whore of his," Kirstyn responded as she raised her wine glass.

We toasted our stemmed glasses and took a sip of wine. We then trash-talked Jake for close to an hour more before Kirstyn picked up the check for the three of us.

"Thank you," I said as we parted ways.

"You're always welcome. Call me before you leave. And be careful driving so late. You can just stay with me if you need," Kirstyn replied.

"I'll call. But I promise we'll be fine. Kinda want to see my mom."

Kirstyn nodded that she understood.

THE LIFE RECAP playing on my personal stage fades away into the night as an eighteen-wheeler sways my car as it passes. I shake my head clear.

The snow has morphed from fresh and powdery to heavy and granular. It falls in large chunks through the beam of my headlights. Typically, I enjoy seeing a new blanket of powder dusted atop a mountainside but increasing precipitation while alone in the middle of nowhere means danger. I keep my eyes peeled along the Montana countryside and watch for wildlife moving along the edge of the snowy road. The last thing I need is a rogue deer to come out of nowhere and halt my journey.

As much as I want to drive all night until we make it to mama's, I know that means traversing an ungodly steep driveway in the dark, and my mother hates people showing up unannounced. An overnight stop is warranted.

I fight to stay alert as I press a fist into my temple to support my drooping head. As much as I hate to admit it, I know I'll be forced to give in and succumb to the exhaustion soon. My eyes water more with every yawn, and the dashed lines in the middle of the highway seem to run together into one solid mesmerizing stripe.

After driving for close to two hours, I finally happened upon Great Falls, the last stop with a full-sized grocery store before the final stretch to mama's house in the mountains.

The quaint town sits nestled quietly between a couple of small distant mountain ranges, and the main drag can get you across town in about twenty minutes with a handful of lights.

We drive into town coasting on fumes, and a small, illuminated motel near the airport shows itself over the hilly horizon. I squint toward the parking lot and see a red sign that flickers "VACANCY" through the snowy haze.

My sedan rattles and sputters slightly as it climbs the hill into the parking lot but finally makes it to the plateau. *Good job, baby.* I quietly scoop Piper up, wrap a fleece blanket around her, and head toward the motel's warm lobby.

A jingle at the handle announces our entry and startles someone with a mop of hair hunched over, napping at the counter. The desk worker hurriedly sits up as if I hadn't just seen him sleeping on the job and wipes a smidge of drool from his lower lip.

"Hi, how much for a room?" I ask the teenage boy. He shakes his head and rubs an eye as he finally comes to.

"A night or a week? A week's a better deal," he explains.

"Um, just a night," I reply. "And I'd like to pay in cash."

"Supposed to leave a card or check. Sorry but it's the policy."

I fork over my debit card.

"Don't worry, we won't run it unless you leave the place a mess," he explains.

I silently smile as I grab the keys and my card. Piper remains tucked into my chest as we venture back into the cold and climb the stairs to our second-floor room.

When the key finally gives way and releases the rusty lock, I carry Piper into our overnight home while feeling a gentle vibration from her deep snore.

I flip on the light switch, and disappointment spreads across my face when I catch a view of our new living arrangements. *I didn't think I would, but I miss the house already.*

The room consists of a queen bed topped with only one pillow and a pea-green quilt coving the white sheets. The bathroom vanity has a wall-mounted hairdryer that hadn't been hung up and dangled freely from its holder, and the bedside lamp constantly flickers against the tacky wall-papered walls in no apparent rhythm.

"Guess I can't complain for only thirty-nine bucks," I whisper.

As I step farther into the room, I catch a lingering smell of cigarette smoke that hangs in the air and wafts out of the worn-out carpet as my feet agitate the fibers. I can smell the burnt wood smell coming off me, but this one is pungent and a scent that will likely leave me waking up with a headache. *I guess it's better than sleeping in the car.*

I gaze down at Piper and all her silent innocence and lay her down on the bed. I slip her out of her winter layers and slowly change her diaper while attempting to be gentle. She's had enough change in her life tonight. I want to let her sleep.

With my teeth unbrushed and my hair pulled back into a high ponytail, I climb into the bed wearing only my bra and underwear and pull a freshly changed Piper in close. The quilt is paper-thin, but I cover us with both it and the crunchy over-washed sheets.

Piper's lips part gently as I stare at her. The slight glow from the motel's sign outside our room shines through the crack in the curtains and lands on her pale skin. I'm still utterly shocked that she slept through a night full of chaos and unusual routine.

Tiny whines escape Piper's lips as I hold her tightly in my arms. Tears involuntarily flood my eyes as I smell the crown of my daughter's head. Subtle hints of baby shampoo and Jake's cologne fill my nose as I close my eyes and allow the familiar scents to seep into my lungs and memory.

My tears continue flowing as the fear that our lives will never be the same again creeps up. I'm worried about what our future will look like and if things will work out for us when the next day's light breaks.

I lay on my back with the sheet pulled to my chin and stare at the popcorn sprayed ceiling. Piper twitches gently near my side as she slips further into dreamland. *He really doesn't care about what happens to us now. It's all up to me.*

After laying on the lumpy mattress for close to an hour with the adjoining room's muffled music playing through the thin walls, I finally fall into a shallow sleep with Piper nestled gently in my arms.

THREE

JOHN

THE HANDHELD RADIO Detective John Waters kept on his dresser squawked, the staticky muffled voice filling the room. A familiar address came across as he was brushing his teeth. *Jake? That's Jake's place.*

John quickly donned a polo and khakis. He kissed his wife and ran out to assist without much argument. Jake was not only a coworker, but a friend, and the call sounded urgent.

He drove down the dark stretch of highway as he traveled away from the heart of town. The snow clouds had left the night sky covered with an overcast layer of wispy clouds. Only scanty bands of moon illumination worked their way through the haze.

He headed toward something the county deputies could handle on their own. Even though a house fire wasn't exactly routine business, they likely wouldn't need his assistance. But he wanted to be there in case Jake needed something.

The night's sharp gusts pushed his car slightly as they rolled off the plains and blew airy dust across the road. He pulled opposite the wind to keep himself between the lines.

The temperature had plummeted suddenly as it often did in December. Every night when the evening sun would begin to fall behind the mountains, twenty to thirty degrees would disappear in what felt like the blink of an eye.

Halfway through his forty-minute drive, a light flurry began to dust his windshield.

"Dammit," he mumbled, realizing he had left his insulated hat and gloves at home. *A windbreaker will have to do.*

John had worked for the Silver Bow County Sheriff's Department for nearly twenty years after retiring and hanging up the pilot wings he had earned in the Air Force.

During his military career, John had flown combat sorties in multiple theaters and pinned on the rank of Lieutenant Colonel before a nasty car accident grounded him for good and ended his flying days long before he was ready.

Butte was where he and his wife were born and raised and where she had been dying to get back to since they left. After twenty years of service, multiple short notice or extended deployments, and eight (sometimes international) moves, he thought she deserved to pick the spot for their forever home.

Since retiring, John had put on close to twenty pounds, gained half a head of greys, and had aches and pains that radiated throughout his body. His wife repeatedly insisted he quit and finally retire for good, but the draw of serving the small community he grew up in drove him to keep working. He couldn't fathom throwing in the towel just yet.

When he thought about retiring, he heard his grandfather's voice ringing in his ears. "Once you slow down and sit your ass on the couch, it goes downhill real fast. Health, mind, everything." Retirement felt too absolute.

The streetlights thinned along the highway and eventually disappeared as he neared the Thacker estate.

He recalled earlier that morning when Jake had stormed into the locker room after using the department's gym. The blank face and grunting tone he displayed was different from his usual bubbly and enthusiastic persona.

John was one of the older people in the department and often felt the need to mentor the younger ones like the Airmen when he served. He tried to pick up on small personality shifts and check in on people.

"Mornin' bud. You doin' okay?" John asked as Jake grabbed some things from his locker.

"I'm fine," Jake grunted shortly without making eye contact.

Jake haphazardly threw a couple of things into his duffle and zipped it closed. He hurriedly tossed the bag over his shoulder. The metal locker door was slammed shut with fury, and John noticed an unmistakable look of frustration spread across Jake's face. He purposely moved out of Jake's path as he headed toward the door.

"See ya," John said in Jake's general direction.

Jake returned an indiscernible grunt.

What was all that about?

Jake continued out the front of the building, and John let him go.

"Hmm, whatever," John mumbled into his coffee. He brushed the encounter off as just a rough morning and went about his day without giving it any more thought.

But now Jake needed him. A housefire likely meant he would need a place to stay, and John was more than willing to extend his guest room accommodations to the young family.

The snow on the windshield increased to the point where wipers were necessary. The clock on the dash ticked close to midnight.

When he finally pulled up the long driveway and arrived at the Thacker's, he saw the ruins of the half-torched house. The left side seemed okay, but the entire right half of the home had succumbed to the hungry blaze.

The people putzing around the truck in their yellow suits and oxygen backpacks had already extinguished the fire and were finishing up whatever they did once the structure was declared safe. The remnants of what had been the place Jake grew up in were illuminated by three cars spaced out evenly in front of the porch, their headlights pointed toward the scene.

In the circular drive sat an ambulance and two other police vehicles. The responders that weren't picking at the home or repacking the truck looked to be standing around bored.

The reflection of John's unmarked car's headlights bounced off the circle of trees that surrounded the house as he slid his car into park and switched everything off.

One of the younger deputies ran across the drive in his down coat as he hurried out to meet John just as he pulled the keys from the ignition. *That boy needs to relax. It's just a fire.*

John rolled himself out of the low car as he grunted through arthritis that pierced through his knees and back. Pain was something he had grown accustomed to.

"It's pretty damn late. You guys better have this thing sorted out fast," John stated with a look of frustration directed at the deputy.

Even though John wasn't the county sheriff, many deputies looked up to him like he was filling the elected seat. He always made an effort to take care of anyone and was more than willing to help when needed.

"Yes, sir. We're uh, working on getting everything buttoned...," the deputy started before John cut him off.

"You guys find Jake yet?" he asked, looking around the crowded yard for the homeowner.

John combed the driveway and didn't see any shadow that resembled Jake's figure. He looked back at the young deputy, who hesitated before answering with a confused look spread across his face.

"That's the thing, sir. He's uh, he's uh, he's in the house."

John rolled over the deputy's stuttered response for a moment and tried to comprehend what he meant. *There's no way it's safe to go in yet.*

"Inside? What do you mean inside? You guys let him back in already?" John asked for clarification.

"Sir, um, well, we uh," the deputy rambled on as he looked down.

"Spit it out, boy," John encouraged while raising his voice.

"Sir, they found his body inside. In the house."

John broke the gaze he had been holding on the remnants of the house and looked toward the deputy for further clarification.

"Say again?" John asked, hoping he had heard the kid wrong.

"His body, sir, we um, found it in the living room. It's close to seventy-five percent charred to hell, but uh, we have no idea what happened yet," the deputy reiterated.

"And you know it's him?" he hurriedly probed.

"Sadly, yeah. A couple of us looked and knew it was him," he responded.

John shook his head slightly as he tried to swallow the emotional lump budding in his throat. His vision narrowed, and his eyebrows pinched toward the middle of his face as he looked toward the house.

"Has Miranda been here?" John asked, worried for Jake's young wife and daughter.

"Who?"

"Miranda. Miranda Thacker. Jake's wife?"

"Oh right, sorry. No, sir, we haven't seen her. It was reported that a woman did call 911, but Brian said he didn't think it sounded like her. But, um, the fireteam has been looking through the house since they put it out. They said they hadn't seen any signs that anyone else was inside. Just Jake," the deputy explained.

"And where are his remains now?" John asked.

"They're still in the house. They're working on getting them out as we speak."

John let out a heavy sigh of relief. *Thank God the girls weren't in there too.*

"Thanks," John said with a swat of his hand as he excused the deputy.

John took a moment to think about his friend. He rubbed his hand across his heart as he felt it thump beneath his dry palm. *Jake, dead,* just couldn't resonate as something factual in his mind. *Miranda is going to be devastated. And Piper, she's just a baby. But now, she doesn't have a daddy.*

John brushed past the litter of first responders that stood in the driveway with solemn faces and made his way toward the house. As he passed, they simply nodded.

Inside the crumbling ruins, he could see the firefighter's flashlights slowly moving around, penetrating the lingering smoke that clouded the air as they combed the home.

The smell of the charred wood hung thick in the air and filled his lungs as he moved closer. Faint wisps of smoke were still rolling out of the front door and down the steps of the house's somewhat spared porch. The flurry that fell and dusted the sleeves of his windbreaker looked to be a mixture of both snow and white ash that were being blustered around in the late evening gale.

"We know what started this whole thing yet?" John asked as he approached the fire chief.

"Not yet. We should be able to figure it out in a couple of days. But I don't know, John. Something just tells me this wasn't an accident," the chief returned as she made eye contact with him. "And I'm terribly sorry for your loss."

He looked at the house for a moment and tried to draw conclusions about how Jake's home could have been set ablaze with him inside. The many possibilities he mulled over were dark and brooding, and he tried to strike them from his mind for the time being.

"Alright, thanks. Lauren, just let me know when you figure something out," he said to the chief.

"Of course."

The firefighters began emerging from the rubble that had once been a beautiful farmhouse nestled on one of the lushest lots in the county. With all the pine leaving the area densely wooded, it was luck that the flames hadn't jumped from the house and set the mountainside ablaze.

John made his way back to his vehicle and realized he had left his bag phone at home in his rush to get out of the door. There was zero cell service out this far anyway. He turned over the ignition to get the heat rolling again and snatched up his dash radio to call back to the office.

"Josie, you there?" he called to the dispatcher on duty.

"Yes, sir, I'm here. Over," her voice crackled back at him.

"Hey, um, any calls about this house fire? Particularly any ones from Miranda Thacker?" he asked, hoping she had called the department.

"Been a few calls. But none of them were from her. Over."

John rolled his eyes. *How many times have I told you? You don't have to say over every damn time.*

"Alright, thank you," he responded.

"Sir, is it really Jake? Over," she asked.

"I don't know yet," he responded quietly and hung up the microphone. He was holding out hope that the deputies were wrong in their identification. *But why would someone else be dead in Jake's house?* None of it made any sense.

Miranda and Piper not being found dead alongside Jake in the house was a blessing. But the fact that Jake's bride was nowhere to be seen and hadn't even called about the fire left John slightly confused about where she had gone.

John had a keen eye and could tell the two seemed to have a rocky relationship that they tried to keep private. Miranda placed a hand on Jake's arm when she laughed at his jokes, but John could see the coldness in her eyes when he kissed her cheek. Even though he knew their marriage wasn't perfect, he wouldn't dare assume that the sweet girl he had met at many office picnics could have killed her husband or set their home on fire with him inside. *But people surprise you.*

The responders inside the building worked as they combed over the wreckage piece by piece. They were slow and methodical in their search, trying to be watchful to ensure they hadn't missed anything or disturbed what had become a crime scene. Based on the number of incidents they had worked together, John knew the response team was good at what they did.

I'll come back tomorrow when it's daylight. Walk the scene, see what I can find. John felt a personal pull drawing him to the fire and its victim. He wanted answers.

The flurry finally slowed, but the night air remained blistering cold and had a cutting draft that whipped through the trees. John stayed in his car, cranked the heat up to full blast, and got comfortable. The current job was for the firefighters, so he stepped back and allowed them to do what they did best.

The clock on his dash neared two A.M., and he fought to keep his eyes open. He sparingly sipped his coffee that had gone lukewarm and tried to convince himself it was keeping him awake.

A flash of white in his peripherals caught John's attention. He looked up and saw three people dressed in fire suits surface from inside the house, carrying what looked to be a motionless body about Jake's size.

He scrambled out of the car and drew his windbreaker tight. He quickly headed toward where the corpse was about to be transferred to a stretcher for transport.

When he made it halfway across the gravel lot, he heard a little jingle as his foot knocked something metal sounding around in the rocks below his feet. He shined his flashlight toward the ground and squinted to see what his shoe had disrupted.

Near his toe, he saw a shiny glimmer in the driveway. He squatted down with his elbow on one knee and slowly picked up the item he'd nearly walked by.

In his palm, he held a dainty gold ring that had been dropped on the ground. He scanned the obscure tree line, looking for anything as he rolled the cold metal band around in his hand.

"Forever and ever," John read as he barely made out the engraving inside the ring.

John loosely dropped the item into his pants pocket to be investigated later and continued his way over to the fire's victim. *For the love of God, please don't be Jake.*

He nervously strode up to the stretcher. He pressed his hands into his hips to silence their nervous twitching. Being calm and collected was important.

A blanket had been evenly draped over the body and hid whatever was lying beneath. An unfamiliar smell hung in the air, one John would never be able to erase from his memory. *Hell, that's gotta be charred flesh.* The pungent odor caused vomit to build up in his throat.

"Excuse me," he said as he took a step back to collect himself before glancing at the casualty.

When he mustered the courage to see what lay on the stretcher, he took hold of the thin covering and pulled it back. The entire motion felt like it took thirty seconds as John silently prayed the figure beneath would be a stranger.

He pulled the sheet to the body's collar bone which inevitably revealed the mostly untouched face of Jake Thacker lying on his back. Patches of charred skin were scatted halfway up his neck, and the flesh along the right side of his jaw was melted clean off. *Dammit.*

"Yep, um, they had it right. That's Jake," John confirmed for the EMT standing with the body as she recovered Jake's face.

The EMT silently nodded her head with a solemn smile and began loading the body up in the back of the ominous ambulance that screamed death.

John walked back to his car and leaned against the hood as he felt the cold metal work through his pants and sting the back of his thighs. He removed his hat and held it over his heart as he studied the destroyed house.

I don't know what the hell happened tonight, but I'm gonna find out.

FOUR

MIRANDA

PIPER STARTS RUSTLING around on the lumpy mattress before the sun even thinks about breaking through the paper-thin curtains. We've never shared a bed before, and I barely got any sleep. Instead of resting after a tumultuous day, I spent most of the night awake, staring at the brownish-yellow water stain on the popcorn sprayed ceiling of the motel room. I tried like hell, but my mind refused to shut itself down. *Fire, Piper, Jake, Allie.*

The darkness left me stressed about our next move, worried about the money running dry, and scared that Piper would fall off the bed onto the dirty Berber carpet if I drifted off.

Piper jabs her chubby index finger into my cheek as she clicks her tongue against the roof of her mouth. I heavily grunt then sigh because it's apparent that she's ready to start the day.

I climb out of bed to get her a sippy cup, hoping she'll suckle the old milk and fall back to sleep. My feet feel heavy as they hit the floor, and I realize how much I miss the days when I could roll over onto my side, latch her onto a nipple, and breastfeed until we drifted off for a few more hours.

When I grab the cup, the smell of spoiled dairy comes out of the spout and hits my nose.

"Dammit," I say quietly. I pour the sour milk down the bathroom sink. I rinse, then fill the sippy cup with water from the tap that comes out with a slightly tan tint. *This isn't going to work.*

I hand Piper the cup, hoping she'll drink it, but she takes one sip, realizes it isn't the whole milk she was expecting, and tosses it to the floor.

"No, mama," Piper yells.

"Seriously?" I tiredly respond with a slightly raised and irritated tone.

Piper's big cerulean eyes look up at me. A broad smile spreads across her face, forcing a soft grin to creep to my lips. Even on the worst of days, Piper always knows how to brighten my spirit and make everything feel okay, even if it's only for a brief moment.

"Let me get dressed, and we will go buy some milk and go to Nana's house. Does that sound good to you?" I ask.

"Milk, milk," Piper answers back with her babbly voice as she stands up and claps.

Before checking out of the hotel and heading another thirty minutes to mama's house, I call and give her a heads up. The phone rings a few times until finally, I hear mama's voice on the other end of the phone.

"Hello?" her feeble voice comes across.

"Hey, mama."

"Miranda, hey, sweetheart. How are you?"

"Well, I've been better. But hey, we're up in Great Falls and gonna come visit you if that's okay."

Mama coughs three times and sounds like she's on the brink of hacking up a lung.

"Mama, you alright?"

"Sorry, I've had this nasty cold for a couple of days. But unfortunately, it doesn't want to seem to quit. Is Piper with you?"

"She is. Why didn't you call and tell me you were sick?"

"Oh, I don't know. I just didn't. I'm fine, you just relax. The doctor told me it's highly contagious, so I'm just trying to ride it out. Got some meds and stuff. I should be fine in a day or so."

"What do you have?" I ask.

"I don't know, just a mean cough and fever. This up and down of the weather gets me every year. The fever refuses to break. You don't need little Piper getting pneumonia or RSV, so why don't you pop on over Friday. I should be fine by then. That sound good?"

I think. Great Falls must have some things for us to do while I wait for Jake to reach out. Mama's house in the country doesn't have anything for miles.

"And according to the news, the plows haven't made it all the way up here. And you know your car won't make it up my drive."

Jake had often told me I needed to trade my Honda in for something with four-wheel drive. For the first time, I found myself wishing I had listened.

"Yeah, so Friday. We can do that. But we plan on staying for a while if that's good with you."

"Awhile? Is everything okay?" mama asks as she resumes coughing. I pull the phone from my ear so I don't go deaf.

"Yeah, I'll just tell you when I see you, alright?"

"Okay, baby. I love you."

"I love you too, mama."

As much as I don't want to admit it, mama's right. Piper doesn't need to catch a rough cold just as winter's beginning and my car doesn't fair well on snowy hills.

"Nana's in a couple of days," I say to Piper, who doesn't understand or care.

I slip one leg and then another into the jeans I'd worn the night before. As the pants' stagnant fibers are agitated, I catch a reminiscent whiff of the fire. *Should we have stayed?*

When I'd hopped into the car and drove away from the burning home, my mind was in an unfamiliar tizzy. It wasn't often I felt like I was out of control, but seeing the fire consuming our house sent me spiraling. A small part of me wonders if my mental state will ever be right again. *Another day of life. This one better than the last.*

I slip my black STAIND t-shirt over my head; it also reeks. But I welcome the smell and allow the smoke aroma to fill my lungs. The scent feels familiar but still surprising.

Piper willingly lets me stuff her back into her multiple layers of tops and bottoms, and I guide her feet into her fleece-lined snow boots. We both don our jackets and feel bundled enough to face the cold winter air waiting for us on the other side of the motel door.

"Ready?" I ask as I slip on Piper's beanie and press my lips to the tip of her nose. She giggles and wipes off my kiss with a gloved hand.

"Okay," Piper cheers as she claps through her mass of padding.

The weather feels more agreeable than last night as we breach the room's threshold and step outside. I peer over the roof of the other side of the building and see the sun finally making its way over the mountain and bathing the small town below in rays of warm light.

Being a Montana native, I'm accustomed to unpredictable meteorological conditions. It's common to start the morning wearing heavy, lined canvas pants and two different weights of jackets and end it in shorts and a short-sleeve shirt at the park. So, although there's a brisk breeze currently, it'll likely be bearable come this afternoon.

With Piper strapped into her seat, I climb into the frigid car and listen to it struggle as it tries to turn over. *Come on. Not now.* Finally, it roars to life. *Wow, this is the only thing we have left.*

The car has a low tap in the engine that Jake had never taken the time to look into, even though I asked him multiple times. The factory gold paint is chipped along the sides, and there are three places where it's peeling on the hood. The old Honda is far from perfect, but I cherish it as the one thing I can label as mine.

Everything Jake and I own is in his name and his only. The house and property it sits on were willed to him. Even after we married, he never added my name to the deed. All of the furniture littered throughout the home was purchased or handmade by his parents. Everything was Jake's.

I've never had a sense of ownership of anything in our marriage.

But the beat-up sedan belongs to me. I came into the marriage with it, and it has nothing to do with Jake or the Thacker name. Miranda Steyn is still printed on the title.

Piper babbles in the backseat as I drive slowly around Great Falls. The dawn quickly wanes into day, and the sunlight reflects off the mounds of snow lining the roads.

When mama first moved up here, we came into town once for dinner, but every other time we usually just skirted the city limits and went straight to her house, where she kept herself holed up.

Now driving around on my own, I realize the town is much larger than expected. Heading down the main drag, I find two large sporting goods stores, restaurants lining both sides of the road, and even a small park on the top of a hill that overlooks hundreds of acres.

When the first gas station finally comes into sight, I pull over and park my car at a pump.

"Milk, milk, mama," Piper cheers as I scoop her out of the backseat.

"Yeah, baby. Milk."

With Piper propped, straddling my hip, we traverse the slushy parking lot carefully to the front of the building. An electronic ding on the top of the door announces our entrance.

"Hi," I say with a gentle nod to the teenage boy working behind the counter.

"Good morning, ma'am," he returns.

I shuffle quickly around the small store and scan the aisles for the things we need. Per Piper's desires, I grab a half-gallon of whole milk from the fridge and a handful of nutritionally lacking snacks.

"It'll be eleven forty-three," the cashier says when he rings up all the items I shoveled onto the counter.

Upon pulling out my wallet, I take note of its weight without even undoing its zipper. I was expecting it to be heavier, but the Vera Bradley fabric pouch in my hand is screaming *YOU'RE BROKE* at me. When the zipper is pulled back, I see the meager contents inside. A small fold of bills and a handful of coins are all that stares back at me. I pull out what I have and pay for the items in cash.

"Thanks," I say and offer a soft smile. I grab the bag of sustenance off the counter and hurry back to the car.

I turn the key, and the car's engine roars to life. The heat starts to fill the cab. *Here we go, back to the motel life.* Before pulling out of the lot, I glance down and see the nearly empty reading on the fuel gauge. *Shit.*

Upon a second peer into my wallet, I see only a five and two ones pathetically tucked in the pouch. I fumble around in the center console, hoping to find more loose money. I push around the excess of fast food napkins and an oddly large number of pens as I run my hand against the felt bottom.

Luckily, I found a half-used roll of quarters tucked under a chew can Jake left in my car. Adding what change I fished out to my cash, I scraped together almost enough to top off the tank.

I yank the keys from the ignition, lock Piper in the car from the outside, and walk back toward the small store.

"Hopefully, this is enough," I say with a forced smile, pushing the small mound of thrown together money toward the cashier.

He quietly counts the bills and coins and adds the total to the pump. *$12.62. Better than nothing.*

"You're good to go, ma'am," he says.

On my way out of the building, I catch sight of an ATM tucked in the back corner. The glowing green "CASH" sign draws me in like a bug to the porch hanging death traps.

I plant a kiss on my debit card and slide the plastic into the reader. The screen comes to life, and I follow the instructions. My fingers move swiftly across the number pad as I enter my pin. I keep looking over my shoulder as if someone will grab the bills the minute they pop out of the machine.

Tick marks pop up and move in a circular motion that continually fold into themselves as the machine connects to the internet. *Please, for the love of God, tell me you haven't drained the accounts already.* The small loading circle continues its rounds as I wait. *Come on, come on.* Finally, the spinning stops and the machine displays additional options.

"Thank God," I whisper to the ATM when it finally lets me pull out cash. I withdraw five hundred dollars from our joint savings account, the daily maximum. I smirk as the machine spits a fat stack of crisp twenty-dollar bills into the collection tray.

I again look over my shoulder before lifting the plexiglass covering and grabbing my cash. *No one.* I pull out the money and shove it into my wallet.

The last time I'd checked our bank statement, we had close to six thousand dollars tucked away in our rainy day fund. I plan to revisit the ATM every day until I've pulled out half of the money I feel entitled to.

One last time I wave at the cashier I have seen too many times for one day and head back out into the cold.

With my feet stationary, I sway back and forth in jeans that provide little to no protection from the gusty squalls as I fill my car. When I'm topped off, I sink back into my seat and hear Piper gently chattering on in the back in a made-up language as she talks to herself.

A smile forms on my face, and I pull away from the pump with a full tank and wallet. The money feels like a symbol of freedom and instills hope for life's potential out from under someone's controlling thumb.

Store signs and lights are slowly turning on as the drag lights up for another day of business. I pull into the Walmart parking lot.

I park the car and drag Piper through another melting parking lot. She fights in my arms, adamant that she can walk independently, but I know putting her down will lead to her slipping and becoming soaked in the oil-saturated slush.

We sort through the aisles, grabbing the things we left behind to turn to ash. The house fire left us starting from scratch, which I think has a cathartic element.

I fill the cart with various foods that are marginally healthier than the gas station snacks. I also thumb through the racks and pick out a few sets of clothes that will better protect us from the impending winter.

We finish grabbing necessities, and I carry Piper on my hip when the boxes of diapers and wipes take up her only sitting room.

"Here you go, baby," I say as I add a couple of simple toys to our almost topped-off buggy. I feel bad that she had to leave everything behind.

We come back to the motel room and lug all the grocery bags up the stairs one load at a time. Both Piper and my clothes fill one drawer of the provided dresser, and I shove the dry food into the other. *It's only for a couple of days.*

Piper sits at the two-person dinette and begins to play with the cheap doll I grabbed while I stare at the phone, unable to pick it up. With a heavy sigh, I finally grab the handset and dial the number ingrained in my memory.

The other end rings and rings, but no one picks up. Eventually, I hear the click of the answering machine.

"You've reached Deputy Jacob Thacker with the Silver Bow County Sheriff's Department. Please leave your name and number, and I'll get back to you as soon as possible. Thank you," the machine says.

When the recording ends and the tone sounds, I pause. Tears instantly flood my eyes at the sound of my husband's voice. I'm still fuming with anger over his infidelity, but I also feel another emotion I wasn't expecting. I miss him. *No, he doesn't love you anymore. Let it go.*

"It's me. Not sure if you're still around. We're going to moms on Friday. Call me then," I say quickly before hanging up. I'm glad he didn't answer. It's easier to face a machine than the man that lied to my face for months.

"Mommy," Piper calls from the bathroom. She'd slipped away when I wasn't looking.

"Coming," I reply as I wipe my eyes dry.

With everything situated, I step into the tub shower combo with Piper and turn the handle until it's as hot as I can stand. The scalding water stings my back but warms the chill that hearing Jake's voice had allowed in.

The steam from the shower billows up from the floor and fills the tiny room with a smoke-like haze that feels somewhat therapeutic. *We're gonna be okay. We just have to be.*

I turn down the temperature and bounce Piper around on my hip. Her smile melts my heart. While we twirl around in the drizzle, I sing nursery rhymes aloud as I spin her in and out of the water's stream.

Our troubles wash down the drain as I lather and rinse Piper. She smiles and giggles at my off-key singing and soapy tickles without a care in the world.

Piper lays her head on my chest. I can sense she's almost ready for a morning nap. Last night was odd for her, and I'm sure she's still trying to acclimatize to her new environment.

My tone shifts. The once upbeat songs become slower and more solemn. I pull Piper in close, feel her growing still in my arms, and sway back and forth as my tame melody transforms into a calm and quiet hum. *He can't take you from me. I won't let him. I promise.*

Jake abandoning us hurts, and I don't want to think about the day I'll have to explain everything that happened to Piper. But, when I do, I plan to tell her the stories of the good days and try to water down the negative details so she can think of her father positively. Tears come into my eyes.

I sit Piper on the tub floor while I pay extra attention to my hair, digging my fingers into my scalp and scratching vigorously as I try to pull out any hint of smoke odor that worked its way into my follicles. I scrub my body to the point where my skin feels raw and I wash off the feeling of Jake's hand on my arm from the day prior.

After I'm clean, I wash and condition Piper's hair while she fights both me and her need to sleep.

When we turn off the water and exit the shower, all remnants of what happened the previous night disappear down the drain, mixing in with all the other horrible things in the sewer. The cleanliness brings a smile to both our faces as I try but fail to wrap Piper's hair up in a towel like mine.

"Silly Mama," Piper says while rolling into a yawn.

"Silly baby," I reply.

I can smell the free motel lavender shampoo and conditioner as I blow my thick hair dry and comb through Piper's tangles.

"Gotta get rid of them rat's nests," I say as I fight with one particularly nasty tangle.

Piper is fading fast, so I lay her down in a circular barrier of pillows while she plays with her stuffed doll and rolls around.

As I walk back to the bathroom, my naked reflection in the mirror catches my gaze. I study myself for a minute and try to figure out if I know the woman that stands looking back at me.

I recently lost quite a bit of weight after having Piper and restarting the regular running regiment I'd neglected for years. I treasured my early mornings while Piper was still asleep and a thin fog rolled over the country hills. I'd brainlessly run for miles until my watch told me it was time to head home so Jake could leave for work. It was my therapy, and one of the few things I did for myself.

Due to my weight loss, a thin boney frame with skin stretched over it now shows. My collar bones poke out noticeably at the top of my chest, and my knees look awkwardly knobby. Most of the size four jeans in my drawer barely stay up, and I often steal one of Jake's belts to avoid buying new clothes.

I cup my hands beneath my breasts and lift them as far as they go before allowing them to fall back down naturally. Pregnancy, then childbirth, and breastfeeding stole the once sexy flop they had. Now they just hang on my chest like trimmed limp chicken cutlets.

I run my boney fingertips down the front of my face pulling at the bottom of the light grey bags that sag under my eyes. Motherhood and the stress of being with someone I knew wasn't happy aged me faster than they should have. With my index finger, I forcefully rub the parallel lines between my eyebrows. I push harder and harder as if I can wipe them away and regain my youthful appearance instantly. *No luck.*

The hair I once took pride in growing and getting highlighted routinely has become long and scraggly. I spy multiple greys peeking out from my part that stand upward in an unruly manner.

I don't see any evidence of the young girl that I should still be staring back at me. Instead, my painful reflection shows a weathered woman that looks closer to her forty than her early thirties.

"Maybe this is why he left you," I mutter to my reflection, briefly feeling guilty.

I walk away from the mirror and try to shake the lingering feeling that I have become an unattractive woman at such an early age. My looks may not be the striking model ones I envisioned this Allie woman as having, but they can't be why Jake ran straight into the arms of a younger woman. That was his fault, and wallowing about it won't fix anything.

When I'm fully clean and ready to face the first day of my new life, I quietly lock the room's door and slip down the outside stairs. I hurry so Piper isn't alone long (even though she's knocked out), drop a quarter into the slot, and grab a thick newspaper from the watertight metal box. I run back to the room and find her exactly as I left her, except now she's snoring with her mouth wide open.

I lay out the local paper on the motel room's carpet and thumb through the ads in the back, searching for a job in town. My life in Butte is done, and I want to see my options if we settle down near Great Falls.

Ad after ad, I read the classifieds word for word as I search for anything that'll cover daycare and basic living expenses. I love my mama and don't mind staying with her for the time being, but it's not a permanent solution, and eventually, we'll need our own place.

I find a snippet stating that the local Albertsons is hiring a cashier with the potential for upward movement in the company. I circle the ad, dog-ear the page, and smile. *This is our fresh start. We're gonna do this on our own.*

FIVE

JOHN

THIRTY-SIX HOURS had passed since the Thacker's secluded home in the woods suddenly went up in flames with its owner inside. People around town were already beginning to devise their own stories about what had happened. The name that slipped from almost everyone's lips was *Miranda*. It's always easy to assume it was the wife.

The two-story shaker-sided house sat on a gorgeous lot that had been coveted by many over the years. The property had nearly three hundred acres of pine woodlands littered with deeply rutted coulees and small mountains, making the land ideal elk hunting grounds. A broad creek ran through the northwest corner, and people often got caught trying to sneak to it from the highway in the hopes of catching the mystifying paddlefish rumored to be breeding in its depths.

Over the years, many locals, and even outsiders, approached Jake's father and then Jake himself with an offer to buy the property. The Thacker men never accepted any proposals, even when they came in well above market.

They loved the place.

John approached the house that was festively draped in yellow plastic caution ribbons. Whoever cordoned off the scene hadn't secured the ends properly, and now the tape was left to dance with the wind as if it was strewn for decorative purposes.

The home was half-collapsed in on itself and was almost unrecognizable. The previous day's falling snow had left behind a thin layer that rested atop the charred mess and glistened like glitter in the sun. The dusting hid part of the burnt wood and made the remaining ruins appear less chaotic. Still, the whole area felt eerie.

A lone rocker remained on the half of the porch that had been spared. John stared at the chair as it slowly moved with the breeze and pictured Jake with a smile, rocking back and forth with his young daughter bouncing up and down on his knee.

The morning after the fire, the fire department was still checking to ensure the house was safe to enter. They tapped on beams, poked through floors, and taped off areas that should be avoided for safety reasons. So instead of going inside, John circled the vast property, looking for evidence that may have been overlooked. Three times he had looped around the nearby tree line and even wandered deeper into the wood's depths where the snow remained untouched.

He looked for something, anything. But nothing looked out of place. The only footprints he happened upon were his own and the tracks of deer and other small game searching for places to burrow.

After abandoning his search, John sat in his car while watching the workers scurry around the house, hoping they would hurry so he could do his own digging.

When the sun finally faded, the team inside the house headed out, and John too went home, ready to attack the scene again the next day.

The following morning, John learned the destructive blaze had officially been declared an act of arson, and the fire chief was quick to locate its point of origin. After hours of cautiously digging around the unstable house, it was determined the fire had been started near where they had found Jake's body.

Evidence from the scene showed someone had haphazardly doused the couch in gasoline and lit it ablaze. The flames danced around the home and devoured fifty-plus years of family history and half of its owner. All that was left was a jerry can that had shriveled up into a small ball of melted plastic.

When the house was released from the fire chief, John volunteered to take the lead on the case and wouldn't hear any arguments against his decision. His first task was to compile a list of possible suspects and start asking questions. *Someone has to know something.* But, the current file of persons to question tucked in his breast pocket was only a blank sheet of lined paper.

"Just please tell me something," John whispered to the charred remains as he stepped closer to the house.

He climbed the porch steps into the home. The biggest question lingering in his mind was finding out if Jake had died before the fire or if it was the reason for his demise. Thinking about his favorite deputy being burned alive broke his heart.

Jake's remains had been carted off to the coroner's office, and John had called to inquire about the status of the autopsy twice already. Unfortunately, they failed to provide a timeline for getting to Jake and kept telling him to be patient.

John cautiously wandered into the house that was finally released from the fire department and searched for any sort of leads. The remnants of the residence that remained looked and felt like charcoal that had been doused in water and left out in the freezing night air. The ice formed over the ceilings' vaulted beams was thick and crystallized the wood's burnt remains beneath its glossy clear coating.

He ambled around more fallen chunks of the ceiling carefully. As he walked, pieces of the burnt home crunched audibly beneath his feet as they turned into puffs of dust.

John had only been in the house twice before, and it had been years since his last visit. But the parts that survived the fire seemed just as he had remembered. *Living room in front, eat-in kitchen to the right, a room to the left, and bathroom, garage, and stairs near the back.*

He didn't dare venture to the second floor that had been roped off with more of the yellow caution tape. Instead, he settled for wandering around the home's front area as he checked out the charred downstairs living room, searching for evidence.

In the middle of the spacious area, he saw the couch to blame for the fire. It was once covered in blue and red vertical stripes similar to the material used to make button-up shirts for cowboys in the nineties. Now, it sat in a barely recognizable shape that looked like it would become dust with just one touch. He walked around its ashen remains and found nothing but burnt upholstery and a grilled frame.

The bookcases adjacent to the fireplace almost touched the ceiling. Their bottoms were charred, and ice hung from the top in long daggers. The books had been sprayed and left in a messy pile on the floor where they'd frozen together into a solid mass.

John glanced at the tile in front of the brick fireplace where Jake's burnt body had been found. The spot of his death looked scorched just like the rest of the house, and he tried to push back the reminiscent smell of his singed flesh out of his mind.

The kitchen was mostly blocked off by pieces of the ceiling that had fallen in on themselves. John tried to weasel his way in under a couple of the planks but pulled back and thought twice before risking his safety to check out another scorched room.

"What's next?" John said as he pushed warm air from his lungs into his hands. The day was colder than the last, but thankfully the remaining frame of the home blocked the majority of the morning breeze.

With his shoulder, John shoved against a stuck door on the west side of the house. When it finally gave and swung open, he heard a gentle popping from the paint that had used the heat of the fire to weld itself to the frame.

Behind the door was a room that remained primarily untouched by the hungry fire. Inside what appeared to be the master bedroom, he found the interior wall covered in a spilled coffee color of brown from the flames that had lapped against its opposite side.

He scanned the room. It appeared as if no one had touched it. It was quiet, barren, and grey. There was only one photo of the small family sitting on the bedside table closest to the attached bathroom.

John moved over to a sage green duffle that lay near the foot of the bed, covered in what looked to be a handmade quilt. He donned a pair of latex gloves and gently pulled on the zipper to see what details the bag would provide.

As he nosed around, he found an assortment of men's clothes that he assumed belonged to Jake, a handful of male bathroom toiletries, and two extra pairs of shoes tucked away at the bottom. *What is all of this for? Where were you going without telling anyone?*

John left the bag rifled through in its place and wandered over to the couple's closet, drawing open the accordion folding wooden doors. On the left side, the men's clothes that remained were half hanging on hangers and strewn on the floor as if they had been recently rummaged through. The other half was a woman's wardrobe that was color coordinated and hung up neatly. It didn't look as if it had been touched in a while. *What did you do, Jake?*

John had always presumed Jake was a clean deputy that kept his nose out of trouble. But the circumstances surrounding the case led him to believe that maybe he was wrong. If Jake had gotten in too deep with someone dirty and they came for him, things could get ugly quickly. He worried Miranda and Piper's safety were also in jeopardy.

He stepped back from the messy closet and walked into the attached bathroom. He pulled open some drawers and nosed around in their cabinets but discovered only the everyday items that would typically be housed in a couple's vanity.

Sitting on the counter between their his and her sinks, John spied a small wooden jewelry box with an "M" hand engraved on its lid. He pulled his glove down at the wrist and slowly opened its top.

Inside the fragrant cedar box, he found a bunch of random women's jewelry haphazardly placed inside and jumbled into a mess. Necklaces, bracelets, and earrings had become muddled into one large ball that would have taken a year to untangle. John stuffed his hand in his pocket, grabbed the ring he had uprooted from the gravel the night of the fire, and laid it down on the counter.

He pulled a solitaire diamond ring from the box and set it next to the small gold band. The two appeared to be very similar, if not the same size. He laid one on top of the other and pictured them as a wedding set.

"Where are you, Miranda?" John asked as his worry began to grow.

After finding nothing else of interest, he left the room and instinctively shut the door behind him.

He wandered into the garage tucked in the home's back. Jake's '96 pickup sat cold and parked in its spot in another mostly preserved area of the house.

John yanked on the door handle and inhaled the aromatic smell of Jake's beloved Skoal chewing tobacco as it hit his nose. He always hated seeing a big wad of chew shoved in Jake's bottom lip but suddenly found himself missing the sight. *I'm sorry, Jake.* He believed a man's truck was a sacred place and felt guilty about violating his privacy. But he was desperate to find some sort of clue.

As he rummaged through the vehicle, he found a couple of sippy cups of spoiled milk that had rolled under the driver seat, some Slim Jim wrappers, and a handful of loose change scattered on the floorboards. *Nothing special.*

He shook an unlabeled tobacco can from the center console and heard something solid tapping around on its inside. He pried off the plastic lid and found the container clear of any shreds of tobacco as if it had been hand washed. Inside, only a rectangular, worn-out business card was folded in quarters. John unfolded the card.

The front showed the name of a local restaurant he was familiar with. The back had a handwritten phone number with a small heart at its end. He slid it into an evidence bag and shut the door after finding nothing else of interest in the vehicle.

The rest of the house was too burnt to explore, and John admitted it more than likely wouldn't give him any answers. He walked out with the few clues he had garnered but no hard leads.

His tires spun slightly as they caught their tread as he pulled out of the drive.

Along the isolated stretch of highway, his mind tried to link the objects from his search together. He was reasonably convinced the ring he found in the driveway had to belong to Miranda. It being discarded at the crime scene left him wondering if she had been there after all and how it came off her finger. *And if she was there, what had she seen or even done?*

The business card seemed tucked away and safeguarded like it was important. The number must have been significant to Jake. *Why else would it be saved and hidden?* John wanted to find out why it was kept so carefully and who penned the small heart on its back.

The duffle of clothes left him curious as to where Jake was heading. The bag looked like he was trying to get away from something or someone in a hurry. *So where were you going? And where's Miranda?*

John believed that Jake's wife had always seemed like a relatively friendly girl. On occasion, she came into the station and brought him lunch, and John's wife had spoken to her at many of the department's dinners. She came across as kind and straightforward but reserved. He remembered her always looking somewhat misplaced in the world but seemed content with her life as a mother and wife. But now, she was nowhere to be found.

Her husband had died in his childhood home, and she was either missing, kidnapped, on the run, or, at worst, dead. Their house was intentionally torched and burnt to a crisp, and John was starting to explore the notion that Miranda would be a critical piece to moving his case along.

John wanted to find her, call her in for questioning, and hoped she could give him some credible answers. He believed she knew something but just wanted to make sure she was alive and okay. But he was at a loss when it came to beginning his search. He vaguely remembered Jake telling him Miranda's mom lived somewhere in Montana but knew it wasn't local.

The morning after the fire, John had made some calls around town. With the help of his deputies, they phoned local motels and determined that she hadn't checked into any of them. While cringing, he also called the area hospitals and prayed that the two girls matching their description hadn't been checked in. But that search had also come up blank.

Few people in town had cell phones due to the lack of coverage in the city limits, and it was even worse out near the Thacker homestead. Reception just didn't reach that far, and people hated the idea of more "skyscrapers" going in and obstructing the scenery. It was likely Miranda didn't have a personal cell either. Jake had been offered a work phone more than once but repeatedly refused to take one.

"They don't do shit out here. Maybe when they put in a couple more towers, I'll take it," John recalled Jake saying.

Taking the next step in locating Miranda, John drove past the office and headed down to the local credit union. He hoped that some financial forensics would help dredge up a lead for him to begin to follow.

He waited in the long line at the busy, small-town bank like everyone else. The tellers were to blame for the delays while they chatted continuously with their never-ending neighborhood gossip. They loved talking about who cheated on whom and which men ended up in the drunk tank the night before.

After close to fifteen minutes of waiting, the woman behind the counter finally motioned for him to step forward.

"Well, good morning, Detective Waters. How are you doin' today?" the teller said with a cheeky smile on her face.

"Not too bad, Leigh. How about yourself?" John returned as his brows pushed themselves together.

"Oh, I could probably complain, but no one would listen," she responded with a subtle chuckle. "What can I do for you?"

"Well, I'm actually here to get some info about someone I'm pretty certain has an account with you all."

"Okay. What name would the account be under? We can start there."

John glanced over his shoulder and peered around the small lobby to see if anyone monitored his conversation. An older woman who had waited in line behind him offered a warm smile, but no one else seemed to have their ear tuned into his words. He leaned towards Leigh and pushed his head between the chin-high partition walls.

"Miranda Thacker."

"Oh... Oh," Leigh repeated as her eyes widened. "Okay, gotcha. Sure was a shame what happened to her husband," she whispered.

John truly hated asking someone else for assistance. Still, he needed to exhaust all avenues to pinpoint Miranda's location before giving up and considering her and her young daughter missing.

"I'm trying to see if she has used any of her cards or maybe even written a check lately. Would you be able to do that for me?" John asked politely.

"Yeah, sure. I'd be more than happy to. Is everything okay?" Leigh asked, trying to pry some decent gossip out of the local detective.

"Yep, all is good. Just trying to check on some things with this house fire," he explained, trying to water down his suspicions that Miranda was somehow involved in its origin. Leigh would make sure *Miranda did it* was the new talk of the town.

"You don't think," she paused and looked around before leaning closer to John, "That she's the one that did it, do you?"

"No, no, no. Not at all," John lied with a subtle chuckle. "Just trying to close out some things."

"Oh, okay. I gotcha," she responded with a skeptical smile and squinty eyes that hinted she didn't believe him.

Leigh hurriedly typed away on her keyboard and didn't look down once as her fingers paraded across the loud keys. She mashed the enter button three times, then the tab key four while continuing her data pull. John stood at the counter and tapped his fingers along the wooden top while he waited. *Are you writing the next great American novel or something?*

Leigh looked up, and John smiled back before she went right back to the keyboard. He watched her head bob up and down smoothly as she searched her database. A few faint "mhm," sounds emanated from her mouth as her finger skidded across her computer screen. Then, finally, her fingers went still, and her eyes landed back on John.

"Alright, so here's what I got. She pulled five hundred dollars out of savings yesterday at an," her voice trailed off as she turned back to her screen and peered closer, "Exxon up in Great Falls. But that's all I can see. I'm sorry."

"No, that's great. Leigh, thank you very much," John responded. "Could you give me the address, please?"

Leigh scribbled down the location over two hours away. She pushed the fluorescent sticky note across the counter to John.

"There you go. Best of luck with whatever you got going on," Leigh stated as she flitted her hand around her shoulder.

"Thank you so much," John responded as he folded up the small note and slid it into his breast pocket.

Great Falls, huh?

SIX

MIRANDA

MY INTERVIEW AT the local Albertsons is in less than twenty-four hours. My experience is slim to none when it comes to working as a cashier, but I'm confident it's a skill I'll be more than capable of learning on the job.

Five times now, I've stood in front of the streaked motel mirror and practiced my introduction and sales pitch. I want it to be perfect. The job is a necessity if we're going to move out of mama's house anytime soon.

I flatten my hair and begin my sixth round.

"Hi, good morning. My name is Miranda Thacker. I'm a hard worker, go-getter, and promise to always be on time," I pause and glance down to see Piper yanking on my pant leg. "Oh right. Please don't mind the toddler that I had to bring with me because my husband cheated on me, burnt down our house, and left me in the middle of the night," I say with a widespread smile that quickly disappears. "Yeah, that'll get you the job for sure."

When face to face with the manager, I plan to rattle off anything I can to explain the lengthy gaps in my employment history. Three years of being a stay-at-home mom are understandable. But if they don't accept my blunt

71

candor, I'll be on to the next highlighted lead while we scrape together pennies and mooch off of mama.

I'd spotted a few other job leads in the twice-read paper that also sounded somewhat promising. I saved a position as a retail associate at a sports store and another as an elementary school lunch lady.

The grocery store cashier position is my first pick, but I'm willing to try again if it means we can stay near family while we get back on our feet. Finding stable employment is my first adult step toward living my own life without a man supporting me, a life I realize I crave more than ever.

Two days of living in the run-down motel on the edge of town is starting to wear on us both. Leaving with only the clothes on our backs was a thrown-together plan, but I'm working hard to make the best of our situation, hoping that our new life doesn't feel like it's starting off in chaos.

I pulled out the five hundred dollars yesterday and plan to continue visiting the gas station ATM until I've withdrawn half of the money Jake and I spent nearly ten years saving. Although I haven't worked out of the home for the money in our account, I've been the one staying home with Piper and making sure the household ran smoothly. I deserve something.

The wad of twenties in my wallet feels thick, but I'm trying my best to use it sparingly in case the slush fund doesn't last as long as I hope.

It's no secret that Jake stands to make a small fortune off the insurance claim and family land when he sells the estate. But I want nothing to do with his dirty money. For all I care, he can have every penny as long as he doesn't try to come after me for custody.

But money is tight, and it will be for a while. I snag extra toiletries off the maid cart in the morning when she isn't looking and fill a plate of food at the continental breakfast that I munch on throughout the day.

Our bed now has sheets I bought to get away from the ones that reeked of bleach and had held hundreds of people, and Piper has her own play yard to sleep on so we can get through the night without flighting for space.

"Money's tight, baby," I tell Piper as she reaches for a thirty-dollar baby doll strategically placed in the checkout line. She twists her face into a scowl and looks away from me. *One day I'll buy you everything you've ever dreamed about, I promise.*

Piper still has a look of disappointment strewn across her face as we pay for our things and head back out to the car.

I grip the steering wheel tight as my other hand is buried in a bag of Cheetos on the passenger seat as we drive into the nearby Little Belt Mountains. The local news anchor had announced that the roads were free of snow, and I thought it was worth a trip. Piper spends most of the drive sleeping, but I'm wide awake, watching how the flat land of the city rises into beautiful snowcapped peaks. I've always loved driving into the mountains and watching the snow grow deeper along the road's edge until it's piled to eye level.

After a sharp turn that feels slicker than I expected, I pull the car over into a cutoff. My front-wheel-drive car is typically dependable, even when there's been a recent flurry, but the growing elevation has turned the roads into a dangerous place. I'm not comfortable venturing any higher.

I step out of the car and feel the quiet of the mountainside. It's both eerie and relaxing at the same time. My foot crunches through the gravel as the ice on top crumbles, and I sink down half an inch. The cold breeze whips its way around the mountain's sharp curves and sends a shiver shooting down my spine. I close my eyes and allow a deep breath of the clean air to fill my lungs. The mountains make me happy.

From my humble spot on the hill, I can see for miles. Other painted mountain ranges are spiked up in the distance, and their snowcapped tips feel almost close enough to touch. The scenery isn't something that can be captured on camera. *This is it. I think we're going to be happy here.*

Ever since we coasted in on fumes, I've felt a growing belief that the idyllic town of Great Falls seems like the perfect place to start over. Everyone we've met has been cheery and friendly with us both, and there are more than enough shopping and restaurants. The beautiful snowcapped mountains are only a short drive away, and there's a modest ski resort tucked within their peaks. It's only been two days, but something in my heart is tugging and telling me we've stumbled into our new home.

I quietly climb back into the car and head back toward town, back to the confines of our hotel room.

Even though I've never crafted any monumental long-term goals, I feel like I've missed out on years of my life. Other women around me worked office jobs previously held by men, and some even went to college and became doctors. They all went off and found their own paths while my identity became centered around Jake and then Piper. I hadn't even thought about what I would do when Piper started school or went off to college.

Jake and I met when we were so young, and my life quickly became so wrapped up in wondering what I could do for my husband. Is he happy? Does he like my grandma's spaghetti recipe? Is the sex good enough? It all happened so quickly that I didn't realize I had forgotten about myself and what would make *me* happy. I stood by Jake's side all those years and allowed him to be the successful one while I lurked in his towering shadows. *And now he's gone.*

Being out on my own and away from feeling the need to constantly please someone else, I finally feel free. I can breathe. It's incredible how much you learn about yourself when you take a step back and view your life from the outside.

Piper runs up the motel stairs with a smile, rejuvenated from her nap. We again walk back into our modest room that's currently home, and Piper immediately heads to the small pile of Barbies in the corner.

While she's occupied, I thumb through the newspaper again, this time looking for a daycare. Mama is old and has a back that spazzes out randomly, and I can attest that Piper's a handful. Asking a sixty-seven-year-old woman to chase an unruly toddler around all day every day just doesn't feel right to me.

I briefly glance up from my search, smile, and watch Piper talk to herself quietly as she plays house with two of her dolls. The larger Barbie seems to be making breakfast for the younger one.

In our sudden departure, I hadn't had the time or chance to grab any shot records or birth certificates required to register Piper at a proper facility.

"Hopefully, they won't ask me questions," I mumble as my highlighter circles an ad for a small in-home daycare in town.

If all goes well with the job interview, I'll stop by the daycare and get some information and see if they have any openings. A chill runs across my shoulders when I think about Piper being in the care of someone that isn't directly related to us for the first time.

The plan had always been for me to stay home until Piper started kindergarten. But, we need money if we're going to start over.

Daddy will kill me when he finds out I put you in daycare.

Piper knows how to say "dada," but I suddenly realize I haven't heard her utter the word in days. Her brain is still at such a formative stage. I'm hoping she probably won't remember much, if anything, about the short time she spent with her dad.

I loved my father deeply, and when cancer took him, it ripped my heart out of my chest and left a gaping hole that's never been filled. He was my best friend, and I still miss him every day. Now that my life is in turmoil, I want him the most. Piper never getting the chance to develop that relationship with Jake makes my heart ache on her behalf. *She'll never know how great it can be.* But that choice hadn't been Piper's. Jake had broken the sacred bond that a father should have treasured with his daughter.

I imagine the school dances and daddy-daughter dates he decided to skip out on. Piper would likely one day ask why her dad had chosen another woman over her, and I'll be the one that'll have to tell her. *Maybe I'll just tell her he's dead. He seems dead to me.*

I shove the thoughts of Jake to the back of my mind. He's no longer worth the space he was once afforded. I scoot off the couch and climb on all fours over to Piper, who's tucking her Barbies under a washcloth comforter for the night.

"You're gonna do so good at daycare," I say to Piper as I try to fight the tears that are actively trying to invade my eyes.

"Kissy," Piper says as she raises a hand towards my face.

I press my lips to her cheek and buzz my lips against her skin before also kissing her doll's goodnight.

SEVEN

JOHN

J OHN RETURNED TO his office with the few details he'd squeezed from the bank teller. Pulling money out of an ATM with her personal debit card didn't seem like she was trying very hard to hide from anyone. *Why are you in Great Falls?*

He pulled out the folded Post-It note with the gas station address and flipped open the thin file folder he was building for the case. There wasn't much tucked in either side yet. Currently, it only housed some photos before and after the fire and statements from the individuals who responded to the incident.

He dusted off the glossy cover of the old phone book sitting in the corner of his cubicle that hadn't been touched in years. John refused to look things up using the internet unless he had no other option. Most people found it odd, but he preferred doing things the old-fashioned way, even if it took longer.

He thumbed through half of the pages in the book until he finally came across the number for the Exxon station in Great Falls, where Miranda had made her withdrawal. *Let's hope they can tell me something.*

John leaned back in his padded office chair and readied his pen and paper for any information the small town convenience store could provide. At that point, anything was better than what he had. Confirmation that the person that pulled out the money was, in fact, someone who at least looked like Miranda and Piper would be a good place to start.

John dialed the number. The entirety of Montana shared the same area code, so it almost felt as though he was calling someone merely a few buildings away instead of two-plus hours north.

The line rang three times, and John prayed the number was still the same as it read in the outdated yellow pages. A dull, monotonous tone ran together into one long hum as he tapped his foot. *Come on. Pick up.*

"Good morning. Thank you for calling Exxon Great Falls," the voice that finally answered said lazily.

"Hi, uh, this is Detective John Waters down in Silver Bow County."

"Uh-huh," the voice on the other end replied.

"Well, uh, I was calling to hopefully talk to whoever was on shift this past Tuesday morning, 'bout five thirtyish." He listened but heard only a perplexed hum come through the phone.

"Hey, Elijah, get over here," John finally heard the person yell as he pulled the phone back from his ear. John gently rapped his fingers on the surface of his desk while he waited patiently for someone else to pick up the receiver.

"Hello?" a different voice said.

"Good morning. My name is Detective Waters down in Butte. I was calling to talk about a young girl in her mid-thirties who came in Tuesday morning. I'm showing she got some cash out of your ATM. There's a good chance she probably had a small child with her. A little girl specifically that's um, I believe just under two years old," John explained.

The clerk on the other end went silent briefly while he pondered John's question.

"Yeah, I think I remember her coming in on Tuesday. She bought a bunch of snacks and like milk and stuff while she was here. I dunno who she is, though. Should I?" he responded.

"No, thank you. That's good. Was she brunette, somewhat tall, and sorta skinny?"

"Yes, sir, that sounds like her. Did she do something wrong?"

"Well, she was down here in Butte the night before she came into your shop. We're just trying to track her down. She didn't say anything about where she was going or anything like that?" John asked, hoping he'd picked up on some small clue she had accidentally dropped.

"No, sir, I'm sorry I can't help you any more than that. She seemed nice, though. Oh, and she did fill up her tank."

"Do you remember how she paid?"

"Cash, I think."

"Great," John paused as he jotted some notes down. "So, she didn't seem upset or anything. Like was she in distress at all?"

"Nah, not really. I mean, I don't think so."

"Did you see which way she turned when she left the lot?"

"No, sorry. I didn't."

"Gotcha, I understand. Well, thank you for all your help. If there's anything else, please don't hesitate to give me a call back," he added.

"Oh, and sir, the daughter looked clean and stuff, but the mom did have a smoke smell to her. It wasn't like cigarettes or anything. It was more like the smell you get after sitting around a bonfire for too long," he explained, providing something concrete that John could add to his notes.

"Okay, thank you, son, that's good to know. Please remember to give me a call if you see her again," he added.

"Yes, sir, will do."

John rattled off his office number and hung up the phone after he thanked the boy again for his time. *So, it was her, and she smelled like smoke. Interesting.*

"A full tank could take you far. Especially if you're running away from something," John muttered as he scribbled down some notes.

He leaned forward on his antique wooden desk and wrote down two small words on his unofficial suspect list in his small legal pad, "Miranda Thacker."

Looking for discrete clues and finding missing people wasn't a standard process for the small-town detective and one he was glad wasn't routine in his jurisdiction. His typical caseload was petty crimes, running background checks, and assisting the livestock commissioner on local cattle disputes. Busy work.

A questionable death and arson was a relatively new game. Most cases that involved someone dying went to the more seasoned detectives or the local police department.

A few years back, John had assisted on a drawn-out case for a young girl that went missing while playing with a soccer ball outside alongside the busy road near her family home. A neighbor that watched it happen recounted that she had seen someone pick her up in the middle of the day in a blue suburban and speed off towards the mountains.

People came from all over the state to aid the search. They searched the mountains, the coulees, and banged on nearly every door in the county but didn't find anything. John lost sleep during the search because he kept imagining his daughter out in the woods, cold and alone.

A couple of weeks after she was taken, her kidnapper silently left her unscathed at a McDonald's near the highway and slipped away into the night. Security cameras pulled the license plates, which led the detectives to the eighty-six-year-old owner who had reported her vehicle missing months earlier. The people that nabbed the young girl were never found.

John's involvement in the case wasn't monumental. He merely helped with the search. He was pulled in to help with the questioning and asked to finalize some paperwork in the aftermath. But his time spent working toward answers gave him some tips to add to his relatively new detective toolkit.

Now, he desperately wanted to find Jake's wife and bring her back to Butte from wherever she had disappeared to. She could be in Great Falls, Canada, or for all he knew, back in town. He believed she had a good piece of information that was pivotal to the case and wanted to talk to her.

John had already drilled Adam, Jake's partner. He asked him about the days, weeks, and months leading up to the fire. What was different about him? What was the same? He figured the person that spent the most time would be able to answer the questions best. Adam answered John's probing the best that he could, but all he had noticed was that Jake had been a little spacey lately, less attentive. He also suddenly realized that Jake often slipped out for lunch alone, coming up with excuses for why he didn't want his partner to tag along. He had taken off earlier than usual and left Adam to finish paperwork, but he hadn't thought of it as something to inquire about.

Again, John thumbed through the phone book and searched for a second number.

"Ah, there it is," John said as his finger tapped a number in the phone directory.

He dialed the number listed for the sheriff's department in Cascade County. A woman he presumed to be the secretary answered the phone promptly and connected him to one of their detectives.

"Hello?" a different woman's voice came through.

"Hi. Good morning. I'm Detective Waters down in Butte. I was calling to ask if you have some time to help me out with a case I'm working on," he asked hopefully.

"Hello, Detective Waters. I'm Detective Herr, Moriah Herr. Good morning. But yeah, we can sure try. What can we do for you?" she responded.

"Well, to keep it short, one of our deputies was found dead, and now his wife has gone missing. She pulled some money out of an ATM there in Great Falls, and I'm just trying to find her."

"Let me guess, you think she's the one that did it?" she asked blatantly.

"Well, I don't really know. I don't think so, but I believe she's involved somehow. Right now, I want to make sure she's not in any sort of danger, and I'm also just trying to find out what she knows."

John provided more details about the fire's circumstances and Miranda's untimely departure.

"Yeah, yeah, wow. That's a lot. I bet we can help you out. Just let me know what you need," Jen offered.

The two worked together and came to a mutual agreement. That afternoon, she would ask their deputies to look for Miranda's vehicle hoping it would be in one of the local motel parking lots. John wasn't ready to issue a statewide alert just yet. A discreet search was the best solution. He rattled off a license plate number that belonged to a gold Honda Accord. She copied it down and read it back verbatim.

"Alright. I'll pull her license. But can you tell me anything else about this Miranda girl?" Jen asked.

John remembered the last time he had seen Miranda and tried to draw an image of her from his somewhat fuzzy memory. They were at the annual department picnic earlier that year. Miranda wore a yellow and white sundress with a frayed edge near her knees, and her light brown hair barely brushed her shoulders. John was talking to Jake about football when Miranda walked over with Piper in trail. She smiled kindly and stood next to her husband.

"She's tall and thin. I'd call her skinny actually. I think Jake, her husband, said she was a runner. So you know, long skinny legs, boney shoulders, probably only an ounce of fat on her. She's young, but something about her makes her look...oh, I don't know, tired," he said, remembering the bags under her eyes that she'd tried to hide with makeup.

He described her as kind and soft-spoken, someone who seemed slow to anger. Not once in the many times had he been around her had he felt she was the kind of woman who would murder someone and burn her house down to try and cover it up.

"And what about the daughter," Moriah probed.

John chuckled as he remembered Piper at the same picnic covered in blue cupcake icing. Even after Jake wiped it off with a napkin, a slight tinge of the dye was left behind, staining her face.

"Piper's a little Miranda. If you told me Jake had nothing to do with creating that little girl, I'd believe it. Looks just like her mom. Same smile and same colored hair, just usually it's atop her head in a wispy little pony. Her eyes are bright and blue, and she's as slender as can be."

John was growing more worried about the Thacker girls as every hour passed. With Jake gone, someone had to be there for them.

"Well, that all sounds good. I'll go out and ask some of the deputies and give you a call back if any of us find anything. That sound good to you?" Moriah said.

"That's perfect. Thank you," John replied.

When he hung up the phone, he fished out the small plastic evidence bag in which he'd slipped the folded card from Jake's truck inside. The cardstock paper's creases were softened as if they had been unfolded and refolded repeatedly. He ran his fingers across the glossy, raised logo branded on its front.

"The Snavely BBQ House," he read, along with a phone number and street address.

John had eaten at the local place a few times and liked all the eclectic objects decorating its walls. It was like a family-owned Cracker Barrel that featured relics from Montana. But he and his wife weren't crazy about the limited options. Almost everything on the menu was pork, fried in bacon fat, or smothered in sausage gravy. She adamantly refused to go back, so he only stopped in there for lunch when work left him on that side of town.

John picked up the phone to call the restaurant. He dialed, and the line rang four times before he hung up. He cross-checked the number with the Yellow Pages and dialed again, slower as if he thought he got it wrong the first time. Again no one answered.

He looked down at his desktop calendar and saw nothing pressing to get done that day and decided to take a drive out to the old dive. He tucked the business card into the case folder, grabbed his keys, and walked down the hall toward Jake's cubicle.

A blinking red light on the desk phone caught John's attention before he even stepped into the five-foot by five-foot area. He had already checked Jake's machine twice, and both times there had been nothing but old saved messages that were insignificant.

He fumbled over Jake's desk chair and snatched up the receiver as he simultaneously hit the voicemail button. A slow static sounded before a voice shut it out.

"It's me. Not sure if you're still around. We're going to moms on Friday," there was a breathy chuckle. "Call me there."

A beep over the machine signaled that the message was complete. He replayed the voicemail three more times and wrote it down word for word in his notepad.

"Dammit, Miranda. Where does your mom live? Hell, what's your mom's name?" John whispered.

He continued digging around Jake's office and found some half-eaten snacks and a mess of pens he seemed to be hoarding. At the bottom of the desk, in between two empty file folders, John pulled out a family photo of the Thackers that had been shoved into the bottom of the drawer.

The photo was covered in a thin layer of dust. John brushed off the glass and saw the image beneath, which showed Piper as an infant. She was too little to smile and just lay in Miranda's arms in a dreamy sleep. Miranda and Jake's cheeks were nearly touching, and the wide grins on both their faces looked genuine.

He flipped over the frame and saw a handwritten note in silver permanent marker on its back. "We love you. Always be safe and come home to us."

He pulled the picture out of the frame. He photocopied it and slipped the scan into his case folder before placing the original back behind the glass and in the drawer.

John popped his head into Jake's former partner's office before leaving.

"Do you know where Miranda's parents live?" John asked.

"I know her dad's dead. And her mom comes to visit from out of town. But I'm not sure from where," Adam replied.

"Could you do me a favor? Pull their marriage license and try to figure out Miranda's maiden name and check for any matches around here," John explained.

"You got it," Adam responded.

John left the office and drove to the small BBQ restaurant on the outskirts of town.

When he pulled into the restaurant's gravel lot, he saw a neon "OPEN" sign brightly illuminated in the window and a few parked trucks. He carefully stepped toward the building with the thin folder in hand, unsure of what he would unearth during his visit but hoping for something.

Inside, the place looked the same as the last time he visited. Under stuffed booths lined the walls, low drop ceilings housed dim lighting above each table, and a thin film coated all the furniture from the overworked fryers.

"Can I get you a table?" a waitress with her hands full asked.

As John brought his body square, she glanced down at the pistol holstered on his hip beneath the edge of his jacket.

"No. No, thank you. I was wondering if I could talk to your manager? I have a couple of questions," John inquired as he flipped open his wallet and revealed his badge.

"Uh, yeah, sure. Just a sec," the waitress replied.

She hurriedly traipsed toward the back of the nearly empty restaurant and returned with a short woman that looked to be in her late forties.

"Detective Waters," he offered as he stuck his hand out.

"Janel," she returned. "What can we do for you, sir?"

"Sorry to barge in on you, but I'm working on a case. I was hoping one of the people in this picture would be familiar."

He pulled out the Thacker's family photo and handed it to the manager. The woman glared at the picture closely and analyzed the three people trapped in the paper. She carefully looked at Miranda and then Piper before returning her eyes back to Jake's face.

"I've definitely seen the guy," she answered as she tapped her finger on Jake's face. "But I don't know anything about the other two. I'm usually in the back, but I know I've seen him here before."

"Is there anything else you can tell me about him?" he inquired, hoping she had more to tell.

"No, I mean, I never talked to him. Did he do something wrong?" she pried. "He's a cop, right?"

"Yeah, he is, was, um. It's just that he's involved in an investigation we're working on," he explained, trying to remain vague.

"Sorry, I can't be of more help then. But, like I said, I really don't know him," the manager explained.

"No, I appreciate it, and thank you for your time. Do you mind if I ask around a little while I'm here?" he asked.

"Go for it," she responded.

Janel headed toward the back, and John approached the first waitress he saw. He again flashed the old photo of the Thackers and hoped for recognition. But, unfortunately, she, too, didn't know much about any of the people in the picture.

"I don't know them, sorry. But you should go talk to her," she added as she nodded her head to another waitress across the room.

John thanked the girl and took his picture back. He walked across the dining room and approached the waitress who had greeted him at the entry.

"Ma'am," John asked.

She stood up straight and stopped wiping down a dirty table. She turned around and looked directly at John.

"Yes, sir?" she asked somewhat hesitantly.

"Hi. I'm Detective Waters. I was wondering if I could ask you a couple of questions, Ms...," he asked, leaving a blank for her to fill in her name.

"Taylor."

"Right. Nice to meet you, Ms. Taylor. Do you have a second?"

"Yes, sir," she replied.

John again pulled out the photo.

"I'm wondering if you know any of these people. Someone said you'd served them here on more than one occasion," he asked.

The waitress went silent for a moment as she looked at the picture of the small family. While she examined the Thackers, John watched and studied her face as she glanced over their photo and gently chewed her bottom lip.

"Well, I know him, um, yeah. I mean, he came here quite a bit, usually for lunch. But I, I don't know either of them," she returned, pointing at both Piper and Miranda.

"Do you remember when he was here last?"

"I don't know, maybe a couple of weeks ago. I don't really remember exactly when it was?" she replied with a questioning tone.

"Did he ever talk about his personal life with you?"

"Uh, no, no, not really. Why?"

"No reason. Just trying to get some more information on him, that's all. If you think of anything else, please don't hesitate to come down to the local office."

"Yeah. Sorry, yes, sir. I will," the waitress responded as she accepted a business card.

John nodded to a few patrons as he walked out and left the restaurant feeling like his trip across town had been for nothing. No one knew Jake well enough to provide anything helpful, and he was no closer to finding any clues as to why he was dead, how the fire had begun, or where Miranda and Piper had run off to.

He returned to his desk and again combed through the case file. He flipped through photos the deputies had taken at the house and tried to see something he had missed as if it would just jump out at him. But all he saw was just what he had seen when he'd walked the place himself.

While staring at the picture of where Jake's body had been found, the ringing of his phone startled him. He snatched it up.

"Uh, hello?" John asked as he cleared his throat.

"Waters, hey. I got some news for you," the Cascade County Detective explained.

"Whatcha got?"

While waiting for her to pass her findings, Adam showed up at John's desk with a sticky note in hand. John raised a single finger in his direction, and he backed around the corner with a nod.

"One of our guys was out near the airport and drove into a motel lot. According to him, he saw a car that's an exact description of your deputy's wife's, license plate and all."

"But no sight of her?"

"No, he watched for a few minutes but assumed she was inside. It's a cold one up here today. But he checked with the kid at the front desk, and room two five eight matches her name. You want us to go up and knock and bring her in?"

"No, but if you can manage it, just keep someone on her for the time being. Make sure she doesn't go anywhere. I'll head that way now to come talk to her if that's alright with you?" John responded.

"Fine by me, I'll have them stay there. Is she considered to be dangerous?"

"I really, really don't think that's the case," John responded, hoping he was right.

John hung up the phone feeling a slight glimmer of hope.

"Hey, Adam, come in," John beckoned.

"Sorry for interrupting," he replied.

"No, not at all. You find something?"

"Yes, sir. Her maiden name is Steyn. I checked the phone listings within three hours, and the only number I found was this one." Adam laid down a printout atop John's desk.

"Here, in Butte. But it's been disconnected," he explained as he tapped the address on the south end of town.

"Alright, thanks. We might have another lead anyways."

EIGHT

MIRANDA

I FIGHT WITH Piper for close to twenty minutes until she gives in and lays down for her afternoon nap. I'd sweet-talked the boy at the front desk, and he gave me some more well-loved pillows that I've arranged into a cocoon to keep her from rolling off the bed.

Her body twitches slightly as I lay down next to her and watch her sleep. I can see her front teeth through her cracked lips that are dry from her mouth breathing. Soft whines come from deep within as her breathing slows. *God, she's picture-perfect.*

I snuggle up next to Piper, draw her close, and plant a gentle kiss on her head. The area where her hair comes in the thickest no longer smells like the tear-free shampoo in her tub back home. Now it smells like lavender and vanilla from the off-brand shampoo the motel provided.

I gently lay my head on the pillow next to her and grab her hand. Her tiny fingers curl around mine, and I close my eyes and try to shut down my busy mind.

Just as I near the brink of joining Piper in unconsciousness, someone knocks on the exterior door to the motel room. My body goes stiff, and

93

my eyes fly open. *Fight, flight, freeze.* I'm in a frozen state, scared to move my head, toes, anything. I know who is on the other side of the door. *Jake.*

"Mama," I whisper. "Dammit."

I'd hoped we'd be situated at mamas when Jake was ready to talk. A stable income and home for Piper sounded like enough grounds for me to be able to fight for full custody. The two of us crammed in a dingy motel room on the outskirts of town will only give him ammunition.

"Shit, shit," I whisper as my body thaws. I rotate onto my back and cover my eyes.

Again, knuckles rap on the door. I sit up.

Trying not to wake Piper, I gently scoot off the least creaky edge of the bed. I stride on the balls of my feet to the room's only door and look through the peephole. The afternoon sun beams through, and my eyes take a moment to adjust to the glare.

Through the fisheye glass, slightly swaying from the cold, is a man in a windbreaker. The breath trapped in my chest billows out of my mouth when I realize it isn't Jake. The man is someone I know, but he's someone that shouldn't know where I am. *Detective Waters? How the hell did you find us? And why are you here?*

The detective had always seemed like a friendly and kind man. Whenever I'd conversed with either him or his wife, they seemed welcoming and trustworthy. Typically, his presence wouldn't have shaken me. But right now, things are different.

I take a deep breath and try to slow my heart rate. *It's gonna be okay; just be honest. You called Jake. You didn't kidnap her.*

Just as the detective reaches up again, I slowly unlatch the deadbolt. The sliding click causes his hand to lower before he can knock for the third time.

When the lock on the handle pops free, I remove the chain and open the door quietly.

"Hey there. Good afternoon, Miranda," Detective Waters thunders with a smile as I stand in the doorway.

A forced smile forms on my face as I silently step outside the room. I leave the door cracked just enough to speak to him without waking Piper. It's teetering just above freezing outside, and I shake gently beneath my thin sweater from my nerves that are doubling with every passing second.

"Hi, detective?" My gaze shifts to the ground. I blink my eyes repeatedly as they adjust to the sun reflecting off the concrete walkway.

"Please, just call me John. It's been a while. How are you doing?"

Really, we're going to do small talk right now?

I grab one elbow with the opposite hand and glance around the vacant second-floor landing. *Just us.* I move over to the metal railing and lean slightly to survey the parking lot below. *Seems quiet.* I turn my attention back to Jake's coworker.

"I know I shouldn't have taken her," I quickly blurt out, my eyes darting up instantly to his. "But, I told him where we were going. And I called. He knew."

"Um, I'm sorry, I'm not tracking. What are you talking about?"

My face shifts to a look of confusion.

"Jake. He clearly wants nothing to do with us anymore. So, I'm just trying to start over and make a life for us. I have a job, well... maybe, hopefully. And possible daycare lined up. Also, in two days we're going to stay with my mom just north of here till we get our own place. And I only plan on taking half of what we had in savings. I swear," I say, realizing I'm rambling defensively.

John briefly stares at me with an astonished face. I place my hands on the landing's railing and shake my head as I look off in the distance.

"How did you find us? It was my mom, huh? No, wait, I didn't tell her what hotel we were staying at. It was the bank, wasn't it? It had to be the bank. Not that I'm hiding," I say as I move from the railing and pace around the deck.

Chill, chill. I rub at the bags beneath my eyes with both index fingers and push the hair hanging near my temples behind my ears repeatedly.

"Miranda, I think you and I need to go have a discussion," John replies with a worry-stricken look.

"About what?" I say, halting my feet. My apprehension instantly triples.

"Well, why don't you just grab Piper and come down to the department here with me. We can talk about it there."

"John, please. He's not taking her. I won't let him," I plead as I point toward the motel room with a shaky finger. "I'm not the one that did this. You know that."

"Miranda, let's just go talk. I promise. No one is taking Piper from you," he assures.

Then what is there to talk about?

My heart thumps heavily in my chest at the idea of going to a sheriff's department. I don't understand what's going on.

I study the soft expression on John's aged face. I see hints of the kind manner my father had always displayed tucked in with his wrinkles. Something about the twinkle in his eyes and the curve his lips make when he smiles feels like home and reminds me of someone I can trust.

"Do I need to call a lawyer?" I ask. I'm nervous Jake is trying to implicate me in a crime I had nothing to do with. He can try all he wants, but I'm not planning on taking the fall for his decisions.

"No, not at this point and time, I don't think so. But you're more than welcome to call one if you would like," John elaborates.

That's a lot of money I don't have. And I'm innocent.

"Okay. I'm gonna have to get Piper up. So uh, can you just give me a minute?"

I stop fidgeting when I realize my nerves are becoming visible. With my index finger, I rub the side of my thumb and feel a wet spot where I've picked my cuticle bloody.

"Yeah, of course. I'll just wait for you out here." John turns around and looks out over the balcony's railing while I slip quietly into the motel room.

Trying to still be quiet, I turn the handle and silently shut the door behind me. I press my back against the surface, sink to the floor, and take a minute to regain my composure. *It's okay. You are okay. Piper is okay. No one is taking her from you. Everything will be fine. Just tell them the truth.*

With a couple of mindful breaths, I feel my heart rate fall into a standard rhythm and open my eyes. I scurry over to the bed and scoop Piper up into my arms. I pull her close and stroke her face with one finger while she slowly begins to wake.

"Mama," Piper says softly when she finally opens her eyes. She places one of her tiny hands on my cheek, and I feel my heart turn to mush.

Piper's touch brings a toothy smile to my face and helps ward off the incoming tears I'm fighting a losing battle against.

"Hey baby, we just have to go somewhere, okay?" I whisper.

Piper lets out one slight whine with tired eyes before sticking her thumb in her mouth. I stuff the diaper bag with baby necessities and shove the wad of cash into my back pocket.

"Okay. Let's just get this over with," I mumble with one last elongated breath before opening the inward swinging door.

"Need any help?" John asks when he sees both of my hands are full.

No, I don't want any of your help.

"Thanks. I'm fine. Can I take my own car? You know, 'cause of her seat and all." I nod to Piper, who's drooled on my neck.

"Oh, yeah. Yeah, of course. You can just follow me."

Getting permission to take my own car helps ease my mind. He'd probably insist that I ride with him if I was about to be arrested. *Right?*

After clipping Piper in, I climb into the driver's seat. My fresh start seems like it's being ripped from my hands as Jake wins yet again. A job, freedom, my independence, it's all gone.

Part of me is expecting Jake to be waiting at the Great Falls Sheriff's Department when we arrive. Piper would gladly run into his arms because she adores him, but she doesn't know the truth. I'm also worried that Child Services will be there to take Piper away. *God, John, please don't be lying.* I breathe in deep and try to stomach either scenario coming to fruition. *He said they weren't going to take her. He wouldn't lie to you. Would he?*

I follow the unmarked Crown Victoria and feel my knuckles going white just as they had when I drove away from the crumbling house. The feeling of freedom that Great Falls brought is now teetering on the edge of a cliff, and I'm terrified that I'm about to be shipped back to my old life or, worse, sent to prison for a crime I didn't commit.

That fear sinks deep in my gut and solidifies into a mass as we pull into the department's parking lot. I park next to John's car.

Piper is groggy, and her eyes are glossed over from not getting a full nap. She reaches for me with wobbly arms when I grab her out of the backseat. I pull her toward me, and she wraps her arms around me instantly, burrowing her face in my neck and begging me to keep her warm. As I shroud her in my embrace, I feel my own hands start to tremble.

"It's okay, baby," I mutter shakily, unsure who I'm trying to calm.

At the moment, Piper doesn't have a care in the world. Snacks and toys fill her mind. She wakes up and smiles widely at John when we approach the front of the building. He holds open the door with a friendly smile plastered on his face.

"Hi, Piper," he says as he gives Piper a two-finger wave.

I nod at him silently, and Piper waves back.

"Right this way," John says as he leads us down a long corridor toward the station's rear.

I follow him willingly down the long hallway that feels endless. I step one foot in front of the other, but every inch forward feels like I'm going nowhere, maybe even backward, and in slow-motion. I can hear every breath resonate in my mind as if the rest of the building is lost in silence and I'm the only one inside. As I walk, the walls seem to narrow in my vision like they're closing in on me.

When we finally make it to the end of the hall, John ushers both Piper and me into a cold and cramped room. The dreary grey walls and panel of one-way glass remind me of an interrogation room on an episode of Law & Order. A shiver runs across my shoulders, and goosebumps suddenly stand up on my forearms. Both the temperature of the room and the nerves coursing through my body sustain a subtle shaking.

"Do you want me to find someone to sit with her while we talk?" John asks as he points at Piper.

"No, thank you. I'd like to keep her with me if that's okay with you," I respond, pulling Piper in closer. *I'm not letting you out of my sight.*

"That's just fine with me. Please, take a seat." John motions to one of the two chairs at the table.

Following his lead, I sit down in a rigid metal chair. It brings a chill to my legs through my jeans. I set Piper in my lap and keep a firm grip on her as she squirms to try to get down.

"Would you like a water?" John asks.

"No, thank you. I'd just like to know what's going on before she throws a fit," I reply and nod toward Piper.

John pulls out a folder, and I strategically place a scattered pile of crunchy snacks on the table within Piper's reach to hopefully occupy her attention while we talk.

"Right, well, let's get started then. I'm really sorry to bring you in like this. And for digging through your finances to find you."

"It's fine."

"I guess I'll start by telling you that your house burned down...well, most of it and...."

I cut him off.

"Yeah, I know. But I didn't do it. I swear to you, I didn't have anything to do with it. I don't want any of the insurance money either. He can have it all. And I'm not trying to kidnap her, but he's not taking Piper from me. She's my daughter too."

"Miranda, just relax."

John pauses as he leans across the table toward me in the dimly lit room. He removes his glasses and lays them down. I watch the breath escape his lungs dramatically. The look I see spread across his face isn't one of accusation but one of sadness that I'd missed earlier.

"I hate to be the one to tell you this," his eyes move from me to Piper, then back to me. "Jake's dead."

I stare at John as I feel the color drain from my face. My mouth slightly opens as I digest the dreadful news. *What?*

"He's dead? I'm sorry. What do you mean he's dead?" I finally spit out with a confused chuckle. My eyebrows pull toward one another, and I shake my head gently. I don't want to believe what John's saying. He must be wrong.

"I'm sorry that I had to be the one to tell you. But unfortunately, Jake was there in the house, the living room, to be exact when it burned down. We don't know how he died yet, but the response team found his body in the house when the fire was finally put out."

John's wearing a look of genuine sadness. *He's serious.* I remain silent as I process the news. My face is undoubtedly twisted into a confused look, and I'm too shocked and baffled to formulate any tears.

"Are you okay?" John asks, trying to break my silence.

"Wow, um," I say and pause. I gently cough as I try to gather my words. "Honestly, I promise you I had no idea about that. Died, no. I just assumed he'd run off on me after our fight."

"Fight? What was the fight about?" John inquires, clearly interested in hearing more.

I fidget in my seat while John pulls out a small spiral notebook from his breast pocket. Even though Jake is dead and the public perception of him has become irrelevant, I don't want to taint his reputation with the painful truth behind his infidelity. But I'm also desperate to clear my name. John needs to know my side of the story so he can use it to help find out who's to blame for my husband's death.

"Allie. We were fighting about Allie. Do you know her, the girl he was seeing behind my back?" I reply as my expression shifts from shock to clarity.

John simply shakes his head in response. He has no clue who I'm talking about.

"I can't say as though I do, no. But please, go on." His face grows more intrigued with where my story is heading.

I adjust Piper in my lap and start my spiel by spouting off the few details Jake had shared about his involvement with Allie. I don't have much to go off, but it's a start. I elaborate on the tough times of our relationship and tell him about some of the healthier points of our seven-year marriage. The tales I weave are all true, and I don't do anything to sugarcoat my testimony to make Jake seem like the perfect angel John believed him to be.

John sits across from me, listening intently and taking notes as I tear through the Thacker family's long backstory. I can feel his watchful eyes paying attention to my quirks and habits as I ramble on. I do everything in my power to sound poised and confident as I speak.

"So, this is yours?" John asks.

He flips to the back of his folder and pulls out a small bag housing a gold wedding ring, *my ring*. He explains that he found the night of the fire buried in the gravel. He didn't even have to pull it out of the baggie. I recognized the band instantly.

"Yeah, it's mine. I just didn't think I needed it anymore," I respond smugly. "I really thought he was gone. But, of course, not in this way."

I sit back in my chair and pull Piper close enough to smell the lavender again. I look across the table at John, hunched over and scribbling. Hopefully, he believes me. I refuse to be the scapegoat or be labeled as the culprit behind my husband's demise. I'll do whatever it takes to get myself acquitted.

"Okay," he says as he stops writing. "Well, we all know a lot of people liked the land. And Jake was holding onto it pretty tight, just like his daddy had. You don't think that someone did this over something like a land dispute, do you?"

"Oh God, no. For the right amount, he would have sold. We were just having issues 'cause the place needed some repairs, and he didn't think there'd be a cash buyer around here. I thought the fire was his way of taking the easy way out to avoid an inspection."

"And you don't think he was wrapped up in anything dirty? Drugs, cattle, something of that nature?"

"Not that I knew of. Did you ask Adam?"

"Yeah, I talked to him. He didn't really have anything to add."

"I mean, he told me he was leaving me," Miranda added at the last minute. *Shit, shut up. That makes you sound guilty. A woman scorned.*

I watch John look up from his notes in shock. *Bet that piqued your interest, huh?*

"Leave you?" he asks.

"For Allie?" I reply quickly. John simply nods and writes something down.

"So, where were you when the fire began?" he asks.

"Honestly, when it started, I have no clue it was well underway when I got there. I spent a lot of time out and about that day. After he told me about Allie, I told him we would be back that night to get some stuff, and we'd be staying with my mom for a week, so I could think. I asked him to not be there that night. I didn't want to see him."

"Okay, and where were you all day?"

"Piper had a doctor's appointment, and after that, we did some shopping, got dinner with a friend, and played at the playground near the south end of town. I just had no desire to go home, not until I was sure he was gone. And when I did finally go home, I saw the house on fire and didn't see his truck in the driveway. So, I assumed he burned down the house for the insurance money. He had joked about it more than once."

John takes down hurried notes as he follows along with my alibi.

"You'll understand if I want to check your story out, right?" John asks.

"Of course. I can write out a list of all the stuff we did that day."

"That would be very helpful."

John tucks away his chicken-scratch notes.

"I'll go get you some paper," he says before leaving the room.

When the door shuts, I feel like all the air has been instantly sucked out of the room. I gasp for a breath and try to fight off a flood of emotions that creep in at once. It's hard for me to admit that I will never again see the man I married. A man I once loved more than anything. A part of me already aches for him even though it feels like he's been gone for years. I want the sweet man I met in the smoky bar to come home and be who he once was again.

Although a part of me will miss Jake, I'll make it through. I'm mostly hurting for Piper. She'll never know the joy of having a father who loves and cares for her. Even though he had been a neglectful then cheating husband, Jake had always been a father that visibly cared for his daughter.

I look down at Piper and smile at Jake's likeness showing on her face as she gazes back.

"You have your Daddy's eyes," I whisper into Piper's ear and kiss her cheek. She squirms in my arms as I pull her close and recall memories of Jake.

Jake loved snatching up Piper while she sat on the floor with her attention directed elsewhere. He would crawl across the room inch by inch while trying not to make a sound. Then, when he was right behind her, he would scoop his hands under her arms and throw her above his head as he twirled her around the living room. Piper's face would instantly ignite with a burst of infectious laughter. He would step back and spin her around the room until his arms started shaking.

I watched and grinned when Piper's cheeks turned beet red and started aching from the constantly giggling. When he became dizzy, Jake would land her on her stomach in an airplane motion and yell, "crash landing," while she rolled to her back. Her hands would come to her face as she pushed him away when he placed his lips between her eyebrows and blew a raspberry.

Seeing the constant and intangible joy between them was something that I didn't even realize I would miss. But as I now gaze into my daughter's blue eyes that make me feel lost at sea, I feel a myriad of emotions wash over me.

I glance upward at the ceiling as I force myself to quit thinking about the pleasant parts of Jake. Tears continue rushing out of me, but I keep reminding myself of the irreparable damage he had brought to our relationship. *He's really gone.*

The door's seal breaks with a scratching sound as John reenters the room.

"Sorry about that. Here ya go."

He pushes a blank piece of paper and a ballpoint pen across the table.

"Thanks," I return with a smile.

I transcribe the various stops I made on the day of Jake's death. As I write, I notice that my penmanship appears jagged, and my hand is subtly shaking. *Just slow down and tell the truth. You have no reason to lie.* I let out a noticeable breath, slow my breathing, and concentrate on writing legibly. I try to be as precise and detailed as my memory will allow to help provide the proof of my innocence faster.

"Here you go." I push my itinerary across the table.

"Thank you, ma'am," John replies as he takes my reproduced day and reads through my stops.

"I hate to ask you this, Miranda. But we will need you to come back to town until this all blows over. I believe your story, but you have to understand how it looks," he pauses before continuing his rationale. "You runnin' off with Piper and all."

A large and painful pit forms in the back of my throat and makes it impossible to swallow. I nod my head smoothly as I try to stomach the fact that somebody would even contemplate the absurd idea of me being a prime suspect in my husband's murder. Although I don't have much loving regard for Jake, the cruel act of setting our house on fire with him inside had never crossed my mind.

I desperately want to shout at the top of my lungs in the cramped room. *I didn't do it! What the hell? I'm making a life for myself, and now you're ruining it. Just let me be.* But instead, I remain silent and try to wait it out while John works through his mandatory process.

I smugly agree to go back to Butte and derail the small steps I'd made toward my independence. Hopefully, cooperating will help my name get erased quickly from John's suspect list.

As we head back toward the front door, I spin around and speak to John again, reiterating something I feel he'd glossed over.

"Please, though, promise me you'll check into her, Allie. I don't know if she has a side to the story that I don't know about, but I have a feeling she's not completely innocent in all of this," I plead.

"I promise, Miranda. I'm going to get to the bottom of this."

John walks us out to the car and follows us back to the motel to collect our few belongings.

I strip down the bed, grab our toiletries, and combine the leftovers we had accumulated into one styrofoam box. As I rush around the cramped room I won't miss, I feel my freedom rapidly fading away. My mind is racing as I think about my innocence, but I'm afraid about how this situation will pan out.

Before checking out, I pick up the phone and call mama to tell her we won't be coming to stay.

"What happened, baby?" mama asks.

"I don't really want to talk about it right now. But, don't worry about us. We're fine."

We talk for a minute longer before I say goodbye and hang up the phone. *All I want right now is my mom.*

I peek out the window and see John still in his car in the lot, waiting on us. I feel like he's just sitting there, trying to figure out if he believes me or not. Part of me is scared he doesn't.

I lug our few things out to my vehicle and offer John a soft smile and single-finger salute before clipping Piper in and falling into the driver's seat. The car roars to life, and I pull up behind him.

As we drive south, I watch my dream town of Great Falls disappear in the rearview mirror as I head back to Butte in the trail of my escort. The ambitions I had begun to plant in the small town had been involuntarily uprooted, and I hoped we would one day find somewhere safe and secure for us to call home.

"Just have to prove I didn't kill Daddy," I say aloud after checking to make sure Piper is knocked out.

We finally pull back into the too-familiar town just as the sun shows the last of its warming rays over the horizon. John helps us get checked in and leads us to our interior hotel room.

I unlock the door, thank John, and reach in as my hand fumbles along the wall, searching for the switch. When the lights turn on, a soft smile cracks across my face when I see the updated room. The lights don't flicker, the bed has an assortment of fluffy pillows, and there's even a tiny kitchenette to use. *At least it's nicer.*

Again, in somewhere new, Piper is agitated with all the drastic changes she's been forced to endure. Her life is now uprooted as well, and I'm in awe of how well she's handling the myriad of adjustments.

"I'm so proud of you," I say as I stroke Piper's hair while she plays in a few inches of bathwater.

After reading and singing to her for half an hour, I finally get Piper to sleep in her foldable mock crib. I'm grateful for her rumbling snore that interrupts the room's silence.

The bed is firm but welcomes me as I lay on my back and close my eyes. My mind tiptoes near sleeping, but the recent developments in my life keep pulling me back into consciousness. A buzz escapes my lips as I release the air from my lungs.

I allow a sad sentiment to creep in for a brief minute when I let Jake slip into my thoughts. I realize I haven't even been sad yet. The tears that I couldn't muster earlier finally flood my vision. *Dammit, Jake, why?*

The memories of our relationship hadn't all been bad, and there had been times when Jake made me immensely happy. A part of me had never stopped believing one day, we would get back to the happy couple we had once been. *Now we never will.*

Jake had a way of brushing the hair out of my eyes that had always sent me swooning. A simple touch could do so much. I now realize I'll miss the little things about him that I previously hadn't given a second thought. *He'll never have my toothbrush ready before bed anymore, and I won't get to hear the sound of his oversized slippers slapping the floor when he walks.*

Tears roll from the corners of my eyes and slide down my temples, tickling their way into my ears. As more memories and moments come to my mind, I start to believe they're just figments of my imagination. *The Jake I remember was cold and unloving.*

I shake the recollections from my busy head. I wipe my damp eyes and move on from the grief I had momentarily let in as I drift off to sleep.

NINE

JOHN

JOHN LAID IN bed and attempted to dissect the extensive story Miranda had presented that afternoon. His wife's obnoxious snore filled the room, but he was so focused on his thoughts he didn't hear a sound. Piece by piece, he worked through Jake's wife's testimony, trying to remember her words and accompanying expressions.

Throughout their discussion, she had been utterly calm and collected. When he'd dropped the news that her husband was dead, she barely flinched, which seemed crazy to him. The idea of anything happening to his wife was too hard to even think about. But Miranda hadn't even seemed fazed.

It also surprised him how quick Miranda was to throw Jake under the bus. Five minutes after finding out he was dead, she was ready to share all of his transgressions in an effort to flip the narrative. Miranda's demeanor came off as callous and harsh, but that didn't necessarily mean she was an arsonist or murderer.

John had a hard time believing Jake cheated on his wife. The Jake he remembered seemed like an honorable man that would have gone to the ends of the earth to be a good husband and father, not someone who would run out on his wife and child for someone else. A part of him even thought Miranda could have fabricated that segment of her story to direct the investigation toward someone else. It wouldn't be the first time a cold-hearted wife crafted a narrative to distract a detective.

It all confused him and kept his mind revolving in a loop.

The Allie woman that Miranda had described was noteworthy. Maybe she was real and had answers, or maybe she was fictionalized from Miranda's need to find someone to take the blame. Either way, finding her was at the top of John's list. He was hoping Allie would be able to tie some pieces of the broken story together.

The following day, John sat down at his desk, overly tired from his night of pondering in the darkness. He readied his spiral notepad and anxiously clicked his pen as he prepared to make some calls. He prayed someone would provide him with new information.

The first number he dialed was that of the county coroner's office, just as he had the past two mornings. Bugging them about the results of Jake's autopsy was becoming the way he started his day.

"Hey, it's me again. Just calling to get the results of the Thacker autopsy," he explained when the secretary finally answered.

"One second, please," she replied as she passed off the phone.

"Sorry, John, it's not ready yet," the coroner stated.

"Dammit, Blake, it's been three days," he returned and paused. "I'm sorry, I'm sorry." Getting irritated with people wasn't going to make things go any faster.

"We're getting there, John. It's not a quick process," the coroner explained.

"Alright, I understand, thanks anyway," he returned.

"I promise, I'll personally call you as soon as we're done," he assured.

"I know. Thank you."

He slammed the handset back to the base.

"Shit." He rested his head in his cracked hands as he pushed the hair in the front of his head backward in frustration.

The autopsy was all he had for the time being. He was anxious to hold the results in his hands. Hopefully, the report would shed some light on the circumstances surrounding Jake's mysterious death and provide John with a new lead to chase.

Deep down, he had a feeling that the autopsy would reveal something else, something dark and painful. He expected to hear that Jake had been killed in some horrific way before his house had been torched or, worse, died from the fire. His stomach churned when he thought about the possibility that his friend had been murdered.

Jake's death was still locked in the questioning phase, where it teetered between an accident and foul play. However, the fire marshal stood firm in his decision that the flames had come from arson and not something faulty that had gone wrong in the home. So, there was someone to blame.

The only person he had on his shortlist was the woman that Jake Thacker was allegedly having an ongoing affair with. Tacking a last name onto *Allie* would be a big help. Miranda's name was also still in his scribbled book, but he believed her alibi would be validated once he had the free time to investigate her day.

John opened his sticky desk drawer and pulled out the somewhat tattered business card from the restaurant he had just visited on the other side of town. He flipped over the bag the card was in. *Dammit, John, how did you forget about the back?*

113

He picked up his phone and dialed the number. The line rang and rang until he heard the click of the machine, followed by a female voice.

"Hey, sorry to miss you, leave me a message," she said in a cheery and singsong voice.

That has to be her. He hung up the phone without leaving a message. *It's got to be.*

He ran his finger along the thin plastic bag that covered the card and tapped on the small, penned heart. Ordinarily, a typical business card from a local restaurant wouldn't have interested him. But its safekeeping and handwritten number made it feel like it meant something to Jake.

He grabbed his desk phone again and redialed the number. The phone rang ominously as John begged someone to pick it up. Finally, the click of the machine again caught his attention.

"Hey, sorry to miss you, leave me a message." A beep chimed.

"Hello, uh, this message is for Allie if she still lives here. This is Detective Waters over in Butte. Please give me a call back. I have a few questions I'd like to ask you about one of our open cases. Thank you, and have a great day."

John rattled off his office information to the machine and sat waiting by the phone. *She'll call back, I hope.* He constantly glanced over at its main body as if it would start ringing from his sheer desire. After five minutes of waiting and staring, John loudly sighed and dropped his shoulders in defeat. He had never been the most patient person.

He figured calling her was a lost cause. Part of him expected Allie to delete his message and move on with her life, but he had her home number. If she failed to call back, he could do a reverse search and find her address. Tracking her down would be simple.

John wore his frustration on his face as he caught up on some needed paperwork for nearly an hour. Then, just as he was about to head out to try and confirm Miranda's alibi, the loud ratting chime of his phone finally sounded from its core and startled him. He quickly snatched up the receiver and dropped it on his desk once as he fumbled with enthusiasm.

"Good afternoon, this is Detective Waters." *Please be Allie.*

"Hi. Um, this is Allie. I think you left me a message on my machine," a soft voice said quietly over the phone.

"Good morning, ma'am. How are you today?" he asked.

"I'm doing fine, thank you. Um, how about you?" Allie responded with a hint of uncertainty in her voice.

"Oh, not too bad, thanks for asking. And thank you for calling me back. I was actually hoping that you had some time today to come down to the sheriff's office and talk to me for a little bit." John cringed and waited for her response.

Allie's voice was silent for a few seconds while she mulled over his request. John ran his foot over the small hole in the office's hardwood floor while quickly moving his fingers from right to left as each tip tapped on the arm of his chair.

"Hello?" he finally inquired, thinking maybe they had been cut off. Or she had hung up.

"Yeah, um, I guess I could do that. Could you just tell me what this is about?"

"Well, it's just something I'd really like to talk to you about in person, if you don't mind." He allowed Allie a moment to provide a response, but he wasn't really asking. *Just say yes. Please, let's do this the easy way.*

"Yeah, um, I can do that," she returned.

"Great, that sounds good," he overeagerly answered.

John set up a meeting with Jake Thacker's alleged mistress, Allie.

With papers spread across his desk, he thumbed through the little evidence he had accumulated since the fire. He dug through Miranda's testimony and came up with his line of questioning. He wanted to know more about the affair, confirmation mostly, but wanted to come off subtly, not flat out accusing her right off the bat.

He also wanted to know if she was around Jake in the days leading up to the fire. Maybe he seemed off or hinted that he was having trouble with something or someone specific. *Just maybe that person was his wife.* Jake may have opened up more to his mistress than the woman with whom he shared a home and child.

But Miranda really wasn't a prime suspect currently. She had been adamant that Allie likely had more information about what happened to Jake, and John was growing increasingly curious about hearing what Jake's alleged mistress could add to his case file.

TEN

ALLIE

ALLIE MADE THE drive into town to meet with Detective Waters shortly after she'd hung up the phone. The roads were reportedly plowed earlier in the day, but they were yet again garnished with a thick layer of snow that covered the blacktop. She drove carefully and kept her eyes peeled for patches of ice.

As much as she hated to think about it, she knew why the detective called. *Jake.* She knew his death was something she would eventually be questioned about and was surprised it had taken a few days to call her into the station. The affair must have been leaked. *Miranda.*

While classic rock played at a low buzz, Allie drummed her fingers nervously on the steering wheel and crept just above the speed limit. She wasn't in a rush to meet with Jake's former coworker and was still unsure how deep she should dive into the background of their messy relationship.

"You got this," she recited as she tried to hush her increasing nerves.

The roads began to clear as she neared the heart of town. She talked over the soft music and repeated her alibi to herself on a loop, trying to make sure it flowed well. She rested her elbow on the car's doorframe and tapped the tips of her fingers on her temple as she tried to memorize her side of the story.

The words she prepared were thought out and detailed. If she could lure the authorities into believing she was forthcoming and her testimony was the whole truth and nothing but the truth, there would be no reason for them to continue to have any suspicions about her.

Jake was gone, and so was her involvement in his life. She had no relationship with his wife or child, and there was no reason that his mistress would be afforded any respect in his death. The role she had played for over seven months was over. *They* were over.

Ever since she'd learned of his passing, she'd been utterly broken. She cried all the time and slipped deeper into depression every day. Jake meant everything to her, and she was the one left behind and alone, emotionally destroyed and forced to find a way to move on.

She pulled into the predominantly empty parking lot and into a spot. The clock on the dash told her she had one minute until their meeting time. She unsteadily shifted the car to park and left her hand on the gear shift as she considered backing up and driving away.

As tempting as running seemed, she knew it wasn't practical nor necessary. A county detective likely had connections all over the state. It would only be a matter of time before he could hunt her down and coax out the few details she was sure about. She wanted to be completely honest but knew she couldn't. She had to keep quiet and keep what she knew to herself.

She straightened her posture and filled her lungs as she readied her mindset to get through the conversation. *You'll be fine, just relax.* Keeping her emotions in check would be critical to making sure she stuck to her rehearsed story.

Allie ran her hands down her face and allowed her worries to wipe off her cheeks. *You can do this.* She took one last look in the visor mirror, applied a light dusting of powder to hide the dark circles of sleepless nights beneath her eyes, and forced a hopefully believable smile to her lips.

She mustered up the shred of courage she had hidden inside and scooted out of her driver's seat. Her boots sunk down as they punched through a thin layer of holey ice that laid in patches across the lot. Every crunchy step seemed to scream as she took the ominous walk toward the sheriff's department's front door.

She stepped into the lobby and took in a heavy whiff of the festive peppermint scent that hung in the room. She scanned the area. Aside from an elderly man with the newspaper open and rattling in his shaky hands, the only person in the lobby was an older woman with half-rimmed bifocals sitting at a small reception desk.

"Hello. Good morning, ma'am," the woman called across the room.

Me, she's calling me. Allie shook her head clear and strolled towards the desk. She hiked her purse back atop her shoulder and pulled it close to her side, tightly wrapping her fingers around its strap.

"Hi, um. I'm here to see Detective Waters," Allie said.

"Yes, honey. Just have a seat, and I'll give him a call."

"Oh, okay. Thanks," Allie stuttered.

She sat down on one of the three couches near the front windows. The cold air outside had created a thin layer of fog on the glass that left her feeling somewhat claustrophobic, trapped even.

The seconds on the clock ticked above her head, and she tapped her foot nervously on the tile. *Tick, Tick... Tick.* Every third tick appeared somewhat delayed, or maybe it was just something her mind was doing to distract her rapidly escalating nerves.

The tapping and ticking finally fell into a synched rhythm. Her foot played along with the delay of the clock.

The woman at the counter glanced over at her a few times as if she needed to make sure she hadn't darted out of the front door when she wasn't looking. *She knows you know something.* A bead of sweat rolled down her neck and tickled her spine before being soaked up by the waistband of her jeans.

Allie found a small hole in the upholstery and dug her finger inside as she nervously twirled the stuffing around. It was chilly in the lobby, but she could already feel a puddle of sweat accumulating in her armpits. *No, I can't do this.*

Allie rose from the couch and prepared to leave. She took one step forward and saw Detective Waters emerge from the single glass door near the front desk that led to the department's back. She froze.

"Mornin'," he said with a muted smile and accusing eyes.

Shit. Too late.

ELEVEN

JOHN

THE SECOND JOHN emerged from the back and stepped into the lobby; he instantly recognized the woman standing near the front windows. *So, I guess it's Allie Taylor?*

Before him, the nervous-looking woman looked more casual than the last time he had seen her bustling around as a waitress. Instead of a cheap embroidered uniform and skid-resistant shoes, she wore an oversized Montana State sweatshirt with a stretched-out neck, and her hands were hidden in its waist-level pocket. Her slightly flared jeans were damp at the bottom and partially covered her waterproof boots. Allie's straight blond hair barely brushed over her shoulders from a part on the left side of her head and looked somewhat messier than their previous encounter. A light layer of makeup was evident on her skin, but her eyes appeared intentionally bare and somewhat bloodshot.

She was noticeably younger than Jake, if not close to ten years his junior. *She's just a kid. Maybe this is all a misunderstanding.* John discerned a masked look of sadness in her eyes and a visible reluctance in her posture as she stood waiting. He approached her.

"Nice to see you again, Ms. Taylor," John said almost sarcastically as he stuck out his hand.

"Yeah, you as well," Allie replied as she awkwardly avoided eye contact. She scanned the room, looking into every corner as if she was checking to ensure no one saw her.

"Come on, let's head back this way," John stated as he pointed Allie toward the back of the building.

She hesitated for a second but eventually pulled her hands out of her pocket and followed John toward the back of the lobby.

Allie's nerves increased as she began to feel as though she was walking into a trap. The strength she had rehearsed on repeat in the car seemed to have flown out the window. A feeling of terror swelled in her gut.

"Right in here, please," John said. He invited her to a room where they could talk.

"Can I get you a water? Coffee?" he asked.

"No, thank you," she replied.

Allie stepped into the square room and only saw a small table in its middle. The stark white walls and concrete grey floor made the room feel cold and intimidating. She pulled out a metal chair and sat down on the far side of the depressing room, facing the door. A poorly illuminated light above her head swung slightly from the non-stop blow of the air conditioning.

Allie scooted her chair closer. It screeched across the tile floor. She flashed a toothless smile at John, fidgeted with her fingers atop the table, and glanced around the empty room.

"Excuse me one minute," John said as he tactfully stepped away.

He quickly scurried around the hallway's corner. He squatted down and observed Allie's monitored behavior from a TV linked to the small black and white camera mounted on the room's ceiling. John intently studied her as she sat silently at the table.

She surveyed the room frequently, and her shoulders lifted as she took multiple overdramatized breaths. Twice, she looked behind her and gazed directly at the camera before quickly averting her eyes. *Tell me something. Please.*

"Sorry," John said as he reappeared in the room. "Had to grab a few things."

He pulled out a yellow legal pad and pen and set them on the table before laying down the folder he was building on the case. He sat down and joined her.

"It's fine," she replied, cupping her hands and forcing them into her lap to avoid fidgeting.

"So, I would like to start this discussion by telling you I don't have any reason to suspect your involvement in Deputy Jake Thacker's death." John watched Allie adjust in her seat at the sound of his name. "And you are welcome to legal assistance. And we can provide that to you at no cost at any time. Understand?"

"I understand."

"Great. Well, I just have some questions and a few other things I need to talk to you about and hear your side of things. Does that make sense to you?"

"Okay, yeah. I guess so. What kind of things?" Allie asked.

Her voice slightly shook as she looked around the room and down at the floor to avoid eye contact.

"Well, for starters, if you don't mind, could you please elaborate some on your relationship with Deputy Thacker," John prompted.

Her eyelashes fluttered, and John watched her neck bulge and swallow a gulp before speaking.

"Um yeah, I guess you could say we were acquainted. He uh, came into the restaurant quite a bit, but you already knew that," she explained.

"Just acquainted?" John asked, probing for more.

"Yeah, I served him quite a few times. So, I guess you could say that we were kinda friends."

"So, you two didn't have any sort of relationship outside of the confines of the restaurant?"

Allie went quiet and looked away from John.

John noticed the beginning of tears building up in her eyes that she was actively fighting. His question appeared to have hit a painful spot and had elicited a reaction just as he had hoped.

Allie's hands moved onto her lap, and she fidgeted more than before as she tried to fight back her impending tears. She picked at her dry cuticles as she tried to keep calm. She had every intention of maintaining her composure but felt her plans crumbling to the floor as her emotions took hold.

"No, nothing more. Just friends, I guess."

"I'm asking because I'm wondering why I found your home phone number on the back of this card in Jake's truck," John asked, trying to lead her into a better explanation.

The color instantly drained from Allie's face as John gently slid the small business card from their first date across the table. She looked down and read the number she had written down for Jake months earlier.

"Um, yeah, uh," Allie responded shakily as her eyes remained focused on the card.

"The heart just makes it seem a little more than just a friendly relationship with a waitress. Do you maybe do something on the side to make some extra money?"

Allie had been avoiding eye contact but suddenly darted her gaze up to John.

"What do you think I am, a hooker?" Her mood shifted, and she quickly became defensive.

"I wasn't implying that. I'm just trying to figure this out. I'm sorry if I offended you." *Too far.*

"No, I'm not a hooker or anything like that. I just...." She paused, trying to formulate a logical reason why Jake had her home number in his truck.

"Sorry, I just wasn't expecting this," Allie said.

"It's alright. Take your time." John remained seated and calm as he allowed her to compose her emotions. *Here we go. Please say something I can use.*

"Do you maybe wanna think again about how close of friends you were?" John asked, giving Allie a chance to change her story.

Allie looked up toward the ceiling and blinked through the tears that had begun to pool in her eyes. Her foot nervously tapped the floor beneath the table, and she kept trying to pop the knuckles at the tip of her thumbs.

She finally looked back at John and allowed tears to release from her eyes and run down her cheeks. The emotions she was trying to keep in check came flooding out like a tidal wave. It was apparent she had more to say.

"I loved him, really, I did. I would never have done this to him. I swear to you."

John clicked his pen and started writing a million miles a minute.

Allie's deny, deny, deny plan quickly went out the window when she realized she was backed into a corner. Trapped. There was no way out. She couldn't create a good enough excuse to justify John's probing, and her poker face was terrible.

"And how long had this affair been going on?" he asked.

"Uh, a little over six months," she choked out.

John witnessed the conviction in her eyes as she repeatedly denied that she was involved in his death. She also rejected having anything to do with the fire while finally breaking her silence about their torrid affair.

The woman sitting before him didn't appear like a killer. John wasn't even sure she was old enough to drink. But she did come off as someone who was heartbroken and had a deeply rooted fear about fessing up to the truth.

"But really, I loved him. I swear I didn't do it," she added.

"I understand that, thank you. But is there anything else relevant to your relationship that I need to know about?" he asked, hoping she would be forthcoming.

Allie sat silently as more tears rolled down her cheeks and fell to her lap. A shiver caused her shoulders to shake, and she grabbed her elbows. Her gaze darted around the room, and she continuously blinked and wiped her eyes while she tried to stop crying.

"It's okay. Take a minute," John said, trying to reassure her.

"I," she took a deep breath that she held at its peak briefly before exhaling. "I don't think so. But I ended it with him the night before you guys found him," she paused again and cleared her throat, "dead." Her crying escalated at the sound of the word.

"You ended the affair?" John asked, growing more confused between the two sides of the story he had heard. Miranda had weaved a completely different account. "Why?"

"Yeah, it was just getting to be too much. I wasn't going to ask him to leave his family or anything. We had already taken it too far, and it needed to be over," she replied as she wiped away the waterfall of tears flowing from her eyes.

"Okay, thank you," John replied as he took down some notes about Allie's recount of the events. Her slow stream of tears was becoming a full-on sob.

John stood and silently left the room. He quickly returned with a box of tissues and pushed them across the table. She kept crying, and her tears were believable.

"I'm sorry," she returned as she dabbed her eyes with a tissue.

"It's all right. Don't worry about it. So, you told Jake it was over, and you were the one calling it quits for the both of you?" John asked.

"Yes, the night before he died," she explained.

"That's good to know, thank you. And how did he take it? You don't think he was distraught and could've done something to hurt himself, do you?"

"Like suicide? No, I really don't think so. The affair was really, really tough on both of us. He was relieved that we could just move on and go back to our own lives. It was a mutual decision."

"Gotcha. Thank you for your honesty," John said with a hint of skepticism.

While Allie talked, John hurriedly took down notes, trying to make sure he caught every detail. His notebook contained two completely different sides of the story, and it was up to him to figure out which one of the women was telling the truth and who knew more than they were leading on.

In some regard, Allie's story felt more concrete and logical. John had known Jake for nearly a decade and thought he knew his character well. He had never taken him as the kind of man to run out on his family for another woman but still believed that maybe he had judged him wrongly. *People surprise you.* However, Allie's confirmation of their lengthy affair left him unsure if he had ever known one of his coworkers like he presumed he did.

"You don't know of him being involved with anything shady, do you? Like maybe something he was wrapped up in that led to someone wanting to hurt him? Drugs? Gambling?" John asked.

"No, I mean, I didn't know everything about his life, but I don't think so. He never mentioned anything like that."

She cited a few more things about how much she cared about Jake and how distraught she had been over his death. Her condolences sounded rehearsed as if she had read them off Hallmark cards at Albertsons before their appointment.

"Was it Miranda? Did she tell you?" Allie asked with a blank look.

"Uh, I'm not really at liberty to discuss that right now," John answered.

"Oh, okay," she replied with a look that said she already knew the answer to her own question.

Allie laid out her alibi, which consisted of a long night of waiting tables with many people bearing witness. There was a timecard that would prove she was telling the truth, and her manager would defend her case.

John took notes to hopefully confirm her story simultaneously while he checked in on Miranda's. Allie's alibi seemed airtight, leaving him to wonder more about the validity of Miranda's.

"Got it," John said when he reviewed her story. "We're gonna need you to stick around town while this all gets sorted."

"I understand," Allie replied. "And I really, really hope you find out who did this."

"Yeah," me too," John said as he paused. "Well, I thank you for your time, and I will give you a call if we have any more questions."

John guided Allie back down the hallway and out of the building.

As she walked down the sidewalk, she glanced over her shoulder toward him twice as if worried she was being watched. Something about her seemed distraught, and all her emotions had come unraveled after the death of Jake.

John went back to his office and rubbed his temples as he glanced over his hurriedly scribbled notes. He repeatedly dissected each story and alibi as he tried to find a hole in one of the women's accounts. *One of you knows something.*

The day's discussion hadn't gone exactly as he had hoped. It didn't end with crossing Miranda off his list, but it did add Allie. Something wasn't aligning between the two women's stories, and John was determined to find out which one had vital information they were keeping a secret.

"Hey, Holly," John called out to one of the deputies.

"Yes, sir?" she asked as she popped into his office.

"Could you start doing some work to get a court order to pull the phone records for these two, please, if you would."

John handed over a sticky with two local numbers written on its front: the Thackers and Allie Taylor.

"Will do."

John pulled out the small notepad from his breast pocket and added *Allie Taylor* right below Miranda's name.

TWELVE

JOHN

JOHN BEGAN DOING his due diligence to investigate both women's stories. He desperately wanted to believe they were both telling the truth. But at the same time, that would leave him with an empty list of suspects.

Miranda's story had some stops he figured wouldn't remember her or have cameras, and he was at a loss when it came to figuring out how to validate that she was at the park as she claimed. He lined through three stops and moved on down the list.

He called the pediatrician's office, and the woman that answered the phone confirmed that Miranda and Piper had made their appointment that afternoon. He placed a checkmark next to that stop.

When John was finished combing Miranda's alibi, he'd circled two different places he believed could confirm her story. He grabbed his keys and case folder and headed out to validate in person.

David Cravotta bought the small restaurant tucked away in the back of downtown for pennies on the dollar when the owner had passed away in the kitchen two years prior. He'd fixed the place up, revamped the menu, and made it one of the most highly rated restaurants in town.

John and David had met over beers at the local VFW nearly fifteen years earlier and have remained friends ever since. They occasionally still met up and swapped war stories over dinner or a pint.

John walked into the restaurant and salivated at the fresh basil smell that hung in the air. David was across the room, conversing with one of his waiters. John waved, and David threw a finger up.

"John. How you doing?" David asked when he was done.

"Well, not too bad, but I've been better. I was wondering if you could help me out with something."

"Yeah, what can I do for you?"

"I was hoping that you'd remember seeing the woman in this picture?" John asked as he pulled out the family photo and pointed to Miranda.

David pulled his reading glasses from the chain that kept them around his neck. He took a few seconds as he studied the woman in the photo.

"Yeah. Yeah, I remember seeing her here. I can't recall what day it was specifically, but I know it was recently. I think she was here with a woman and maybe a baby?" David explained.

John nodded his head slightly as he heard Miranda's story halfway validated.

"Well, do you have any cameras or anything I could check?" John asked, hoping to get hard proof.

"I'm sorry, I don't. Those are just up for show. They don't actually work," David explained as he pointed to the bulky wall-mounted surveillance cameras.

"You've always been such a cheap ass."

"Hey, I make it work."

"Well, Dave, thanks for your time, and good to see you. We should get together sometime," he offered.

"Of course. Hey, do you want to leave that photo with me? I'll check with my night crew from that evening. Maybe see if any of them remember her?" David suggested.

"If you don't mind, please give me a call as soon as they confirm her story."

"Wilco."

He handed the owner a copy of the Thacker family photo and left the restaurant hopeful David would call and solidify Miranda's story. But, while he waited, he was going to keep working toward trying to find information on his own.

He drove to the home of Kirstyn Anderson, the friend that Miranda claimed to have had dinner with the night of Jake's death.

As John headed across town, the small run-down houses and single wides became more sparse as the developments grew into expensive Tudor Style homes. He eventually came to a wrought iron gate that stopped him from following the rest of his printed MapQuest directions.

He pulled over to the side and was about to get out and scroll through the list of residents when a red Mustang pulled up and opened the gate. John quickly slipped into the neighborhood behind the car.

The metal knocker on the overly tall wooden door was ice cold to the touch. John lifted it and banged it three times, the echo sounding through the expanse on the other side. A smell of smoke hung in the air from the many fireplaces roaring nearby. He took a step back and surveyed the modest mansion while waiting on the stoop.

After a brief wait, a brown-haired man that looked to be in his mid-thirties opened the front door and greeted John with a tentative smile.

"Hi, uh, can I help you?" the man asked with a hint of confusion in his tone.

John was all too familiar with the perplexed look stricken across the man's face. It was the standard blank expression he was always greeted with when he knocked on someone's door, and they opened it to see a person with a gun on their hip, especially when they weren't expecting someone.

"Hi, I'm Detective John Waters. I was looking to talk to Ms. Anderson if she's home," John explained as he stood out in the cold.

"May I ask what this is about?" he asked as his eyebrows slanted toward one another.

"I just need to talk to her about a friend of hers regarding an open investigation. Are you her husband?"

"Yeah, I'm Tyler. Come on in."

Tyler stepped out of the way and allowed the detective to enter their home. John offered to leave his snowy boots at the door but was told, "don't worry about it," and was escorted into the living room. He took a seat on the couch, and Tyler took his large overcoat and hung it on a rack near the door.

"So um, I'll go upstairs and grab her. Please, feel free to make yourself at home."

"Thank you."

When Tyler disappeared upstairs, John looked around the grand living room he'd been invited into. Flames danced around in a red brick fireplace in front of him and made the room feel homey, and movement from a small train circling the base of the Christmas tree caught his eye. He got up to check out the lush Fraser Fir positioned in front of a large picture window.

It was covered in eclectic Hallmark ornaments. They were hung in an evenly spaced manner that seemed almost methodical, so just the right amount of greenery and lights peeked through. The sentimental pieces made the tree feel more personable than one decorated in color-coordinated balls and garland. While he was busy examining the decorations, a tall woman with long black hair silently slipped into the room.

"Hello, I'm Kirstyn."

John flinched at the voice. He stood up straight and turned to the homeowner, nearly knocking a small Lion King ornament off the tree.

"Sorry about that. Hello. I'm Detective Waters. Nice to meet you."

"Nice to meet you as well. Please, have a seat. What can I do for you, detective?"

John sat down on an uncomfortable tufted bench while Kirstyn took a seat in a grand wingback chair covered in a tacky floral print.

"Well, I'm here to talk to you about your friend Miranda Thacker."

"Okay. What can I tell you about her?" She crossed her legs and leaned back into the chair.

"Well, I'm sure you're familiar with the situation involving her house and husband," John stated.

"I know. It's terrible what happened to Jake. I always thought he was a nice guy, but evidently, there was more to him than I knew."

"What do you mean by that?"

"Well, Miranda told me about what happened earlier that day while we were at dinner, about the woman he was seeing and stuff. I just never thought Jake had that in him."

"Yeah, I think that surprised us all. Can you tell me more about Miranda's state of mind after she told you everything?"

Kirstyn stared at him for a moment and crossed her legs. She leaned deeper into her chair and placed her hands on her lap.

"Detective, are you trying to ask me if I think she did it?"

"No, no. Not at all. I just was wondering if you tell if she was upset, relieved, angry...," he led.

"I would say she was all the above. I mean, her husband treated her like shit, well, did something really shitty, and told her he was leaving her. I don't think anyone in their right mind wouldn't feel the whole gambit of emotions at that point."

"Yeah, I understand, but...," John stated before he was cut off.

"But no, I don't think there is any doubt in my mind that Miranda is innocent. She wouldn't hurt a fly. Was she upset, yes? But did she murder her husband? No."

"Okay, I understand," he paused as he nodded toward her. He, too, had the same theory about Miranda's innocence. "Anyways, uh, Miranda claims you, and she met for dinner that night."

"Yep, we did, at Nick's around fiveish, I think," Kirstyn replied.

"Great, so can you give me the details of her story?"

John listened intently and took some hurried notes as Kirstyn spoke a mile a minute. She didn't spare any details. The story she laid out for him was nearly word for word identical to Miranda's as if it were rehearsed. Her speech had no awkward pauses or breaks as she rattled off the details John had been searching for.

"Miranda told me she would call me before she hit the road, but she never did," Kirstyn explained. "I was worried something happened to her when I saw the fire."

"You saw it?" John asked for clarification.

"Well, I drove over to her house to check on her when she didn't call me that night. But she'd promised she would. And that's when I saw it was on fire. So, I was the one that drove back into town and made the 9-1-1 call. I always forget that stupid flip phone thing. It doesn't work out that way anyway."

John recalled the dispatcher describing the caller's voice as a middle-aged-sounding woman. But unfortunately, before they could pull any other identifying information about her, the line had been cut off.

"Oh, I didn't know that," John said as he scribbled the tidbit down.

"Yeah, called from a payphone and ran out of spare change. But I didn't see anything or anyone else there. Miranda's car wasn't in the lot, and neither was Jake's. The house was well lit up by the time I showed, and I instantly left to call it in. After dinner, I had gone home and didn't go back out until I started to worry about her," she added. "That's all I really know."

John took down Kirstyn's information and gave her a business card in case she remembered something else. He donned his coat, exited the large house, and pulled out of the gated community.

Kirstyn had validated the majority of Miranda's story. *What about Allie's?*

He drove past his office and continued following the road out to the edge of town. He pulled into the gravel lot of the place where Allie spent her time waiting tables for minimum wage.

John entered the restaurant and directed his eyes to all four corners of the dining room, looking for Allie. Based on what he could see, she wasn't working. He strolled over to the first waitress he saw and kindly asked her to direct him toward a manager.

"I'll be right back," the waitress responded as she disappeared.

He gently swayed back and forth in his boots while waiting at the restaurant's entrance for nearly five minutes. Eventually, a person who wasn't wearing a cheaply embroidered polo and dirty black slacks walked toward him.

"Hi," said a man who looked to have some authority.

"Hi, I'm Detective Waters, and I'm just here to talk to Janel."

"Sorry about that, Janel is off today, but I'm Mark, the assistant manager. What can we do for you today?"

"Nice to meet you, Mark. Well, uh, I'm here because I'm trying to validate a story for one of your employees."

"Yeah, sure. Whatever we can do," Mark returned as he clasped his hands together at his waist.

"Are you familiar with Allie Taylor?" John asked as he showed him the picture the department's secretary had dug up of her.

"Oh yeah, Allie is a great girl. Did she do something?" he replied with a genuine look of concern.

"Well, I'm really hoping that isn't the case. She claims she was here the other night, and it's directly linked to something we're working on, so I was hoping you would be able to back up her story."

"Yeah, please, follow me," he said while directing John towards an office in the back of the restaurant.

The two worked together and checked Allie's timecard against the story she told John. The alibi she'd given directly matched the hours she claimed she was working. *So maybe it wasn't you.*

"Well, that's good news. Glad we could help," Mark responded as he tucked her card away.

"Yeah, it is. But uh, is there anything you can tell me about any of these people," John prompted as he showed him the family photo and tried to leave the question open-ended.

Mark looked at the picture, and his eyes moved right to Jake. He quickly spoke up without needing a minute to think about it.

"Allie did seem a little off that day, just so you know. She looked pretty emotional, and that guy, yeah yeah, um, he came in here all the time and often asked to sit in Allie's section," Mark explained.

"So, they were friendly?"

"Oh yeah, if I didn't know any better, I would have thought the two had a thing for each other. But hey, I could have that all wrong."

"Great. Is there anything else?" John asked.

"No, I don't think so. Sorry, I didn't talk to the guy," he responded.

"Well, thank you so much for your time, sir. You've been very helpful. Please don't hesitate to let me know if you think of anything else," John replied before tucking away his photos and handing the assistant manager one of his cards.

"Sure thing."

As John walked toward the restaurant's front door with his notes in hand, he felt his shoulders drop at the thought of both women's stories leading him nowhere. Now he was left with an empty suspect list.

As the sun was setting, he finally got back to his office with more questions than he'd left with.

"Sir?" the department's secretary asked as he passed by her desk.

"Yeah?" he responded as he stepped toward her. She pulled out a little sticky note as she slipped on her reading glasses.

"Dave from Nick's called while you were out. He said his evening guys said she was there."

"Okay, thank you."

He rested his head in his palms. *Great, they both told the truth.*

THIRTEEN

MIRANDA

MY ANXIETY IS spinning out of control as I sit at the foot of the bed. I put my palm on my thigh to stop my leg from bouncing. It keeps driving up and down as if strapped to a rogue piston. It's been close to twenty-four hours since I provided my alibi, and I'm dying with anticipation, waiting for John to call and tell me it checked out, which it will.

I'd already wandered around the room when the satellite TV went out, and Piper was napping. I'm beyond familiar with the contents inside our four walls that are beginning to feel like a prison. There are three spots where the flat white paint is chipping, two of the blown-up stock photos aren't glued to the wall level, and there's one place beneath the table where it looks like someone had put a cigarette out on the carpet. *Come on, John, call.*

Someone laughing in the hallway or a car laying on its horn in the intersection causes me to look at the phone. But my mind quickly reminds me that it's not ringing, the sound was just crafted by my imagination. Part of me feels like I'm stepping closer to the edge of insanity.

All I want to hear is the deep, monotonous voice of the county detective. *Everything checked out just like you said.* The sound of him clearing me from the case is the freeing words I'm desperate to hear.

The longer we sit in the hotel room, the more it feels like a black hole. I'm trying to escape, break free and live my own life, but it refuses to let me go and keeps pulling me deeper. The bright, exciting future I once saw for us is just dangling in front of me, begging me to latch on and get whisked away. But, with every passing hour, the chance of starting over seems to drift further out of reach.

Many people in the community had loving regard for Jake, and his passing saddened many, but I never received a single casserole or condolence card. Jake's family had lived in Butte for more than a century, owning businesses and running fly fishing charters. Every Thursday, his mother sewed quilts with a group for children with cancer, and his father went to the city council meeting as if it was as sacred as church service. The Thacker name is well known and respected. Jake may have been loved, but I've always been the silent member of the marriage that no one really knew.

After Jake died, our family photo was plastered on the paper's front page alongside one of him and his parents when he was a pre-teen. Jake, in his youth, always made me smile. He had chubby rosy cheeks, constantly windswept hair, and teeth the size of Chicklets. I enjoyed looking at his childhood photos more when I realized how many of his genes had been passed down to Piper. Even though everyone thought she looked like me, I always thought little Jake with a costume wig could pass as Piper.

A short story was typed beneath the black and white pictures where the columnist painted Jake as a loving family man and loyal deputy. I read the article three times and saw the words "not foul play," "mystery," and "killer still at large." A handful of shivers ran down my spine.

After the story had run, I often saw the sideways glances people shot my way when I wandered around town. Their eyes and sharp glares burned accusing holes into me as I walked through the grocery store or simply enjoyed the warm afternoon weather in the park. It got to the point where I didn't want to leave the hotel.

Going out may be a pain but being stuck in a cramped hotel is absolute hell. Piper and I are accustomed to having our own space and privacy, and the single room we're sharing has neither luxury. She's no longer sleeping through the night and often fights with me when I try to get her back to sleep. Our mini fridge is stuffed to the brim with containers of leftovers we'll never finish, and the complimentary breakfast is always predictable and bland.

My patience is growing thinner every day. I've even noticed that my irritation has started escalating to the point where it's become noticeable. I've loudly snapped at Piper on a few instances when I would have typically allowed myself a moment to cool down before flying off the handle. But she's been unusually needy, and while I understand, I'm desperate for a break.

At the house in the woods, I would take Piper outside and let her wander around the front yard when I needed a few minutes alone. I'd grab a book and relax on the porch steps while she'd venture a few feet into the treeline and collect sticks and rocks to present to me as gifts.

But in the hotel, I find it difficult to create personal space in the small area we occupy. Sometimes I step outside of the room while Piper naps, just far enough where I feel alone. Even though I quit years before Piper was born, I sit on the other side of the door and imagine taking a long drag of a cigarette drag to talk myself off the ledge.

I've begun to anxiously rub a small spot where my hair meets the back of my neck. I keep unconsciously digging my index finger into the follicles, and I sometimes even pull out a strand or two when I feel unable to cope. The area is starting to thin and even bald from the constant attention. It's the closest thing I've ever done to what a therapist would call self-harm. *Don't lose it, girl. Keep it together.* When I catch myself doing it, I pull my hands from my scalp and shove them under my butt.

The following day, I fill the tub halfway, sit on the floor outside the shower room, and read a novel. I just need five minutes somewhat alone. Piper's splashing and babbling just on the other side of the wall drones on like white noise until it's interrupted by the screaming ring of the room's phone. At first, I ignore it, thinking my mind is again generating sounds that aren't there. But I realize it isn't a facade on the third ring and keep one eye on Piper while I sprint to grab the phone.

"Hello?" I say as I haul the phone from the nightstand to the bathroom entrance. I lean against the frame as if I might need it to hold me up if I get bad news.

"Hey, Miranda," the grunting voice of Detective Waters responds.

"John, good morning." As much as I've awaited this call, I'm tired and annoyed with the entire process.

"Hey, um, I was hoping you'd be able to come back in and talk to me some more," John explains.

"I can. But this time, do I need to bring a lawyer?" I ask and bite my bottom lip.

"You are entitled to if you choose, but no, not unless you really think you need one."

"Alright. I'll be there."

I coordinate to drop off Piper with my friend in town to spare her from the headache of sitting in the sheriff's department for hours on end and to give me a few minutes of freedom.

My finger floats above the bell as I stand in front of Kirstyn's glass storm door. I glare at the woman looking back at me. Even in the dull reflection, I notice the utterly exhausted woman standing on the porch, staring back at me.

My hair is tied atop my head, thrown in a messy bun that looks like it hasn't been washed in days. The dark bags that hang below my eyes stand out more prominently than I had realized, and the baggy sweatpants I'm wearing don't do anything for me.

Piper pulls at my hand, and I stop staring at the mess of a woman I've become. I ring the doorbell and sigh.

"Hey, girl. Whoa," Kirstyn says as Piper pushes past her in the doorway and runs into the house.

"Sorry about that. Thank you so much. I just didn't want to have to drag her along," I explain, leaving out that she's slowly driving me deeper into madness.

"Miranda, I am just so sorry. I know he was a piece of work, but I just can't believe this happened. You must be absolutely devastated," Kirstyn offers.

"No, I...," I say, then instantly pause. I quickly realized that the entire time the investigation had been going on, I'd come off as cold and unemotional when it came to Jake's death. My face had often been expressionless, and I had yet to shed a single tear in public. Of course, I was sad in private a couple of times, but in general, I hadn't shown the signs of devastation a widow was socially expected to portray.

Standing on the front steps, my friend glaring at me with concern, my demeanor instantly flips when I realize my lack of emotion toward my dead husband is likely making me look more guilty. To be convincing, my face suddenly drops, and I put on a deep look of sadness as I try to force the emotion. *Come on, make some fake tears.*

"Oh, I know. It's been really hard. Thank you so much for helping me out. It's just been so much to handle," I lie. I watch the empathetic look on Kirstyn's face deepen, and her eyes become misty. *There you go. That's how you need to be.*

"Anytime, girl, really, just ask," Kirstyn responds as she pulls me into a hug.

I bring my arms up to her back and relax in her embrace to make the sympathetic hug seem genuine. While my eyes are out of Kirstyn's sight, I roll them from the irritation of my faked emotions. But I know the grieving widow card is my new part to play in the show of my life.

"You know a Detective Waters came by?" Kirstyn asks as I pull away from her embrace.

I shoot her an inquisitive look.

"He did? When?"

"Yesterday. He asked if we actually went to dinner at Nick's that night. And how you seemed."

"And what did you tell him?"

"I told him you were upset as any woman would be that found out her husband was leaving her. And I confirmed that we were at Nick's. He seemed like he believed it," Kirstyn said with a slight shrug.

"Thanks. That's probably what he wants to talk about."

"Hey, if you need something or someone, please call me," Kirstyn says, code for *you to look like shit.* I offer only a smile in response.

With Piper safe and out of my hair, I head toward the sheriff's department for what I hope will be the last time. *Please tell me something good.*

When Jake was still around, I'd been to the department multiple times. I didn't mind stopping by and bringing him lunch or his gym bag when he asked. But, with all my new visits in, it has become the looming black hole in town I desperately want to avoid.

I stroll into the building I'm all too familiar with. The suspicious eyes of three deputies glance my way as soon as I step into the lobby. Their voices go silent at the sight of me, and they stare me down as I usher my way toward the front desk. *What the hell are you looking at?*

"Here to see John," I bluntly tell the receptionist.

"Deputy Portlock, can you take Miranda back?" she asked, calling to one of the men huddled in the corner.

Frank Portlock, look at you. You hated Jake for being promoted before you. But now it seems like you've drunk the "Miranda killed her husband" flavored Kool-Aid as well.

I follow him with a smile as he ushers me into one of the department's back rooms. He refuses to look me in the eye.

"Thank you so much. Tell Tessa I said hello," I say smartly as he shuts the door with nothing but a grunt.

147

I sit alone in the chilly room and stare at the blank walls. A gentle hum slips from my lips as I try to break the deafening silence. When I've sung through three of my favorite country songs, John finally comes into the room.

"Miranda," he offers as he sits with a grunt. A loud thud echoes off all four walls when he sets down a large folder. "Sorry to keep you waiting. Thanks for coming in."

"Yeah, can we just get this over with?" *Please be good news.*

John nods silently.

I lean back and hug my elbows. I gaze across the table and notice John looks more haggard than usual. A glossy look of exhaustion is spread across his eyes that sag in the corners, and the apparel he's known for keeping pristine isn't up to par. There's a slight coffee stain near his collar, and his pants look like they haven't been ironed or washed.

"Yeah, sure," he replies as he thumbs through his file. "Alright, well, for starters, do you recognize this woman?"

John pushes a newspaper clipping across the table. I pick up the square cutout and read the caption typed out below. The story is about a local woman that collected four hundred blankets for the county homeless shelter. The person captured in the paper is beautiful, but nothing about her looks familiar. I glance back at John and shoot him an annoyed look that I think he quickly understands.

"No, am I supposed to? Who is she?" I ask as I shrug my shoulders.

John takes a deep breath.

"That's Allie Taylor," he explains.

I pick up the photo and gaze at it again. I study the girl in the black and white image. The Allie in the picture doesn't look remotely like the woman I'd crafted in my mind, the one I'd pictured taking off her top and laughing at my naivety. Her breasts look perky beneath her turtleneck, and her perfectly straight short hair makes her look younger than Jake. *A lot younger.* She's attractive, even I can admit that.

"Yeah, I don't know her," I reiterate as I push the photo back to John.

"I didn't think you would, but I did talk to her. I've got some good and bad news," John offers.

I slide my hands under my butt to avoid picking my chewing my nails off.

"I'm all ears."

"The good news is I talked to your friend Kirstyn, and she was able to validate your story. So did the manager at Nick's. The bad news is, I was also able to confirm Allie's. I'm glad to hear that neither of you guys are prime suspects anymore, but I'm at a loss as to where to look now."

How was I ever a suspect? I swallow his words and feel them weighing on my gut. It hurts to think anyone could have imagined I could commit such a heinous crime.

"Yeah, me too," I reply. "Have you guys heard anything from the autopsy?"

"No. But, I've been on them, though."

"Got it. Please let me know when you hear something."

"Of course. Another tidbit I wanted to tell you about, though...," John says, then pauses. "Allie told me that she ended their relationship the night before the fire. She claims that she called it all off and that Jake was in agreeance."

My face shifts from relieved to blank. An exaggerated scoff escapes my lungs, and I purse my lips into a flat line as I ready a charged comeback.

"You do realize she's lying to you, right?" I ask as I elevate my voice and slam my fists on the thin metal surface. The feet bounce, and the table rattles in the wake of my anger. I stand and press my fingers alongside my eyes.

"Miranda, please," John says, trying to calm me down.

"No, this is complete bullshit. She's lying to you, and look at you," I say with a scoff as I point at John with open palms. "You're falling for her cute girl act just like he did." Tears are beginning to build from my frustration.

I walk back and forth on my side of the table while running my fingers along my scalp. My mind is racing.

"Miranda, I don't know what to believe, but I do know there's nothing either of us can do to prove what she told me," John explains. "Will you please sit?"

"Whatever, fine. I don't even care who believes me. Everyone thinks I did it anyway. Portlock and the boys out there basically see murderer written across my forehead in Jake's blood. And the looks I get in town... don't even get me started on that. So what does it even matter?" I cross my arms as I join him back at the table. *Jake wouldn't have lied to me about this. I know he wouldn't have.*

Our marriage was undoubtedly rocky. But I don't believe that Jake would have left me unless he had someone there waiting as a backup. He always liked having someone around to take care of him and be there when he got home. He would have endured our sham of a relationship forever if Allie hadn't tempted him. And I would have too.

"It's not that I don't believe you. Because I do. I promise. Just know right now, there's nothing that I can do to validate what she's claiming," he reiterates.

"Yeah, sure," I reply shortly. I do my best not to make eye contact with John and look everywhere in the room except at him.

"Just relax, okay? We're doing what we can. Leave it up to me. I'll get to the bottom of it, I promise."

"Yeah, okay," I reply, still visibly annoyed.

"But the good news is that I'm going to clear you officially as a person of interest in the case."

I finally look at John. I quietly pump my fist beneath the table.

"Well, how about you tell your guys about that news. I don't appreciate how they've been looking at me," I respond and wave my hand toward the lobby.

"I promise I will."

"Thank you," I respond, feeling slightly less irritated.

We shift topics and discuss Piper's and my future. John seems genuinely interested and offers to do whatever he can to help us get back on our feet and figure out where our lives are headed. I still have big dreams, and the cloud of haze they were trapped in is finally starting to clear.

The more we talk, the more I relax. I'm no longer sitting straight as a board with my palms flat on the table. I feel comfortable now and have leaned back and placed my right leg over the left, my hands lightly resting on my lap. I even laugh a few times as we swap funny stories about Jake.

"Thanks again," I say as John walks me toward the building's exit.

"Of course," he responds with a warm smile.

I'd been so wrapped up in worrying John would unearth something about me that could be misconstrued that I forgot how kind and familiar his smile was.

With a final thanks, I breach the threshold of the building and feel the cold air fill my lungs. My shoulders relax as if an enormous weight has fallen off them, and I close my eyes. I take a deep of the chilly winter air. *I'm finally free.*

FOURTEEN

MIRANDA

I HURRY OUT of the sheriff's department and nearly skip I'm so happy. I even contemplate running because I'm scared if I move too slow, John will change his mind and lock me up.

A smile is plastered to my face, and I'm not sure I'll ever let it drop. My breath is shuddering, and I can feel my heart fluttering. The tips of my fingers are tingling with the possibilities of my new freedom.

I sink into the seat of my vehicle, and my mindset does a one-eighty. As soon as the door slams, tears roll down my cheeks as the weight of what just occurred takes hold. *Why Jake? Just why?*

Within thirty seconds, my nose is stopped up, and my eyes burn. I try to blink from the tears, but they keep flooding from somewhere deep inside. I don't know if I'm sad or just relieved. Maybe a mixture of both.

I could probably sit in the sheriff's department parking lot and cry all day, but I have to stop. Jake's gone. Even though I'm cleared of suspicion, someone still needs to pay for killing the father of my child. I just have no clue who that could be.

When John had finally spat out the declaration of my freedom, my first instinct was to grab Piper from Kirstyn's, leave Butte, and never look back.

153

We could throw the few possessions we have in the trunk and dart out of town without a single goodbye. There's only a handful of people that would miss us anyways. We'd just keep driving until we found someplace that felt like home again.

I'd even considered that maybe our lives need a change of pace, somewhere completely new. A few times, I'd pictured us settling down in Florida. I love daydreaming about Piper playing in the white sand and green waters of the Gulf Coast, seagulls trying to nip at her snacks. Montana's home, but I'm slowly finding myself more open to the idea of trying something new and going somewhere no one knows my name.

I stop crying and wipe the tears from my cheeks.

"Ugh," I groan as my forehead contacts the steering wheel again. I pull my head back and bang it lightly three more times.

As tempting as it sounds, I know I can't leave town just yet. But I'm confident we'll pack up and go another day when we're more prepared. My decision to run from the fire was a quick one and one that initially made me look guilty. But now I know I can't just rush off without a trace. I have unfinished business to take care of first.

Now that I'm no longer a suspect, there's insurance paperwork to file, land to sell, and a funeral to plan. I'm the only person left to settle Jake's estate, and I couldn't do it while the law suspected me of murdering my husband and committing a felony to cover it up.

A shudder dances across my shoulders when I think about organizing a ceremony to honor Jake's life. It just doesn't seem possible. I'm still having a hard time believing he's gone, and the idea of putting him in the ground makes it feel real.

I rub my eyes dry with the back of my jacket sleeve and pull out of the parking lot.

As I drive through downtown, heading to get Piper, I catch sight of a slender dirty blonde female walking a black lab on the sidewalk. Her knee-high winter boots tread carefully with a dainty gait, and she stands tall in a waist-length wool coat. As I pass by, I quickly do a double-take as the lady's face comes into view.

"Allie?" I say before realizing the woman's face doesn't resemble my husband's mistress. *You're losing it, Mere. You can't lose it now. Hold it together.*

I lightly slap my cheek three times as if I'm trying to wake myself up from a dream that won't let me go. Jake's mistress and the lies she shared with John are now at the forefront of my mind. *Now she's not only a homewrecker but a liar as well.*

Something in my brain clicks as I feel a moment of clarity relax my demeanor. Jake was my husband for years, and I loved... love him still, and so does Piper. Yet, even with how we treated each other, I know if I had committed a similar sin and wound up dead afterward, he would still have gone to the ends of the earth to figure out who had harmed me. Now I'm the one that has to make sure that Jake gets justice and that Piper and I can have some semblance of closure.

I know I'm not to blame for his death, and I don't know of anyone else that would have wanted to harm a hair on his head. I've racked my brain and looked through our accounts but still can't think of any disputes he was a part of or outstanding debts that would have led to someone murdering him. Allie, the only other person I can imagine that would have

155

a motive, is also claiming innocence and apparently has a solid alibi to back up her claim. *So, who did it?*

After what John told me about Allie, I have more questions than ever before, but I know most of them will probably remain unanswered. She clearly knows how to craft a believable lie, and I bet John listened to her tales, smiling like a pathetic little puppy just like my husband had.

Jake may have been a liar and a cheat, but I know he wasn't a stupid man. This affair had been happening for over half a year, and I was none the wiser. If anything, I look like the idiot now for believing that the late-night calls and extra duty hours were real and not just an easy way to slip out. *What else were you keeping from me?*

"She can say what she wants. I know nothing was called off," I mutter to myself as I speed out of downtown.

I don't know how, but someone has to find proof that Allie's deceiving John. She can deny her involvement all she wants, but I know Jake's mistress knows a lot more than she's putting on, and I'm confident it'll eventually reveal itself. I want to be there when it does.

I smile again, knowing I can relax after picking up Piper and heading back to our room. Being cramped still isn't fun, but the looming threat of being carted off to jail for something I didn't do I gone. I can breathe.

"Thank you so much," I say happily when I pick up Piper.

"Any time," Kirstyn responds. "You seem... better."

Evidently, the improvement in my mood is visible.

"I feel better, I do. I think that we're gonna get this all figured out," I return with a smile.

"Good. You deserve that."

"You're right. I do," I beam. I'm ready to catch a break.

Later that night, Piper falls asleep with a full stomach of fruit and yogurt while I settle down on the couch. I sip from a heavily poured glass of red wine and prop my feet up on the coffee table.

"Salud," I say as I toast the air in celebration. I close my eyes as I drink, and my mind begins to wander.

Although I would have never even dreamed that Jake would die, I'm starting to find positive things that have happened since. We'd hid our sham of a marriage and played an exhausting game for the public eye while keeping our divorce desires locked inside, afraid to say it aloud. I wanted out, and so did he. We just refused to admit it to one another. Half of a house is all that's left of our painful past.

"The house," I whisper as I imagine our home in its former glory. The white exterior, dark green front door, and wrap-around porch I had always pictured Piper running along with friends when she was older are all gone.

As much as I hate to admit it, I have to go back. According to John, some of the house is still intact, specifically our bedroom. I can grab birth certificates, family heirlooms, and almost two grand in government bonds that should still be shoved in the closet safe. But first, I have to muster the courage. The idea of stepping back into the crumbled home where Jake was killed makes me sick to my stomach, something I'll have to get over because there are possessions inside that I want to save.

The money from both the land and Jake's life insurance policy should be enough for us to have whatever we want within reason. I can buy us a place (somewhere far, far away), and Piper will have enough money for college.

The wine hits my mind, and I picture our life. I envision preteen Piper running around the yard, ensuring she doesn't step in the flowerbeds where I'm growing azaleas, chasing a yellow lab puppy. She's happy, and

I watch her laughing from the porch; I am too. *That's home. That's where we need to be.*

As my second glass of merlot runs dry, I sit down on the edge of the couch and flip on the TV, careful to keep the volume at just above a whisper so I don't wake Piper. Nothing interesting is on, but the soft white noise fills the quiet and calms my fluttering thoughts better than the heavy silence.

As my first night as a free woman ends, I thumb through a real estate booklet, looking for a new place for us to live.

"If we're staying here, then we ain't staying here," I slur with a drunken smirk.

I comb through the many pages of rentals in the handout I'd snagged at the Walmart checkout. I love the look of the vaulted ceilings and houses scattered along hillsides and know Piper would enjoy the apartment complexes with a pool and playground. I currently can't afford the majority of the places in the book, but hey, it's still fun to dream.

My search leads me to a small one-bedroom apartment downtown that offers a month-to-month contract. I highlight the snippet with an unsteady circle.

The rent on the apartment is much more affordable while we figure out what's next. Hotel life isn't sustainable anymore for both our sanities and my wallet. I'm ready to get comfortable in somewhere that has privacy for Piper and me while we try to find out what happened to Jake.

I quietly hum an N*SYNC song while counting out the cash I still have left on the room's dinette table. I set aside enough to cover the first and last month's rent as explained in the listing and write out a detailed budget with what remains.

"Thirty days sounds like fun to me. Right?" I whisper to Piper, who is sucked into a deep sleep across the room.

The money left from savings should last us for a while until we can file claims and get the hell out of dodge. An idea that brings a smile to my face.

"It's almost over," I say as I kiss Piper on the cheek before falling into bed. My head sinks into the fluffy pillow. The idea of our lives finally heading in the right direction helps me drift off to sleep.

FIFTEEN

JOHN

THE FOLLOWING DAY John flipped through the stale file of information he'd compiled on the Thacker case. He had photos of the wreckage, testimonies from neighbors and friends, Miranda and Allie's testimonies, and various other paperwork inside. But nothing he had was the smoking gun he was hoping to find.

Pages turned, pictures were stared at, and he reread everything just as he had the day earlier. John believed there was a lead hidden in the file, and if he just kept looking, something interesting would eventually turn into a groundbreaking discovery.

As he combed the last of Allie's testimony, the department's secretary walked in as if she were in a hurry. Rarely did she ever move at a rate beyond a stroll, so he was shocked to see her in a rush.

"Yes, Diane?" he asked in a monotone voice without looking up from his papers.

"John, it's the coroner's office. They're on the line," she said softly.

John's eyes swiftly darted over the tops of his reading glasses and looked at Diane. Her hands were cupped near her midsection, and a broad grin was spread across her face. She hurriedly nodded when he looked at her.

161

"Thank you," he responded as she smiled and slipped out of the room. *Here we go.*

He snatched up the phone's handset and held it to his ear, hoping something productive would come out of the call—an accident, suicide, murder, something that'd tell him what happened to Jake.

"Hello," John greeted.

"John, it's Blake," the coroner said.

"Blake, good to hear from you," John returned. "That autopsy ready for me?"

"It is. I could just fax it over, but I was hoping you had some time to come down and talk to the medical examiner about what we found. And sorry it took so long. We had a couple ahead of him and some people out sick."

"I understand. I'd like to just come on down. I'll can be on my way in a minute," John quickly spit out.

"Great. We'll see you soon."

John hung up the phone without another word and snatched his keys and notepad off his desk. He threw on a pair of fleece-lined gloves and rushed out the door without telling anyone where he was headed.

He grabbed the switch in the car and threw on his flashing blue lights as he sped through the small town. A few vehicles puttered in front of him and finally moved when they saw his signal. In his rush, he ran two red lights, a stop sign, and finally parked his car in a handicap spot in front of the coroner's office.

His knees popped like bubble wrap was tucked in between his joints as he climbed out of the car. John winced and pushed through his pain as he raced to the door, desperate for answers.

When he made it to the front of the building, he placed a hand on the handle and hesitated. *I really, really hate this damn place.* With a deep breath, he pushed open the door and stepped into the building.

He looked around the room. The only person he saw in the lobby was a young woman that stood alone with her hands shoved into the pockets of her jeans, her eyes fixated on the local news. The door shut, and she turned his way. John walked across the lobby toward her.

"Detective Waters, hi. This way," she said, noticing John was in a rush. "Sorry, Blake had to run out."

"It happens," John returned.

She shot her hand out to John, "Kristin."

"John," he replied, returning her handshake.

She increased her pace to match John's and directed him to follow her. They quickly walked down a brightly lit corridor toward the building's back after Kristin typed in a combination to get them through a secured door.

John could hear his heart racing in his chest with every step. Each beat sounded as though it was echoing off the walls. He wasn't sure if his increasing nerves were from the idea of seeing a dead body or the excitement that this could be the break his case needed.

After two hallways and another locked door, his guide finally entered a room and held the door open.

"I just need a second," John explained. Kristin silently nodded and continued into the room, giving him a minute of privacy. He had been in this area of the building once before.

When he was fifteen, his parents were hit broadside when another car rammed into them at an intersection in the middle of nowhere. The other vehicle had four passengers, three of whom made it after a hospital stay, and a woman that was thrown from the passenger seat and died on the scene.

While his dad was hospitalized and in a medically induced coma to slow brain swelling, John was forced to differentiate between his mother's body and the other woman. Their faces were almost unrecognizable, but John could pick out his mother's veiny hands and knobby knuckles anywhere. The cold mortuary room felt even cooler as he gazed at his mother's body and saw blood oozing from her scalp and tainting her golden hair.

The woman who rocked him to sleep and made the world's best banana bread was lying lifeless on the metal table, and he couldn't do anything to bring her back. That was the last image he had of his mother, and the memory of her mangled body still haunted him.

The officers took care of John until his grandma arrived and tried to comfort him. Although he was already set on being a pilot, especially since he had already accumulated twenty-seven flight hours in a Cessna, he saw law as a possible backup plan one day. Making sure drunken idiots like the one that killed his mother see their day in court sounded like a good idea. He thought maybe he'd be a lawyer if pilot training didn't work out. Little did he know that he'd no longer be able to fly one day and wind up being a small-town deputy, then detective, and back in the room where he said goodbye to his mother all those years ago.

"Love you, mama," John said as he rubbed the small airplane keychain that she had given him in his pocket.

"Sir, are you okay?" Kristin asked, breaking him from his painful memory.

"Yeah, sorry," he replied.

John followed Kristin into a large, brightly illuminated area. When he broke the threshold, he saw all four walls covered in countless tools and devices that reminded him of something that would be used to chop someone up in a horror movie.

The room had a lingering odor from all the chemicals they used during their process that burned John's nose with every inhale. As strong as the smell was, he was grateful he didn't catch wind of the cooked human flesh scent that had filled his lungs at the scene of the fire.

A vibrating chill ran down his spine when his gaze landed on the body-shaped figure in the middle of the room. Although it was covered with a thin white top sheet, he could make out the edge of a chin, the curve of an abdomen, and toes poking upward.

The cold room was still and silent. John could sense the heavy feeling of death looming over his head as if it were watching him as he moved toward the late deputy. *Dammit, Jake.*

"I'm going to pull this back and show you some things," Kristin explained. "He probably won't look like you remember him. Is that okay with you?"

Fear kept John's voice trapped inside. *Hell no, it isn't okay.* He motioned with his hand for her to proceed.

She pulled the top of the sheet back just past Jake's collarbone. His face had almost no color, and both his lips and eyes looked as though they had been super-glued shut. Only a trace amount of charred skin peeked out from beneath the cloth and worked its way up to his chin. He saw the friendly face of the Jake he remembered.

John smiled as his mind played a hurried montage of seeing Jake alive. In his usual fashion, he was joking around with the guys in the locker room,

165

playing pranks on the new deputies, and always willing to stay late and help with paperwork.

He felt pressure building up behind his eyes from the tears fighting their way to his vision. A gentle shake of his head staved off the emotions and the past he had remembered. He fought back the grape-sized lump in his throat and the tears that slowly crept back into his eyes.

"Detective Waters?" Kristin asked.

John snapped out of the gaze he had locked on Jake.

"Yes, sorry. Please, go ahead," John replied as he rubbed his hand down his chin.

"Yes, sir."

The medical examiner grabbed a clipboard off a desk that looked identical to the table where Jake lay. She ran her finger downward and read a few items silently before addressing John. When her silence broke, she rambled on about a few things from Jake's medical history. They had discovered some minor underlying conditions while his chest was wide open that she felt the need to babble on and on about.

John didn't want to come off as rude. But, in his desperate rush for information, he cut her off. A hint of fatty liver disease and Jake's slightly inflamed prostate weren't things he was interested in learning about, nor did he think they were relevant to the case.

"I'm sorry, but can you please just get to the cause of death?"

"Yes, sorry. I apologize," Kristin responded as she flipped a couple of pages on her clipboard.

"Um, blunt force trauma," she said as her gaze went from her notes to John. His mouth instantly fell to the floor.

John forced his lips back together as he looked at the lifeless body. He tried to comprehend that his house fire case had spiraled into a full-on murder investigation.

"So, he didn't die from the fire?" he clarified.

"No, sir, we're pretty sure he was dead shortly before the fire started," she answered. "Time of death around five."

John rolled the newly obtained information around in his mind while he stared at Jake's still face. His suspect list had recently been emptied, and with his case now intensifying, he felt even more determined to look for someone new. But he had no clue who that someone could be.

"Any idea what the weapon was?" John asked.

"Looks like it was documented as something with a sharp corner, not too large, possibly wooden, and not overly heavy," she explained.

She flashed something toward John, and he looked to see a picture of the wound on the back of Jake's head. The image almost caused him to vomit. He coughed once to combat nausea. *Good lord.*

In the photo, he saw the crater that someone violently dug in the crown of Jake's head that led to his death. The image didn't do a good job of showing the wound's depth, but anyone with decent vision would be able to tell the trauma wasn't from a gentle action.

"Okay, yep. I got it," John said as he looked away from the picture when he couldn't take it anymore.

Kristin grabbed a plastic tape dispenser off her desk and elongated her arm as she raised it over her head.

"Based on the entry location and angle of penetration, it looks like it was done in this sort of motion," she stated as she moved her arm downward in an arching motion.

"Could you please do that again?" John asked. He moved so he could see her motion from the side. She swung again.

"Can you please keep doing that?" he repeated.

Her arm continued moving up and down as if she were hammering a nail into a wall. John's mind drew a person-shaped silhouette directly at her twelve o'clock. While she repeated the motion, he intently watched and studied her moves while analyzing the tape dispenser's consistent trajectory.

"It almost looked as though he had just hit his head on the corner of the hearth during a fall. But when we looked further, we could see the angle at which the wound was delivered. And we didn't find any traces of brick," she explained.

"Gotcha."

"So based on all of that, it seems like the wound was inflicted by someone his height, or possibly even taller," Kristin concluded.

John silently nodded his head in her direction. He'd reached a similar conclusion. Both Miranda and Allie were significantly shorter than Jake, and whoever had the gall to kill him in such a brutal way more than likely wasn't someone that had ever had feelings for him.

"Again, we didn't see an apparent amount of smoke in his lungs. So, we don't believe he was breathing when the fire began," she added.

Thank God he wasn't burned alive.

"But there was a decent amount of gasoline present on his skin, particularly on his feet. So, I do believe someone tried to cover up the body."

"Hmm, okay, I understand."

"Also, if you look here," she hovered her finger over a spot on Jake's neck. "It's hard to see, and we almost missed it. But can you see the slight irritation on the skin?"

"Yeah."

"It looks like someone choked him. Not too hard, and probably not for a long time. But someone had their hand wrapped around his neck just long enough to leave a faint mark."

Jesus.

"Okay, thank you," he replied, trying to stomach the facts.

"Of course. Sir, there is one last thing. We also found some skin cells under his nails that don't belong to him. But unfortunately, there was no match in our county database, so we sent it down to the state lab hoping that they can come up with something," she said, adding icing to the mystery cake. "We should hear back in a couple of days."

"I guess that's good news," John said, hopeful the skin cells would turn up something. "Thank you for your time."

"We'll find whoever did this. I know we will."

SIXTEEN

MIRANDA

MY FACE TWISTS into a look of shock when I find out that Jake had taken out a seventy-five-thousand-dollar life insurance policy. Once upon a time, we had agreed to forty thousand each to make sure Piper would be well off, but I supposed he upped his at some point without asking me.

"Just here, and here," the woman at the agency says as she points at two blanks on an official-looking document. I've already signed about twenty other spots: what's two more.

Ever since I told her my story, *dead husband, no clue what happened, burned down home,* the woman's been wearing a forced smile and apologizing as if I need her sympathy.

"Just get a copy of the death certificate, and we can process this for you," she says. I nod and smile in understanding.

A slight pang of guilt creeps in as I step out of the insurance office. The money is a good start, and I feel bad it's exciting even. It doesn't seem appropriate to be happy about getting rich from my husband's death. But knowing it won't bring Jake back to take care of us, I shake the feeling. *He would want us to do better.*

Jake had always dreamed of Piper going to college and making something of herself. She always gravitated toward dogs, particularly the small annoying ones, so Jake always saw her being a veterinarian one day.

"I don't want her being a stay-at-home wife or dependent on a man," he often said, making me feel like he was declaring that staying home and taking care of *his child* meant my life was unfulfilling. But it was quite the opposite. In fact, being a stay-at-home mom has been the most rewarding career I've ever had.

I hate the idea of Piper leaving one day, but I know it's inevitable and for the best. Butte, Montana only offers so much, and Piper deserves the world. I plan to tuck away some money from the house payout for her to use when it comes time to head off to school.

The rest of the cash is my chance to finally figure out *my* life goals. For years I'd toyed back and forth with the idea of one day enrolling in community college. I'd spent hours flipping through brochures and scanning through programs but never found anything that clicked as something I wanted to do forever. As easy as it would be to apply for a waitress job, I know a career is a smart move. Stabilizing ourselves with something concrete and consistent will be essential to making our new lives as successful as possible.

With the things quickly piling higher on my plate, I got Piper set up at a local daycare so I could spend my days venturing around town and planning our eventual escape.

On her first day, Piper runs into the colorful room full of toys without so much as a smile in my direction. I watch through the window briefly before sprinting back to my car, where I sob until my head hurts.

When I get back to our dull hotel home, I miss Piper even though I was dying to get a break from her. I suddenly feel the heavy weight of loneliness and feel even worse when I look around and realize we're still in temporary lodging, nearly a week after the fire. *No, we're not doing this anymore.* I snatch up my keys and purse and head to my car with a magazine in hand. I head downtown.

A neon poster sign with helium-filled balloons on its top directs me to the leasing office for the apartment I found that fits our budget. Quiet hours after ten, reserved parking spaces, and a playground in the back, it sounds perfect.

In the office, an older lady at the counter reads over my filled-out application line for line while I sit near a window and bounce my leg incessantly.

"Okay, ma'am," the lady beckons me over.

"Yes?" I respond as I hurry over to her desk.

"So, um, it says here that you don't have a job?"

"No. Not currently, but I'm looking. And I have the money. I'm good for it."

"Oh," she said shortly as her eyes glanced back to the lengthy application.

Dammit. She's gonna turn us down. Let's make her cry.

"Ma'am, it's just that my husband just died, and our house was burned to the ground. I don't have a job because I'm just waiting for the insurance money, and then we're moving away. It's just too hard to stay here after he...," I pause for effect. "Died. But I have the money." *Let's hope the sob story works.*

"Oh sweetheart, was it the deputy?" she asks.

"Yes, ma'am," I reply as I again tap into my scripted widow emotions as if I have them programmed on a soundboard. "We just miss him so much. We're just taking it one day at a time."

"I'm so sorry. I heard about that from a friend. But, I understand," she replies as she flashes me saddened eyes.

"Thank you," I respond. The woman rises from her worn-out desk chair. "It's been rough."

It takes all my might, but I let a single tear fall from my eye. It tickles as it rolls down my cheek, but I don't dare wipe it before the woman sees it. Then, finally, she looks at me, and I watch her eyes move to the drop as I rub it away with my pointer finger.

"I'm sorry. Just talking about it is tough," I say.

"I bet it is, baby. How about you move in first thing in the morning," she says as she slides a double set of keys across the desk to me. "Number thirty-three."

"Thank you so much." I kindly smile.

As soon as I'm out of the woman's sight, a wide grin spreads across my face. Having an apartment with more space is exactly what we need.

"I think you'd be proud of me," I say under my breath as I walk out to my car.

Although he had often been cold, Jake loved celebrating my successes in our early years. I'd once earned employee of the quarter when I worked at the school, and Jake took me out for a steak dinner to celebrate. He was so proud, so I didn't tell him there were only four people in the office and the award rotated quarterly. When I completed my first marathon, it was *him* at the halfway point with a sign cheering me on, then *him* at the end to help me carry the mounds of swag the sponsors forced into my arms the second I crossed the finish line. He *was* my biggest cheerleader. The supportive version of him is something I hadn't even realized I missed. *I wish you were here to tell me I'm doing the right thing.*

The quaint apartment isn't anything special. But it's the foundation for the new lives we're building for ourselves without Jake. I'm just happy I'll be able to put Piper to bed in a closed-off room while I enjoy some evening TV with the volume higher than a whisper.

Knowing Piper is situated for the day, I drive to the local funeral home. It's something I know I have to do whether I like it or not.

I force myself out of the car and head into the building's office. Even the outside of the stucco-covered structure looks depressing, and I can't imagine it's much cheerier on the inside.

A resounding gong-like bell announces my entrance, and a man quickly emerges from an office right off the foyer. The backs of his cuffed suit pants drag the floor near his heels as he shuffles toward me. *Is that a mustard stain on his shirt?*

"Hello," says the elderly man in an oddly high-pitched voice.

I hunch over slightly as I reach out and shake his stubby hand. He talks for a few minutes, telling me the funeral home's history, and I learn he inherited the business from his father. I listen politely even though I just want him to give me some information and shut up.

When he finally stops talking, I tell him my story, and he passes me a handful of pamphlets from a plexiglass rack mounted to the wall. He guides me into his office, where I sit on a chair that I almost swear spits dust as I sink into its cushion.

As he throws more information and choices at me, I quickly realize just how much work goes into planning something to signify the end of a life cut short. Plates, tablecloths, music; I'm responsible for choosing it all, and the cost is rising with every decision. It feels odd to worry about things so trivial when my husband's killer is still out wandering the streets.

When I've made all the decisions and picked out invitations, I painfully hand my Visa to the man, knowing this will cost me a fortune.

Thankfully John told me that the deputies had started a small pool of funds that I could tap into to curb the debt. Once they realized I wasn't the culprit behind Jake's death, they were willing to do whatever they could to help. Department spouses came by the hotel room day and night, passing off condolences and casseroles I had to reheat in chucks in the microwave.

With my day finally complete, I head back to the daycare to pick up Piper, only partially hoping her first day without me had been a success (I secretly hope she hated it and never wants to go again).

"Mama," Piper says with a smile as she runs toward me.

I pull her close and nuzzle my nose in her neck. I can't believe how much I missed her. She smells like sweat and sunscreen, my new favorite scent.

"She did so well," the daycare worker, covered in paint and looking utterly exhausted, assures me.

I thank her and promise that Piper will be back in the morning. *She might be. I dont' know yet.*

Piper fights me through dinner, then plays happily in the bathtub while I finish rushing around the room and picking up the meager life we built. In the week and a half since we left home, I'm shocked at the amount of stuff we've both purchased and had donated to help us get back on our feet.

The only thing left to pack is the pathetic excuse of a bed surrounded by mesh walls that Piper has become accustomed to passing out in. I smile as

I lay her down quietly and pull up a chair. I watch her sleeping blissfully while the hotel furnace roars next to her and the outside temperature plummets.

I reach in and stroke the top of Piper's warm cheeks, realizing how resilient she is. We'd endured living in two motels together, countless fast-food restaurants, and two long drives across the state of Montana.

"I'm so proud of you, baby," I whisper. *And I'm proud of myself.*

When Piper is fast asleep, I call mama and share the details of everything that has happened. I listen through the line as her hacking quickly morphs into a subtle sob.

"No, he didn't," mama mutters.

"I know. Trust me, I know," I reply.

Mama had always loved Jake, partly because I had never said an ill word about him. Jake was always lifted and set on the highest pedestal and could do no wrong in her eyes. Hearing all the hurt he brought me finally shed light on the struggles of our marriage. *He ain't so perfect now, is he?*

"You sure?" mama asks.

"Sure what?" I ask for clarification.

"That there was another woman."

I let out an irritated sigh. She still thinks he's a damn saint.

"Mama, I've seen the other woman. She fessed up to it."

"I just can't believe it. Not Jake."

"Well, believe it."

I tell her about our plans. She extends an invitation for us to come to stay in Great Falls, but I currently have too many loose ends to think about leaving town just yet.

"Hopefully, soon we will," I reply.

"I love you, baby. You'll be stronger for going through this."

"I know I will. It's all up to me now."

When our call is over, I switch off the lights, climb into bed, and close my eyes. I breathe a sigh of relief that our troubles are finally coming to an end.

SEVENTEEN

MIRANDA

THE NEXT DAY, with the help of a few deputies, I move us into our seven hundred square foot apartment while Piper's at daycare.

The front door opens into a living room with a small sofa. Beyond that, there's only a tight kitchen with an oven stove combo and microwave, and down a short hallway is the bedroom and bathroom. It's not much, but it's home.

The apartment's bedroom is small enough that my air mattress and the play yard Piper is sleeping in butt up to one another. In the quiet of the night, I can hear every dreamy whimper she makes and feel a nudge every time she stirs.

Some of Jake's coworkers and others around town were happy to provide us with some basics to help us get back on our feet once they realized I hadn't been the person behind my husband's death. They generously passed down used pots and pans, a small TV, a set of silverware and plates, and some mismatched furniture to help us feel more at home.

On our first night in the apartment, Piper quickly falls asleep in my arms. I lay her down gently in her play yard and enjoy a glass of merlot while chuckling through reruns of The Tonight Show. It's the best night I've had in years.

Two days later, and after countless decisions I never imagined I'd have to make. I finally jumped through all the hoops of planning a funeral and wake for my dead husband.

Jake had a plot next to the local Catholic church already designated, right next to his parents. He had never taken the time to make sure there was room for me to be buried with them, which was fine because I wanted to be cremated and have my ashes dusted along the mountains in the early stages of fall.

I picked out the marble headstone that will sing the praises of how he was a loving son, husband, and father for eternity, something that I cringed while agreeing to inscribe. Other people probably wouldn't think *cheating bastard* was a proper homage to his memory, no matter how true it was.

The half of our savings account I had expected him to take and run off with Allie paid for his casket. The solid pine box was cheap but still nice enough to show at his funeral.

Due to his physical state, the director recommended, and I agreed that the ceremony should be closed casket. He no longer looked like him, and I don't want a pale corpse with caked-on makeup to be the last image people have of him. But I still wanted Jake buried in something nice. The only suit he had was close to a decade old and probably wouldn't fit over his biceps that seemed to have doubled in size since he'd last worn it.

A somber numbness spread throughout my body as I thumbed through the racks at the mall and picked out the last clothing Jake would ever wear. Black shirt, black jacket, and a navy tie, the same color combination he wore the day we got married.

The cold-hearted nature I had adopted from the minute the name *Allie* slipped from his lips has slowly begun to fade as I've allowed myself time to grieve the marriage chapter of my life. A part of me had started to miss just being in the same room as my husband, even when an awkward silence loomed between us.

After I drop off the last of the meat and cheese platters for the reception, I head home to Piper. Mama came down for the funeral, and even though she's still hacking as if she'd smoked unfiltered cigarettes for the last thirty years, she's happy to play Barbies and have tea parties while I rush around town.

While they're occupied, I repeatedly rehearse my role as the grieving widow in the mirror. I've gotten pretty good at crafting a believable sad face but am also finding it becoming less forced as time goes on. Lately, there have been more times where I find myself missing Jake than resenting him.

I don an all-black dress with lace around the hem and top it off with a dark grey cardigan, just like a wife in mourning should. There's a good chance I'll cry during the ceremony, so I decide to keep my eyes void of eyeliner or mascara.

Now that I'm ready, and mama is also sporting a dark-colored pantsuit, I fight the mist in my eyes as I slip Piper into a tiny black dress. She still doesn't comprehend what happened, and I'm still dreading the day I'll have to break it all down for her. *I'm so sorry this happened, Piper.* I smile at her and try to act like everything is right in the world.

"Dada, bye-bye," I say to Piper as we prepare to leave for the ceremony.

"Dada, bye-bye," Piper echoes with a smile.

We're the first to arrive at the funeral home. The director welcomes me inside with a muted smile, and mama folds her hands at her waist and nods at me, saying, *I'll wait here.*

I take a deep breath and smile back, adjusting Piper on my hip. The director opens a heavy wooden door that leads into the atrium. I slowly walk inside, ready to have my last few moments alone with my husband's remains.

The room is still and quiet as the lingering feeling of death carries me into its fold. I make my way to the front, where the casket is on display surrounded by flowers. A large, framed photo of Jake in his dress uniform rests on a tripod on the right. *God, he was so handsome.*

I stop right in front of the casket. The hand I'd slipped my gold wedding band back on gently rests on the closed pine box as I speak to him one last time.

"It wasn't all bad, was it?" I say with a soft chuckle wishing he could laugh with me. "Jake, I never wanted this for us, and I'm sorry it went the way it did. I loved you, I still love you, and I'll always miss you. I know you didn't mean for this to happen. I promise to raise Piper right and tell her good things about you," I say honestly with a tap of my hand.

I adjust Piper to my other hip as I finally gather some tears and let them fall down my cheeks. I step back from the casket and stare at the wooden box sitting front and center, ceremony ready, in the funeral home's open room. I nuzzle my nose into Piper's hair and kiss the crown of her head.

I hear the door open and turn around to see mama peeking through the crack, checking on me like always. I nod at her to come to join us.

"Dada, bye-bye," I say in a hushed voice and wave at the casket.

"Dada bye-bye, dada bye-bye," Piper mimics as she says goodbye to her father for the last time.

Piper, mama, and I take our seats in the front row, and ten minutes later, guests come flooding in as soon as the doors open. *Here we go. Try to make it through.*

"Thank you for coming," I kindly say to everyone who comes up to offer their condolences and shake my hand. I swear some of them look more distraught than I am. *People really loved you, huh?*

Right before the start of the ceremony, I look around the room. The attendees fill every seat, and those without a chair stand around the edge. The audience looks like a sea of a depressing mix of grey and black attire.

The ceremony is on schedule but may quickly run over with the number of people coming out of the wickets to make their way to the microphone. It seems like everyone has something thoughtful to say about Jake. Some people cried through their chuckling while telling stories of comedic moments they'd shared with my husband. I, too, eventually find myself tearing up as I smile inside, remembering some of our finer moments.

The speakers make him sound like the model husband and friend, like someone who would have never done anything wrong. But to me, the accolades sound foreign. In my eyes, he hadn't been that guy in years. As I listen to their stories with a half-smile, I try to block out our bumps in the road and rely on their old positive memories.

The funeral I'm watching doesn't feel like one thrown in my husband's memory, but one that I'm attending for a complete stranger. I hadn't realized how much of Jake I'd lost as our relationship declined until strangers began to drone on about how incredible he was. Tears start to roll down my cheeks.

Piper starts fussing and crying halfway through the ceremony as it nears the time for her afternoon nap. I empty the seemingly bottomless diaper bag and hurriedly dig through its main pouch, trying to find something to soothe and silence her. But, the snacks, toys, and juice-filled sippy cup aren't enough to calm her frustrated exhaustion. Her high-pitched whining soon begins to cause a scene.

"I can take her out," mama leans over and whispers. I can see by her misty eyes that she has been pretty upset by the ceremony, especially since she is still convinced there must be a misunderstanding. In her mind, Jake could never and would never cheat.

"No, no. I got it. Thank you, though."

I pull Piper close and excuse us, so we don't disrupt the endless stream of people that keep speaking about Jake. The director is in the back of the room and offers me a nod as I slip through the wooden double doors.

As soon as the doors shut behind me and I'm alone in the lobby, I feel the heavy weight from my chest release as if someone just took one of those lead aprons used during an x-ray off my shoulders. I can finally breathe.

I step out of the lobby and into the afternoon's cool breeze. Piper is fighting with me, but I finally win and pull her into my chest and wrap my cardigan around her tired body. It's been a long day for both of us, and it's not over yet. She slips her thumb into her mouth, and I feel her slightly loosen in my arms.

"Shh," I say as I sway back and forth and try to calm Piper down. The ceremony should only have about twenty minutes left, and I'm expected to thank everyone for coming at the end.

The outside is quiet, but the sound of an engine roaring to life breaks the calm. Piper twitches at the rumble, and I realize she's fallen asleep. I survey the parking lot. It's full of vehicles and marked patrol cars, and some are even parked in the grass on the side of the building.

I catch sight of a black SUV sitting fifteen feet in front of the building as its running lights flip on and beam in my direction. I squint as I look closer and make out the outline of a woman sitting in the driver's seat.

I shift Piper to my other hip and quickly walk toward the running car. After making it a few feet, the SUV begins to back out. When it's perpendicular, I see Allie staring back at me as she rapidly turns her steering wheel. *You bitch.*

I stop moving forward when I realize Allie will outrun me, and Piper is finally knocked out. A look of shock is stuck on my face, and heat is raging in my cheeks. I stare the car down as it finally pulls out of the parking lot.

"You've got some nerve showing up here," I whisper, even though I want to scream.

I make my way back inside the building and don't say a word as I sit. Mama looks over at me and takes Piper from me. I cross my arms and try to hide my scowl as I listen to the ceremony's ending with Allie's face burnt in my mind.

When Jake's casket is successfully lowered into the ground, I take a reenergized Piper to the hall where the wake is being held. The walls and tables are decorated with faux flowers and a few cheesy banners that look like they've been used for fifty other funerals.

People are clanking beer bottles, smiling, and sharing stories of Jake. He wouldn't have wanted a funeral where people sat around crying and missing him. He would have liked a party just like this in his honor. *I should have bought a keg.*

I secretly take a shot of tequila into the kitchen and throw it back. The room temperature liquid slides down my throat and brings a pucker to my lips as it takes the sting off the moment. Hopefully it will help me get through the rest of the day.

I thank people when I hear an "I'm so sorry for your loss," and reply with a kind "yes sir," and nod when someone says just how great Jake was.

All the people in attendance are still locked into the false reality that we were a couple with a deep, undying love for one another. We'd played it well. I keep up with the role to offer Jake dignity in his death and casually walk around the room and shake hands like a good wife should, while all the while remembering his betrayal that's still fresh in my mind.

EIGHTEEN

JOHN

JOHN SAT AT his desk two days after Jake's body was placed in the cold winter ground. The Thacker case was at the forefront of his mind. Many deputies had come by and patted John on the back, thanking him for taking the lead and offering their help to locate whoever killed one of their own. John always thanked them and told them he had it under control. *I hope I do, at least.* Jake's investigation was pressing, but so were the other assaults, accidents, and murders currently sitting on the department's docket.

The other things he had on his plate before the fire had been inadvertently thrown to the wayside. Jake got all his attention. He'd sifted through the files and divided his open cases among other deputies and detectives willing to take on the extra work. Although he tried to improve at delegating, it wasn't his strong suit.

The photo of the Thacker family at the creek, with broad, genuine smiles on their faces, poked out of the case folder. He pulled on its edge and slid it out of the plastic sleeve. Miranda had provided three more photos that he kept with the picture of the family. He felt a lump of emotion bud in his throat. *Why are you taking this so personally?*

The deputies were like family to him, and he considered Jake both a coworker and a friend. He would have generally handed off the case to someone more qualified, but he just couldn't. Jake needed him.

He went to tuck away the photo when his eye caught sight of the playground in the distance. There were three swings, a tube slide, and a small pirate ship atop a wooden frame shaped like a brig. *Hannah. Hannah loved that playground.*

John's daughter Hannah loved anything and everything that had to do with the outdoors. She constantly begged to go hiking, fishing, and on bike rides down country roads that never seemed to end. Every year or so, when they came home to Butte when John was on leave, that playground was the first place she wanted to go. Atop the wooden frame, she was the captain. She sailed treacherous seas, imprisoned her father and the other playground children, and soared as high as she could pump herself on the swings.

Hannah had always been the light of his life and was he and Trish's only child. Although she was now grown and starting a family of her own, he could still picture her playing at the park, absolute happiness in her eyes. *Piper will never have what Hannah and I do.*

That's when John realized the reason he was so adamant about closing the case was for Piper. The little girl had already lost her father in a terrible way, just like he had lost his mother. John believed justice for Jake would help Piper and Miranda both have the closure they deserved.

There were instances when John was deployed overseas where he wasn't sure he'd be coming home. Of course, his wife would be devastated, but he couldn't even begin to fathom the pain in Hannah's eyes if she had sat front and center at his funeral as Piper had.

John's phone rang and startled him.

"Hello," he said. He tucked the photo back into the file.

"Hi, is this Detective John Waters?" the voice asked.

"Speaking."

"Good morning, sir. I'm Heather from the state lab. I was just calling regarding the results of the inquiry you put in."

"Yes, uh, please, go ahead," John replied as he adjusted himself in his chair and grabbed a pen.

The current way forward with his investigation had been idling as he waited patiently for the call he was on.

"I'm sorry to tell you, Detective, but there just wasn't a match in our system."

His heart plummeted and suck deep into his pelvis.

"Well, thank you anyway," John returned as he closed his eyes and sighed.

He hung up the phone and rested his head in his hands as he pondered his next move. The immense stress the case had put on him personally and professionally was starting to toll on his overall health.

He hadn't been eating much and could feel some noticeable slack around the waist of his uniform pants that typically fit snug. There had been many late nights at the office and at home while he combed back through the file folder repeatedly as he tried to find something that he'd missed. He looked line by line through the reports and statements and continually came up blank.

While he stayed up working long into the evening and going nowhere, John routinely heard his wife's words echoing in his head, telling him it was time to hang up his public service hat and quietly slip into the life of a retiree. *Maybe she's right. Perhaps it is time.*

"Sir," John heard, followed by a knock on his door.

He looked up from the scribbled notes in front of him and saw one of the deputies standing in the doorway of his office.

"What is it, Holly?" he asked.

"I got that court order approved and got a hold of the phone records for the Thacker and Taylor homes," she explained.

John's demeanor instantly piped up when he realized the phone records could provide relevant information about the case that had run dry on his end.

"Thank you," he said as he grabbed the sheet of paper.

John scanned the paper and looked at Jake's calls from the day of the fire. On the short record, he saw one outbound call to his partner's desk line not long after he had stopped in and grabbed his gym bag. That morning there was also one outbound call he recognized as Allie's home phone number. Later in the evening, there was a third incoming call that belonged to the Snavely BBQ restaurant and a fourth call from the Taylor house. Allie's phone records were also slim and only showed a few incoming 1-800 numbers and the calls made to Jake.

Upon realizing the owners of the various numbers, he stared at the record, perplexed about the timeline that ran through his mind.

"You called it off the night before, then called him three times the next day? And once while you were supposedly at work?" he spoke aloud as he tried to talk through the evidence.

He leaned forward in his chair and scribbled "Allie's phone calls" onto his notepad. John grabbed the records and walked away from his desk as he hurried across the station.

"Why did Jake call you the morning of the fire? He was off that day," John asked as he slammed the print off on Jake's partner's desk.

"Uh, Jake called and said he left his locker unlocked. He just wanted me to close it up for him," Adam replied as he looked at John with a confused gaze.

"And that's it?" John probed, hoping there was more.

"Yeah, that's all, I promise," he responded.

"But how did he sound on the phone. Upset, happy, what?" he asked, sounding like he was interrogating Adam.

"Uh, he sounded okay to me, just like he always did. Just, I don't know, Jake," Adam responded shakily as John leaned toward him on his desk.

"And he didn't say anything else?"

"No, really, that was it."

"Alright, thanks," John said as he backed into a less threatening stance before walking out of the room. He was halfway down the hall when he realized how abrasive he had been.

"Sorry," he added as he peeked back into Adam's office.

"No worries, sir."

John dialed Allie's number, realizing he almost had it memorized. It rang and rang, but no one answered. He hung up before he got the click of the machine.

He snatched a few things off his desk and shoved them into his case folder that was slowly but surely thickening. He again drove out to the edge of town to Allie's place of employment, hoping she was there. John was convinced he had finally reached the tipping point of her testimony, and the discovered calls would eventually force her to finish telling him the snippets of the story that she was hiding.

He rapidly scanned the dim room when he walked into the nearly empty restaurant. Allie was nowhere to be seen. John grabbed the first waitress he saw.

"Allie, Allie Taylor. Is she working today?" John asked.

"Yes, sir. She's here somewhere. Hang on a sec," she said as she strolled toward the back of the building.

As the girl slipped into the kitchen, John saw Allie come out of the bathroom in the back corner of the dining room. Her hair was a mess, and she looked flush. Her eyes popped open when she noticed John. He nodded at her, and she began walking toward him.

"Detective?" she asked.

"You alright? You look sick?"

"Yeah, I'm good. I just ate something that didn't agree with me. As you know, life's been a little rough lately."

Besides looking flush, John took note of Allie's changed appearance. Her cheekbones stuck out more than they had before, and the skin around her nails looked chewed on.

"May I please have a word?" he asked.

"Um, yeah, I guess. Let's walk out back."

The two walked out the restaurant's side door and stopped where the large drum smokers were operating at full speed. The smell of burnt ends and brisket made John's mouth water.

"So, we were able to pull the phone log from Jake's house the day of the fire. We saw a call from here, and two dialed from your house," he explained. "Do you care to elaborate on either of those?"

Allie squinted her eyes and let out a noticeable breath as she appeared to think about how best to answer John's question. Then, a light suddenly seemed to click on in her mind.

"Oh, yeah, I made all of them. I just wanted to check on him," she explained as she lightly shrugged her shoulders. "I broke it off and just wanted to make sure he was okay."

"But one of those calls was made while you were allegedly here on the clock," he returned.

Allie looked at John like she was confused momentarily. She gently shook her head as her hands came up to her eyes before lowering them with a nervous smile.

"Ah, that's right. I ran home 'cause I forgot my dinner and didn't want to pay to eat here, so I called him again while I was home."

"And what did he say?" John probed.

"Um," she searched for her response. "He said he was fine, no hard feelings kind of thing."

Her only saving grace was that the call from her house had been made hours before the documented time of death and before the fire had been ignited.

"Please don't tell my boss. I didn't clock out, someone just covered for me, and I was only gone for like twenty minutes. I swear," she explained as her smile faded into a face of worry.

"And there's nothing else you want to tell me?"

"No, really. I promise."

John thanked her again for her time. He wasn't sure what to believe when it came to Allie. She seemed shaken all the time. But she was young and had gotten wrapped up in something big. He pulled out his spiral notebook and circled her name that had been recently scratched through. She wasn't off the hook just yet.

NINETEEN

MIRANDA

THE SELECTION HANGING in one corner of my apartment's only closet is an array of disappointment. All I have to choose from is the mismatched attire I'd purchased at the Walmart in Great Falls when we were scraping by. None of the tops or pants I grabbed in a hurry appeal to me, and I'm itching to get back to my usual wardrobe.

John had previously given me a rundown about the state of our home. According to him, our bedroom and garage were just about the only rooms saved from the flames. Everything else was unsalvageable.

A trip out to the house would give me back the clothes I was comfortable wearing, which was, more often than not, workout clothes. Anything would be better than the baggy pants and shirts I'd picked off the clearance racks.

I haven't been actively looking for employment and check the mail at least twice a day, hoping to get the house payoff soon. Once the money comes through and Jake's case is solved, I'm ready to cut ties with Butte and never look back.

The last thing on my to-do list is giving up the property that Jake loved. As much as I wanted to get rid of it years ago, I slightly regret thinking about selling it now that Jake has no say in the matter. But it has to happen.

Before the wooded land and burnt home go on the market, I have to find the courage to go back to the scene of the crime one last time. There are odds and ends in the house that I hope have been saved from the flames, things that hold sentimental value to Jake and me that I want to pass down to Piper one day.

I fall backward onto my slightly deflated mattress, close my eyes, and listen to the tiny hiss of the escaping air. *You have to do it. You have to go back to the house.*

"Ugh, but I don't want to go alone," I say aloud.

I reach down and wave my hand around until I grab the phone next to the bed. I shamefully dial the number of John's desk and close my eyes as I wait for a response.

"Hey, John. It's Miranda," I say when I get him on the phone.

"Hey. Good morning. What can I do for you?" he asks.

I scratch at my temple with my pointer finger, still uneasy about seeing our house again.

"Well, I'd like to go in the house and see what I can salvage. We have some important paperwork and stuff I'd like to get because I'm selling the land."

"Wow, well, that's pretty big news," John says, a noticeable shock in his tone.

"I never wanted to live there anyway, and it's worth a small fortune, as you know."

"That I do. I might have to throw my hat in the ring for that one," he says with a soft chuckle.

Yeah, you and half the town. As much as I know he'd love it, it's un-likely John will be the highest bidder category. *And there ain't no special discounts.*

"Well, I was wondering if you would mind taking me out there. I don't really want to go alone." *If you say no, I just won't go.* Going in the house alone sends a chill down my back.

"Yeah, I can do that. How does this afternoon work for you?"

"That sounds good. I'll meet you at the house at two?" I reply.

"Two works for me. See you there." I hang up the phone and let out a sigh of relief that I won't have to face the ominous crime scene alone.

I'd carelessly walked through the front door for years and didn't think twice about my life without the house. On more than one occasion, I threw up drunk in the bathroom while Jake held my hair and scratched the small of my back, and we'd danced and cried in its kitchen multiple times. The house may contain many great memories, but the thought of stepping back inside shakes me to my core. *You can do it.*

My knuckles go white as I grip the steering wheel tightly and take the long drive from town out to the property. I tap my left foot and try but fail to force my nerves down through my toes. I suddenly realize I'm biting my already chapped bottom lip raw as I traverse the final stretch of highway.

As I near the gravel driveway, I feel guilty about giving up the acreage, but I have no plans or desire to build a new house on the plot of land. The long trek out of town to the house in the woods had been one of the main reasons I'd never liked living in the handed-down home. It took nearly twenty minutes just to get to a small grocery store, and at one point, I'd driven almost an hour for a waitressing job on the other end of town.

It's time for something new, somewhere new.

My eyes slowly grow misty as I survey the surrounding tree line and mountainous backdrop in the distance. I'd spent so much time taking the place for granted I sometimes failed to see its beauty. But now I can see why Jake never wanted to let it go. *Let's hope whoever buys this place does it justice.*

I drive up the long driveway. John's tire tracks are gently pressed in the thin dusting that's covered the gravel. The last time I'd been on the drive, our home was being devoured by violent flames as I pulled away and fled the scene.

The home comes into sight as the trees welcome me into the front yard. The ruins that sit in the back of the circle parking area look eerie and quiet as I pull up next to his car.

"Hey," John says when I climb out of my sedan.

"Hey," I return with a huff, realizing I sound exhausted. My hair is haphazardly brushed and thrown into a messy bun on the crown of my head. My clothes hang loosely on my slender frame, and there's a fresh stain on my sweatshirt. The grey bags resting beneath my eyes make it look like I haven't slept in days.

"You doing, okay?" John asks.

"Yeah, I'm fine." I lie. I'm struggling mentally and physically. "Why?"

"Just checkin'."

I'm desperately trying to emulate the persona that I'm doing okay. Yet, inside, I'm slowly crumbling away piece by piece, and my head is just barely above water. My life was spinning out of control even before the fire, and I'm ready to fix my issues and start fresh somewhere I don't have a ragged past. But John doesn't need to know all of that.

As I look toward the half-burnt house that had once been beautiful, I remember the first night I'd spent here with Jake.

"Come on in," Jake said cooly. He smiled at me and leaned against the doorframe as if he was the only thing holding the house upright.

"Wow, this place is beautiful," I complimented.

His house felt warm and inviting when I walked inside. At my place in the city, my roommates and I struggled to pay our bills. We often relied on layers of blankets and space heaters instead of turning on the furnace.

The house I'd grown up in was nothing special, and the cramped apartment I shared with two other girls was even smaller. Jake's place felt like a mansion.

"Yeah, I do love it out here," he replied and elaborated on the home's backstory. "Something about the quiet and the night sky just makes me want to live here forever."

I inch toward the ruins of the home and feel the memory of his supple lips moving upward along the center of my back. They slowly work their way up to my neck until they reach the base of my jaw. My body reacts with a shiver, and as I stand watching the house.

In the early years of our relationship, Jake would pull me close when one of our songs played on the CD player. We would dance happily in the kitchen while the water boiling on the stove roared on without attention. His eyes would beat a hole into me as if I was the only person in the whole world who mattered.

Seeing the house also reminds me of the day Piper took her first steps in the living room. Jake had leaped off the couch to block off the edge of the sharp brick fireplace in case she toppled backward. He then followed her around the house on his hands and knees as she explored anywhere her feet would take her.

A smile cracks across my face as I push the lonely nights and arguments to the back of my mind. Even though there was pain, I can admit there was good in our relationship. Those are the times I'm focused on remembering.

"He's gone," I quietly remind myself as my breath billows out visibly. "It's just a house."

My throat feels like it's slowly closing as I choke down my sadness. I try to fight back the tears that want to fall from my eyes when I replay both good and bad memories on a quick loop. Regardless of our broken relationship, the father of my child is dead, and someone burned down our family home with him inside.

"You ready?" John asks as he approaches me. I realize I've slowly crept up toward the ruins.

"Uh, yeah, I suppose." *You can do this.*

"You can do this," John says.

We walk toward the torched home. I slowly climb the steps to the porch landing and try the door. It sticks a little on the bottom like it always has. Knowing how to fix it, I wedge my foot against the frame, turn the handle, and force it open.

The heavy door swings open, and I peer into the darkness before me, where a stale smell of pent-up smoke hangs in the air. I place one foot inside the frame and pause briefly to rethink my decision. *I can't do it. But I have to.* I close my eyes, hold my breath, and enter the house entirely.

Once inside, I see the rubble of the house that's been in Jake's family for three generations. The three-hundred-and-sixty-degree view is painful. Parts of the ceiling have fallen in, and a few spots allow me to see the gloomy afternoon sky above. The walls that held the home together through good and bad times have failed. The interior is almost unrecognizable.

A sharp chill shoots down my spine when I see the extent of the damage. As much as I wanted to sell the house and move away, I never wanted to see it like this. The kitchen where we'd shared family meals is destroyed, and the living room where Jake loved building a fire is covered in soot and fallen beams.

I take a deep breath and walk toward the bedroom I'd slept in for nearly nine years. Using my shoulder, I nudge the door open. I jump back at the sound of a deep grating above me, thinking the roof is about to collapse. But, when everything remains in place, I continue forward and walk into our room.

The first thing that catches my eye is a bag sitting on the end of the bed. I tug on the zipper and realize Jake stuffed it full of the things he would have needed to ride off into the sunset with Allie. *Guess you were ready.*

I pull out one of my old duffels from the back of the closet and begin to shove my entire wardrobe inside. The clothes left behind have an embedded musty smell of week-old smoke that reminds me of what I was wearing the night of the fire.

"Hopefully, that washes out," I say, trying to breathe through my mouth.

When the bag reaches capacity, I dump out the contents of Jake's duffel to use it as well. The clothes, shoes, and toiletries fall into a pile. The last thing to come out is Jake's tungsten wedding ring.

I bend down, pick up the grey band, and hold it loosely in my palm. It's been years since I've seen it on his finger, and I assumed he'd tossed it off somewhere or lost it. Tears involuntarily flood my eyes. I move my hand up to my heart and feel a wave of emotion hit me.

"You bastard," I say.

I close my eyes and sob. All I want is to go back to when our love was palpable. But I'd come to grips with the fact that our reconciliation would never happen years ago, and now there really is no going back.

I wipe the tears from my eyes and slide Jake's ring into the pocket of my jeans while I continue to gather things around the house that still have value to me.

In my nightstand drawer, I find a pressed penny from the time Jake and I visited the Space Needle, a takeout menu from the restaurant where we had our first date, and the small bracelet that was wrapped around Piper's tiny ankle the minute she came out of the womb. I shove the various items into my bag with the clothes.

"Thank God."

I fall to my knees in front of our safe. It was tucked away in the back of the bathroom linen closet and remained untouched from the fire's blaze. I rummage through the metal cabinet and pull out our birth and marriage certificates, the house deed, vehicle titles, and bonds. I thumb through the rest of the file folders and grab a couple more documents that might warrant keeping.

Before putting my jewelry box into the duffle, I add Jake's wedding band to the small cedar case next to my diamond engagement ring.

"I promise I'll give your ring to Piper," I say as I close the lid.

I fish out three family photo albums from the bottom drawer of my dresser. The pictures in the books are in chronological order, and the spines are numbered. The laminated photos stuck on the pages are now all we have to document our family history. I want Piper to remember what her dad looked like.

Life as I know it is over, and that reality hits me after I grab a few more things and take one last look at our house. Everything Jake's parents and their parents before had worked for is nothing but ash. *I can't believe this is all gone. The good, the bad, it's all gone.*

"Bye, house," I mumble under my breath. I step back onto the porch with John and don't even bother shutting or locking the door.

"Did you get everything?" John asks.

"Yeah, I think so," I reply, tucking one last thing into one of my over-stuffed bags. I stand, toss my hair behind me, and brush some soot off my shoulder.

"How the hell did you get so dirty?" John asks.

"Well, I know how much Jake loved this stupid clock. He would have wanted Piper to have it. I knew it was in the living room somewhere, so I reached under the bookcase some and found it wedged underneath; looks like it survived," I say as I pull the clock from the bag and wave it around.

John's eyes become the size of saucers as he stares at the clock.

"Miranda, put that down."

"What?"

"Just, just put it down."

"Okay, okay," I say. My eyebrows pinch toward one another as my face contorts into a puzzled look. I kneel, place the clock on the porch, and step back as if it's rigged with explosives.

John walks out to his car without a word and comes back with a plastic bag and a pair of gloves. He steps back up on the porch without saying a word.

"John, what's wrong? What's going on?" I legitimately have no idea what's happening.

Silence hangs between us as John slips on a single glove and places a knee on the porch. He reaches down, grabs Jake's beloved clock, and gently puts it in the plastic bag. I stare at him, bewildered.

"What the hell was that all about?"

John zips the evidence bad shut. His shoulders droop as he exhales.

"Well, um, we got the results of Jake's autopsy back, and...," he pauses briefly. "Someone killed him," he goes quiet again. The thumping in my chest doubles in speed. "And the description of the weapon they used sounds somewhat like that clock."

My hands instantly shoot up and silence the gasp that slips from my lips. I shake my head back and forth quickly in disbelief. *Murder? No, not murder.* Even though I already knew this was a possibility, hearing it aloud makes it real.

"Are you sure?" I ask shakily.

"That's what they think. And it lines up."

"How?"

"Miranda," John says. He avoids the question, thinking it'll stop me from continuing to probe.

"How?" I say, raising my voice and deepening my tone.

"Blunt force trauma to the back of the head." John's neck goes limp while I turn around and look at the front door.

I sit down on the front porch steps of the home and allow myself to sob in the presence of somebody else. Jake dying had already been terrible, but the fact that somebody bashed his head in with one of his most beloved family heirlooms breaks my heart. *I loved him. I did.*

John groans as he sits down next to me. Warmth envelopes me as he drapes his arm over my shoulders and tries to offer some comfort. I lean into his chest and bury my face in my hands as tears continue falling.

"I know. I know. I'm so sorry," he says as he pulls me in tighter.

While John strokes my shoulder with a thumb, there's a familiar feeling of safety, like when I was a little girl curled up in my dad's arms as we watched the thunderstorms roll in over the mountains. My dad would always hold me close and reassure me that we'd get through anything together, no matter how bad something looked. But, I'm not sure this is one of those times.

I nuzzle into John's side as my sobbing intensifies. *He loved that clock, and he adored this house.*

I finally pull out of John's embrace and look back toward the front of the house. In my gaze, I imagine Jake in the living room with a look of fear spread across his face when he realized he was in the last moments of his life.

"But how? Who?" I ask.

"I don't know, we can run it for prints and see if anything comes back, and I hate to say it, but I'm not gonna hold my breath."

"I get it, but I want this bastard to pay," I respond, feeling my cheeks flush with red.

"I know, trust me, I'm doing everything I can," he responded. "Also, his truck is in the garage if you want to come back and get it sometime," John offered.

It was here the whole time. I was here. If I'd just seen it, I could have helped him. Dragged him out. Saved him. I shake my head and fight back more tears fighting their way into my eyes.

"Would you guys be able to get his truck for me?" I ask, choking through my obnoxious sobbing.

"Yeah, I'm sure we can get someone to do that."

I gather up the bags of clothing that I'd been able to salvage and stuff them into the back seat of my car. John places the bagged clock on his passenger seat and walks over.

"But maybe it was Allie. Talk to her again. She has to know something," I plead, hoping my words don't fall on deaf ears.

"We've talked to her. Her alibi was even tighter than yours. I'm sorry, Miranda."

I close my eyes and take a breath of the fresh air to calm my anxiety. Getting all worked up again won't help anything.

"Okay, sorry. Thank you for everything," I say.

"Don't be. It's okay. We're all here for you. Whatever you need. Just call," he replies with a warm smile.

I softly smile. Things have changed so much between us in such a short time. John had once seemed like a possible menace to my happiness, but he's quickly become somewhat of a father figure.

John closes the door to my car, then, with a nod, heads to his own.

I head down the drive for what I hope to be the last time I'll ever see our house. The crumbling ruins grow small in my rearview mirror as I blink through the damn tears that just won't quit.

Soon the house will be torn down with everything else inside, and the land sold off to the highest bidder. I hate knowing that my decision would break Jake's heart, but it's what we need to give us the best chance of starting over somewhere new. *I'm sorry. I just can't keep it.*

I close my eyes and compose myself before taking the long drive back to town. The chapter that included the farmhouse in the woods has finally come to a close, and the next one will soon open.

I wipe my eyes with the back of my sleeve and pull out onto the highway, John in trail.

TWENTY

JOHN

JOHN PLACED THE evidence bag containing the small clock on his desk. He crossed his arms in his chair and scooted forward to study the possible murder weapon. The only sound that broke the silence was the rhythmic tapping of someone's keyboard in the farm of cubicles down the hall. He focused on the item.

He looked around the bagged object, turning it over repeatedly while searching for any sign the clock was the weapon someone had sunk into Jake's skull.

One corner had minor charring, while the rest of the cherry wood was in relatively good shape. The glass on its face had been slightly yellowed from the intense heat but still clicked away and read the correct time. The small brass plate riveted to the back showed the inscription that had been engraved on it when it was given to Jake's father:

"To Caleb Thacker,
Thank you for your forty years of
service to Butte Electric.
You will surely be missed."

The item didn't have any instant indication that it had been used as a murder weapon. It just looked like a regular clock meant to be displayed on a shelf. John checked it multiple times and didn't notice any blood or dinged edges. From his view, it seemed relatively standard compared to most of the other things he had seen in the house after the fire. *There's gotta be something.*

Just as John was ready to take the clock to the lab, he noticed a minor discoloration on the bottom of the item. *Is that blood?*

His mind instantly flashed to an image of Jake in his living room fighting for his life against an unidentifiable assailant. He watched the blank-faced murderer grasp the weapon firmly as they ran toward Jake from the rear. John closed his eyes and cringed when he envisioned the weapon sinking softly into the crown of Jake's skull like a knife into warm butter, silencing the look in his eyes.

John deeply sighed as he opened his eyes and tried to erase the violent and disturbing image from his mind.

He hand walked the possible murder weapon to the lab and hoped they would get some results that would lean in his favor. The DNA under Jake's nails had led him nowhere, and the jerry can had been too melted to find any evidence. He crossed his fingers in the hopes they would be able to lift some prints off the clock that would provide him with an answer.

"I need this stat. Please," John said to the lab technician.

"Yes, sir. On it," she replied.

Nothing seemed to be going right with the case, and he was starting to worry that it would soon run cold. The idea of someone going away for life weighed heavily on his mind.

The lab was his only hope.

While he waited for results from the clock, John walked the charred house two more times after he and Miranda had gone there and salvaged her things. He picked up fallen chunks of wood, pushed around furniture, and reached under the areas that wouldn't budge in a desperate attempt to find even a hair that he could link to a suspect. He felt that if he kept going back and picking through the rubble piece by piece, he would eventually unearth something. But sadly, it didn't seem like there was anything to be found.

"Dammit, dammit, dammit," he screamed out of frustration when he again came up with nothing new. John walked out the house's front door and sat down on the porch steps. He buried his head in his hands and said a short prayer.

"Lord, I know I've done some things, not been the best person I could have been, hell not even close. I'm not the world's best detective; I know that. But I'm trying, God, you know I'm trying, and I need something," he said as he stared up into the overcast winter sky.

John waited for close to twenty minutes, hoping God would drop some evidence into the gravel lot. He sat there until the cold became too much, and he could barely feel his toes in his boots. When no divine intervention showed up, he worked his way down the stairs, into his car, and back to the office.

The next day, the lab called John back with the news he'd been waiting to hear. *Please.*

"Tell me," he said.

"I'm sorry, sir. There just wasn't anything on it," the woman explained.

"Nothing, you didn't find anything?" he asked, hoping he had heard the woman wrong.

"We found two prints, one was his wife's, and you told us to expect that one. We matched it to her records from the school district. But the other was just a partial," she explained. "But we did find his blood on the clock, and it seemed like someone had sloppily wiped it off."

"Can you guys run the partial?" John asked.

"Sir, we did, and we didn't get anything back," she replied. "I'm sorry."

"Alright, thanks," John said as he hung up the phone. *Thanks for nothing.*

John left the office close to three hours earlier than usual and headed home for the evening. He was frustrated with the lab's answers and emotionally drained from the last three weeks he'd spent searching for a murderer who didn't want to be found. The time and effort he had vested in the case had gone nowhere, and his evidence trail seemed to have run dry.

John always tried to shed his frustrations before going home to his family. When he was an instructor pilot, one bad day with one particularly mouthy Lieutenant had sent him home fuming. He stormed into the house angry, which turned into an all-out fight with his wife over something menial. But he learned his lesson that day. *Work doesn't follow you home.*

He climbed out of the car and felt Jake haunting him like a shadow hitched onto his back. No matter how hard he tried, he couldn't shake his emotions.

He blew through the front door in a hurry. His wife witnessed his emotionally charged entrance and hurried over to console him.

"Just don't," he said as he raised his hand and halted her approach. She crossed her arms, and he saw the look of both concern and *oh hell no* in her eyes.

"I'm sorry. Just, I need a second," he added.

John pressed his palm against the wall and hung his jacket on the wire hook mounted near the door. He took a step back, looked at the sheriff's department emblem, and thought perhaps his wife had been right all those years. *Maybe it is time to call it quits.*

The disturbing case had taken such a toll on his body that he barely recognized the man he saw in the mirror anymore. He wasn't eating right, laid in bed late at night for hours, unable to fall asleep, and hadn't placed an affectionate hand on his wife since its onset.

During years of service, he had seen some things from the war that still crept in and haunted his memory from time to time. Things he thought he would never be able to forget and fought to keep in the back of his mind. But as hard as those moments were, the image of a clock viciously burying its way into Jake's skull seemed to be the one that hurt the most.

"I'm sorry," he quietly muttered to his wife, still standing in the hallway staring at him.

"What do you want me to do?" she asked with concern evident in her tone.

"I don't know. I just don't know what to do anymore. I'm out of ideas, I don't know where to turn, but I don't want to give it all up. Jake didn't deserve to be murdered, but I have absolutely no idea who did it," he said as he fought back the tears pricking at his eyes.

"I know, babe. He was a nice guy. I know you'll find something. You always do," she responded as she inched toward her husband.

John sat down on the bench near their entryway as he began to untie the shoes that had walked the Thacker home close to ten times. His wife joined him and draped her arm around his shoulders. John leaned into her embrace that smelled of sourdough and honey, and closed his eyes as he tried to go just a few short moments without thinking of Jake and the case.

TWENTY-ONE

MIRANDA

I DROP THE phone when John says the words *clock* and *murder weapon*. I collapse against the wall and limply sink to the floor. My temples throb almost instantly as I throw my head into my hands and begin to cry.

The dark and painful image of Jake being brutally murdered right where our daughter had taken her first steps is just one I can't shake no matter how hard I try. It hurts to even think about.

Ever since John escorted me to the house and all my memories flooded in, I've started to feel guilty about our broken marriage, what could have been. Images of our failed relationship find their way into my head, and I hear a whisper telling me I could have saved him.

Maybe if I'd wrapped my arms around his waist when he came home from a hard day and told him I loved him or seduced him while I was still wet from an evening shower, I could have kept him safe. Because for some reason, I know that even though it might not have been her, Allie is involved. But I can't go back now.

Deep down, I can admit, even though it rips me in two, that there was nothing I could have done differently that would have led to him staying.

No matter what I'd done, Jake wanted out, and he had for a long time. He would have never been willing to do the work needed to get our marriage back to its glory days. *It's not my fault.*

The case is still dragging on without any new leads emerging. The clock had led them nowhere after Allie provided prints that didn't match the partial. Her cheek was swabbed, but her DNA sample also didn't match the cells found under Jake's nails. So, John was back to square one.

I can tell John's frustrated that he's essentially out of people to question. He's already talked to Jake's barber, insurance agent, and even the grumpy neighbors across the highway that we never spoke to. No one knew anything. If it were up to John, he would run around town and fingerprint and test everyone until he found a match.

With his case still up in the air, I feel compelled to stay in town while I sell the land and hope answers surface. I don't feel right leaving and knowing the person responsible for Jake's death is still at large.

The apartment allowed me to renew the lease for six more months. I didn't even have to put on a show of emotions this time.

I finally bought Piper and me proper beds to sleep on and little things to make our residence feel more like home. We now have Corelle dishes, a framed photo of the three of us next to the couch, and a spider plant near the window.

I've been waiting patiently for John to call and tell me that everything is solved, that Jake's killer (whoever they may be) is finally behind bars. But the phone has been eerily quiet. The only person that ever calls is mama.

I finally landed a job in town, working as a secretary at the front desk of a family doctor's office. The position pays well enough to cover our basic living expenses and Piper's daycare. But it doesn't leave much else at the end of the pay period, and I often have to dip into Jake's death benefit money to provide for us. It's not the renewed life that I'd been dreaming of, but I can still see a beaming light at the end of a tunnel, even if it grows longer every day.

When I pick up Piper from daycare after a long day of checking in patients, I have to pull her away from the wooden blocks she's playing with, which leads to a fit of dramatics. As we walk out to the car, Piper screams in my ear until I'm tone-deaf.

"Would you just stop it?" I yell at Piper, who won't stop fighting me as I try to clip her into her five-point harness.

"Want Dada," Piper screams.

Tears flood my eyes when I realize how little I'd thought about Jake's and my relationship in the previous days and even weeks. I've spent so much time licking my own wounds that I haven't even thought about the prolonged lasting pain that my daughter will grow up with.

"I know Pipes. Dada's gone," I reply.

Piper looks up at me. As I gaze back at her, I see Jake's eyes staring at me. *Baby, just be happy you don't understand.*

When we arrive back at the apartment, I plop Piper down in the living room with a fresh sippy cup of apple juice.

"You wanna see Dada?" I ask.

With her cup suctioned between her lips, Piper simply nods. I grab the family photo albums from the top shelf in the closet.

"Okay, let's see, Dada," I say as I sit down next to her.

The pages crack as I peel apart the plastic lining of the family photo albums that made it through the fire. Piper scoots in close and rests her head on my shoulder.

I start with the oldest book. Piper looks up at me and smiles as she flips past the cover page and finds various photos arranged like a five on a die. The album has a faint smell of smoke that wafts off its upholstered cover that I bet will never fade. I run through the pages and admire the photos pasted beneath the film.

The first book shows Jake and me back when we were still dating. We did everything together, and I was adamant that we documented our outings with my old Nikon. Piper touches every picture as we go through the pages. There are skiing expeditions, a trip to the Black Hills, me smiling in front of IKEA in Denver, and Jake posing with the multiple trucks he had before we married.

"Hemorrhoid with a Polaroid. That's what Daddy used to call me," I say with a chuckle. Piper just looks at me, oblivious.

Even through the bad times, photos of Jake's smile draw me in as a warm spot in my heart still misses him. He once knew how to make me laugh and crave just being around him for five minutes. I may hate Allie for their relationship, but I understand how intoxicating Jake's smile and personality could be. She probably couldn't resist him, just like I couldn't.

In the rest of the album, there are photos of us eating, hiking, and Jake kissing my forehead in front of the tree on our first Christmas together. In every picture, a believable look of happiness is spread across both of our faces. I can't help but smile as every page turns.

"Mama and Dada," I say to Piper as I point to us in a picture.

"Dada," Piper repeats as she rubs her Cheerio-dusted fingers over the page covering.

"Yeah, Dada, good job," I say. Tears instantly begin welling up in my eyes.

Piper seeing her father brings a smile to her face that I reflect. They really were great together, and I'll always miss the love and laughter they shared. Now, the photo albums are all we have left that documents the early years of our relationship and the short time we'd spent as a family of three.

I tuck the first album away back in the top of the closet out of Piper's reach, so the memories will stay nice for years to come. The pictures are all Piper has left of the father she will never know or get the chance to form her own opinion about.

I bring out a second album and thumb through the pages to show Piper more of our family's history in chronological order. The book has pictures of my father before he died and the house in the woods before we'd slapped on a fresh coat of paint.

"Nona," Piper says as she points to a picture of Mama and me from when I moved in with Jake.

"Nana," I correct, reminding me how much I want to leave Butte and run home to my mom.

I point and explain the images that hold the few photos of our courthouse wedding and the small after-party with friends. As we near the middle of the book, the exciting days of the two of us living in Jake's parents' home as a married couple show. The house suddenly looks more beautiful than I'd ever remembered.

Again, tears come to my eyes as my memory flashes back to the live version of the photos I desperately want to relive. The more time passes, the more I've permitted the bad parts of our marriage to fall from my mind and allow me to reflect and lean on the positive moments. *There were good times. There really were.*

We sit on the carpeted living room floor until Piper loses interest and wanders off into the corner to play with her basket of toys. I move to the couch and look through the rest of the album, picking through the memories I hadn't thought about in years. When I reach the end, I close the book and squeeze it tight against my heart with a softened smile before finally putting it back on the shelf.

We'll be okay, Jake. Believe that we will.

TWENTY-TWO

JOHN

SIX MONTHS PASSED, and nothing further surfaced in the Jake Thacker case. Although he was still trying to dig up something new, John was forced to slow down on his search for new clues or suspects. The country sheriff decided to pause the investigation for the time being and leave Jake's case a mystery.

Upon the case's suspension, John handwrote a letter and put in his two-week notice with the department. The investigation and other various things on his plate had run him ragged, and he was ready to throw in the towel.

Lately, he had been more agitated and often short with people in his life. He verbally snapped at others before hearing them out, and his use of profanity had nearly tripled. He didn't think his wife could take much more of the man the stress of the job had turned him into. It was time.

John was looking forward to retirement. He planned to spend his days fishing the local creeks with his daughter and coming home with fresh steelhead trout for his wife to smoke. Between his time in the military and his time with the department, close to forty years of his life had been spent in the public service realm. It was hard to admit, but it was time to hang it all up and enjoy the time he had left with the people who loved him most.

For the time being, Jake's murder would remain unsolved. But it seemed like more technology was coming out every day, allowing cases that were once cold to be reopened and criminals to pay for their crimes. Also, new DNA was being added to databases that might lead to an answer eventually. He hoped that one day, a flag would trip, and something incriminating would surface.

Unfortunately, there was nothing he could come up with to answer any of the case's open questions. He didn't know who started the fire, why, or who else in Jake's life was involved.

Before it ran cold, he'd even tried handing the case over to the local police department, hoping they would see something he'd missed. The city detectives checked and rechecked everything in the file but ran into the same roadblocks as John. They too quickly ran out of leads to chase.

They had again questioned Miranda, Allie, and the various other people that had inadvertently gotten wrapped up in the small-town murder investigation. DNA was pulled again, and the crumbling house was ransacked by a fresh set of eyes. But unfortunately, the stories remained unchanged, the lab work returned the same, and the ruins still held no answers. The other detectives came up blank, just as John had.

It tore him apart that the case had gone unresolved on his watch, but he had done his best. He'd dug and dug but didn't know what more he could do to unearth evidence that didn't want to be found.

The little bit of information he'd managed to gather was filed away in a cardboard box and placed on a shelf in the department's evidence room. John expected it would sit there for years and collect dust until it became buried and forgotten like so many other unsolved cases. The person responsible for the murder and fire would never see their day in court, and Jake would never get the justice he deserved. Leaving things open didn't sit right with John, but he was out of options, and the sheriff was adamant it was time to file it away and move onto something else.

Some residents of Butte had a few moments of hysteria when they first learned that the town had an unknown killer on the loose. Not long after the fire, John got calls day and night from random citizens calling to pass the blame on anyone they could find a reason to accuse of the crime. He looked into many of the calls, but none led him to anything concrete.

The fear seemed short-lived and quietly faded away with the cool winter air as they snapped out of it. Everyone went right back to their daily lives once the initial shock factor wore off, even though the murderer remained at large.

John repeatedly insisted she stay out of it, but his wife began planning an event for him to celebrate his time in service to both his country and the state of Montana. She was adamant that he needed a party to signify his final retirement, while he would have preferred to slip away without a shindig.

Even though he loved working for the community and knew he would miss it, John adored the light he started seeing shine again in his wife's eyes when she thought about him being home for dinner every night. The air around her was noticeably happier, and she had begun flipping through foreign travel magazines and circling locations for them to start visiting.

Three months earlier, John had started meeting Miranda and Piper in town for a meal to catch up on the events in their lives. They tried to meet at least twice a month, sometimes for lunch, other times for breakfast. He had grown rather attached to the two girls and felt like they were adopted members of his family.

"Wait a second. You're retiring?" Miranda said with a shocked profile when John shared his news over a Denver omelet.

"Yeah, it's time. I'm not getting any younger, and I think Trish might leave me if I don't. I'm sorry I never figured out anything about Jake," he responded as he solemnly hung his head.

"Hey, you did your best. Everyone knows you tried. And I'm sure the case will be reopened and solved one day. Jake knows you did everything you could," she responded as she placed her hand lightly on his.

"Yeah, I really hope so."

Miranda smiled back, knowing that John had indeed tried his best. She'd witnessed him run himself ragged, trying to find answers to a case that had no clues or trails to follow.

"So, I closed on the property last week," Miranda stated. "It's in the hands of a Kurt Murphy now. Former Marine Special Forces, I think. Seems like a nice guy."

John's head instantly perked up when he heard the news about his favorite lot in town. He had tried and failed at convincing his wife that they needed to scrape together the money to buy the coveted land.

"Eight...hundred...thousand, for the land and insurance," she quickly added.

"No shit?"

"Yep. When our lease is up at the end of the month, we are out of here," Miranda said with a smile as she looked over at Piper.

John was happy that Miranda was leaving the small town she was born and raised in and finally making her own way. Terrible things had happened to her in the last year, and she deserved a fresh start somewhere new where no one knew her name or story. But he knew he would miss their frequent diner meals that he eagerly looked forward to.

"So, where are you guys gonna go?" John asked.

Miranda looked over at Piper, roughly gnawing on some apples with her new molars, and chuckled.

"I'm not sure yet, even though I've had plenty of time to think about it. We really liked Great Falls, and my mom is close by. I've been thinking about giving it another try. Maybe this time you won't come and make me leave." Miranda said with a smirk.

John narrowed his eyes across the table.

"Only kidding," she returned.

"More, more," Piper begged as Miranda scooped more food onto her daughter's plate.

"Jokes aside, I think you would love it up there. You guys will do great no matter where you land," John replied genuinely.

"Thanks. I sure hope so."

As usual, he snatched up the check before she had a chance to argue with him. After paying for breakfast, he walked the two girls to their car. Piper stretched her arms out wide and pulled him tight around the neck for a hug.

"Bye-bye, Papa," Piper said.

Piper started calling John *Papa* about a month earlier, and no one corrected her. John realized how much he liked the nickname.

"Bye-bye, Pipes," he replied and kissed her forehead.

"Next month? Maybe in Helena? It's sorta halfway," Miranda asked.

"Well, I'll be retired and bored. So, you just let me know when, and I'll be there," he responded.

"I promise," she returned with a smile.

"Oh, Trish is planning some fancy retirement party for me, so she might call you about that soon. Feel free to tell her you're busy or just flat out no," he said with a gentle eye roll.

"I will most definitely be there cheering in the back," Miranda replied with a smirk.

John hugged Miranda and felt tears of happiness build up behind his eyes. Jake was a great friend, but John had enjoyed taking his family under their wing when they needed him the most.

Miranda sank in her driver's seat and rolled down the window. With a flippy wave to John, she pulled away from the restaurant.

TWENTY-THREE

MIRANDA

I **PICK UP** speed as I roll through the country mountains. The mid-morning summer air brings in a therapeutic feel as it moves around the car. Whether on the road or in the house, I believe it's a sin to have the windows closed if it's nice out.

The road bends as I edge into town. I pass by the diner where John and I ate the previous month and realize how enjoyable our meals are. I know I'm going to miss him when we finally leave town.

I drive through the quiet afternoon, enjoying the breeze and listening to Piper talking to herself. I turn toward downtown. As much as I hate being cramped in a small apartment, I love that living in the city's heart means we can go for a walk and grab early morning doughnuts and coffee when the weather is nice.

I glance over at my favorite boutique, hoping to see a sale sign posted in the window. I still try to save money where I can, but I've enjoyed spending money buying this for myself. Something I didn't do for years.

Instead, I spot a woman standing near a black SUV on the sidewalk that catches my eyes. I quickly look back. The blonde hair that skirts her shoulders is familiar. I stare as I pass by and realize why I recognize the woman. *Allie.*

I focus on Allie's face as I see it for the first time since her odd appearance outside Jake's funeral. I hadn't really been able to make out her face well in the parking lot, but I remember my husband's mistress vividly from the image John had shown me months earlier. Even from a distance, her face is even prettier than in the picture, although her cheeks appear slightly chubbier.

Allie's casually leaning up against an SUV pulled up and stopped next to the curb. She's just standing there alone with her arms crossed as if she's locked out. I veer into a metered spot and park my sedan. Her back remains visible in my rearview mirror.

The image of Allie and Jake joyfully walking down main street and holding hands like a regular couple surges into my mind. He looks happy with her hanging on his arm, probably happier than he was with me.

As much as I wanted justice for Jake, I, too, gave up in my search for answers. I knew John was doing the best he could and even outsourcing to the police, so all I could do was wait, and eventually, I just lost hope.

But seeing Allie brings an entire gambit of emotions back.

"Stop it," I say quietly to myself as I try to fight against my feelings. I wipe away the few tears that formed and continue watching the woman I know in my gut had something to do with my husband's death. I've thankfully never run into her in town before, and the thought hadn't even crossed my mind about what my reaction would be if I ever saw her in person. *Maybe it isn't her. Maybe I'm just making this up. But I really think that's her.*

My first idea is to get out of the car, rush over to her, and confront her. My hands instinctively form into fists in my lap when I think about asking her why she lied about everything and what she did to Jake. I know she's involved somehow and talked her way out of it. There's no way Allie broke it off as she had suggested to John. *If she had, Jake wouldn't have admitted to anything, and he'd still be here.*

If I walk over to her, I hope she'll break down and spill her guts to me and then John, finally not holding back the things she must know. Piper and I would finally have the closure we need, and Jake's murder case will be closed. But I know whatever secrets Allie is holding in are staying tucked away. It's unlikely I'm going to be the one to coax a confession out of her.

My gaze stays locked on Allie, who remains glued in the same position on the car. She turns her eyes upward toward the early spring sun and allows the rays to beat down on her face. Her shoulders are rolled back, and the delicate curves of her face's profile give her an elegant appearance. I understand why Jake she'd caught Jake's eye.

I reach out to the door handle, ready to exit the car and confront Allie when a tall man in a button-up and jeans emerges from the store and approaches her. *Who the hell is that? Probably another married man she's trying to steal.*

I scoff and clench my jaw, my teeth grinding against one another. The man lightly places a hand on Allie's closest shoulder and kisses her on the forehead between her eyes. *Took you long to move on.*

The moment the man's lips touch her skin, I see Allie visibly flinch and slightly recoil from his touch. She pulls the shoulder closest to him up to her chin as if she's avoiding any further affection.

I sink down slightly in the driver's seat. Deep lines form between my eyebrows as I watch the two people from a distance and anxiously wait to see what will happen next.

The man turns and begins to walk over to the car's passenger side. Allie follows behind him. As she turns, I finally catch sight of her face head-on and know without a doubt it's the woman my husband was planning on leaving me for.

My mouth nearly falls to the floor when I see Allie's body come into full view as she rounds the front bumper. Underneath her black crewneck shirt and boot-cut jeans that cling tightly to her body, I see something that completely changes the narrative.

"You've got to be shittin' me," I say aloud. *She's pregnant? Like very pregnant. Like about to pop pregnant.*

I watch Allie's hand grab onto the hood of the vehicle. She steadies herself and steps off the curb, putting the majority of her weight on her hand as if she doesn't trust that her growing belly won't send her tumbling into the street. I blink and shake my head as I try to reset my vision. *Maybe she just gained some weight. No, that's not fat. That's a baby.*

Piper makes soft noises in the back of the car as she pretends to rock her baby to sleep. I reach back and flip my hand around blindly while I try to silence her as if it will help me hear the words passing between Allie and the man.

When Allie finally waddles over to the passenger side of the car, the man helps her inside and shuts the door.

"Sorry, John, I'm not leaving this all up to you," I say under my breath as I watch the man walk back around and climb into the driver's seat.

I silently work out the timeline in my head and compare it to the size of the stomach bulging out beneath Allie's clothes against Jake's death. Although I was tiny for nine months, I know that the size of a baby bump can vary. So maybe my timing is wrong, but Allie looks like she'll be popping soon.

"That's Jake's baby," I finally mutter as I look back at more living proof of his fertility. "It's gotta be."

When the man climbs into the car, I slump down in my seat as if they'll be able to see that it's me. From my slouched position, I see the car lurch forward and head east toward the outskirts of town.

I sit up in my seat, shift my car to drive, and make an illegal U-turn, the tires slightly squealing against the blacktop as I head in the same direction as the SUV. I follow them out of downtown and keep a liberal car length from theirs as I try to remain discreet about my tailing.

A smile creeps onto my face. I feel like I'm working to solve a crime that the law couldn't. I don't know what I'm doing or where I'll end up, but the thought of stepping in and getting answers is exciting. *Let's do this.*

Piper begins talking more in the backseat and snaps me back to reality. Not only am I illegally stalking a pregnant woman, but I'm dragging my toddler along.

"Looks like you get to come too," I whisper. I push the pedal more to keep up with the SUV I'm dead set on following.

The car comes to a stop at a red light. The person in front of me shifts into the other lane at the last second, and I'm forced to pull up directly behind Allie. An older man in the car next to me looks over, making eye contact and offering a timid smile. *Shit.* I quickly pull down the visor and slip on the sunglasses I'd forgotten were resting atop my head. I glance down at the floor and avoid looking in front of me or to my right. *Green. Green. Go green, dammit.*

When the light finally switches to green, I hold back briefly before continuing my stalk. The vehicle continues its drive out of town.

A few miles later, the SUV stops in front of a barbeque restaurant out near the county line. The thick smell of cooking meats is being wafted around by the spring breeze as I drive past the restaurant, trying to be inconspicuous. I'd eaten there once many years ago but never felt the urge to return. On the other hand, Jake loved the place, and I often found lunch receipts from the establishment shoved into his pants before I threw them in the wash.

I make a U-turn roughly a mile down the road and stop on the shoulder. I quickly count to ten before driving back and pulling my car into the parking lot across the street. I still have a vantage point of both the SUV and the building's entrance from my stakeout spot, but it doesn't look too obvious. I lean my seat back until I feel it bump against Piper's knees and peer over where the door frame meets the window's glass and try to remain out of sight.

For nearly a minute, the car sits still in the half-full lot as if there's no one inside. I hold my breath, waiting. *Maybe you've officially lost it. Maybe you didn't see what you thought you did. No, no, you did. She's definitely pregnant, like super pregnant.*

The car sits there for an additional minute, and nothing changes. *Time to let it go.* I place my hand on the gearshift to drive away when I see Allie finally climb out of the passenger seat. She shuts the car door and begins walking toward the restaurant's entrance with a black waitress apron in hand. When she's about five paces from the car, she quickly snaps her attention to her rear and turns around.

She leisurely strides back toward the driver's side of the car with an apparent reluctance in her gait, which is more of a shuffle. As she rounds the back bumper and is hidden behind the vehicle, I see her shoulders drop as if she's irritated about something.

Allie stops at the driver's window and listens to the man for a moment. I watch her nod a few times as he speaks inaudibly. He then leans out of the window and kisses her cheek.

I again see an uncomfortable smile spread across Allie's face as she allows his lips to meet her skin. As she looks away from the driver, her eyes shift to my place across the street. I quickly sink down even lower in my seat and count to ten before resurfacing. My heart is speeding a million miles an hour.

When I work up the courage to look over toward the SUV again, I barely peek over the edge of the doorframe. I watch Allie wave at the driver and pass in front of the vehicle. She heads back toward the restaurant.

The driver stays parked in the lot until Allie enters the building. Then, when she's safely inside, he pulls out of the gravel lot, kicking up rocks in his wake.

I keep my hand on the gear shift for a brief second while I toy with my two options. *Do I follow him and see what is going on? Or do I bust in there and force her to sing like a canary.*

The anger boiling inside of me causes me to ponder my decision. Aggressively confronting and accusing an overly pregnant woman in a public establishment probably isn't the best idea. Also, involving Piper in my affairs isn't appropriate. For all I know, one of the two people in that black SUV could be dangerous. *I know you did it, you bitch. But, let's go see who this guy is.*

I pull out of the lot and continue my tail. I follow the man as he heads back toward the heart of town. I presume he's a local with how comfortable and familiar he is as he drives quickly through the winding mountain roads without riding his brakes. I speed up to stick with the car.

As my endeavor becomes too apparent, I feel the need to abandon my hunt and head home. But then, the SUV flips on its blinker, and the driver pulls into a small cutout in front of a duplex with streetside parking. While still fifty yards away, I immediately pull into a spot in front of another duplex out of sight. I watch the vehicle as it parks, and its brake lights disappear.

The driver climbs out of the vehicle and grabs a few grocery bags from the back seat. He walks through the home's grassy front yard and enters the southern half of the duplex.

I take note of the lovely outside appearance of the building. The two-story house I've driven past plenty of times has brand new siding, Montana climate-appropriate landscaping, and a nice hanger on the door that reads "Welcome." *If it wasn't Allie, it was you.*

This man clearly cares about Allie, and if they were together before she met Jake, that's motive in my mind, especially if the baby isn't his. Also, John said the person was probably taller than Jake, and this man probably has three or four inches on my late husband, leaving me more convinced this is worth looking into.

I scribble down the house number, and street name on one side of a stashed away fast-food napkin. Then, for five minutes, I sit in the car and watch the front door as if the man will come out in clothes covered in Jake's blood with a typed-up confession in hand.

But as I wait and watch the house, the street remains still. Only two middle-aged women with a tiny poodle walk by, and I look away to avoid being seen. The house stands quietly while I hope for something monumental to happen.

Piper's fallen asleep in the back, and I hear her stuffed up nostrils whistling as they try to suck for air. Eventually, she begins breathing through her mouth, and the car falls silent.

I continue watching the house for close to twenty minutes. I don't see curtains move, lights change, or anyone step outside. I don't know what I'm hoping to see, but I know it will make sense to me when something shows itself.

Piper starts rustling around in her seat, and I snap back to reality, realizing I need to give up and get her home. *Well, you tried.* I drive back to our apartment with a wide grin.

When we get home, I rush inside and get Piper situated in front of the TV with a bag of Goldfish. I don't even care if she makes a mess right now. With Piper mindlessly glued to her cartoons, I grab the phone and dial the number to John's office.

"Come on, John. Come on," I beg over the phone and tap my hand rapidly on the kitchen counter. The line rings and rings some more, but no one answers. I snatch the business card pinned to the corkboard adjacent to the phone and flip it over to reveal another number inked on the backside.

"Zero Zero Two," I say aloud as I dial his home number and hear the line ring again.

"Hello?" I hear a woman's voice say across the line.

"Hi, um, I was calling to talk to John Waters?"

"Yes, may I ask who this is?" his wife questions.

"Uh, this is Miranda, Miranda Thacker."

"Oh, Miranda, sweetheart. How are you doing?" she asks in her always kind voice.

"Oh, you know, life is going."

"I understand. I'm so sorry I haven't reached out or anything. I still feel terrible about what happened with your husband," she says as I hear her breath escape as if she's sitting down and getting comfortable. *No lady. Get up and take the phone to John.*

"Oh, it's fine. So, uh, is John home?" I hurriedly ask, hoping she'll understand I'm not interested in small talk.

"Yeah, yeah, he's here. Hang on a sec," she responds as I hear her grunting as she stands back up.

"Thank you," I reply. I hear footsteps as she travels through their home, looking for her husband.

"John. John?"

I gently roll my eyes while I wait. Trish repeatedly calls his name until she finds the room where he's holed up. The phone transfers hands with a scratching sound.

"Hello?" he asks.

"Hey, it's Miranda," I respond.

"Oh, hey Miranda. What can I do for you?" he inquires.

"I tried you at the office, but you didn't answer. I'm sorry to call you at home, but I needed to tell you something," I explain.

"Don't worry about it, that's why I gave you the number. I just took the rest of the day off. That omelet didn't sit well with me. Is everything okay?"

"Yeah, uh, after we had breakfast, I was driving around and saw Allie. You know, Jake's Allie," I say.

"And?" he returns.

"John, she's pregnant, like happened before Jake died pregnant. And I saw her with a guy. He kissed her, and she didn't seem too keen on him doing so."

I stretch the phone's cord and sit down at the kitchen table, waiting for John to respond to my news.

"Well, that's interesting," he finally returns.

"What is?"

"I'm sorry. What did you say?" I can hear football playing in the background, distracting him.

"The baby John, keep up. I bet it's his," I interject.

"Well, come on. Let's not be too hasty."

The John that I knew months ago would have jumped out of bed in the middle of the night to hunt down a possible lead in Jake's case. He would have stopped at nothing to chase down any track he could if it even had a slight inkling it could be Jake related. Unfortunately, the man I'm currently talking to doesn't seem overly excited about the revealing information.

"John, what are you talking about?" I cry. "You have to talk to her. Go get her to confess. That's got to be his baby. That's a new motive."

"Jesus. You're right. I'm sorry," he responds as he snaps out of his jaded moment. I hear the clicking sound of the footrest on a recliner being stowed. "I'm gonna head to the office now and see what I can come up with."

"Okay, thank you. Please let me know what you find out," I reply.

"Of course. You know I will."

I return the phone to its cradle. I smirk as the idea of Allie again being brought in creeps into my mind.

"Sorry, Piper," I whisper toward my daughter, knowing she'll never get to meet her new sibling.

TWENTY-FOUR

JOHN

JOHN HUNG UP the phone and stared at it for a moment. He shook his head clear and hopped out of his chair like crippling arthritis hadn't destroyed his mobility. He quickly threw on some slacks and a polo and snatched his keys off the hanger near the door.

After his breakfast with Miranda, John had called in and headed home to watch the football game he'd recorded over the weekend. The rest of his day was already clear, and all he had to do was come back in for an afternoon meeting with his wife's retirement party committee, a meeting he was attending under duress.

The revelation of Allie carrying a baby that Jake could have possibly fathered had thrown him off guard, but Miranda was right; he hadn't sprung into action like he should've. The version of him who had lost twenty pounds and countless hours of sleep over the unsolved case would have jumped out of his recliner and chased down any lead. John felt a slight disappointment when he realized how lackadaisical he had become. Jake deserved better.

When he made it to the office, he searched through the mass of paper on his desk, shoving away the case files he'd already passed on to others

239

in preparation for his retirement. Beneath the piles, he found the yellow sticky note that he'd written Allie's home number on months before.

This is it. He clenched his teeth and sucked in air that whistled between his molars as he readied himself to revisit the case that had caused him a tremendous amount of mental and physical strife.

He grabbed the phone off his desk and dialed a number he never thought he would again. The ominous rings on his end seemed to mesh into one long tone. He slowly closed his eyes and rested his head in his hand. The droning sound ran on and on without cease.

"Come on. Pick up. Please," he quietly begged. A tone sounded, and his shoulders sagged in defeat.

"Hey, sorry to miss you, leave a message," he heard Allie's high-pitched voice say when the ringing finally ceased.

"Dammit," he said as he laid the phone back down on its cradle. He instantly redialed the number to Miranda's apartment. She answered on the first ring.

"Where did you see her?" he asked.

Miranda remained silent while she gathered her thoughts and tried to tone down her stalking escapade. The BBQ restaurant was on the opposite side of town from where she had just finished having breakfast with John not two hours earlier.

"Uh, I saw her like forty-five minutes ago. She was walking into where I'm guessing she works. It was that shitty barbeque place out on the edge of town."

"Okay, that makes sense, thanks."

He got off the phone with Miranda, and a soft smile appeared on his face. A second discussion with Allie wasn't likely to suddenly reveal all the hidden clues that he had missed during his investigation, but just maybe, it would give him something. John looked up the Snavely BBQ restaurant in the local phonebook and dialed the number listed.

"Snavely Barbeque, this is Charlotte," a woman's voice answered.

"Hi, I'd like to talk to Allie Taylor, please. If she's around," John explained.

The woman made a groaning sound as if she were stretching to look around the dining room.

"Well, she's with a customer right now. Can I take a message and have her give you a call back in just a few?" she asked, smacking her gum into the reciever.

"No, um, this is kinda important," John persisted. "I don't mind holding."

"Uh, alright, I'll get her for you in just a sec."

John patiently waited as he heard the usual sounds of the restaurant's afternoon crowd bustling around in the background. He rapped his fingers lightly on his desk and grabbed a pen in case Allie said anything noteworthy. *Hopefully, this takes us somewhere.*

"Hi, this is Allie," she finally said.

He sat straight up in his chair and swallowed the lump in his throat when he heard the familiar voice.

"Allie, hi. Detective Waters," he said and cleared his throat.

"Hi, uh, what can I do for you?" she said, lowering her voice to just above a whisper.

"Could you please come down to the station? I think we have something we should probably discuss."

A sigh emitted from Allie's mouth, and it quickly faded like she had pulled the phone away from her ear. An elongated verbal pause followed her expression.

"Um, yeah, I guess I can stop by after my shift," she said as John heard a slight shake in her voice.

"Yeah, I'd like to do this now if you don't mind. I can talk to Janel or Mark if need be," John countered.

"No, no, it's fine. I'll just take my lunch now."

"Alright, I'll see you soon." A smile cracked in the corner of his mouth. *Progress.*

"Oh, um, do I need a lawyer?"

"As always, you're more than welcome to bring one if you would like to."

"Okay, thank you."

John hung up the phone, and his little smile built into one that reached across the entirety of his face. He darted out of the cubicle farm that smelled of burnt coffee and headed back to the small room of archived cases. He sorted through the cardboard boxes.

On the shelf labeled *T*, then specifically *TH*, he found the folder he had spent hours building on the Thacker case. The lid landed on the floor as he began skimming the documents he hadn't looked at in over a month: Allie's testimony, Miranda's alibi, the phone records, and pictures. Everything was still there just as he had packaged it. As he tried to refamiliarize himself with the details, a gentle knock on the door caused him to turn around quickly.

"Sir?" a voice called out.

"What is it?" he replied without looking up from the file.

"We're waiting in the conference room if you're ready to talk about your retirement ceremony. Trish just showed up."

John looked up and saw one of the deputies glaring back at him as he tore apart the file like a madman.

In the wake of the news Miranda had brought to light, he had forgotten all about the party planning tiger team his wife had put together to iron out the details of his retirement celebration. They were three weeks out, and she refused to accept that he wanted to slip away into the night and leave the department behind quietly.

He rubbed his hand across his forehead, trying to figure out how to get out of the meeting tactfully.

"Thank you, can you please tell my wife I'm gonna have to reschedule? Something came up. Something important."

"Will do."

The look on her face meant she knew just as much as he did how upset his wife would be that he was again choosing work over something she wanted him to do. But he couldn't walk away now. He could feel it in his gut that he was finally getting somewhere.

When the deputy disappeared from the doorway, John went back to skimming Allie's previous testimony. He ran his finger along the text as he scanned it word by word as if he'd missed something minute the first seventy-five times he'd read the story.

When he felt refamiliarized, he took the box back to his office and the file to an interrogation room. He pre-staged the area, checking the black and white camera. He lined up three black pens, three blue pens, and enough paper to transcribe the Bible twice.

John walked back and forth in front of the lobby windows that looked out into the parking lot. Across the room, the secretary watched his feet pace as though he was digging a rut into the tile. He was anxious.

After nearly ten minutes of nervous pacing, a blue Ford Escort finally pulled into the lot. *Maybe that's her.* The car parked and sat in a spot with its back end facing the building. John watched it from the rear, assuming it was Allie and waited for her to get out and hopefully prove Miranda right. He tapped his left foot and crossed his arms at his chest while he waited. But the vehicle's driver sat motionless as John stood there with his nerves proliferating.

Finally, the driver-side door swung open. John saw one leg swing out from the seat and extend toward the pavement. Then, using the handle on the roof, another foot was slowly lowered to the ground.

When the person finally pulled themselves up and out of the car, John saw Allie standing in the light of the spring sun with a large belly that stuck out underneath her work shirt.

"Holy shit. Miranda was right," John whispered.

TWENTY-FIVE

JOHN

JOHN HELD THE door open for Allie as she waddled up the sidewalk. The woman who'd once been put together and spry now looked like she'd aged five years and gained fifty pounds.

"Mornin'," John said when Allie reached talking distance.

"Hi," she said through her labored breathing.

"Well, come on in."

Allie kept her gaze aimed downward as she stepped over the threshold of the building and entered the lobby. She looked around before looking up at John. Her expression looked exhausted, and her smile muted. She no longer looked like the girl that broke down in tears after speaking about a man she loved.

While John studied her, she used her hand to lean against a couch. The ring wrapped around her swollen pointer finger looked like it was cutting off her circulation. John stopped staring.

"Oh uh, we're gonna be back here," John said as he showed Allie toward the back of the building.

A noticeable look of apprehension was on her face as John ushered her through the glass divider door that led to the back of the building. *Let's hope this is it.*

When they made it to the room he had set up, John pulled out the chair for her. Allie dragged it back farther, hearing it screech against the floor, before gently lowering herself into it. She scooted slightly toward the table until her belly brushed against its side. She adjusted her backside in the seat and winced once as John noted her discomfort.

An awkward stillness hung between them while they both refrained from speaking. John just didn't know where to begin, and Allie's expression made it clear she had no interest in getting roped back into the case.

"So, I'm guessing I'm here because of this," Allie said with a hint of attitude as she disturbed the silence. She waved her swollen hands above the large belly protruding from her shirt.

Per what his mother had taught him, John always knew it wasn't proper to ask a woman if she was pregnant. He'd once asked one of his teachers if she was having a baby, which led to his mother smacking him across the head at the grocery store. But looking at Allie and knowing what she had looked like six months earlier, he knew there was no reason to assume he would be wrong. *Sorry, mama.*

"Well, honestly," he nervously coughed. "I would like to talk about that," he added as he pointed to her belly with the tip of his pen.

Allie's hand came up and rubbed the crest of her belly where it met the table. Her shoulders shrugged as she pushed out a heavy breath.

"Alright then. Go ahead. Ask away," she replied as her eyebrows inched closer in the middle.

"Well, how are you?" John asked.

"John cut the shit. Just ask."

"Alright. Well, uh. I know it's odd to ask you this, and I apologize, but is it Jake's?"

Allie gently rolled her eyes and then took them on a tour of the room as she avoided looking at John. She let out a slight scoff that quickly morphed into a subtle chuckle.

"No, they aren't Jake's," she responded as she looked down.

"They?" John asked.

"Yeah, I'm having twins, boys actually," she answered.

As much as she tried to fight to keep them at bay, John could see her hiding behind a small cloud of foggy tears forming in her eyes. He didn't fully believe her about the paternity of the babies but knew there was nothing in his power he could do to prove she was lying. Even if he could verify that the children growing in her womb were Jake's, it didn't mean that she could be implicated in his murder simply because she was carrying his children.

"So, whose are they? Do you have a boyfriend or something?" John returned. *Why did I not think of that sooner?*

"Honestly, I know who their father is, but I don't believe that's any of your business," she responded sternly.

He couldn't probe for too long without charging her with something and booking her and the nearly delivered twins. He needed to select his questions methodically before she stopped talking and walked out.

"You're right. I apologize," John backtracked. He flashed his palms at her defensively. "How far along are you, if you don't mind me asking?"

"Again, I actually do mind."

She crossed her arms and rested them atop her stomach. John studied her glare and saw a slight look of fear behind her darting eyes. She avoided every question he asked, and it seemed like she was trying to rush through the inquiry. *What are you so scared of, Allie?*

"Right, um again, sorry, and uh, my apologies," John said, feeling fire creep into his cheeks.

"Yeah, so, are we done here?" Allie questioned.

"Um, for now, I suppose. You haven't thought of anything else to help us with Jake's case by chance?" John replied.

"No."

She looked tired and annoyed.

"Well then, you're free to go."

"'Kay, cool."

She turned her body ninety degrees and placed one hand on the chair's back and the other on the table. She pushed upward and leaned forward with a grunt as she tried to get her large frame out of the seat.

John noticed her struggling and chivalrously walked over to help her out of her chair, assuming it must be challenging to be carrying twins. He reached a hand toward her.

"Here," he offered.

"No thanks. I got it," Allie snapped at him as she raised a hand, causing him to retreat.

John led Allie out of the building without another word passing between them.

"Thanks again for coming in," John said as they stood at the building's exit.

"Sure. It was a blast as always," she replied as her lips formed a flat smile.

With a close of the glass front door, Allie was gone again, and no concrete evidence had surfaced. Sure, it was interesting that she was pregnant and didn't want to talk about it, but it didn't mean she was guilty of murder, and John had nothing on her. *Guess I'm gonna have to figure out who the father is.*

John watched her waddle back down the sidewalk toward her vehicle. From the rear, he saw her head bob around slightly and her fists clench a few times as if she was muttering to herself.

When she was out of sight, John rushed back to his office. He snatched the phone up in a hurry to share the news with Miranda. He dialed her number wrong at first, then slowed down the second time.

"Hello?" Miranda said.

"She claims they aren't Jake's. That's her side, at least. But she wouldn't tell me anything else," John blurted out instantly. "I tried."

"They? I'm sorry. Did you just say they?" Miranda said, repeating John's reaction.

"Yep, there's two of them in there," he replied. "Boys, actually. But she was also very cagey in her responses, and I could tell she wasn't interested in talking. I don't know. She almost seemed... scared."

"Jake had two sets of cousins that were twins. I bet it's genetic. But she has like a boyfriend or something. Maybe he's new; maybe he's not. I don't know. But, if it's not Jake, it has to be that guy I saw her in town with. And I swear something about the two of them looked odd if you were to ask me," Miranda explained.

"Yeah, we can look into him. I'm gonna dig through the files again," John added.

Miranda rattled off some of the basic things she remembered about the odd man that Allie seemed to have a distaste for. He was probably six-three to six-four and had short-cut dark brown hair. He was on the thicker side but more muscular than fat.

"How did you find that?" John asked when Miranda told him Allie's address.

John looked it up in the phone book months ago but never went inside once her alibi lined up. Maybe that had been the wrong call.

"I kind of followed them."

John didn't say anything but subtly chuckled.

"Be careful, Miranda."

"I will. I promise."

"I'll let you know what I find out," John said as he excitedly scribbled down some information. "But, let me do my job."

"Fine," Miranda replied and hung up the phone.

TWENTY-SIX

ALLIE

ALLIE WALKED BACK to the car and released her tears as soon as her face was out of sight. She tightly clenched her fists that had started shaking when she heard John's voice over the phone and hadn't stopped since. She cursed under her breath, angry that she had willingly come in, even though she knew she didn't have a choice.

On top of her personal problems, her ankles were swollen to the size of her calves and were getting puffier every day, and getting her shoes on while maneuvering around an oversized bowling ball had become a chore that took her breath away. Lately, her hair fell out in chunks, and she was constantly irritated. But the most uncomfortable part was the twin sitting directly on her bladder and kicking it repeatedly. She abhorred being pregnant.

I swear to God I am never doing this again.

Allie was beyond fed up with carrying two children that felt like the size of watermelons. She didn't know how to muster the strength to do it for another month before her scheduled cesarian.

As she replayed the meeting, she thought she handled John's probing questions with ease. She kept calm and didn't break down in tears as she had anticipated. Of course, she knew her deflected answers wouldn't shut him down for good. He'd be back. But at least she paused his suspicions about the babies being Jake's and made it clear she wasn't interested in letting him glimpse into her personal life.

As much as she wanted everyone to know that sweet, gentle Jake was the father of the two babies swimming around in her womb, she couldn't tell anyone. It only made her look guilty, and she was trying to steer clear of anything Jake-related. Besides her, only one other person knew the truth, even if he didn't want to believe it.

Allie climbed into the car. She leaned into the headrest and sighed as she took the pressure off her struggling limbs and tried to regain a normal breathing pattern. Every step hurt, and she admitted her days of whisking around the restaurant waiting tables and slinging drinks were coming to an end.

She screamed out the emotions that had been locked in her chest. She beat her fists against the steering wheel of the borrowed car as her screaming continued and her tears escalated.

"I hate you. I hate you," she yelled on repeat.

When her throat ran dry from her stressed vocal cords, she laid her head down on the wheel and finished sobbing.

"It's all your fault," she whimpered. "Not mine."

So much in her life had changed since she lost Jake. Her heart broke more every day that his twins grew inside her without him around. She wanted him, needed him back in her life, but he was gone, and she had to pick up the pieces all by herself.

Dylan was all she had left, and the one convinced the twins were his. Allie closed her eyes and tried to understand how she had reached this point. Her life felt like a failure.

Allie met Dylan in high school during their sophomore year, and they had stayed together since. The two lived together in the modest duplex Allie purchased herself after saving enough tip money for a down payment. Over the years, they opened a shared bank account for their bills and adopted a small lap dog that Dylan never really cared for. They looked like an average domestic couple on the socially average path.

Allie spent years wishing Dylan would get down on one knee. Every year when Valentine's Day or Christmas came around, she hoped there would be a velvet box with a diamond ring inside. She'd always seen her future full of kids, a house with a wraparound porch, and herself being a stay-at-home mom who volunteered with the PTA. But years came and went, and not once did she hear him even hint at the idea of proposing.

For the first couple of years, their relationship was fresh and exciting, and everything about Dylan felt right. He tried to do nice things, bought her gifts that never failed to bring a smile to her face, and constantly reminded her how incredible and precious she was to him.

When he finished his two years at community college and went off to an out-of-state university, they maintained a long-distance relationship, often splitting the four-hour drive to see one another on the weekends.

After graduation, Dylan accepted a job back in Butte as an architect, and the two combined their households into Allie's duplex. She willingly shared her space and hoped moving in would mean a proposal was on the horizon.

Dylan became increasingly lazy and dull once he started his new job and had Allie caring for him daily. She found her role in his life quickly became less of a girlfriend and more like a friend. He never went out with her, even when she begged, and Dylan didn't know any of the people she hung out with. As time passed, it was difficult for Allie to discover new ways to fall in love with him every day like she used to, and subconsciously began to drift away from him. His lack of desire to get off the couch, and Allie's inability to stand her ground, caused their life to spiral into constant boredom.

As time went on, she began going through the motions in their relationship. They still had sex occasionally, but she hated every minute of it and tried to avoid the act at all costs.

She wanted out years ago but stayed because it was comfortable. Dylan made almost three times what she did and took excellent care of her financially. He paid all the bills and gave her pocket money whenever she asked. As dull as their life was, Allie really believed he could change for the good and that he would become the man she deserved one day.

But then she met Jake, and she realized she wanted more than anything to be with someone who loved and adored her. His attention made her feel seen for the first time in years.

When she found out Jake was dead, her heart instantly fell out of her chest. The man she had placed all her betting money on was out of her life forever, and she was stuck with Dylan.

Dylan was there for her, but things were different between them. She didn't love him anymore. Whenever he touched her or made a move to kiss her, she tried to wiggle out of his contact if she could. Dylan still insisted on them being intimate, and when Allie couldn't talk him out of it, she just laid there like a doll and closed her eyes until it was over.

As much as she wanted to leave Dylan and never lay eyes on him again, she knew she didn't have enough money to raise a set of twins on her own. And he'd threatened her.

She had toyed with the idea of going to live with her parents. But staying with them would have ended with a lot of, *I told you so's,* and *maybe if you hadn't been living in sin* comments.

Mr. and Mrs. Taylor were very religious and had never agreed with their daughter's life choices. The three of them had no real relationship anymore, and her parents still had no clue she would soon be having their first grandchildren. The idea that their only daughter would birth a child out of wedlock would stain their carefully maintained saint status at the church.

She'd also considered the idea of adoption. The twins could go to a friendly family that wouldn't lie to them about their father for the rest of their lives and get to live a life with a couple that loved each other. But, as easy as that option seemed, she knew Dylan would never go for it, and she feared how he would react if she even brought it up.

Dylan was convinced the twins were his, even though Allie knew they weren't. He often talked about them and how they would look just like him and all the things he was excited to experience as a family. In his mind, they were his, and no one could ever convince him differently.

"I wish you were here," Allie said through her sobbing, hoping that Jake would speak back to her.

Allie gazed out of the window and stopped the tears falling from her eyes. She had to compose herself and get back to work before her manager cut her shift short.

Lately, she had tried to spend as much time as possible at the restaurant to avoid seeing Dylan. Even though her entire body ached, she picked up every extra shift available and tried to poach as many tables as possible to make some extra money and stay out of the house.

Allie pulled out of the sheriff's department's parking lot and headed back to the restaurant. She breathed in and out in a rhythmic manner while trying to stop crying. Her nose was already stuffed up, but if she calmed down, she could finish her shift without puffy, bloodshot eyes.

She pulled into the parking lot and looked at the visor mirror. Tiny little veins of red worked their way through the whites of her eyes to her pupils, and she kept sniffling. *These damn allergies.*

Her appearance was as close to normal as it would get. Most people didn't even look at her face anymore, they were too busy gawking at the overinflated basketball tucked into the XL shirt she was barely squeezed into.

"Let's get through the day," she said, rubbing the crest of her stomach as she shuffled through the gravel lot and into the restaurant.

"Hey, we're slammed. Can you take table two?" a waitress with full hands asked before Allie could even set down her purse.

Allie nodded with a grin and pretended nothing was wrong. She spent the rest of her shift bussing tables, running food, and filling pint glasses while maintaining a forced smile and cheery attitude. She looked okay on the outside, but inside, she was falling apart more every minute.

A brown-haired man sitting in a back booth alone caught her eye on a trip back to the kitchen. His short fade haircut and broad shoulders reminded her of Jake from the back and took her back to the first time she saw him.

ON A PARTICULARLY dreary Tuesday, Jake Thacker casually strolled into the restaurant. He sunk into a booth meant for two in the back corner, all by himself. Allie looked his way, and his good looks snagged her attention.

She stared for a few seconds. His hair was perfectly cut and slowly faded into being longer on top, and he had thick eyebrows that sat just above a set of big blue eyes. The white t-shirt he was wearing hugged his frame just right, and the sleeves wrapped around his purposely sculpted biceps. By her guess, he was in his mid-thirties, and Allie presumed he was nearly ten years older than she.

She intentionally directed her attention down and noticed no band on any finger of his left hand. Not even a tan line was present.

His gaze left his menu and scanned the restaurant, where he caught Allie staring at him. When Allie realized the union, she immediately moved her attention from him and went back to wiping down the table she was bussing before being distracted.

Jake sat quietly at the table for a few minutes, waiting for service. He looked around the room and tapped his fingers in his lap while no one came to serve him. *Here's my chance.*

Allie knew the waiter responsible for that section of tables was outside sucking down at least two cigarettes. She peeked out the side door and yelled at the workers crowded onto a picnic table at the smoke pit.

"Hey, Matt. Do you mind if I take one of your tables? It's just one guy," Allie asked.

"Sure. Go for it," he responded.

Allie adjusted her underwire to perk her breasts up and tucked her hair behind her ears. She walked over to the table where Jake sat.

"Good evening, and welcome. My name is Allie, and I'll be taking care of you tonight."

Jake's eyes broke from his menu. Allie felt her stomach flip when she saw how blue they were. She'd never been to the beach before, but the iris' looking back at her reminded her of the coastal waters she'd seen in magazines.

"Hi," he responded shortly as his eyes met hers. He flashed her a toothy smile.

She smiled back.

"Hi, um, can I get you started with something to drink?"

"Oh yeah, um, just whatever light beer you have on tap should work. I'm not too picky."

Allie caught him looking at her hand.

"Okay, easy enough. I'll be right back."

Allie walked away from the table to grab the draft and felt him eyeing her backside as she made her way across the room. While the bartender filled the frosted pint glass, she watched Jake look around and study the restaurant's eclectic wall decor.

Allie slid the chilled glass across the table. Before she could get a word in, Jake spoke up.

"So, are you from around here?"

"I am. How about you?" she asked as she leaned against the end of the opposite side of his booth.

"Yep, born and raised, sadly."

"Oh, it's not that bad around here," she retorted.

"Not when there are pretty girls like you in town."

Allie shyly looked at the ground. She smiled and pushed her hair over her shoulder as she gazed back at him.

"So, um," Allie stopped and chuckled. "Are you looking to get something to eat?"

Jake placed his order, and Allie walked away from the table. The tempting image of his tongue gently running across his lips spread through her mind.

She grabbed him a second beer when his glass ran dry. Again, he shot her a warm smile that caused her stomach to contort and red to rush into her cheeks.

When his pulled pork sandwich and fries were ready, she quickly snatched them off the warming window and rushed them over. When he saw her coming his way with a plate of food, he shot her a half-smile that reached up to his eyes.

"Is there anything else I can get for you?"

"I think I'm good for now, thanks," Jake answered.

She replied with a smile as she backed up slowly.

She returned to check on him once while he ate and then again when he'd finished. Allie cleared his table, laid his check face down with a smile, and took his used plates and cutlery to the kitchen.

When she returned to the dining area, her smile flattened when she glanced across the room and realized her customer had left. Jake had paid for his meal in cash and slipped out while she was back in the kitchen. On the table, Allie found a twenty-dollar tip and a penned note that read, "It was nice to meet you, Allie."

Three days later, Allie clocked in and walked out into the dining room to see Jake finishing a meal again at a table by himself. He smiled at her from across the room, and she returned the grin. A few moments later, he left the restaurant without saying so much as a word to her. For some reason, she felt her heart sink.

"Hey, that guy over there left this for you," one of the other waitresses said as she nodded toward Jake's empty table and handed Allie a small note.

Allie opened the pocket-sized sheet and saw a handwritten invitation, "Drink's at The Peak Bar at eight?" Again, she read the small note, and a broad smile spread across her face.

Hours later, when her shift ended, Allie ran home quickly and changed into something that didn't smell of constantly running deep fryers and BBQ sauce. Her hair was brushed and thrown into a high bun with a cotton scrunchie. She dabbed a streak of brown powder on her eyelids and ran a stroke of mascara through her stubby lashes.

Dylan sat on the couch with a beer in his hand, watching TV, and caught Allie as she was darting back out the front door.

"Where are you going?" he grunted from the couch, his eyes never leaving the TV screen.

"Just gonna go out and have some drinks with some girls from work," she lied as she flung her purse over her shoulder.

"Oh, okay, have fun," he replied with a slight wave.

I plan to.

She drove to the bar with a wide grin glued to her face as the exhilaration of spending time with the attractive man from the restaurant sank in. A fleeting bout of guilt almost caused her to turn around and head home when she thought about lying to Dylan. However, a quick shake of the head dismissed the notion, and she talked herself into going and just classified it as a harmless night out. *It'll be fine. He'll never know.*

Allie had never done anything like this, but she desperately craved company with the opposite sex and hadn't even realized it until she saw the sweetness in Jake's eyes. Since the man she lived with refused to give her attention, she decided she deserved to go out and find it with someone else.

When she arrived at the bar a town over, she walked in alone. She quickly spotted Jake seated at a booth in the back that overlooked a field. The intimate corner had a dimly lit hanging light that showcased Jake's sharp jawline in its shadows. A floating candle bobbed around in a low-cut vase on the round table. The whole set-up screamed *romance*.

Jake waved across the room when he saw her standing in the doorway. Allie released the apprehensive breath that had been caught in her chest and sauntered toward him. *Just be cool. You got this.*

"You look great," Jake said, standing as she joined him.

"Thanks," Allie replied, feeling her cheeks flush from the compliment. She sat down at the booth, and Jake did as well, their knees slightly tapping beneath the table. A shiver ran down her arm as she felt sparks dance across her back.

The outing went smoother than she expected. Jake and Allie spent most of the evening laughing and drinking together as they allowed time to be ignored. She learned things about the handsome man that enjoyed mediocre barbeque and loved the subtle look in his attentive eyes while she talked. The two chatted about everything under the sun, but both kept the vital information about their significant others wrapped up tight.

When the waiter came by, Jake snatched up the check and paid for the drinks that had brought them to an apparent level of tipsy. He gallantly shouldered the door and insisted he escort her out to her car.

"I had a good night. I'd like to do this again sometime," Jake said.

With a smile, he reached up and brushed away the stray hairs the summer breeze had blown into her eyes. Allie felt her core tighten as she tried to contain the excitement brewing in her stomach. His simple touch ignated a flame in her that had been dormant for years.

"Yeah, me too," Allie responded as she quickly leaned forward and pressed her lips against his. She pulled back and suctioned her hand to her mouth, panicking about what she had just done.

"I'm so sorry. I shouldn't have done that," she said. *I can't believe you did that.* The darkness of the parking lot hid the crimson red filling both of her cheeks.

"Really, it's okay," he replied with a chuckle. "Don't apologize."

Her vodka-induced buzz provided her with confidence she wasn't used to having. Typically, she was timid, the last girl to ever do something spontaneous. It seemed she was more shocked by her boldness than he was.

His lips formed into a curve and Jake lightly wrapped a warm hand around the base of her neck and the other on the small of her back. He pulled her close, and she could smell the Jameson on his lips. He leaned in, she closed her eyes, and when his mouth pressed against hers, she felt as if she was floating.

Goosebumps made their way across Allie's skin as she reached her hand up toward Jake's cheek and felt the gentle sandpaper feeling of his five o'clock shadow brush beneath her palm.

Allie hadn't felt anything emotionally in a while. The undivided attention she got from Jake just felt right. She missed the days of someone kissing her passionately and enjoyed the bulky feeling of a man's embrace. The excitement in her wandering hands and lips caused her to realize the affection was something her body craved more of.

Jake released his lips from Allie's, and she took a step back. They both smiled in the soft glow of the overhead parking lot lights.

"Goodnight," he said. "And here."

Jake reached into his pant pocket and passed Allie a business card with his desk number embossed on its front.

"Thank you," she returned with a smile, unable to formulate any other words after their kiss.

Allie reached into her purse and pulled out one of her restaurant's business cards she found rolling around loose in her bag. She wrote down her home number with a small heart at its end and handed it to him. Dylan never answered the phone, and she figured if Jake called, she could explain it then. Part of her also assumed he wouldn't call, and this was all just a dream.

"Well, goodnight," Allie said with a smile.

Jake kissed her one last time as she climbed into her SUV.

Allie drove home with an intentionally muted smirk and laid down next to Dylan, who violently snored. She stared up at the ceiling and realized she had no love for him anymore. Her heart raced in her chest for the first time in years, but it was for someone else. *I'm sorry, Dylan.*

It didn't take long for Jake and Allie to find every reason they could to meet up. They loved being together, and their affair silently became fun and exciting.

Eventually, Jake broke the news about Miranda and Piper, and Allie shared the details about her personal life. The two found that their unhappiness in their relationships was just something else that connected them.

"I want out. I really do. It's just hard with Piper. But I don't want to do the wrong thing and lose her," Jake explained.

"I know. I want out too. I just don't know what Dylan would do without me. And I guess I feel bad. But when I do it, I know I'll be happier," Allie added.

"You make me happy," Jake said. He kissed Allie on the forehead and pulled her close.

"Same," she replied and nuzzled her lips into the skin just below his ear. His embrace made her feel safe.

"We'll figure us out. I know we will," Jake assured.

It took a little more work for Jake to slip away from Miranda and get out of the house, while Allie could just stroll out of her front door unnoticed. The two met at obscure restaurants in neighboring towns, cheap motel rooms that charged an hourly rate, and even a few times at Allie's house when she was confident Dylan was at work.

Allie knew she loved Jake after just a couple of weeks. Even though it seemed rash, something about the tender way he cared for her felt right. Her heart ached when she thought about him sleeping next to Miranda, but she also knew she had to be patient. One day she'd have him all to herself.

When Allie realized the consistent day her period always started had come and gone, panic shot through her body. She was never late. *No, no, no. I can't be.*

With trembling hands, she drove out of town on her day off to an inconspicuous gas station in the next county. She wore dark glasses and a Montana State University ball cap as she purchased a pack of three pregnancy tests. A fake smile spread across her lips as she paid in cash while different options whirled around in her cloudy head.

She tapped her foot on the tile of the dirty bathroom of the gas station after peeing on two of the white sticks. The second hand on her watch seemed to tick by slower than it ever had as she waited the grueling five minutes for something to appear on the tests she avoided peeking at.

Here we go. God, please be negative. With her eyes closed and her heart praying, she flipped the plastic pieces over and saw the double pink lines displayed in the small windows of both sticks.

"No. Come on. Not now," she cried as her head fell into her hands.

She broke down and started sobbing while sitting on the toilet covered in single-ply paper. Allie believed the child growing inside her was more than likely Jake's, which meant the options rolling around in her head doubled when she thought about the two men in her life.

"Dammit," she whispered through her sobs. She discarded the tests and their wrappings in the trash can and headed home.

As she drove, she tried to break down the timeline to figure out the father of her child. She was pretty convinced the baby was Jake's but knew she couldn't be one hundred percent certain. Dylan's twenty-fifth birthday had passed the month before, and they had gotten pretty drunk that night. She woke up in only her bra and couldn't remember if they had slept together or not. *I have to tell him. But how?*

The night before the fire that destroyed all the plans she had built for them, Allie finally broke the news to Jake about the baby.

"It's yours," she said cringing into a half-smile, fearful to hear his response.

"Are you sure?" he asked.

"I'm positive." *Mostly positive.*

Jake pulled Allie close and wrapped his arms around her. He kissed the top of her head.

"Are you mad?" she questioned.

"No, no, baby. Not at all," he replied. "It's not going to be simple. I don't want to lie to you. But I promise. Together, we will make it all work out."

Those words and the passionate kiss that followed reassured her that Jake would be there for her and their baby, no matter what.

A VOICE SNAPPED Allie out of her daydream.

"Hey, Allie. You okay?"

She blinked twice, remembered her swollen ankles, and felt one of the babies kick her in the ribs.

"Yeah, I'm fine," she replied. *I'm not fine. I'm never going to be fine again.*

TWENTY-SEVEN

ALLIE

ALLIE SAID GOODBYE to a select few of her coworkers when her shift ended and rode home with a friend.

Every day, it seemed to get more laborious to wedge herself into a car, especially when they sat low to the ground. She slumped down in the passenger seat and waited while her friend made out with a guy at the bus stop like a high schooler. Even Joe, the cook on work release, seemed better than Dylan. She pushed her bun onto the headrest. *Another day.*

Finally, Malisa got in the car, using her sleeve to wipe off her chapped lips.

"Ugh, I'm so ready to go home," Malisa huffed as she put the car in drive.

"Me too," Allie lied.

Malisa drove while Allie stared out the window, watching the streetlights passing in tiny blobs of light and trying to avoid conversation. After talking to John, her whole day had been spent in a haze while she tried to control her ever-changing emotions.

More than ever, Allie wanted out of her relationship with Dylan. She'd been planning it for months, but she took it more seriously as her due date drew nearer. She had been skimming some money off Dylan's accounts for months, and he was none the wiser. Almost three grand was stashed in a jar in her locker at work. So, when she did finally muster up the courage to end their relationship, she would at least have a cushion to fall back on.

Allie was ready to throw in the towel and accept her defeat. At that point, anything would be better than staying in her current situation. *I'll just go stay with mom and dad and live the quiet country life.*

Her parents would undoubtedly have their opinion about her out-of-wedlock pregnancy. *Unholy, disappointment, shame* were just some of the words she expected to hear. But she believed that their comments and judgment would be worth it to be rid of Dylan.

Her father had always been protective. Every boy she went out with, even if he was from her youth group, had to be vetted and have her home by eight. No handholding or kissing was allowed in the Taylor house, making Allie want to rebel even more. Her parent's devout mindset wouldn't approve of her choices, but she knew she would be safe under their roof.

"You okay?" Malisa asked as she parked the car in front of Allie's duplex.

"Yeah, just beat from these two," Allie replied as she rubbed her belly. She had gotten good at lying and masking her true feelings.

Malisa offered a smile, and Allie thanked her for the ride. She climbed out of the car and waddled up the sidewalk as Malisa pulled away.

When Allie was five yards from the front door, tears flooded her eyes again. The mixture of her misery and the swarm of hormones racing through her body caused her to cry for no reason, no matter how hard she fought it.

She slowed her breathing and tried to compose herself. If she went into the house with tears visible in her eyes, Dylan would undoubtedly drill her about what she had been up to that day. He would push until she broke down and told him why she was so distraught. She didn't want to give him any reason to suspect that she had been talking to John or that the detective knew about her pregnancy.

Since she had started to show, she avoided going into town as much as possible. Work was typically the only time she left the house. The restaurant was rarely packed, and she never thought about someone seeing her and telling John.

No one had any reason to suspect anything was odd about her pregnancy. Most people didn't even know she and Jake were aquainted, much less sleeping together. As far as anyone knew, she was the same sweet, innocent girl who poured their sweet tea and smiled warmly. She figured they just assumed she was just another knocked-up twenty-something working for minimum wage.

When Jake was buried in the ground, so was any trace of their relationship. Their romantic moments and days of hurried hotel sex were over. He was gone.

Allie focused on her thoughts and continued to slow her breathing. She pulled out her scrunchie and rubbed her hair down as she tried to flatten it out.

"Just another night, you can do this," she repeated and wiped her eyes.

She slowly finished walking toward the house that felt like it was on a railway rolling away from her as she stepped closer. She expected the door to creak open and show Dylan passed out on the couch with six or seven empty beer cans littered across the coffee table. *I don't want to be here.*

Her hand hesitated over the knob as she thought about making a run for it and heading off to her parents at that exact moment. The freedom she desired felt so close she could taste it, but she had to tie up some loose ends, and the only car they had was in Dylan's name.

Allie squeezed her eyes shut and gritted her teeth as she forced her hand to turn in a clockwise motion. The door squeaked loudly, and the sound echoed off every wall in the hall as she allowed it to swing open. She breached the threshold quietly and stopped just inside the frame as she waited for the flooding sound of sports playing to hit her ears.

Instead of the usual chatter from the TV, only silence hung heavy in the hall as Allie shut the house's front door. It was peculiar that Dylan hadn't been waiting up for her. *Maybe he's out with friends.*

The hallway that opened before her stood full of hollow darkness, only broken by a soft glow from the kitchen at its end. The light bounced off the walls toward her and created a dimly illuminated path.

She gently placed her keys down on the entryway table, laying them down silently as if she were already worried about waking up two temperamental infants. She hung her purse up on the hook and heard its buckle hit the wall. The sound seemed to reverberate throughout the entire frame of the house.

"Shit," she whispered as her face contorted into a grimace.

She glared toward the soft white glow of the kitchen light at the end of the hall. They always made sure to turn off all the lights when they went out or headed upstairs to bed. Allie squinted toward its source and slowly moved forward. She rubbed her hand against the wall to support her waddle.

As she tried to tiptoe, every footstep echoed in her mind. *Fe fi foe fum.* She was nearly fifty pounds heavier than she had been six months earlier. No movement she made felt quiet or discreet anymore.

She finally reached the end of the corridor, where the light poured through the doorway. She peered around the corner and looked into the kitchen.

Dylan sat at the table with his hands wrapped around a coffee mug. He stared into the contents as if he was reading tea leaves. Allie took a step closer, and the loose floorboard at her swollen feet creaked and signaled her entry.

Dylan looked up from his slouched position and made eye contact with Allie. The tiny vessels in the whites of his eyes were red and stringy as if he hadn't slept in days, while the rest of his profile was blank. She tried but failed to decode the flat emotion he flashed her way as he stared emptily in her direction.

As she glared back, Allie felt as though Dylan's eyes were looking through her and not at her. They had an eerie hollow look that was unfamiliar. A sharp chill shot down her spine.

She had half a mind to wrap her arm around her belly in support as she raced back down the hallway she had just breached. Something about his look gave her the impression that Dylan was emotionally in a wicked place, and she had a growing fear of where his anger would be directed.

"Hey," Dylan finally said.

He brought the Disney World coffee mug to his lips as he took a small sip and rested it back on the table's surface. Allie's pregnant nose could detect even the slightest scents like a bloodhound. *Canadian Whiskey.*

"Hey," she returned as her grip on the door frame tightened.

Dylan's eyes looked up from the table and met Allie's.

"So, where were you today?" he asked.

"At work," she replied. "We had a couple of good rushes."

"Not all day you weren't."

"What are you talking about?"

Allie felt her heart fall, and her hands began to tremble.

"Well, Paul and I came by for an early lunch today. I went inside and didn't see you there," he explained. "So, do you wanna tell me where you were?"

Dylan took another swig of his whiskey and placed his palms flat on the kitchen table. His glare remained fixated on Allie.

Allie stood in the doorway silently and stared back at him. Her mind flipped around as she hurriedly tried to formulate a coherent response. *He only comes in maybe once a year for lunch. Why did it have to be today?*

"I was uh...," she paused and gently coughed as she cleared the fear from her throat. "Just out."

"Just out? That's what you're gonna go with?" he returned, his tone coming off as angry.

"Yeah, why? It wasn't a big deal," she returned. "I just ran out to grab something to eat."

"Because I believe that for one second," he returned as his eyes rolled. "Were you out screwing some other guy again?"

"Are you kidding? Look at me. Who wants me like this? I'm as big as a house," she replied as she used her hand to showcase her large midsection.

Dylan closed his eyes and loudly released a breath. Allie watched his eyebrows come toward one another in the middle as one of his hands morphed from a flat palm to a gripping fist.

"Well, I'm gonna ask you again. Where were you this afternoon?" he repeated as his hands loosened. "And I would prefer it if you didn't lie to me this time."

Just as Allie opened her mouth to speak, Dylan violently slammed his hands down on the table.

"Dammit, Allie," he thundered.

The coffee mug they had picked out together nearly bounced on the wooden table when his fists made contact. A loud screech shot across the room as he pushed his chair back and came to a standing position.

Allie's entire body flinched at his angry stance. She gripped the door frame harder as if she could pry it off and employ it as a self-defense tool.

"I. I...," she stuttered through her growing fear.

"Where were you?" he yelled louder.

"I um, I was at the sheriff's department. Okay?" she replied and allowed herself a moment to take a deep breath. "The detective found out I was pregnant and wanted to know whose it was."

"And what did you tell them?" A creepy half-smile cracked across his face.

"I, I, I told him it was none of his business. I told him that they weren't Jake's babies. But I didn't tell them whose they are," she returned. "I swear."

Dylan moved out from behind the table and casually strolled over to the doorway where Allie was still standing. She was frozen in fear. Her nails dug into the wood. *We need to get out of here. Now.*

Allie tried to back up slightly, but she knew the wall was close behind. As much as she wanted to sprint down the hall and out the front door, there was no way she would be able to move her pregnant feet fast enough to outrun him, no matter how drunk he was.

He gently placed his hands on Allie's shoulders when he came into arms reach. Dylan's eyes met hers as she looked upward at him. Beneath his grip, she trembled with fear as his whiskey breath billowed in her face. *He's hammered.*

He pushed her backward. Her breath cut short, and a soft grunt escaped her mouth as her back hit the wall. Again, she saw nothing but a hollow gaze in his eyes and felt him using her as support while he swayed drunkenly.

"So, if that's all it was, why didn't you tell me that in the first place?" he asked.

Allie's gaze remained locked on his silent eyes. Her lips parted slightly, and her head silently shook back in forth. She searched for the words locked deep inside, but nothing came out.

Her pregnancy and apparent disinterest in being forthcoming about paternity would likely stir an insatiable drive in John and Miranda. So, naturally, they would be desperate to find out who was the father of the twins she would soon deliver. Allie knew it was only a matter of time before they put two and two together and realized she and Dylan were cohabitating. A smile cracked silently in her mind when she thought about Dylan being hauled off for questioning, and she could finally break free of his sadistic grasp.

While her mouth silently sputtered back and forth, unable to formulate a response, Dylan raised his meaty hand and struck her across her left cheek. Instantly, water filled her eyes as the pain flooded in.

"How about next time we start with that?" he demanded.

Allie rubbed her afflicted cheek, shock rippling through her body. *He's not gonna stop.*

What had initially been water formed from the impact of his hand quickly became fear-induced tears that began running down her cheeks. Her breathing deepened as she felt panic taking hold.

With her back still to the wall, Allie stood with her mouth open as she stared in Dylan's direction. Her shoulders rose and fell as she gasped through her sobbing. She was out of viable options and stuck defenseless in the hallway.

Dylan moved his hands and placed them on the wall on either side of her head on the wall He leaned into the stance. The smell of whiskey was more pungent now that he was close enough to breathe on her.

"What happened to us, Allie?" he asked, resting his forehead on her shoulder.

He drunkenly rocked back and forth, swaying as if the entire house was riding over whitecaps in the middle of the ocean. Allie trembled beneath his weight, too scared to move an inch.

The ice maker kicked on, rattling as it dropped a fresh batch of cubes into the reservoir. The sound caused Dylan to bolt upright. *Was he just asleep on my shoulder? Did I just miss an opportunity?* At that moment, Allie decided she wasn't going down without a fight.

Dylan took a step back. He swayed and grabbed the doorframe as he steadied himself. Allie looked up at him and saw the beginning of tears forming in his bloodshot eyes.

"Dyl...."

His other hand came upward as she drew a response and latched around the middle of her neck. Dylan pushed her head back as he pinned her to the wall. She moved both hands up to his as she clawed at them with the dull nails she'd been stress chewing. His grip was tight but not cinched to the point where she fought for every breath. The mix of adrenaline and fear coursing through her body was helping her lungs expand and contract.

"And what else did you tell them? I know you're not telling me everything," he whispered in her ear.

Allie again opened her mouth, but no words came out. Dylan kept his hand locked onto her throat tight. She could have spoken, but fears of him collapsing her trachea and what was to come had rendered her silent.

When no words came from her mouth, he finally released her from his grip. She sank to her knees and hit the hardwood floor. She stabilized herself on three limbs and brought one hand up to her stomach to ensure the large belly holding her twins was still there.

Fight Allie.

"Nothing, I didn't say anything else. Dylan, I swear," she finally said as she tried to resume a regular breathing pattern.

Dylan knelt next to her and placed a gentle hand on her back. He ran his fingers across her shoulder blades, down her spine, then in a circular motion just above her beltline.

"Shh, it's okay. I'm sorry," he said, slurring his s'.

Allie shuddered at his attempt at a loving touch and felt her motherly instinct kick in. *Now's the time to fight, mama bear.*

Dylan backed away from Allie, whose knees were digging into the hardwood floor, and braced himself at the doorway. He stared at her broken state.

"I'm not gonna say anything. I already told you that, and I meant it," she said firmly.

"Because you don't have anything to say?" he asked.

"Yes."

"Good."

She reached upward and used the bookshelf next to her to return to her feet. She gently shook as she tried to guess what would happen next.

As soon as she was upright, Dylan stumbled forward and again slapped her across the face. The college ring he refused to stop wearing landed on her cheekbone and split her skin.

Allie fell to her right side and caught herself when her elbow hit the bookcase that had just supported her. There were photo albums of memories the two had built lining the shelves and other trinkets they had picked up during their years together. A snow globe they got on their trip to Denver fell to the floor and shattered, creating a puddle of glass and glitter.

In a fit of rage, Allie grabbed one of the marble bookends that held up some of Dylan's college textbooks. She gripped it tight and swung it like a club in his general direction.

Her first swing missed his face. She held onto the bookend and braced herself with her hand on the shelf, fighting for every breath. He took a step back and chuckled slightly.

"Come on, Allie," he said coyly.

It's now or never.

His chuckle caused her anger to boil. Allie gripped the bookend tighter and felt one of its sharp corners dig into the meat of her palm. Dylan walked back over, thinking she didn't have any fight left.

"Come on, Allie. Just put it down," he tried to reason as he reached for the hunk of stone.

When he was within distance, Allie again swung toward him, using all her strength as she brought herself upright. This attempt landed the corner of the heavy bookend directly under Dylan's right eye.

Blood instantly came spurting out from his wound as he reached up to grab it. He groaned loudly as he collapsed to his side in the middle of the hallway and left the door to the kitchen unguarded.

Allie's flight drive kicked in. She hopped over her groaning boyfriend and darted into the bright kitchen. She was in a complete daze, and everything looked blurry. Her tunnel vision and adrenaline rush left her unable to remember where the wall-mounted phone was. *I don't see it. I don't see it.*

Her breathing was shallow and rapid as she searched. She took a deep breath and found the phone hanging on the wall in the same place that it had been for years. She snatched it off the receiver. Her fingers shook violently as she quickly dialed 911.

"Help!" she screamed, followed by slurred words when a woman finally answered.

"Ma'am, I can't understand you. Please try and slow down," the woman on the other end of the line said. "Can you please tell me where you are?"

"Help, please. I'm pregnant. Need help, my twins that need," she spoke incoherently as she choked through her labored breathing.

"Ma'am, can you please tell me your address?"

"812a Cedar."

As soon as Allie said the *R* in Cedar, she saw Dylan stepping into the doorway. He held the sizable gash she'd created underneath his eye socket as blood dripped through his fingers and covered his Nirvana shirt. The eye was already beginning to swell. He groaned as he stumbled toward Allie.

She instantly dropped the phone to the tiled floor, and it swayed back and forth by its cord. Allie surprised herself at how quickly she shuffled across the room. She snatched the largest knife out of the middle of the holder and tucked the rest of the block under her arm if she needed a backup. Shakily she pointed her weapon horizontally toward Dylan.

"Come any closer, and I swear to God I'll throw this at you or stab you with it," she screamed, hoping the person on the phone could hear the urgency of the situation.

Dylan shook his head silently and said nothing as he stared at Allie's threatening position. Blood rolled over the tops of his lips and slipped into his mouth.

Just hold him in the kitchen till they get here.

"Don't," she yelled when Dylan took one step toward her.

Allie's hand shook outward at Dylan. He took two steps back and raised both palms in a nonthreatening manner.

"Alright, alright. I'm going okay. I'm sorry it ended up this way. That was never what I wanted," he slurred as his hand returned to his wound.

Allie remained silent as Dylan moved into the hallway and stepped out of sight. Even when he was gone, the knife remained pointed at the door as she backed up and felt the edge of the counter meet the small of her back.

Sounds echoed from within the crawlspace as he retreated down the hallway. The jingle of keys followed by the loud slam of the door allowed her to catch her breath.

Fear continued rippling from her body even after she heard the screeching sound of tires pulling away from the curb. She lowered her shaking hands but kept a firm grip on the knife as she slowly inched toward the doorframe where Dylan had just been standing. She held her breath and count to five as she listened. *Nothing.*

With no tact, she stuck her head through the frame and gazed down the long dark corridor that seemed to stretch out for a mile. The front door was shut, and from what she could gather in the dark hallway, Dylan was nowhere to be seen.

Allie slowly stepped back into the kitchen and sank down onto the floor near the phone. She set the knife block down near her hip. Her breasts moved up and down as she began to gasp for breath and finally felt the pain from her cheek wound. *He's gone.*

"Hello? Ma'am, are you there? Hello," she could hear the woman's voice calling through the phone's earpiece.

Allie raised her shaking hands from the floor. She positioned one on top of her stomach and the other near her rib cage. She counted by twos and tried to slow her breathing to a normal rhythmic pace.

"Kick, babies, please kick for me," she cried as she leaned her head back and concentrated on trying to find even the tiniest movement.

She desperately begged through her tears for any form of a motion to come from her stomach. The babies were all she had left of what had been her beautiful life with Jake, and she couldn't bear the thought of losing them too. *Please be okay.*

Allie waited on the cold floor of the kitchen she and Dylan had once enjoyed cooking in together back when they were happy. Now it was a scene from one of the worst days of her life.

"Please, please," she continually muttered as tears ran down her cheeks in wide paths. Their lack of movement grew more worrisome for her the longer she sat there and experienced no internal flutters.

"Ma'am, they are almost there. Just hold on, okay?" the dispatcher said over the line.

Allie grabbed the dangling phone and shakily brought it up to her ear. It took everything she had to stop sobbing for a moment and speak.

"Please tell them to hurry," she cleared her throat. "I can't feel my babies moving."

"I promise you they are coming, just keep talking to me," she said in a soft, calming manner.

"I just don't, don't know," Allie stopped and leaned her head back as her quiet tears turned into a roaring sob.

"Ma'am, I'm here. Talk to me," the woman coached.

She had yet to feel any movement beneath her hands, and her anxiety doubled as every minute passed. She released the phone and allowed it to dance back and forth on its leash as it hung loosely. *Come on, babies. Do it for me. We're gonna be okay. Just hang in there.*

As her finger passed just below her navel, she felt the tiniest of kicks, a flutter that she would have mistaken for a bout of gas months ago, but now, it was a glimmer of hope.

Allie twitched slightly from the contact but didn't dare move. Moving might cause the twins to adjust, and she would never know if the movement was real or not. She stared down at her stomach and prayed the motion wasn't a figment of her imagination. *Another, please.* She closed her eyes and waited as she silently prayed.

After feeling two more soft nudges from varying sides of her abdomen, she smiled and laughed through the tears still cascading from her swollen eyes.

"You're okay," she whispered through her crying. "You're both okay."

She leaned back into the cabinets.

"Thank you. God, thank you," she said as she looked downwards and rubbed her belly from top to bottom.

TWENTY-EIGHT

JOHN

JOHN WAS HEADING toward Allie's house when he heard the dispatcher's voice coming across his dash-mounted radio. He'd been caught up in the office all afternoon, digging through the Thacker file and skimming the contents to refresh his memory. But now, he finally had some time to spare. He was planning on driving by Allie's house to make his own assumptions about the pieces of the story she was refusing to share.

The blanket broadcast called for any cars in the area of Cedar Street. At first, John didn't pay any attention. He was off duty and working on his own issue. But then, "pregnant woman with twins" caught his attention and struck a chord. *No, it can't be.*

He flipped a switch and turned on the light bar mounted inside his windshield.

"This is Waters #343. I can be there in less than a minute," he said over the radio.

John pushed on the gas pedal harder, and the engine roared as it shifted to the next gear. Within a few seconds, his speed had doubled as he drove down the city roads and hurried to an address he'd driven by countless times before. His heart raced in his chest. He was worried Allie had done something to hurt herself.

Various other officers chimed into the call and weren't far behind John. But he wanted to get there first.

The brakes skidded as he pulled up to the duplex and threw the car in park. The front porch sat still and illuminated by a single porch light, nothing looked amiss. John was the first person on the scene.

Flashing blue and white lights bounced off the houses that lined the road, the darkness making them almost blinding. As he climbed out of the car, he saw a curtain move out of the corner of his eye and looked up to see children peeking out of a nearby second-story window, hoping to see something interesting.

John left his car parked in the street, blocking the right of way, and unholstered his pistol. He ran toward the left of the double-sided building.

He stood bracing himself with the house and grabbed the door handle. With a twist and turn, he pushed the door open and repositioned both hands on his firearm.

He turned into the house, gun raised, and scanned the entryway. The floor creaked beneath him and echoed down the hall. The weight of the weapon in his hand was nerve-wracking. Besides his trip to the range for annual qualifying, John hadn't shot it in years.

After a closet and entryway table, the foyer opened up. There was a straight staircase to the right and a small living room on his left, both cloaked in darkness. John turned into the room and worked through the corners. *Empty.*

A soft glow poured out of a doorway at the end of the hall.

"Hello. Hello, Allie?" John yelled as he moved toward the light.

After speaking, he stopped and pressed his lips in a long silent line. He held his breath and took in the stillness as his heart thudded deep in his chest. His ears rang from the ominous silence.

"Back here." A muffled crying voice broke through the silence.

John hurried down the corridor with his pistol still in the ready position, heading toward the low voice in the back of the house.

When he reached the end of the hall, he put his toes on the frame and pivoted into the room. With his finger elongated on the trigger guard, he scanned from left to right and only saw a typical kitchen.

Behind a table, Allie was sitting on the floor near the phone that hung loosely from the wall. Her hands were resting lightly on her stomach as she sobbed uncontrollably. Her crying escalated when she looked up and laid eyes on John. A small smile broke across her face, and she began to chuckle through her tears.

John paused his advance momentarily and looked closer at her. The beginnings of a large purple bruise were forming under her eye, and the redness on her neck looked as though someone had their hands firmly wrapped around it. A sizable amount of blood was sprayed on her t-shirt in a messy pattern, but he only saw a small gash on her cheekbone. *Who's blood?*

He kept his pistol ready and chest facing the room's only entrance. Using the wall as support, he sank into a squatting position next to Allie. He placed a hand on her shoulder. At the feeling of his touch, Allie flinched slightly and pushed her back further into the cabinet.

"Sorry, sorry," he said as he pulled his hand back and flashed his palms toward her innocently. "Talk to me. Are you okay?"

Allie swallowed the growing lump in her throat and took a deep breath before she was able to respond.

"I, I, I think so," she finally sputtered out.

"Okay, just relax. There's an ambulance on the way. They're almost here. Who did this?"

Allie's head fell into her hands as she resumed crying.

"It was Dylan. My... my boyfriend," she muttered through her tears.

"Okay. And is he still in the house? Do you know where he is now?" John groaned as he stood up. The suspect could still be in the house.

"He um, he's gone. We got into a fight, and he ran out."

"Okay, that's good. Just try and relax."

John took a knee next to Allie while they waited for medical help to arrive. She remained seated as her tears continued falling. As much as he wanted to ask what happened, try and pry something out of her, he remained silent. *Now isn't the time.* The broken woman before him was in no state to begin answering the thousands of questions lingering in his mind.

The two sat there in the home's quiet while they waited for the ambulance. John saw little smiles pop across Allie's face a couple of times as she gazed lovingly at her stomach.

"They kickin'?" John asked.

Allie simply nodded, returning them back to silence.

A few minutes later, the wailing sirens of deputy cars and an ambulance finally grew louder as they pulled up in front of the house.

"They're here. Do you hear them? You're gonna be okay," John assured her.

Footsteps echoed at the front of the house as deputies stepped through the door and began searching the house. Just as protocol dictated, they were working room by room, but John wanted them to hurry.

"We're in here," John called out to them. He stood to go toward his fellow deputies, and Allie grabbed his wrist.

"Please don't go. You can't leave me."

"Okay, sorry," John replied as he sat back down. Her grip tightened on his arm.

Tears began to stream down Allie's cheeks as she smiled. Two uniformed men entered the room, and upon seeing John, they holstered their weapons. Allie nodded that it was okay, and John stepped away to talk to them. Three EMTs followed and helped Allie up as they took her out to their vehicle to evaluate her and the babies.

After giving the other first responders the few details he had, John nosed around the house while trying not to disturb anything. Pictures of Allie and a man he assumed to be her boyfriend, Dylan, were adorning the shelves and lining the walls in the hallway. Everything looked normal. There was a *live, laugh, love* sign, loveseat with a crocheted blanket, and two sets of slippers near the front door. *His and hers.* All mundane things you would expect to see in the house of a young couple.

John called one of the junior detectives and asked her to start taking pictures and bagging up the evidence. He specifically pointed to the coffee mug on the table and the bloody bookend that sat at the end of the hallway.

He stepped outside and watched from the sidewalk as the experts spent ten minutes checking Allie out and making sure she and the babies were safe to transport. When they cleared her, she was put on a stretcher and loaded into the back of an ambulance.

Just as John turned around to walk back to his car to provide an escort, Allie called to him.

"John," she said somewhat weakly as she sat up on the stretcher. "Would you ride with us?"

He mulled over his response as he tried to gather his current thoughts about Allie. For nearly a year now she had been lying to him, hiding what she knew. But she was a scared woman with a story that John wanted to hear, so he politely offered a counter.

"How about I meet you there, I don't wanna leave my car in the middle of the road," he replied with a soft chuckle.

"Okay," Allie said. She flashed him a slight grin before grimacing from her emerging shiner. "Thank you."

TWENTY-NINE

JOHN

THE LATE SPRING winds pushed John's car side to side along the town's road as if they were playing with him. He took the lead in escorting the ambulance to the hospital, lights flashing and speeding through reds.

When he had pulled up to Allie's, he heard a second call on the radio, calling for assistance with a fender bender. As he passed by the accident location, he saw a giant blob of blue lights at the end of the road. *Kinda overkill for a little bump.* He shrugged and continued heading toward the hospital.

With time to think, he began to formulate his own story. He believed the babies Allie was carrying were Jake's and hoped she would fess up to the paternity when her boyfriend was found and brought up on domestic violence charges. She didn't have anything left to lose.

A puff of air buzzed through his lips as he shook his head slightly at the amount of drama he quickly found himself wrapped up in. The easy transition into retirement seemed to be further away as he again got himself involved in Allie's affairs.

"Miranda, Allie, Piper, Jake, and now some guy named Dylan?" he asked himself with a confused look. "What the hell have you gotten yourself into, John?"

The bright white and red lights of the county hospital came into view. A beacon of safety on the hill. John escorted the ambulance to the front door and brought his car to a stop. Four medical personnel rushed out of the building to accept the transfer of Allie.

John climbed out of the car and walked over to the back of the ambulance. Allie was being unloaded, a faint smile on her face.

"Still doing okay?" he asked.

"For now," she replied.

"I'd like to talk to you when you're ready."

"I figured."

"Sir, we will come and get you once we've checked her out. Okay?" one of the nurses said.

"Alright. Thank you. I'll be in in a minute."

Allie was quickly carted off through the hospital's entrance, and the doors shut with a hydraulic hiss. John took a deep breath and leaned against the trunk of his car. *You really made a mess of things, Jake.*

He stood under the building's protective overhang and closed his eyes while he listened to the rattling of the ambulance's diesel engine running. Even if it took all night, John was determined to weasel his way into Allie's room and finally get to the bottom of the story he believed she knew.

Foliage separated the emergency unloading area from the visitor parking lot, and some of the plants had begun to bloom. John meticulously picked a couple of flowers from the blossoming spring bushes to take home to his wife. He felt terrible for flaking out on her retirement planning meeting and thought maybe a couple of wildflowers would make up for his absence.

As he dropped the loose bouquet into the empty cup in his cup holder, a second group of emergency vehicles pulled into the bay.

The escorting deputy fumbled with his dash before getting his screeching siren to turn off. Just as John rounded the back of the ambulance, the white double doors swung open, and the EMTs quickly jumped out of the back. An additional team came rushing out of the building, pushing a medical cart.

"He's in and out," the EMT in the back of the ambulance yelled to the nurse that arrived at the stretcher first. She pressed her fingers to his wrist and found a pulse.

John peered around the corner of the vehicle and saw the mangled body of a man lying lifeless on the stretcher. Blood was everywhere, and there were multiple deep lacerations on his face and arms. His breathing was severely labored due to the giant chunk of metal lodged in his chest.

"My God," John said quietly to himself.

"Sir?" the deputy called out to him and redirected his attention.

"Yeah, sorry. What's up, Austin?" he replied as his attention shifted. "You handle that? What happened?"

"That was the alleged fender bender on Moss Street," Austin replied.

"Looks like a little more than a fender bender to me," John responded.

"Yeah, the guy wrapped his SUV around a light pole and wasn't wearing a seatbelt. We could smell the whiskey on his breath as soon as we neared the car."

"Geez, yeah, sounds like someone reported it wrong."

"But you want to know what the interesting part is?" Austin led.

I'm not sure I can handle any more interesting tonight.

"Well, spit it out," John encouraged.

"His ID has the address of the house we were responding to when we got diverted to help him. The Cedar Street house."

John looked at him while he pondered what he was saying and putting together the puzzle pieces in his mind.

"Is his name Dylan?" John asked as he looked at the driver being pushed on a gurney across the hospital's threshold.

"Yes, sir," Austin replied.

A wave of clarity rushed into John's head.

"Post a deputy outside of his door. We've probably got him on a felony DUI, and we might just get to tack on the murder of Deputy Thacker," he instructed.

"What?" Austin replied.

"Just do it."

"Yes, sir," he responded as he rushed off to follow the unconscious suspect.

John gently bit his bottom lip as he watched the deputy chase down the man's stretcher. If this played out as he hoped, his suspect had been right under his nose the whole time. *How the hell did you miss him?*

THIRTY

JOHN

JOHN WALKED INTO the hospital and used the phone at the nurse's station to make a call. Within a few minutes, he'd received approval from a local judge to pull DNA from Dylan and called the lab to make sure they were checking the cup found at the scene. They would attempt to match it to the archived cells from under Jake's nails and use his prints to cross-check the partial from the clock. *It's gotta be a match. It all makes sense.*

"Sir, she's ready for you," a young nurse said as she grabbed John from the waiting room.

"Thank you," he responded as he stood.

He followed the woman in clean navy scrubs through double doors. The white walls and fluorescent lights blinded him as she weaved around the building. She took John on what felt like a tour of the entire hospital before guiding him up two flights of stairs. They finally came to the maternity ward.

"She's right down there, sir," the nurse said as she pointed down the hall to a room where a deputy was sitting in a chair just outside the door.

John thanked the nurse and headed down toward Allie.

"Sir," the deputy said with a smile.

"Hey. Can I go in?" John asked, not that he really needed permission from the new deputy. A nod answered his question.

John stood at the door for a moment and allowed a bout of fear to creep in. All the things he had spent months working on then tucking to the back of his mind had reemerged all in one day. It felt like too much to handle, but he anxiously awaited to hear incriminating words spill from Allie's mouth. He hoped that a conversation with her would close out the Thacker case.

Here we go. He turned the handle and stepped into the room.

Monitors beeped from every direction as the various machines hooked up to Allie worked. The room was cold and had a sharp smell of disinfectant. A shiver slipped from his shoulders to his fingertips as he stepped closer to the reclined bed.

"Hey," Allie said quietly from the side rail bed they had her tucked warmly inside.

"Hi," John returned.

John looked away and glanced around the room. It had been years since he'd been in a hospital. He looked at the wide strap looped tightly around Allie's belly.

"It's just the babies' monitor," she stated.

"Ah, gotcha," he responded as he cleared his throat.

"Do you wanna sit?"

"Uh, sure, yeah."

John walked over to the side of the bed and pulled up the single-seat chair that looked like it belonged in a stuffy waiting room. His knees popped as he lowered down and sat on the lumpy cushion.

"So," John stated.

"So?" Allie returned.

"So, are you ready to talk about what happened tonight? And are you ready to tell me about anything else you know?"

Allie brought her hands up and rested them on her belly that poked out from beneath the white hospital sheets. She rubbed up and down as John watched a small smile spread across her face.

"They're fine," she said.

"Good, I'm glad to hear that," he returned sincerely. *Guess I should've asked.*

She stopped looking at her stomach and directed her attention to John. Her chest heaved as tears welled up in her eyes. She silently shook her head in his direction and frowned at him.

"They're Jake's," she finally choked out.

Holy shit.

"Okay, so tell me more then. I know you have something that you aren't telling me," John said as he pulled out his faithful breast pocket notepad.

Allie looked away, and her head fell back into the pillow of her angled bed. Her hands left her stomach and came up to her eyes as John listened to her sob. He sat patiently and waited for her to speak.

"I didn't... I just didn't know what to do," she said as she spoke through the gaps in her fingers.

"Do about what?"

Using her elbows on the mattress, Allie sat upright and crossed her legs beneath her stomach. The back of her hands rubbed across her eyes, and she winced when she brushed her thumb against her bruised cheek.

"It's uh, a long story," she said as she rubbed her hand across the top of her head and through her hair.

"I'm ready whenever you are. I don't have anywhere else to be," John replied with a click of his pen.

"It was Dylan. All of it was Dylan. At least, I think. I'm pretty sure it was," she explained, then took a deep breath. "I woke up and uh felt like complete shit."

THIRTY-ONE

ALLIE

ALLIE QUIETLY BOUNDED down the stairs of her two-story duplex and locked herself in the half bath tucked beneath the steps. She dropped to her knees, threw her head into the toilet, and vomited violently. Her hair hung loosely in waves around the outside of the bowl as she heaved.

Even though her stomach ached, it was completely empty. She'd only picked at her food at dinner the night before, and when she thought about it, she realized she had skipped lunch. All her body could muster was burning acid to discard.

When her puking stopped, she sat against the wall with her knees at her chest and wiped her mouth. Her head throbbed as she closed her eyes and tried to relax. *Alright, suck it up.*

She used the vanity to pull herself up and stared at the person she saw. The same girl she had always known stood gazing back at her, but she was different. Her eyes were swollen to the point puffy bags had begun to form underneath them, and her skin looked disheveled. The rapidly changing hormones were causing her acne to flare up. *So much for "glowing."*

Between her heightened emotional state and the stress of her life problems compounding, she had been in a constant state of tears for close to two weeks.

The chaotic mess she saw in the mirror was a girl who threw her hopes and dreams out of the window the night before after finding out the man she loved was dead. She closed her eyes and leaned forward on her palms as she braced herself on the countertop. Her thoughts were scattered as she relived the moments that felt like a lifetime ago but had happened less than twenty-four hours earlier.

ALLIE RAN TO the phone in the kitchen as it rang, hoping it was Jake.

"Hello?" Allie said in her usual peppy voice.

"Hey babe," she heard Jake over the line. A smile illuminated her face, and she breathed a sigh of relief. The clock on the microwave read 10:47. *Dylan's at work.* She twirled the phone cord with her index finger.

The night before, she'd told Jake she was pregnant, and he left asking for time to digest the news. He promised he would, but she wasn't sure he'd call.

If he'd picked Miranda over her, she'd understand. Leaving his wife and child for a random girl he'd knocked up didn't make sense. But that would leave her back at square one, trying to decide where her life would go next.

But he called. *He's choosing me.*

The stress was heavy in his voice. He explained that he broke the news about their affair to Miranda. She pictured him pacing, phone in one hand, the other in his hair, tousling it into a mess. For a moment, she felt guilty, like this was all her fault. *No, Jake wants this too.*

"I haven't told her about the baby," he said.

"Are you going to?" Allie returned.

"Yeah, eventually. I just gotta make sure the time is right. I just wanna be with you," he said, causing a chill to roll over her shoulders. "I know it won't be easy, but we'll figure it out."

The more she said it, the more their situation (a man leaving his wife and child for his pregnant mistress) sounded like the Monday afternoon feature on a telenovela. It was going to be messy, but Jake and their soon-to-be family was worth it.

"Good, I'm glad. I wanna be with you too."

Allie smiled, realizing she was getting everything she wanted. She'd landed her dream man and was on the brink of starting a family. Being with Jake got her out of the monotonous life she had created with someone she no longer loved.

Jake was doing the same thing. As bad as she felt for being the home-wrecker that broke up a small family, she knew he wasn't happy. But he deserved to be, and she wanted to be the one to brighten his day. *If we can be together, we'll both be happy.*

Jake said Miranda had left the house after he admitted to the affair. They planned to sit down with her in the coming weeks to hash out some details moving forward. Treading carefully was important. He didn't want to lose any rights or time with his daughter.

A few months into their relationship, Jake had brought Piper to a few of their playground meetups, and Allie quickly took a liking to the toddler. Knowing they had a future together, her heart beamed when she thought about her new role as a stepmom.

"I love you. I'll call you tomorrow," Jake said as their phone call ended.

"Okay. I love you too," she replied with a smile. She hung up the phone and grabbed a soda to settle her morning sickness.

On the fridge, there was a picture of her and Dylan at Disney World, standing in front of Cinderella's castle. His arm was draped over her shoulders, and she was beaming with happiness. *Oh, how things have changed.*

"Dammit," she said when she realized she would have to break the news to her boyfriend.

She didn't expect Dylan would be heartbroken when she said it was over. Not that he'd be relieved or happy, but okay with it, willing to move on without a fight. The last few years they'd spent together had been almost a blur while they both avoided admitting their relationship had run its course.

Allie sat on the couch, her leg bouncing up and down from her nerves, waiting for Dylan to come home for his lunch break. The kitchen faucet was still leaking, and she could hear every drop echoing down the hallway. *You have to do this.*

A car stopped at the curb, and a door slammed shut. Allie's back went stiff as a board. She held her breath and listened to his keys fumbling with the lock. It finally gave way, and Dylan broke the threshold. He set his keys down and took a step before seeing Allie sitting in the living room with the TV turned off.

"Hey. Um, what are you doing?" he asked with a confused expression.

An enormous pit formed in Allie's stomach when she looked over at him. She tried to spit out the story she had rehearsed countless times but remained silent.

"Helloooo?" he asked.

Allie shook her head and offered a tentative smile.

"Hey," she replied.

Dylan looked at her as his eyebrows edged closer to one another. She stared back, blank-faced.

"Are you gonna say something?" He began to walk toward her, and Allie sprung out of her seat.

"Lunch break?" Allie asked.

"Uh, yeah," he replied, still vaguely perplexed.

She stepped in front of him in the hallway and started walking backward.

"So, uh could we talk for a second?" she asked

"Sure? What's up?" Dylan responded.

The two continued their momentum toward the kitchen at the end of the hall while Allie kept backtracking. She smiled at Dylan and took a couple of deep breaths while trying to rattle off the speech she had recited in her head close to ten times. Even though she knew what to say, ending a seven-year relationship was hard.

"Um, I just think we need to talk about us," she explained.

Dylan rolled his eyes and pushed past Allie, taking a direct route to the fridge.

"Come on. Do we have to do this right this second? What is it this time?" he asked, pulling out cold cuts and cheese.

"Yes, right now," she returned, knowing that Jake had already talked to Miranda. *Once I tell Dylan, we'll both be free.*

"All right then. Get on with it," he replied, rotating his hand around in a charismatic motion.

"Okay, um, well, Dylan, I think you and I both know that this relationship has changed a lot over the years," she said. Dylan sat down with his plain ham and cheese sandwich. "It's not either of our faults. But we've grown apart over the years, and I don't think we make each other happy like we did years ago. I know there's someone out there that would make you happy for years to come, and I don't wanna hurt you. But, I don't think this is working anymore." *Why did I say years like fifteen times?*

Dylan squinted in her direction and gently bit on his bottom lip as if he were confused. Allie's breathing quickened as she waited for his response.

"So, basically, what you're saying is that you're breaking up with me?" he asked casually.

"Yeah, I guess I kind of am," Allie admitted. She shoved her hands into her pockets to hide her trembling.

He sat quietly for a moment, then chewed another bite of his sandwich.

"Honestly, is there someone else? And I swear to God, Allie, you better not lie to me. At this point, I'm pretty sure I deserve the truth."

Allie's bottom lip quivered, but no words came out. Lying would be easy. But, in a small town like Butte, it would only be a matter of time before Dylan caught wind of their affair and her pregnancy. Maybe it would hurt less if she admitted it up front.

"Yeah," she finally said.

Dylan gently nodded his head, adjusted himself at the table, and took another bite of his sandwich. He looked toward the picture window in the back of the duplex and remained eerily silent while he chewed his food.

Allie watched him and waited for a response; anger, sadness, acceptance, something. But instead of lashing out or saying he understood, he just stared at the afternoon storm brewing for close to two minutes while he finished his sandwich without uttering a word. After taking the last bite, he rose from the table and placed his plate in the sink.

Silently, Dylan strolled across the room, closing the gap between them until he was directly in front of Allie. He stood so close she caught hints of his Old Spice deodorant and saw the hairs he had missed that morning when he'd shaved. His eyes stared into hers, slightly darting left to right, with his lips squeezed into a tight line. She looked at his face, trying to read his expression.

Without saying a word, Dylan reached out and pushed Allie up against the kitchen wall forcefully. Every muscle in her body tightened when she realized he was laying a violent hand on her for the first time.

"Do you maybe wanna talk about this some other time?" Dylan asked.

Fear surged through Allie's body. She trembled beneath the hand on her shoulder that had her pinned firmly to the wall. Her head shook sideways and up and down while her voice remained caught in her throat.

Dylan's other hand reached up and pushed her jaw closed before laying across her lips and covering her mouth with his palm.

"Now, let's try this again. Don't you think maybe we should talk about this tonight?" he repeated.

Allie stood silently against the wall. Large tears formed in her eyes and rolled down her cheeks. She was utterly terrified, and she couldn't find the right words to respond.

"Mhm," she mumbled through his hand and gently nodded her head.

Dylan released his hand from her mouth and raised it in frustration. Allie cowered, believing it was aimed to hit her.

"Please, don't. I'm pregnant," she admitted. She bent over to protect her stomach and raised a hand toward him.

As he'd intended, Dylan grabbed the back of his neck and took two steps back. His angry expression was instantly replaced with sadness as his face twisted into a frown. Dylan realized that his girlfriend of seven years was pregnant with a baby that might not be his.

"Wait. What?" he asked.

"I'm really sorry. It wasn't supposed to happen this way, but I want to be with him." Her voice shook as she spoke through her tears.

"How. How do you know that baby's not mine?" he asked as he pointed at her flat stomach.

"I. I...," Allie stuttered out while searching for the right words.

He was right. She wasn't sure who the father was. But, it didn't make a difference. She wanted to be with Jake and was pretty confident the baby was his.

"I said, how do you know that baby's not mine," Dylan repeated as his voice rose.

Allie flattened her palms against the drywall. Her body trembled while her mind searched for the right words to calm him down. Dylan took a few steps to her left and then to the right as he ran his fingers through his hair.

"Dammit. Answer me, Allie!" he yelled, using his hands as tools for emphasis.

She shrank at his elevated voice.

"I don't know, okay! I just don't know," she screamed out as her tears turned into sobbing.

The truth had come out quickly. What she had meant to say was *I just know it's his.* Which also wasn't very convincing.

Dylan cracked a faint smile and stopped pacing. He walked over to Allie and brushed a wispy bang from her eye. He smiled at her as if nothing was wrong.

"Okay then. We can figure this out. But I can tell you one thing, you're not leaving me while you're pregnant with my child. That baby comes out, and it's not mine; that's a different story. But until you know that for sure, I refuse to let you go. And I promise, you don't wanna try. Got it?" he asked in a creepy and threatening tone.

Allie felt like her eyes were going to explode. She nodded her head in short bursts.

"Who is he?"

"Dylan," she pleaded. Her shoulders dropped.

"Allie, you tell me who he is! I need to know," he yelled, slamming a fist on the doorframe.

Her entire body flinched at his aggression.

"His name is Jake," she replied.

"Jake, who?"

"Thacker, Thacker. Jake Thacker."

Dylan shook his head gently and went over to the sink. He rinsed the crumbs and mayo off his plate and put it in the dishwasher. A soft smile cracked across his lips as he passed by Allie and walked toward the living room.

The subtle suck of the couch broke the silence as Dylan sat down and flipped on a show. Fear kept Allie glued to the spot on the wall. She was scared to walk away, scared to stay, and scared of Dylan for the first time in her life. Something in the tone of his voice caused her to shiver and feel a chilling fear creep up her back.

"Hey, do I need to drop you off at work, or is Malisa coming to pick you up?" Dylan hollered from the living room.

"Muh, Malisa is going to get me," she finally sputtered out.

"Okay, cool," he responded.

Allie left the kitchen and hurried past the entrance to the living room, hearing Dylan chuckle at whatever he was watching on TV. She climbed the stairs to the second floor and ran into their bedroom, and shut and locked the door.

She slumped down against the nearby wall and pulled her knees into her chest. She cried until her eyes felt like they had run dry, and she had to blink through the swollenness.

"No, no. Please no," she whispered.

While sitting in her vulnerable position on the floor, the door handle jiggled. When it didn't give, Dylan knocked.

"Hey, Allie. I'm heading back to work. I'll see you tonight when you get home," he said casually, as if nothing had just transpired between them.

Allie sat quietly behind the closed door and heard his footsteps head back down the stairs. Her whole body jerked when she heard the front door slam and the ignition of his SUV turn over.

She stayed on the floor and cried for five minutes. *Now what? He's going to want to talk about it when I get home.* It had been hard enough to say the words she already had. What more could she come up with to say later?

Going to work after what just happened was the last thing she wanted to do. But, Allie stood and got ready for her evening shift at the restaurant. She was unsure of what her future looked like and knew she would need money to make sure it worked out for her and her baby.

Allie washed her face and applied a light dusting of powder and colored in her eyebrows. She avoided adding any mascara or eyeliner. *It'll get figured out.*

With a deep breath in and then out, she put on her work uniform and looked at herself in the mirror. The cheerful and welcoming persona she usually had at work was replaced with a look of sadness and frustration. But money was waiting.

She donned a winter coat and stepped out of the house.

"Hey, what's wrong?" Malisa asked with a concerned face when she saw Allie's swollen eyes.

"Nothing. Just some BS drama with my family," Allie responded as she climbed into her friend's blue Ford Escort.

Allie sat in the passenger seat and stared out the window while she contemplated how to get Dylan to accept their situation. *He has to let me go. Right?*

THIRTY-TWO

JOHN

A **KNOCK CAUSED** llie to stop talking. Someone in scrubs cracked the door and peeked inside. Allie nodded her head, *it's okay*, and John cursed under his breath as the doctor entered the room.

They were just getting to the good part of the story, the part he thought would provide some answers, and the interruption had come at the worst time.

John sat quietly and grinned at the woman. She smiled back, fiddled with the IV bags, and grabbed a sheet of paper nearly a mile long that had been slowly spilling out of a printer.

The doctor touched Allie's belly and spoke just above a whisper while Allie nodded in response. John tried not to listen, but the quietness of the room caused even the faintest of sounds to echo. He caught *the twins are great*, and *mucus plug in place*. He looked away and hummed softly to avoid hearing any more.

When the woman left the room, John went right back to his questioning. Allie looked over. She appeared to have calmed down significantly since he found her on the floor in her kitchen. Her face had softened, and there was no longer a terror-stricken look in her eyes.

"So, you told him about Jake," John stated. "And how did he react when you got home?"

"Well, I didn't even see him until later that night. I did call Jake from the restaurant, as I told you, but he didn't answer. But I didn't go home and call him from the house like I said. I was at work the entire time. I don't know who called him," she explained.

"So why did you lie?"

"I assumed Dylan must've made the call. I was just trying to keep him out of it when I lied to you. Because this is what happened when he thought I said something."

With both hands, she motioned from her head to her toes.

"But why lie for him? He threatened you," he replied.

"I know, I know, and it all seems so incredibly stupid now that I look back on it. But I just didn't know what else to do," she said as a floodgate of tears hiding behind her eyes opened. "I mean, he legitimately scared me. And he threatened the babies and me," she responded as she stroked her stomach. "I don't have much, and with Jake gone, I didn't know what else to do. I thought he would hurt the babies and me, or worse."

"You could have come to us," John explained.

"I know, I know that now, okay?" she replied as she wiped her eyes with the back of her hand. "I was just scared. No, I was terrified."

She sat silently in her bed for a moment and just listened to the rhythmic beating of the army of machines. They played in a rhythmic beat that had begun to sound like the opening to Queen's *We Will Rock You*.

"I don't have anything. Yeah, I have my house, but besides that, I have nothing. Dylan made all the money and paid all the bills. I wasn't planning on staying with him, but I was trying to save up enough money to make sure we would be okay when I finally came forward. It's stupid, I know, but it's the only thing I could think of," she explained.

Her tears escalated as she talked. John took down hurried notes as she continued spilling information.

"Don't you have parents or something? A family member that we can call?" John offered.

"Yeah, I mean kind of. They live in Kalispell. But they would have shamed me like a whore for getting pregnant," she cried. "I haven't told them. We don't talk much. I'm young and stupid. I felt stuck, okay? I can't justify it any more than that."

John couldn't imagine his daughter being alone and pregnant in a hospital room. He suddenly felt a wave of sympathy for Allie. *She really has no one.*

"I'm not trying to call you stupid. Just tell me what happened when you came home from work," John prompted.

"Okay," Allie responded as she leaned her head back and dug for the details she had tried to forget.

THIRTY-THREE

ALLIE

ALLIE STARED INTO the TV and became mesmerized by its blankness. The dead channel she'd landed on provided nothing but a pixelated black and white screen and scratchy static. She kept her eyes on the glass and sat on the couch, waiting for Dylan to come home. *He should have been home by now. He probably went out for drinks, and I'll have to go pick him up, dammit.* She didn't want to have the rest of the conversation with him intoxicated.

She was ready to hear him out but didn't want to fight. Even if he begged her to stay, she was determined that she didn't want to try to fix things with him. It was time for them both to move on. Their relationship had run its course, and Dylan needed to understand that.

The easiest way it could go would be for him to accept that things were over and agree to move out of the house. Or it could go like it had that afternoon; anger, tears, violence.

A soft smile peeked on her lips when she thought about selling her modest duplex and sharing a home with Jake, Piper, and their bubbly addition in the not-so-distant future. Allie had seen a picture of Jake's house in the woods once and couldn't wait to see it in person.

Trying to remember the look of the place, she crafted a beautiful image of the four of them, *the new Thacker family*.

She saw quick little feet in rubber rainboots playing in the yard into the evening when the summer sun refused to set until close to ten. Jake kissed her on top of her head and smiled while they watched their girls chasing butterflies and shrieking at spiders.

In the winter, she imagined him building a roaring fire in the hearth and the flames dancing and reflecting in his pupils as they sipped hot cocoa in the living room. It was a real family. A family she loved and one who loved her back. *It's so close.*

The faint creaking of the front door awoke Allie from her charming daydream and snapped her back to the troubled reality she lived. The room was dark, and a musty smell hung in the air. *He's home. Now what?*

"Dammit," Dylan whispered as he fumbled trying to pull his keys from the lock. "Thank you," he said when he pulled them out.

He walked into the house.

Allie turned toward the sound as Dylan stepped into the soft glow emitting from the screen. Upon seeing his silhouetted figure enter the room, Allie stood from her seat, ready to talk and prepared to fight.

"Hey," she said.

Dylan didn't respond and hung his head low. Allie could hear labored breathing.

"Dylan?" she asked.

"What?" he snapped, in a tone, she couldn't interpret.

Allie flipped on the floor lamp beside her and brought light to the room. Dylan squinted as his eyes adjusted. Allie gasped and covered her mouth with her hands.

Blood was sprayed haphazardly across his shoulder and collected in deep maroon circles near his collar bone. A disheveled look darkened his gaze. A bruise had begun forming beneath one of his eyes as he stared blankly at Allie.

Her hands began trembling, and she pushed them into her cheekbones. She shook her head, and her stomach sank into her pelvis, knowing whose blood was sprayed on her boyfriend.

"What... What did you do?" she asked.

"Nothing."

"Dylan. What did you do?" she repeated, raising her voice slightly.

No, no. Please don't say it. Please. Not Jake.

"You don't wanna know," he responded as he broke eye contact. He picked at a spot of dry blood on his thumb. "It was an accident."

Tears welled up in her eyes. *Jake.*

"Dylan, no," she said as she gently shook her head.

"What? Don't even start, Allie."

"Dylan, no. Please no." Tears cascaded down her cheeks in a heavy stream.

Dylan turned away and walked toward the stairs with a scoff. She chased after him, catching a faint whiff of gasoline every time he lifted his foot.

"Dylan, tell me. What did you do?" she screamed at him as he continued up the stairs. He trudged on without so much as a mumble, holding onto his silence and continuing toward their bedroom.

Allie followed him, skipping stairs as she tried to catch up. Her lungs felt small and constricted. Every breath was a chore.

Dylan made it to the landing and stopped. Allie was right behind him, her tears still falling but words trapped in her throat. When she too stepped

315

onto the second floor, Dylan turned around and tightly grabbed her by the shoulders. His grip instantly loosened as if he was worried about scaring her. His eyes looked softer than they had downstairs. He hung his head, took a deep breath then looked up to face Allie.

"Listen to me, okay. Are you listening?" he asked.

Allie simply nodded.

"Stop crying, okay? Please," Dylan said. He used a thumb to wipe the tears from her cheeks. She flinched at his touch, and he removed both hands from her shoulders and placed them by his side.

Allie looked into his familiar eyes. She saw both sadness and regret. He, too, looked like he'd been crying.

"Wh... what happened?" she stammered.

Dylan knocked at the sides of his head with his fists and swayed gently.

"Just don't. I swear to God it was an accident. But I'm not gonna lose you, Allie. For your sake and our baby's sake, I want you to keep your mouth shut. Nothing happened."

"But, what do you mean?" Allie asked.

"You're not leaving me," he added.

A hostile glare reentered his eyes and caused a chill to shoot down her spine. She realized he was threatening her.

"Got it?" he asked.

Allie gently shook her head. Even though she didn't want to, she understood she had no other option but to agree.

Dylan smiled softly and turned around. He walked into the bathroom, silently stripped down, put toothpaste on his toothbrush, and climbed into the shower.

When she was finally alone, Allie hit her knees at the top of the stairs. She placed a cupped hand over her mouth and sobbed as her back arched up and down. *This is my fault. It's all my fault.*

THIRTY-FOUR

JOHN RUBBED A hand across the top of his head and flattened his hair. Even though it hurt to hear, Allie was finally providing the answers he'd wanted to find months ago.

Allie sat still in the bed with her legs crossed, the machines continuing their electronic beeping and her eyes swollen with tears. She wouldn't even look in John's direction. She just stared at her hands that were slightly shaking.

"So that's all you know? He didn't tell you what happened when he was with Jake?" he asked.

"No, I'm sorry. I asked him the next day, and he told me never to bring it up again. So, I dropped it. It was clear he was serious about not talking about it," she explained.

John felt a wave of emotions as he tried to process the idea of finally finding Jake's killer. Bringing Dylan to justice would allow the Thacker family to leave town in peace and live their lives.

"Well, we're running his DNA, so we should have confirmation soon," John explained. "There were some cells found under Jake's nails. Here's to hoping it was Dylan." John raised an empty hand as if he was offering up a toast.

"What do you mean his DNA? Like from his toothbrush?" Allie asked.

"Well, we grabbed some stuff from your house. But also, he's here. He was in a pretty bad accident tonight. They brought him in an ambulance right behind you. Now, I'm not a doctor, but I'm not really sure he's gonna make it based on how he looked."

John watched Allie's face shift and her shoulders soften as a look of relief washed over her. She was petrified of him, and his death would liberate her.

"Good God. Okay. Am I safe?" she asked and looked around the room as if Dylan had snuck in and was hiding out in one of the dark corners.

"Yeah, of course. Last I heard, he was unconscious. But I'll make sure there's someone here with you round the clock."

"Thanks, John." She stared at her hands and fidgeted. "Again, I'm sorry about all of this. It's all my fault. Dylan killing Jake, me staying with him, him getting into an accident... Wait, he didn't hurt anyone else, did he?" she asked and finally made eye contact with John again.

"No, thankfully, it was just him and a wooden light pole."

"Still, it's all my fault. I should have never gotten into this mess with Jake. Then Piper would still have a father."

"Listen, there's nothing you can do about it now. So you might as well just move on from here and worry about you and them," John stated as he pointed at her belly. "Jake was a grown-ass man and made a decision as well. It takes two to tango."

Allie let out a forced chuckle.

"I'm sad he's not here with us. You know?" she added.

"Yeah, me too. He was one of the good ones."

John felt happy tears coming to his eyes but fought them off. Allie swiped a tissue across her cheeks and then beneath her nose before adding it to the growing pile near her lap.

A gentle knock on the door caused them both to turn their heads. John watched Allie tense up as if she thought Dylan would walk into the room.

"Ma'am, I'm sorry to bother you. But, you're Allie, right?" a woman in scrubs asked.

"She is. What do you need?" John asked, speaking on her behalf.

"It's about a man named Dylan. He called for you once before we put him under. The deputies said you were his girlfriend?"

"Yes," Allie coughed. "I am... was. I'm not really sure what I am now."

"Well, ma'am, I hate to be the one to share this with you, but due to his state, we're trying to contact the next of kin. They'd be the ones that could make decisions on his behalf."

"What kind of decisions? We've been together since high school. Can I decide?" Allie asked.

There was a good chance he was probably on life support and hanging on by a thread. John could tell Allie assumed the same thing. He figured she'd pull the plug without thinking twice if given a chance. That's what he would do if it were his call.

"I can't really discuss anything with you. I'm sorry. Direct family only."

"Okay. I understand. Um, his parents live in Billings. I have their number at home, but their names are Ben and Kayla Pupkiewicz. I'm sure they're listed in the phone book."

"Thank you. We'll give them a call and let them know about his situation."

"Oh, okay. Thanks," Allie returned.

The woman exited the room, and Allie faced forward, staring at a blank wall. John watched her and waited for a reaction, but she remained as still as a statue, processing the news.

"Wow," she finally said with a gentle shake of her head. "Just wow."

"I'm sorry, Allie," John said.

"What? Oh God, no. Don't be. He deserved it. I hope he's gone soon. And I hope he suffered. I don't know what I'm gonna do now when the twins come, but it's for the best. I was going to leave him anyways when I figured out what we would do."

"Yeah, but that's a lot for you to handle. A lot of loss."

She shrugged.

"I know. I'll figure it out."

The two sat in silence for a few minutes while only the rhythm of the monitors sounded. It felt uncomfortable, and John wished he could climb inside of Allie's mind and read her present thoughts.

"I'm uh gonna go make a couple of calls," John said as he excused himself from the awkwardly silent room.

THIRTY-FIVE

DYLAN

WHILE ALLIE LAID out the details of the affair and events that followed, Dylan lay in a hospital bed a level beneath her. Every inch of his body ached, and his limbs wouldn't move no matter how hard he tried. His face would twitch slightly when he focused, but it was a chore that caused a surge of pain to run through his head when he tried to open his eyes.

The fluorescent light hanging above his body burned his pupils when he managed to crack his eyelids. He kept his eyes squeezed shut as he tried to escape the brightness.

"Dylan, can you hear me?" The gentle voice of a woman called out to him.

He let out a soft mumble that buzzed through his lips. He squeezed his eyelids harder, which brought on another ache that felt like fluid rushing through his brain, cutting out crevices in the soft tissue. The woman pressed her thumb into the palm of his hand, and although he could feel it, all he could do was wince to let her know.

A few seconds later, he felt the pressure from a needle being slid into a vein atop his hand, followed by the cooling rush of the saline entering his bloodstream. He soon began to slip into an unconscious bliss as his pain began to subside.

Before he passed out, he peeked through his eyelids and saw someone identical to Jake Thacker messing with his IV line. He tried to open his mouth to say something but nothing intelligible came out. He'd been trying to say, "I didn't mean to. I'm sorry."

"What was that?"

He looked through the crack in his eyelids and saw that the person he thought was Jake was really a woman in purple scrubs with short locks twisted into her hair.

"Allie," he uttered before his eyes rolled into his head, and he allowed the cocktail of drugs to lull him to sleep.

DYLAN SLAMMED THE car door of his SUV and enclosed himself inside the vehicle. He screamed at the top of his lungs and felt his vision fade as his lungs emptied. The metal frame silenced his frustration as he vented his anger the only way he knew how. He closed his eyes and breathed in and out, trying to compose his rage. *I can't believe this. I cannot believe this. No, this is not happening.*

"Dammit! How could you?" he yelled as he slammed his fist onto the dash.

He was big enough to admit he hadn't been a great boyfriend. It was true that he had been neglectful as of late and didn't do romantic things like he once had. But he couldn't accept that his shortfalls justified her infidelity.

The blood in his veins boiled when the image of Allie being with another man flashed into his mind. Her laugh, her smile, her lips on his skin, things that were meant for him and him only. The idea of Allie kissing and having sex with someone else was incomprehensible.

She always kept their small home neat, cooked his favorite meals, and was constantly there for him anytime he asked. Upon reflection, he played their relationship out in his mind and realized how poorly he'd treated his girlfriend for at least three years prior. A switch in his mind flipped, and tears fell from his eyes as he accepted his shortcomings.

"It has to be yours," he said aloud as he tried to convince himself the baby Allie was carrying was his. "It's gotta be."

He wiped the tears from his eyes and knew he wasn't letting her go, not without a fight. He looked out the passenger window and saw what was once a house but being with Allie made it home.

"I love you, A," he muttered towards the house.

Dylan went back to the office and finished the building plans he was drafting as if it were just another typical day. He was still fuming, but he tried to talk himself off the ledge. Taking some time away from Allie would hopefully cool him off. He regretted his immediate outrage and couldn't wait to apologize for his actions.

He sat at his desk, unable to concentrate enough to even draw a line as he thought about how they could make their relationship work. Allie was worth the fight, and so was the family they would soon have together. He was finally ready to put in the work and hoped he could do something to convince her to do the same. *I gotta get that Jake guy out of the picture, or he's gonna pull her back. He's trying to be in our lives, and I know it isn't going to stop.*

Dylan left work early and drove home with a soft smile, excited to see Allie when she got off that evening. His anger from the morning had faded, and he was ready to talk things through calmly. *I'm just gonna call this Jake guy first.*

"Thacker, Thacker," he mumbled as he ran his finger down the *T* section of the white pages. "Ah, there you are."

The address he read in the was for a house on the opposite side of town. Dylan stared at the phone. *How many times did you drive all the way out there, and I didn't even know?*

"It's fine. It'll be okay," he said as he shook off the ill feelings creeping into his thoughts.

He took a deep breath and mashed the buttons of the phone. It rang, and he waited. The pack of gum in his pocket was slowly ripped to shreds as he fidgeted through his anxiety. After three rings, a voice finally came across the line.

"Hello?" he heard a male say through the receiver.

Dylan stood quietly while he listened to the deep voice of the man who had been sleeping with his girlfriend for God knows how long. He tried to picture what he looked like, but his mind failed to generate an image.

"Helloo?" Jake said again as he elongated the last vowel.

Dylan stood in his kitchen, listening to Jake's voice while remaining silent. Just as he was about to speak up and recite the threatening speech he'd worked on all afternoon, Jake spoke.

"Allie? Is that you?"

Dylan slowly lifted his head and stared at the wall-mounted phone as if he was looking at Jake himself. His breathing intensified as a fury of red rushed into his cheeks. He twisted the mouthpiece upward and gritted his teeth. What he planned on saying to Jake quickly went out the window as he felt his anger double.

Jake heard nothing but a crackling silence on the other end of the line. "Miranda?"

Dylan instantly hung up the phone and then slammed it back down two more times before punching a hole in the nearby drywall.

"Dammit!" he shouted as he pulled his hand out of the wall. He paced clockwise around the kitchen table, muttering aloud while trying to calm down.

There hadn't been many times when he had felt that infuriated. He'd been heated over pranks in college and even got into a fistfight that left him with a broken hand. But nothing compared to the anger brewing in his mind.

"Chill, chill," he repeated as Jake's voice saying Allie's name repeated in his ears.

His efforts to relax appeared worthless, and he only grew angrier as time passed. Images of Allie laughing and kissing a faceless man kept popping into his mind as he spiraled. Instances, where she had slipped out unnoticed played on repeat when he realized his oblivion.

And Miranda, huh?

"So, it's not just my girlfriend? There's a Miranda too, I guess?" he asked himself, thinking Jake was seeing two women. "She deserves better. God knows she does."

In his moment of rage, Dylan snatched his keys off the entryway table and hopped into his SUV. He drove slowly through town and stared out of his windshield with an angry glare. *I'm just gonna talk to him. That's it. Just a chat.*

He made it to the outskirts of town and merged onto the highway, heading west. Snow fell in a gentle flurry that blew off the treetops with every passing gust. Dylan lowered his visor to cover the rays of the early evening sun. Ten miles later, he turned down the long gravel driveway.

The two-story farmhouse came into sight as the driveway terminated in a circle. His brakes made a sharp squeal, and he skidded to a stop near the front steps of the home. The gravel driveway was empty, and the garage door was closed. Two lights shone through sheer curtains, one upstairs and one downstairs.

Dylan stared at the still house. He had a brief notion of turning around and heading back home. Some flowers and an apologetic speech sounded acceptable in his mind. If that didn't work, he could get down on one knee, propose (something he now realized he should have done years ago), and try to apologize for how he had scared her. But the more he looked at the house, the more he thought about the man inside. *Just a talk. That's it. There's no harm in that.*

He slid his car into park, and took his foot off the brake. The decision to confront Jake became an idea he couldn't abandon. He had already threatened Allie, and something inside forced him forward to approach Jake.

Every step crunched as he swiftly moved forward in the icy gravel. He glared at the home's front door. He was angry before but seeing a house where Allie had likely slept with Jake brought his emotions to a head.

"He doesn't get to have her. She's yours," he assured himself.

The wooden door was only inches from his face. He rapped against it three times and felt pain in his knuckles when he pulled his hand back and placed it by his side. The house was still and quiet. The only sounds breaking the silence were the cars speeding along the highway. He pulled his jacket tight and knocked again.

Footsteps from inside the house echoed through the crawlspace as someone approached the front. "Coming," he heard from inside.

When the steps neared, the porch light flipped on. Dylan looked up and listened to the person on the other side fumble with a handle lock and deadbolt.

A man, who Dylan assumed to be Jake, opened the door. Dylan looked downward at him and smirked when he realized he had a good three inches and thirty pounds on him.

"Can I help you?" the man asked as his eyes peered around Dylan and surveyed the driveway.

"You, Jake?" Dylan responded.

"Uh, yeah. What's up?" he asked.

Dylan's hand shot up from his side and wrapped itself around Jake's throat. He pushed him into the house. They moved across the room as their feet alternated like a dance.

When they neared the opposite side of the living room, Jake's back was slammed against the wall. Dylan's grip on his neck kept him pinned down. Jake reached up and grabbed Dylan's wrist and clawed at his skin, digging small gashes into the top of his hand. When he saw Jake begin to gasp for every beath, Dylan loosened his grip and finally released him.

"Who are you?" Jake asked as he bent at the waist and sucked for air.

"I'm Dylan. It's nice to meet you, Jake," he responded.

The color instantly drained from Jake's face, leaving him white as a ghost. He stood up straight and looked Dylan in the eye. Jake understood who he was facing and returned to the wall where he was cornered. Fear entered his eyes.

"Okay, okay. Can we talk about this?" Jake stuttered as he raised his hands innocently toward his attacker.

"What? Talk about what?" Dylan asked, raising his voice and feeling red flush into his cheeks. "There's nothing to talk about. You're gonna leave her alone, and you're not gonna come around anymore. Is that understood?"

Jake stood silently as his eyes slowly rotated to each corner of the room as he gathered his thoughts.

"But uh...," Jake finally stammered out.

"No," Dylan said as he talked through his clenched teeth. "There isn't a but option. The answer you're looking for is 'okay.'"

Dylan could see Jake's hands shaking loosely by his side in his peripherals. His jaw quivered. Jake was at a loss for words, but Dylan was happy to see he his tactics were working.

"I... I can't do that to my kid," Jake answered.

"That baby is not yours, and it's never gonna be yours. That's what I'm trying to tell you," Dylan replied, jutting his hands out in short rhythmic chops for emphasis.

Dylan took a couple of strides back from Jake and looked down as he paced behind the couch. He rubbed his forehead, trying to figure out what to do. The emotions coursing through his body were new, and his rage left him scared and confused.

Jake pulled himself off the wall and slowly started walking to the home's front entrance. Dylan looked up and over at Jake, who had inched his way closer to the door.

"Just stop," Dylan screamed.

Jake froze in place. Dylan walked over to the front door, shut it, and secured both of its locks. Sweat rolled down his forehead even though it wasn't hot in the house. Jake's entire body shook visibly as Dylan stared at him.

"Listen," Jake started.

"Listen, what. Please do tell," Dylan said.

"Allie's a grown woman. If she wants to be with someone, we shouldn't be the ones to decide that or stand in her way. If she doesn't wanna be with me, that's fine. I just want her to have the option," Jake said with his hands raised at waist height, reasoning with Dylan.

Dylan instantly charged. He grabbed Jake by the shoulders and pushed him against his living room wall, Jake's elbow sinking into the drywall. Dylan pulled his hand back and formed it into a tightly clenched fist that he swung in an uncoordinated manner. His first blow landed right in Jake's stomach, and he cocked back and threw an additional one that hit right below his eye.

Jake utilized the training he received as a deputy and threw three aimed punches back. Two of his fists successfully landed on Dylan's face, and the third was a miss. When Dylan's hands shot up to touch his affected cheek, Jake grabbed him by the shoulders and threw a knee into his stomach that sank hard and deep.

Dylan instantly bent over at the waist and groaned like an injured animal. Red flooded into his vision as he unsteadily propped himself up using the couch as a crutch. His eyes squinted into a sliver, and his hand shot out as he grabbed the only thing in his reach.

Jake evaded Dylan's grasp and sprinted to the master bedroom to grab his pistol. Dylan stood, took two large steps, and caught up to him. With one heavy swing of his hand, he moved the object he had picked off the end table in an arching motion. He felt his hand stop as he made contact with something.

Jake's feet stopped. His face went blank, and his eyes rolled back as the blunt object effortlessly sank deep into the crown of his skull. His body fell to the floor near the fireplace and flinched once before falling still.

Dylan stared at Jake for a moment, waiting for him to move, get back up and fight, do something. But he just laid there as a small stream of blood began to run out of his head and pool on the tile in front of the fireplace.

Jake's collapse sobered Dylan and his rage instantly faded. He looked around the room as if there was someone else that had witnessed the entire altercation but saw no one around. He kicked the bottom of Jake's boot twice as he called his name, waiting to see if he moved. *Nothing.*

"Shit, shit, shit, shit, shit," Dylan repeatedly said, growing louder as he said it. "No, no, dammit, no."

He kneeled and pressed two fingers where Jake's jawline met his neck. For close to two minutes, he pushed down, released, then pushed again as he desperately begged for even a slight pulse to beat beneath his clammy skin.

"Come on. Come on. I'm sorry. Don't do this."

He stood and walked around the room as he tightly tugged at the hair on top of his head. A wave of nausea crept over him as he stopped pacing and stared at the dead man in the living room.

"All I wanted to do was scare him. That's it," he yelled as he swallowed his encroaching vomit. "Shit!"

Dylan sank into Jake's couch and looked at the photo on the end table that had been knocked over. He saw Jake, a woman, and a relatively new-born baby looking back at him.

He walked to the kitchen, trying to decide what to do. There was a copper kettle on the stove, a box of mac n cheese on the counter, and a high chair next to the pantry.

A round wooden table sat in the middle of the room, and a circular basket held what looked like a month's worth of junk mail. He picked up the stack and thumbed through the various envelopes.

"Jake. Jake. Miranda. Caleb. Miranda. Miranda. Jake. Miranda," he dropped the envelopes back into the basket. Every piece of mail had the name Thacker on the end.

Realization crept into his mind, and tears formed in his eyes. Dylan put two and two together.

"Miranda is his wife? And they must have a...," Dylan went silent. He quickly realized he killed a man who wasn't only a husband but also a father. "No, come on, no," he pleaded.

Dylan bound up the house's stairs in a hurry. There was only a room and a small loft at the top of the landing. Inside the room, he saw an empty crib and pastel pink painted walls with PIPER spelled out in large decoupaged letters. He fell to his knees and shoved the meat of his thumbs into his eyes before folding his hands into a prayerlike position.

"My God, I'm so sorry," he said as tears streamed down his cheeks and fell off the edges of his jaw. He sat on his knees and cried for nearly five minutes.

When he composed himself, Dylan meandered back down to the crime scene. Briefly, he thought about calling the police and turning himself in. *Maybe he's still alive. It was an accident; they'll know that. Won't they?*

Dylan mulled over many things he believed he could use to save his soul when the police arrived and got to the bottom of the story. But, once he laid out the facts, he knew there was no way of escaping his crime of passion.

"I was the one who came to his house. I attacked him. He tried to run. My girlfriend is pregnant with his kid. Shit, this doesn't look good for you, Dylan, not at all," he said as he looked at Jake's body.

He opened a couple of doors using his sleeve before he finally found the one that led to the garage. Three stairs took him down, and he flipped the light switch on the wall. Jake's truck sat before him untouched, and tears again welled up in his eyes when he saw the car seat resting in the back.

"I swear I didn't mean to," he said as he wrestled with his tears.

He looked around for a wheelbarrow but didn't see one in the garage. Jake's land was coveted around town, and years earlier, even Dylan's dad had made an offer on it before they decided to move to Billings. It wasn't until he pulled up to the plot that he realized the place belonged to Jake.

With its vast thatch of rocky wooded mountains, he figured he would be able to find a place to drop Jake from a rock cliff and make it look like a hiking accident. *Guy probably doesn't even hike.*

Dylan walked back into the house and tried to pick up Jake's lifeless body. The dead weight was heavier than he'd expected. He wedged his hands under his armpits and tried to slide him toward the door.

The two only made it about a foot before Dylan felt something in his lower back pop and burn and radiate up his spine. He grabbed just above his knees and gasped for air as he tried to stand back upright.

"Ow, no, no, no," he said, realizing he was in no state to carry a two hundred plus pound man anywhere, much less up the side of a mountain.

With tears in his eyes, he sat down on his knees and slowed his breathing as he tried to formulate a plan B. He grabbed the clock that he had used as a weapon and wiped it off with his shirt before sliding it underneath a bookcase. *I'm just gonna leave him there.*

He mustered every ounce of strength he had and climbed to his feet. Slowly he shuffled back out into the garage to wipe down the light switch when his eyes caught sight of the bright yellow and red gas can sitting next to an ancient lawnmower. With the container in hand, he wandered back into the house.

"I'm sorry. I can't think of anything else. I didn't want this to happen, I swear. I just lost my temper. I'm sorry. I promise I'll take care of her and the baby," Dylan said as he spat out his last words over the body.

The sharp smell burned the tiny hairs in his nose as he doused the couch in fuel before setting it ablaze with the lighter in his pocket. Dylan stared as the flames quickly engulfed the tacky fabric.

The fire quickly took hold and roared at eye level. Dylan took one last look at Jake's still body. It hadn't moved an inch. *He's dead.*

He hurried out of the house as he grimaced through his pain. With his shirt sleeve, he closed the door, wiped down the handle, and stepped back into the cool night air.

He shivered as he wrapped his arms around himself tight. He turned around and stared into the fire. *I should have let the fire have me too. But Allie's gonna need me.*

A sigh of relief escaped his mouth as he looked up through the yard's halo of trees and stared into the sky. The quietness of the land in the country brought a feeling of calm to him as he felt light bits of snow fall onto his cheeks.

"I'm sorry," he quietly muttered one last time.

He hopped into his SUV, high-tailed it out of the icy gravel, and sped down the drive. He gripped the wheel tight as he maintained the speed limit to avoid getting pulled over.

His heart was racing, and his breathing was heavy as he drove through the dusk. The snowfall steadily increased as he neared town. He passed by one car along the road, then another as the city's lights finally came through his windshield.

As much as it hurt, he kept thinking about the gut-wrenching idea that he'd brutally murdered someone and then set his house ablaze to cover it up. The violent man Allie's revelation had turned him into was foreign. *I didn't mean to. But, God, what have I done?*

Dylan sped through town and pushed his foot farther down as he rushed to get home before Allie. The smell of smoke was dusted atop his clothes, and he could feel dried blood stuck to his face. When he pressed his hand to his temple, he caught a slight whiff of gasoline. A decent amount of blood had landed on his shirt, and he didn't know if it was Jake's or if it had fallen from the gash hidden just beneath his eyebrow.

He expected that if Allie found out, she would run to the police and instantly turn him in. But it was an accident, and he wasn't ready to go to jail. *She'll never know it was me. I'll shower, start a load of laundry and act like nothing is wrong. Have a beer, blame a bar fight.*

He held the wheel and felt his hands shaking as he pulled his vehicle up to the curb. He looked over at the house and saw the porch illuminated and a faint light visible through the blinds of the front window.

"Dammit, she's home early," he whispered, knowing he wouldn't be able to pull off her not finding out. *I'm not telling her anything. Ever.*

THIRTY-SIX

JOHN STEPPED OUT of Allie's room and quietly closed the door. He took a few steps down the hall and rounded the corner to avoid being seen by the deputy sitting outside of Allie's door. He pressed his back against the wall, closed his eyes, and took a moment to reflect on everything she'd shared. *We got him. We finally got him.* He clenched his jaw and lightly pumped his fist.

Once the lab confirmed that Dylan's DNA matched the cells under Jake's nails, the case could be closed. They'd probably even be able to check his print to the partial. Jake and Miranda would have their justice, and he could retire knowing the biggest crime of his career was solved.

Miranda deserved to know, but he wanted to wait until he was sure they had their guy. If it hadn't been for her calling about Allie's pregnancy, the chain of events might have never happened, and Dylan would still be wandering the streets.

John wandered down to the lobby and politely asked the nurse to make a call. She kindly handed over the phone, and John dialed the number to the lab.

"Yes, sir. We're going as fast as we can," the tech explained.

"You understand this is very important," he reiterated.

"Yes, sir, really we're trying."

"Alright, sorry."

John took an elevator down to the ICU and followed pointed fingers around the hallways until he came to a room with a deputy posted outside. It was nearing midnight, and the kid had fallen asleep in the chair sitting beside the door.

Years ago, John had been the new guy tasked with watching over people that only the Lord himself could revive. He knew it was often a tiring and pointless task. Dylan wasn't getting out of bed anytime soon, if ever.

"Mornin'," John said as he kicked the leg of the chair.

"Hey, Detective Waters, sir. Good morning. Sorry, I didn't...," he replied.

"Just don't let it happen again."

"Yes, sir."

John peered in through the glass window on the top half of the door. Dylan was still lying motionless with cords running to him from every side.

"Anything new?" he asked.

"No, sir. As far as I know, nothing's changed. But they haven't really said anything to me."

John grunted and then stepped inside the room.

The air felt different, as though he could already feel Dylan's body decaying in the bed. There was an intense smell of rubbing alcohol, and the room felt a few degrees cooler than Allie's, causing goosebumps to rise on his arms.

Dylan was tucked under a few layers of blankets. Multiple machines beeped back and forth, and a tube inserted in his throat was forcing his chest to rise and fall. *He's gone.*

"His parents are on their way. But I'm not sure he's going to last that long. His body is shutting down pretty quick."

John flinched at the voice.

"Sorry, I didn't mean to scare you. I'm Doctor Shrestha. I'm currently attending to him. His parents gave me permission to share his status with you," he explained.

"Oh, okay. So, what happened?"

"Well, to make a long story short, multiple injuries. He has a brain bleed, and the majority of his organs are shutting down from the trauma. There's really nothing we can do at this point but wait," he explained. "From what I hear, he wasn't even wearing a seatbelt."

Good. John nodded that he understood.

"Okay. Can he hear us?" John asked.

"Well, maybe, maybe not. Scientists can say what they want, but who's to really say what happens when you're in a coma? Especially if you never wake up." He shrugged. "It's worth a try if you have something you want to say."

This guy thinks I'm gonna say something sweet and reverent.

"Thank you. Do you mind if I have a moment alone with him?"

"Absolutely. I'll be just down the hall. Please have one of the nurses grab me if you need something."

The doctor quietly slipped out of the room while John walked over to Dylan's bedside. The picture of him and Allie in their hallway had shown a put-together man wearing an honest smile. But the person he saw lying on the bed was almost unrecognizable.

His face was pale but battered to hell, and he was covered in lacerations and purplish-green bruising. His eyes were swollen to the point he couldn't open them even if his brain would allow it.

John leaned in close to the side of his head and whispered in his ear.

"I don't know if you can hear me, but I really hope you can, and I hope every second you have left hurts like hell. You got what you deserved; you piece of shit."

THIRTY-SEVEN

JOHN

ALLIE REMAINED IN the hospital for two days following the incident per the doctor's request. John stayed by her side the entire time. *Someone* was watching over her just as he promised.

He ate the bland cafeteria food and doused it in hot sauce to cover its cardboard taste, slept on a narrow pull-out sofa, and tried to keep Allie calm.

They sat around and talked, often sharing stories about Jake. Allie was witty and charming, making his extended stay in the hospital bearable. The more he got to know her, the more he liked her and began to forget that she'd lied to him.

Dylan's parents had arrived before the sun rose the morning after the accident. They had driven all night, desperate to make it in time to say goodbye to their only son. Dylan didn't move, blink, or squeeze his mother's hand when she talked to him through her sobs.

John watched from the door as his mother buried her face in Dylan's torso and cried. His father stood behind her with a hand on her shoulder and tried to be the strong one. But, if there was ever a time to break down

343

and cry so hard, your soul felt like it was leaving your body; it was when your child's life was only continuing only due to machines.

Although he was glad Dylan was paying for his crime, he couldn't imagine the immense pain his parents were feeling.

When Dylan's mother was able to compose herself for more than a minute, John had a long discussion with his parents. He explained the theories he was playing around with that he believed would soon prove factual once the lab work was returned.

"Your son killed him, crime of passion sorta thing, then burned down his house to try and cover it up."

He tried to sugarcoat it, to make it less painful to a mother in mourning, but it was challenging to it sound gentle, and frankly, he didn't care anymore. Sometimes the truth hurt.

Hearing her son was even a suspect, Dylan's mother cried, and his father took her in his arms as they listened to John's paraphrasing of Allie's story.

"Would you like to see Allie? Maybe hear the story from her?" John asked.

"I want absolutely nothing to do with that girl. She ruined our son's life," his mother said as she choked through tears.

"I understand," John returned.

After over fifty hours of life support, Dylan's parents made a decision no parent should have to make. To ease his suffering, they signed the paperwork, the staff switched off all the machines keeping him alive, and he was allowed to drift off peacefully.

Mr. and Mrs. Pupkiewicz made plans to take his remains to Billings and have a small ceremony. They were still holding out a snippet of hope that Dylan's DNA wouldn't come back as a match and he would be afforded some dignity in his death. But they could hope all they wanted. John was convinced he'd found Jake's killer.

Everything with the twins checked out, and the medical team finally released Allie. Her scheduled cesarian was less than a month away, but they expected her back earlier due to her size and blood pressure.

In the meantime, she was directed to go onto bedrest for the rest of the week. No stairs, no unnecessary walking, and no working. Money was the thing she needed the most, and now that she was confined to her home, she coundn't earn any.

Allie's friend Malisa had straightened up her place while she was laid up and volunteered to help her out. She cleaned up the kitchen where Dylan's blood had pooled on the floor and let his parents in so they could grab the last of his effects. The house was ready to go when Allie was released.

She was reluctant to go back into the home where she'd been attacked, but John finally coaxed her inside.

"Thank you, John. For everything," Allie said.

Allie had lied to his face on more than one occasion, but John was drawn to her. He cared about Jake, and Allie was all alone. He couldn't stand the thought of something happening to the twins one of his friends unwillingly left behind.

"You're welcome," he replied with a genuine smile.

John dropped off Allie to get settled and returned to his office. As he climbed out of his car, he could smell the multi-day stench that staying in the hospital had caused. *God, I need a damn shower.*

He walked toward the building and felt the aches and pains that had set in from sleeping on a makeshift bed. His back was tight, and his hips felt compacted. When he stepped into the front door, the first thing he saw was Miranda sitting on the couch in the lobby, waiting for him.

"Hey. What are you doing here?" John asked. He stood tall and tried not to limp.

"I heard she was being released. Trish didn't answer, so I figured you'd come here eventually," Miranda said.

"How did you hear she was getting out?"

"Don't worry about it. I have friends," she subtly smiled. "So, was it him?"

"I don't know yet. I think so, but I'm not sure. We're still waiting on the lab," he explained.

"So, what do we do until then?"

"We wait. That's all we can do."

"And you'll call me?" Miranda asked.

"Of course."

John watched Miranda walk back to her car. Telling her about Allie's paternity confession felt like the right thing to do, but he held back. There was enough confusion and stress in her life. At that moment, he didn't want to tack on anymore. *She'll know if and when she needs to.*

John refused to leave his desk while waiting for the lab to call. It had been days since he bathed, he needed something wholesome in his stomach, and he missed the warmth of his bed. His wife begged him to come home, but he knew the results would come through the second he left the office. He had to be the one to hear the news first.

The third night after the attack, John fell asleep on his desk and was startled by the sound of the ringing phone.

"Hello? John asked as he cleared his throat.

"Sir. They were a match. An exact match," the young man at the lab explained.

"And you're sure?" John asked.

"As sure as we can be. I'll fax it over so you can see for yourself."

"Thank you. I really appreciate it."

John hung up the phone and rested his head in his palms. A few scoffs escaped his mouth that eventually built up into a gentle chuckle. *It's over. We did it.* Tears of joy fell from his eyes and dropped on the photocopied picture of Jake, Miranda, and Piper on his desk.

He packed up his stuff and headed home, feeling like his work for the department was finally complete.

THIRTY-EIGHT

JOHN

THINGS MOVED QUICKLY once the DNA came back as a definitive match. The case was considered closed, and Dylan was determined to be the sole perpetrator of the murder and arson. Two men had been at the scene of the crime that night, and both of them were now dead and buried. John had come to grips that he would never know the events that unfolded and led to the fire.

John tried reaching out a few times to Dylan's parents, but they never picked up, and eventually, the line was disconnected. They'd cut ties with the local area and weren't looking back, and John didn't blame them.

Allie said she had also attempted to call in the hopes she could offer her condolences, but they refused to speak to her. They asked her to box up anything else she found that belonged to Dylan and they'd be back around Thanksgiving to pick it up.

"That's it then. It's really over," Miranda said when John gave her the news.

"Yeah, it's pretty good to know it's finally done. But still, wish we could have avoided it all," John responded. "Miranda, I didn't tell you before 'cause I wasn't sure if I should, but Allie said the twins are Jake's." John

349

listened while the other side of the phone remained silent. Finally, she sighed.

"You know, I didn't want to admit it, but I figured as much. Sorry but I'm not interested in her or her kids being around Piper."

"I get that."

"Because at the end of the day, it was all her fault. If she hadn't slept with my husband, gotten pregnant, and told her boyfriend about it, Jake would still be alive."

"I know, it's terrible. But just know she feels awful. I think she really did love him."

"Well, I hope she can come to terms with it one day. Because now we both have kids growing up without a father."

"You know, I know you don't want to hear it, but Allie really could use some help. I know you made a lot off the house and stuff."

Miranda huffed.

"I know. I'll think about it, okay?"

"Thank you."

As John's retirement date neared, so did the party his wife planned for him. As much as he begged and pleaded for her to cancel it, she refused to budge. The closure of the Thacker case sealed the deal, and she believed he had to have a celebration.

A local hall had been rented and decorated. Blue and white streamers were twisted and hung from corner to corner. A balloon archway welcomed you in, and a "Thank you for your Service" banner was strewn across the back wall. Various food lined one side of the room while little butane lighters kept it warm. Mementos selected and signed by other members of the department and community leaders sat on a table on the opposite side. Nine round tables covered with white cloths sat in the center of the room, and a rectangular wooden floor had been pieced together in the back.

"This looks like a middle school dance," John whispered to the department's secretary when he walked in.

"Stop it," she returned with a swat. "Just enjoy it."

John chuckled to himself as he walked across the room.

"You did great, sweetheart," he said as he planted a kiss on his wife's forehead. "Thank you."

"I'm so proud of you," she returned.

His wife walked over to greet some of the first guests that filed into the room. John stayed back and flipped through the photo album she left on the table full of pictures and newspaper clippings showcasing his career.

The first chunk of the book had pictures of him when he first joined the department and still missed the freedom of flying fighter jets. He wasn't sure he'd ever get over the feeling of practicing emergency landings by cutting off the engine at ten thousand feet and gliding to the runway in a spiral. But, eventually, he admitted those days were over and began to love his new job in law enforcement.

The rest of the book was in chronological order and showed the hundreds of moments his wife had captured over the last twenty years.

One of the sandwiched photos showed the ceremony when Jake pinned on his Sergeant rank. John stood there, arm draped across Jake's shoulders, both men smiling from ear to ear. From Jake's first day with the department, John had always seen potential in him and even believed he could be elected as sheriff one day.

"We'll always miss you, Jake. You should be here."

John tapped the picture of Jake and continued flipping through the curated album. The final photo was a picture of John, Miranda, and Piper outside of a diner after one of their lunches. His eyes got misty. *Don't be doing that here, John.*

"Hey stranger," John heard from over his shoulder. He turned around to see Miranda with Piper bouncing on her hip.

"Hi girls. You look great. Thank you so much for coming," John replied as he wrapped his arms around them.

"Papa," Piper said as she reached out toward John. He grabbed her hand and shook it gently with a smile.

"Thanks for having us. I'm glad we got to be here for this. Honestly, John, thank you for everything you've done. Our lives have closure now. And I didn't realize I needed it until it was over."

"It's what he deserved, Miranda. I'm just glad I get to retire knowing I was able to finish the case."

As he held Miranda, he looked around the room and saw the crowd full of people there to honor his service. John didn't believe he deserved all the recognition but was grateful for what he and his team had accomplished over the years. Then, just as he started to release Miranda from his embrace, he saw an overly large woman step through the door and into the party. *Oh shit.*

"Enjoy the party," John said as he stepped back from Miranda.

He quickly backed away and walked over toward Allie. The twins that were due any day couldn't be hidden under her maroon chiffon dress and black cardigan.

"Allie, hi. Thanks for coming," John said with a forced smile.

"Oh, thanks, your secretary invited me the last time I stopped by. The doctor said it was okay as long as I sat as much as possible. They've eased up now that my stress has gone down."

John looked at the deputies, detectives, and even the county sheriff in the ballroom and thought through his response before he opened his mouth. He didn't want to come across as rude, but she wouldn't be welcome by many of the party guests, especially Miranda.

"Honestly, Allie, I'm so sorry, but I don't really think this is the right place for you. Some of the guys still... well... you know," John grimaced.

"Oh, yeah, duh. I get it. I understand. I should have known better," she responded with an awkward chuckle.

"I'm sorry it has to be this way."

"Really, I get it. I thought I shouldn't come but did anyway," she awkwardly laughed. "But now I realize I should've just stayed home."

"Thank you for stopping in, though. And you have my number. Please give me a call if you ever need anything and when the babies come."

"Yeah, of course, congratulations John, you deserve it."

John offered one last smile and headed back into the party, feeling guilty he'd turned her away. She was a lovely young girl who had gotten caught up in the wrong situation and was now alone. Her life had changed just as much as everyone else's, but she was the one left as the pariah, picking up the pieces of her broken life.

THIRTY-NINE

MIRANDA

IT'S HARD NOT to spot the overinflated beach ball trying to be hidden beneath the dress Allie should have thrown away in the second trimester. But she's still trying to make it work, even though the seams are screaming and hanging on for dear life. I look away, pretending I didn't see her but instantly look back. My curiosity always gets the best of me.

I watch from across the room as John has a hurried discussion. There's a noticeable amount of discomfort in his stance. He never moves his hands that much when he talks. It's apparent he's trying to hurry her out as quickly as possible before anyone can see her.

The corner of Allie's lips tug upwards in a forced smile, and she turns and heads toward the building's exit. *This isn't your place. How the hell did you not know that? Well, Jake, this is what happens when you get into bed with a twenty-something-year-old. They don't know any better.*

As I stand across the room glaring at the young woman that looks like she is about to explode, a lump forms in my throat. The urge to confront Allie creeps up, and I try to suppress the temptation.

John told me the horrid details of what Allie went through with Dylan. I feel a slight pang of sympathy for her, even though I shouldn't. She did it

355

to herself. But, being pregnant, alone, and labeled as an outcast on top of it sounds terrifying.

As hard as it is, I've forgiven Allie. I just haven't told anyone. It's easier playing the angry scorned woman. But Jake was just as much to blame for their affair, and I feel kind of bad that Allie is the one still facing the constant criticism and small-town gossip.

It takes two to tango. Right? My dad used to say that embarrassing phrase before I went on dates in high school.

Based on the small details John leaked, she was due to have the babies soon, and she was all alone. I know small tidbits about Allie's financial hardships and solidarity with her immediate family. It sounds rough.

Jake had been by my side while I labored for eighteen hours with eight-pound thirteen ounce Piper. I couldn't have done it without him. I feel bad knowing she's about to push out not one but two kids without a support system. *Dammit, Jake, dammit. Fine, I'll talk to her. You happy?* I look up at the popcorn ceiling, feeling Jake's stare from above burning a hole through the plaster.

"Do you mind taking her for a second?" I ask one of the other deputy's wives.

"Of course not," she responds, and I hand over Piper.

As Allie turns her back and is nearly at the door, I skirt through the entryway and follow her down the hall. I double my pace, practically running on the low pile carpet and cursing myself for wearing heels, trying to catch up before she leaves the building.

From the rear, I can see the energy it takes her body to move forward. There's an obnoxious waddle to her gait as she walks. Her swollen ankles are nearly the size of her calves, and every step looks like she almost can't bear to take another.

When I'm only a few paces from Allie, I can hear her muttering under her breath.

"Stupid. How are you so stupid? Why did you think that you'd be welcome here?"

"Hey, Allie," I call out to her.

The sound of my voice causes her to stop dead in her tracks. She rolls her shoulders upward from their hunched-over stance and adjusts her posture to stand up straight. I remain silent while I stare at her backside, waiting for her to respond.

"Yeah?" she finally asks, breaking the awkward silence between us.

"Would you at least do me the decency of turning around and talking to my face? I think I deserve that much."

Allie turns around. I see her close up for the first time, not even seeing hints of the girl I'd seen in the picture months earlier. The baby weight is showing in her thickened neck and hidden cheekbones. Her eyes are puffy and pink, and the makeup she haphazardly threw on is asymmetrical and barely covers the bruise Dylan caused. The front of her hair is full of flyway's that stand up in every direction, and spots of her scalp are noticeably thinning in some areas. *Jake would hate seeing you like this.*

"Look, Miranda...," Allie starts.

I close my eyes, dip my head, and raise a hand in Allie's direction.

"Don't. Just don't. Because I really don't wanna hear it," I reply. "Listen, what's done is done. You made this bed, and now we all have to lie in it. But I know Jake, and I know what he would've wanted. You bring me proof that those are his babies, and I'll give you some money from the house

357

sale. He wouldn't want you guys to struggle," I offer. *Look at you being...
benevolent.*

Tears well up in Allie's eyes. I can see she's trying to keep them hidden
but is losing the battle with her emotions.

"You don't have to...," Allie starts before I cut her off again.

"Again, just please don't. I'm not gonna ask again, and I'm not gonna
make the offer again. Take it or leave it. But that's honestly all I have to say
to you," I say. "Do you have something of his? For DNA."

Allie thinks for a moment.

"I do and thank you."

"Good luck," I say before turning around. I don't hear anything else as
I head back into the hall.

When I'm back near the dessert table, I look back down the hall and see
that Allie has left.

"You're welcome," I mutter at the ceiling. I almost feel like I can sense
Jake patting me on the back.

I enjoy the rest of the evening, feeling like an enormous weight has been
lifted off my shoulders. It's not that I particularly want to help Allie out,
but I know it would have made him happy. Taking care of his kids was
always important to him, and leaving Allie high and dry while I have plenty
of money to get by doesn't feel like the right thing to do.

John spends the night dancing with his wife, both palpably happy. They
sway back and forth as I watch the love light up their faces. I miss that
feeling.

After dinner, John gives an elegant speech that he has to pause more
than once as he chokes down tears. People stand at the microphone in
the front of the room and drone on and on about his accomplishments.

Throughout the night, I heard various stories about his early detective years and even watched a small clip of when he flew an F-16 for an airshow.

"You did it all, John. Now go enjoy being retired," I say, holding a passed-out toddler who gets heavier by the minute.

"I'll try. But you know what? It was worth every minute. I wouldn't change any of it for the world," he replies with the most beautiful twinkle in his eyes.

FORTY

ALLIE

T HE TWINS MADE their appearance late on a Tuesday evening while Allie had a popcorn bowl propped atop her belly. She had yet to see the movie Big Daddy and finally found a reason to laugh again. One of her chuckles ended with a subtle popping sensation, and then a rush of fluid spewed from between her legs and soaked the couch cushion. *Oh shit. Here we go, boys.*

Allie immediately phoned a taxi and almost didn't make it to the hospital in time. When she arrived at the maternity ward, she was too late for an epidural, and a cesarian was no longer in the plan. She was going to have to push the good ole fashioned way.

Six men barged into the room at different times to feel around her vagina. One finger, two fingers, they wedged them up inside her and said a different number almost every time until one of the numbers told them she was finally ready to push.

Her ear-piercing cries and screams could be heard down the hall as she labored with Malisa by her side. Malisa tried to coach her through the contractions even though she had never had a child and honestly had no clue what she was doing. She just fed off Allie and tried to be a good friend.

As she pushed, sweat poured down her temples. Allie screamed till she was hoarse, and the nurses kept trying to put a mask over her nose to help her breathe easier. Every time the small woman attempted to strap the plastic oxygen bowl around her head, she threw it to the floor, grabbed the bed rails, and continued to bear down.

After thirty minutes of crying, yelling, and almost giving up, two healthy baby boys came into the world three minutes apart.

The babies were quickly cleaned off and placed on her chest, where they nuzzled against their mother's warm skin. Then, one at a time, they slowly opened their slitted eyes and saw Allie's face, which was covered in tears of joy. She looked at each boy individually and saw Jake's deep cerulean eyes looking back at her.

"You both look just like your daddy," she said as she spoke through her heavy sobbing. *God, Jake, I wish you were here.*

The babies were given the name's Jake and Caleb after the father and grandfather they would never know.

Three days later, she was sent home to take care of her two newborn babies all by herself. There was no guidebook, instructional pamphlet, or even self-help videos that could've prepared her for the new life she was facing. The boys cried, screamed, and then screeched when they were done crying and screaming. No matter what Allie did, she could never seem to soothe them simultaneously.

She constantly tried to breastfeed them, which seemed like more of a chore than it was worth. Her nipples were raw and sometimes even bled through tiny cracks that caused her to cry out when one of them did take a breast. Their refusal to latch made her worry that they weren't intaking enough calories. Eventually, she grew tired of fighting with them and switched to formula.

Allie often pictured what her life would look like if she still had Jake as a support system. Maybe if he were around, she wouldn't have on two-day-old clothes with spit up on both shoulders, and her hair would get washed more than once a week. But she was determined to do it alone, and she also put on a good show when the few friends she had stopped by to hold the twins.

Allie fought an exhausting battle with postpartum depression for months. She cried in the shower, cried in the bathroom when she returned to work, and cried in the car. The heavy weight of the emotional pain that she didn't understand left her feeling like she couldn't bond with her baby boys.

At an appointment with her OB/GYN, she voiced her symptoms as she poured her heart out. The doctor knew how to help and wrote out a prescription to provide some relief. A few days later, Allie started feeling somewhat normal again and could smile when the twins did something new.

When her mood leveled off, she cleaned up the house and tried to create a routine. The twins were thriving in daycare, and she was waitressing again, but the bills just wouldn't stop coming in.

She struggled to pay both daycare and her mortgage and barely had enough money left for necessities. At work, she would scrape her customers' barely touched food into styrofoam to-go containers and slip outside to eat it in her car so she wouldn't get caught.

As much as she fought to be a strong, single mother, she knew she was failing. The money she had been skimming off Dylan's account and saving up while she was pregnant had finally run dry, and she was starting to worry she wouldn't be able to make ends meet for much longer.

She had to do something.

"I see Caleb's eyes are turning brown. It looks like Jake's might be, too," the twins' new pediatrician said as she gazed into their pupils with a scope.

The last pediatric clinic she had taken them to had shunned her for giving the boys formula. She agreed *breast is best,* but formula-fed babies turned out just as bright and healthy as every other kid. She was quick to see what other places her insurance would cover.

"What?" Allie asked as she looked into her boys' eyes.

"Yeah, most babies are born with blue eyes. Usually, by their first birthday, they change to brown if they are going to."

No, those are Jake's eyes.

"I didn't know that," her stomach churned with worry. "But, um, I'm just curious. How would I go about getting a paternity test?" she asked, even though she'd already done her research so she could take Miranda up on her offer.

"Well, is the father here? We can do a cheek swab," the doctor explained.

"No, he's uh, dead." *They're both dead.*

"Oh, my goodness. I'm so sorry. I didn't know."

"Thank you. It's okay."

"Well, um. Do you have something of his? Something with his DNA on it?"

Allie reached into her purse and pulled out a toothbrush sealed in a Ziploc baggie.

"Yeah, this was his," Allie explained as she handed it over.

"Great, thank you. I'll get the tech in here, and she can swab the boys' cheeks, and we will call you when we get the results."

For two weeks, Allie waited, hoping the doctor's office would call with her results. Once they sent her the proof she needed, she would painfully ask Miranda for some money to better provide for her boys while she figured out what was next.

As she thumbed through the mail she hadn't checked in five days, Allie saw an envelope that stuck out to her. "PELICAN LAB CORP" was printed in the return address. *It's the results. I thought they were going to call.*

She tore through the envelope in a hurry. She opened the triple folded paper as her eyes skimmed left to right. Word for word, she read through the document three times, trying to see if she read it correctly.

"The DNA obtained from the child(ren) CHEEKSWAB(S) and the DNA obtained from the parent TOOTHBRUSH BRISTLES have been tested. The two forms of DNA came back as a 98.2% POSITIVE match. The adult that provided the DNA is a direct match to the child(ren)."

Allie dropped the paper in her driveway, and the toothbrush fell from its pocket. Tears filled her eyes as she gently bit her forearm. She stood outside and cried for five minutes while her children wailed in their car seats.

Allie walked into the house, leaving the kids in the car, and opened the hall closet. Inside was a cardboard box labeled "DYLAN'S THINGS." She dropped the toothbrush inside and went back to her life which was quickly falling apart.

The next day, she called a realtor and put her half of the duplex up for sale. It had gained value since she bought it, and if she could sell, she would stand to profit close to fifty thousand dollars.

"Are you sure this is what you want to do?" her friend Malisa asked as they hammered the FOR SALE sign into the front yard.

"I don't want to, but I have to. I don't have any other choice," Allie responded.

"But what are they gonna say?"

"They're my parents. I guess I hope that it doesn't last too long. Hopefully, I find a good job down in Helena and move out and get my own place."

Allie was under contract in a week and closed on the house the following month. Her parents came down to help her, and the twins move. Her mother refused to look at her and barely acknowledged the twins.

Here we go. My new beginning. Just don't let her see you cry.

FORTY-ONE

MIRANDA

I T'S TIME, WE'RE actually doing it. The light at the end of the tunnel and a future I thought would never happen is no longer miles away but is right in front of me in the form of a sign.

The brown sign reads "Welcome to Great Falls" in one long line, with some river-looking swirls carved behind it, hinting at the town's namesake.

This time we're rolling up confidently in a brand-new white Force Explorer, not sputtering into town in a beat-up Accord with the law chasing our trails. *No more coasting in on fumes ever again.*

A calming feeling washes over me when I feel at home again. I roll down the windows and feel the last few days of the summer breeze blow through the car. The pungent odor of the oil refinery doesn't even bother me as we head down the town's main street. The beautiful mountains in the distance are basking in the afternoon sun, and I'm already excited about teaching Piper how to ski this winter.

"We did it, Piper," I say, feeling tears pressing behind my eyes. She's awake but playing with her Barbie in the backseat, not caring about a single thing I say.

After selling Jake's family land, his truck, collecting the insurance money on the house, and cashing in on his life insurance policy, I found myself with more money than I needed to start over. My bank account is full, my wallet has plenty of cash, and my confidence has shot through the roof, knowing I no longer have to answer to anyone else for money. The smile on my face could reach across the entire state of Montana.

I drive by the rundown motel where we'd run away to less than a year earlier and throw it a gentle wave.

"No thanks," I call out to the glowing VACANCY light.

This time, we're checking into a quaint boutique hotel with two thousand thread count sheets, complimentary breakfast, and an Irish pub just off the lobby.

"How long will you be staying?" the blue-haired lady behind the counter asks after I haul our bags inside.

"Well, we're just gonna start with a week. But we plan on staying in Great Falls forever. We're supposed to close on our new home next Thursday," I explain as the lady extends a welcoming glass of champagne.

"Congratulations, sweetheart, that's exciting news. You look like you deserve it," the lady says with a wholehearted smile.

"I do, I really do," I return, finally believing it. "Thank you."

When the woman tells me the total, I feel comfortable swiping my card, knowing good and well the account is overflowing with cash. I pick out a sectioned room where Piper and I can still have personal space and happily take the keys from the woman's hand and usher Piper onto the elevator. Behind her, I roll in three large suitcases that contain almost everything we own.

"Yay," Piper cheers when I open the door to our temporary home.

Piper runs in and begins jumping on the fluffy bed immediately. A few tears work their way into my eyes when I see the luxuries of our room. *We're gonna be okay here. More than okay.*

The following week, we close on our quaint three bedroom, two bath, two-story house, and we finally have our own space again. It's within walking distance of a playground in the heart of town, and there's an ice cream truck that drives by every other day.

Piper begged, and I finally gave in, and we ended up rescuing a small brown dog that enjoyed being outside as much as we did and named him Toby.

At first, I applied for a few small jobs around town. But when nothing excited me, I decided I was ready to do something more with my life.

College. Daunting, expensive, and time-consuming, but worth it.

I thought about it for a while and realized I loved the days I spent with Piper, watching her learn and grow. I want to see the same bright light click on in other children's heads and a smile spread across their faces when I offer them positive affirmation.

So, I gathered up the required paperwork, applied for a couple of scholarships, and submitted my application to the local community college to pursue a degree in education. Being an elementary school teacher just fits me, and I've started dreaming about my future role in molding the minds of America's youth.

I'm finally happy. I feel like my life has finally reached the point I'd always believed it would. In the years I'd spent with Jake, I was locked in a mentality of contentment. But now that I'm on my own and making my own choices, I realized I'd never noticed how unhappy I was until I was free of a man's control.

The new and improved me has finally put on a couple of pounds and filled out the malnourished frame I'd earned from constantly running and barely eating. I've cut the many inches of dead ends off my hair and started going back in for regular colorings. A smile is permanently plastered on my face, and I finally feel like people believe me when I say I'm only in my mid-thirties.

I still feel sorry that Piper will never have any relationship with her father. But, I plan to provide her with as much love and care as she would have received from two parents. She's my whole world.

One day I'll have to explain our dramatic family story to Piper, but I plan to leave out most of Jake's imperfections and highlight his noble traits. Of course, he had his flaws, but he was once kind, hilarious, and loved his daughter passionately.

Now and then, I'll see a blonde woman on the street and do a double-take, thinking I've seen Allie. But a second glance tells me my eyes are just playing tricks on me. The deal I'd made with her has still gone unclaimed, leaving me to believe my husband died for no reason. *I bet they weren't even his.* I thought about asking John but decided it wasn't worth my time, and I'm not sure I even want to know the answer.

Every day I finish up with classes and pick Piper up from daycare. She loves the small classroom of other kids her age, and I get at least three colored drawings on printer paper as a gift daily. When she sees me at the door, Piper always runs toward me with a smile spread across her entire face, and I see every feature I once loved about Jake. She then drops her stuffed "beebees" and enters a full sprint while screaming "mama" at the top of her lungs.

Every night we go home and complete our nightly routine. We always start with dinner, then a bubble bath filled with Barbies, and end the night with wild tales that I make up on the fly (I can't wait for the day she's ready to read Harry Potter). I then lay in her big girl bed next to her, lightly scratch her belly, and quietly watch her eyes slowly close as she falls into a deep slumber.

When Piper is all tucked in and snoring, I often pour myself a glass of Merlot and grab a plate of crackers and cheese. The rocking chair on my porch always welcomes me as I close out the night alone.

I enjoy sitting on the stoop and rocking back and forth. Sometimes I read or simply hum the country songs that I'd heard on the radio that day. I sit there and sip my wine and typically have a second glass and realize I've finally made it. Even without Jake or the societal norm of a woman with a child having a husband, I'm free to do what makes me happy.

Every night I eye the houses that line the street. Their lights turn off one by one as I stay up until the stars come out.

The various styles of homes on our street are modest but elegant, and our neighbors have welcomed us with loving arms. Yet, as much as I enjoy having people nearby, I sometimes still miss the farmhouse in the trees and the man I shared it with.

ACKNOWLEDGMENTS

First, I'd like to thank anyone that picked up this book and took the time to read it. Supporting self-published or Indie Authors is incredible, so I thank you for buying into the genre. There are so many other excellent books out there that have been published non-traditionally that have blown me away! So please, buy Indie just like you shop small and support those that write passionately!

Self-publishing is a lot of work, and I'm sure there are still some errors in this book. I tried to catch them all (I've read this book probably 100x), but that's what happens when you DIY and use creative freedom to make your dreams come true and your ideas come to life. I have a story I wanted to tell, and I wanted to tell it my way.

Adam, thank you for listening to me talk about this book almost every day and rolling your eyes when I ramble about my plot and don't make any sense. You're my favorite reader, and although you usually take a year to read one book, I appreciate that you get through mine in a few days.

Thank you to my other friends and family, that have been nothing but supportive. I get so many questions and love the excitement people get when they hear I'm working on something new. And Paul, thanks for listening to me blabber on during our lunch breaks

My biggest thank you is to Lisa Chappel. Thank you for working with me through the editing process of this book and helping it get polished into something readable. Your words and advice really helped mold the story in a more captivating way.

ALSO BY LIZ GORDON

The Bell of The Bar

Made in the USA
Columbia, SC
12 June 2022

61639400R00231